# ESCAPE

## A F Hurst

**ISBN - 978-1-0682725-0-9**

# Author's Note

Before becoming a writer, I am wholeheartedly an avid reader. It is my opinion that at times, as a reader, I can sometimes feel a little disappointed when reaching fresh into a book and seeing triggers listed at the start. While I support that these help us, as readers, to understand any sensitive subjects that the story contains, and where content may upset the individual reader. For me, these warnings can lead to indications of the story to come and this can affect the enjoyment I feel when reaching into a book for the very first time.

Therefore, any trigger warnings for this story are located on the very back page of the book or you can contact me via social media or email. Please be assured that any content contained indicates reference too and does not go into in-depth detail.

@a.f.hurstauthor
a.f.hurstauthor@gmail.com

I truly hope you enjoy reading this book as much as I have enjoyed writing it.

To all those who think you can't.

You absolutely can.

You just have to start.

# Prologue

Luck.

If I didn't have bad luck, I don't think I'd have any luck at all. In all my years of therapy, it's like I've developed my own mantra. One which encourages me to find the rainbow amongst the dark skies. It is both my ally; and by far my biggest nemesis.

This trip to see my best friend has been on my mind and I've finally decided to just do it. I managed to pack my bags and leave America for the first time in 7 years.

But honestly, this is the tip of the iceberg.

I'm stood on the streets, not sure what is happening in front of me. My mind is racing.

*What. The. Fuck.*

I have spent the last 5 years of my life thriving. Well, sort of. Until recently I guess.

I've been working so hard towards my goals and achieving them, going from strength to strength. I am so close to living life to the fullest.

Yet here I stand, speechless.

How quickly it happened to put me back at square one. I need to breathe, take a step back and rationalise what is happening. Remembering back to therapy, Dr Rene always said, 'A cloudy mind makes for mucky decisions' whenever I forgot the path we were on.

I start my counting exercises and take a deep breath.

That's when I notice the tears flowing down my cheeks.

I never cry.

I don't know what I am supposed to do next. But maybe that decision is about to be made for me.

# Chapter 1

## Present Day

I wake up startled.

Glancing at the clock across the room it reads 03:23am.

For a moment, I can't quite gather my bearings. I'm used to being woken from my nightmares but this doesn't have that dreary hangover feeling.

Like I've woken up from '*slumber-hell*'.

No, more like something has prickled my senses. Blinking I chatter to pull myself together Mollie. I realise my iPad is vibrating from across the room and I scurry across in a haste to pick it up, coherent thoughts hitting me into reality hard.

I can't miss it.

Reaching it, I see 'Max' is wrote across the front screen. I quickly press the green camera button and Max's face enlarges across the screen.

"Hey Babe!" I say with excitement, my smile spreading across my face.

"Hey," Max replies smiling back at me through the screen. "I haven't got long today, coms is screwing up and I don't want the conversation to cut without saying goodbye." Max says woefully as he looks at me disappointed.

"It's ok, some time is better than no time remember," I prompt him, trying to hide my disappointment for yet another short conversation.

Max is my boyfriend. We have been together now for 3 years. His large frame fills the camera frame as his 6ft4 towers over. He has bright blue eyes and short dark hair, his skin always tinting a bronzed tan from his time away. He is most definitely all muscles, he is gruff and full of testosterone, but while his cheeks sport tiny dimples to those who know him properly, we know on the inside he is pure teddy bear snuggles.

He is every woman's complete wet dream.

I often pinch myself at the thought that this man actually fancies me. He just oozes sexual tension.

We met by chance, at the end of a chapter in my life that I was definitely happy to see the back of. It felt like fate to me. A moment that was written in the stars and I fell head over heels almost instantly.

Max works overseas in the military, so it can sometimes be a while between when we see or speak to each other, in person and over the phone.

"You look different, have you changed something?" Max asks, his brows pinching together in the middle.

"No, maybe it's just the lighting." I reply, not sure why there is a slight tremble to my voice.

I am not a short girl, 5ft9 with natural curves, I'm far from small. I have naturally deep red hair although there are streaks of blonde which complement my pale green eyes.

I stretch over to turn on the lamp.

"What are you wearing?" Max asks continuing to frown at me through the video.

*Fucking hell, I've just woke up in the middle of the night, why so fucking critical.*

"Erm, just my pyjamas, a t-shirt and pants. Why?" I respond, hesitantly not really sure why this is relevant.

"You just look…" he pauses, thinking of a word to choose, "…a little unkept." He finishes.

Wow.

I sigh. Feeling like I'm a million dollars now, not.

Max continues the conversation like he's not just ruined my confidence in a swift 30 seconds.

"How's things on your end?" he asks.

"Not to bad, work is hectic as always, but we should be completing on the next book instalment soon, I'll hopefully have some time to visit Sara." I reply.

Max frowns, "Don't put pressure on yourself to fly Mollie. There isn't a rush to put yourself out there if you don't need to." Max states, looking concerned.

"I know, don't look at me like that, if I need to, I'll get a boat across the Atlantic, it'll be fun." I reply sarcastically, but keeping my spirits up.

We carry on chatting, and I fill Max in on all the details of work, friends and life outside of the war zone. The conversation lasts around 20 minutes before we're cut off from the call, but Max promised me he'll be home for my 25th Birthday in 2 weeks time and that's all the reassurance I need right now.

I tuck myself back into the bed covers and salvage whatever is left of the night before tomorrows busy day.

****

My alarm goes off first thing in the morning and I instantly want to pull the covers over my head. That late night call has completely knocked me off my game today.

I am used to having broken sleep so usually I'm not affected by interruptions but lately it has been so calm without any nightmares to keep me awake, I think I've  finally got used to a full nights sleep. I pull myself together as unfortunately sleeping in doesn't pay the bills.

I live just outside of New York City, in a small cul-de-sac of houses set away from the busy hustle and bustle of city life. It's a small street, with just a handful of homes and families living on it. I share the street with eight other houses and everyone knows everything. You can't even fart in the wind without it being popular street gossip. It's the only downfall, but honestly, I love living here, despite the commute into the city being exhausting.

My closest best friends live on the street with me, they house share together. I've known my best friends almost all of my life, aside from Sara, who we met whilst travelling on the gap year holiday following university.

With Sally and Gina living so close, it is in actual fact a complete godsend at those times where Max is away fighting in a place I'm not privy to knowing. We can struggle to lock down Sara as she moves a lot with work also. It can be a nightmare to even know what timezone she's in these days, but on the whole we always try and make Zoom nights together every Thursday.

I have always had a passion for words on a page and I currently live in my dream world as CEO and editor in chief of MR Publication Studio, where we publish and support upcoming writers to find their feet between pages of their own creation. My girls Gina and Sally work alongside me, Gina is Chief of Design and Sally is Chief of Finance and both girls are totally irreplaceable to me. I am hoping that Sara will come back and join us when she's ready to, but she's always been the 'Dora the Explorer' of our group.

I meet the girls as they jump into my SUV ready to commute to work. We each car share most days when our calendars align and we are all due in the same place at the same time. It makes the long journey much easier when I have these girls to keep my mind occupied.

"Girl! You look rough." Gina exclaims as she flops down into the passenger seat. I look into my rear view mirror and I have to admit my hair closely resembles a birds nest.

"Ergh, Max called through the night and you know I'm not good when I've had broken sleep Gee. But I did speak to him for the first time this month, so I suppose it was worth it." I respond excitedly, the smile spreading across my face instinctively.

"Oh really? I'm glad he was able to drop in a call before you really lost your shit." Gina said with a smirk pulling at her lips.

"Oh piss off Gee, honestly I think I've coped better than expected of myself this time. It has been three long ass months, but he's hopeful he's going to return in two week's for a month before he's redeployed, just in time for my birthday celebrations!" I tell Gina, giddiness oozing from me.

Gina smiles back at me. "Good for you sweetie, it's about time he came back, his deployments just keep getting longer, how are you going to keep on this future together if he's never here?" Gina asks, and I sense she's sincerely worried about this for me.

"I know. Maybe we need to have a chat, he has been saying he was going to retire soon, he's already done 14 years service." I begin, trailing off what feels like a rehearsed speech, "But I can't complain, I knew he was in the services before I made this commitment." I finish, looking around for Sally so we can get moving and I can feel less interrogated. Although, that's unlikely when Sally hears the topic of conversation.

Sally runs from the front door and jumps in the back of my SUV "Sorry! Let's go!" She announces and I put my foot down and we head into the city to start the day.

We arrive in the office on time surprisingly. We have to focus today. There is a client meeting in 5 minutes and we definitely need a miracle for this to be approved.

I put my things on my desk before heading out of my door and over to Gina and Sally's offices.

"Girls, be ready to bring your 'A' game this morning. Coffees in hand, stomachs full, bladders empty. We have the meeting this morning and hopefully we will be ready for print." I shout as I turn and stride across the wooden floors. I look towards my assistant, Meryl, "Is the meeting room ready Meryl?" I ask, knowing full well she's set it to perfection.

"Of course Ms Rutter." Meryl responds as polite as always.

I look at her deadpan, "Meryl, you've been my assistant for 2 years, I wish you would call me Mollie." I laugh and Meryl gives off a small smile.

"If I'm not professional in my role Ms Rutter, I am not worth my position." She responds, and I smile wryly towards her knowing I'm again on the back of losing this battle. I gather my items and head into battle - I mean, to the meeting.

The meeting ends after 4 long hours but we've finally finalised the finishing touches and the client is happy with our choices. This means we are finally going to launch and we have high hopes for another successful publication. Gina smiles at me, we're proud of this one, we've published several stories but this one is by a well known author and should bring us so much more business which will allow us to keep expanding.

"I think we should go get shit faced." Gina exclaims as she plonks herself down on my office sofas.

"Gee, it's lunch time, we can't just up and leave now." I laugh.

"Why the fuck not? You're the boss," she winks at me with the best come-fucking-drink-with-me eyes I have ever seen. I laugh and Sally comes into my office squealing with joy.

"Yes, girls!" She shouts, shaking her arms in the air. We all jump up and come together in a hug. "I've got us a table in Reggie's for 1pm, let's go celebrate!" Sally continues and I laugh at my two best friends. For the first time in forever I have the best feeling that everything is falling into place.

We grab our belongings and head out for an afternoon of merry antics and ruthless ladies.

We sit on our usual table at our favourite food and cocktail place 'Reggie's Bar'. The drinks are flowing. My brother Graham, or 'Gray' as we call him and his best friend Joey joined us after their work days have ended. We have all been laughing and reliving some of our best childhood memories. That always seems to be the go to when we've had one too many alcoholic drinks.

We all originate from England, in a small village in the heart of Yorkshire. Gray and Joey have been inseparable since they were 5 years old and having Joey grow up with us is like having a second actual brother. I look around at my friends and family, and I swear despite everything I have been through, nothing could take away the happiness I feel right now. I feel complete, which is strange since Max isn't here. It makes me wonder why.

I decide that I feel happy because I am quite literally 'merry'. The drinks have been flowing since 1pm and it's now midnight. Leaving my SUV in the underground garage at the office, Gray and Joey make sure that us girls are safely tucked into a cab and we head back to our happy little cul-de-sac.

****

My pulse is racing. I'm tossing and turning in bed.

"Stop!" I shout, panic rising and flooding through the veins in my body, like a river overflowing its banks.

I can feel my body tensing, as goosebumps prickle along my skin, the sensation of hands roaming over my skin, the smell of cigarettes and whiskey lingering around me.

I can't move. I am frozen to my core. Stuck lying in the same spot.

I know I need to get myself out of this, but my instincts just can't seem to interact with my brain, with the need to survive and

I'm just frozen. I can feel his hands trailing up my body, he grips my throat and I think for sure, that this time, I am done.

My eyes fling open, gasping for breath, as my chest rises and falls rapidly. Paralysis has taken over my body, as I lie in my bed, my eyes open and aware. I run through my routine that I have done for the past 5 years, counting myself down.

Five things I can see: "*my bedroom, my light, my ceiling, my wardrobe, my window*."

Four things I can hear: "*my clock, the wind, the pipes, a train*"

Three things I can smell: "*my fresh laundry, my perfume, my lavender incense sticks*."

Two things I can touch: "*my bedding, my legs*."

One thing I can taste: "*my blood*."

I feel my heart-rate starts to slow and I push my positive thoughts through, reminding myself, you are at home Mollie, this is just a nightmare.

Just.

Fucking.

Breathe.

I sit bolt up right, suddenly back in control of my body. I gasp, as though there is just not enough oxygen within my cells. Grabbing the drink from my nightstand, I take a big gulp to wash away all of the blood coating my cheeks from biting down on them. I jump up and out of bed, heading for the en-suite. I instantly need to jump into the shower, as the urge to wash myself crawls along my skin.

As I stand under the flowing water, I press my back against the wall and slide down, sitting on the floor whilst the shower rains down along my skin. My breathing is heightened and I need to continue to remind myself to relax. Balling my hands then relaxing and tapping my fingers, I count as they tap my palms.

I haven't had a nightmare like that one for years now and I wonder what has triggered it this time. I reach for my phone and shoot the girls a message in the group chat.

**Mollie** - "Reset the counter. Nightmare 1, Mollie 0"

I hit send and a couple minutes later a response pings on my phone. I glance at the clock which reads 01:32. I wasn't expecting a response as I knew it was late and I know, at this time, it's likely Sara who has messaged back.

**Sara -** "Shit girl! Any idea what your trigger was this time? You were doing so well."

I sigh reading Saras response, knowing how disappointed I feel with myself and I know my girls will feel it for me.

**Mollie -** "I'm not sure, maybe it's work? Maybe it's the drinks we had last night, I really have no clue. Maybe it's that I'm on my way to the latter half of my 20's :'( "

**Sara -** "Mol, you're 25 in 2 weeks. Don't go picking out your coffin yet. xx"

**Sally -** "Do you guys not know what sleep is? It's almost 2am assholes! P.S. sorry about your nightmare Mol. Sending vibes your way, but seriously shut the fuck up, it's Cilla-Zilla day tomorrow Mol, we need 'A' Game!"

I smile at Sal's crass. I can just imagine how grumpy she is about being woken up at this time. I instantly feel bad. I head downstairs to make myself an Ovaltine in the hope that I'll get myself back to sleep sooner than I anticipate. I grab my phone and respond to Sally.

**Mollie -** "Sorry Sal! You're right, tomorrow is a big day. Ignore the nightmare and head back to the land of nod! See you in the morning. And Sara, I hope you're home for my birthday celebrations. I will not accept no for an answer xx"

I place my phone back on the bedside cabinet and my brain starts to race thinking of how I got myself back on the path of nightmares after almost two years of none. I decide to type out an email to Max, hopeful that he will reply when he gets signal of some kind.

It's frustrating as hell living in a relationship where we can go weeks without a word, but when we're back together it's always worth it. Although, this time I definitely need to get myself back in the gym because hell, this body could make a troll cry and I swear, I'm a turn off even to myself.

I finish up my Ovaltine and tuck myself back into bed. I know I can't think about the nightmare again before I settle back to sleep or I will just take myself right back into it. I start thinking about the new books lined up for publishing in the upcoming weeks at work instead to focus my mind elsewhere. There are some real exciting stories and I can't wait to support the girls with their dreams.

It's a long night and I toss in my bed throughout, feeling afraid to fall into a deep sleep. At 05:00am, I opt to make a start on my new physique before Max comes back into town. I head down to the gym, close to the city and near to my office building. Having packed my office attire for the day so I can head straight to the office when I'm finished.

I arrive at the gym and get myself ready. The hope is that I'll work on my body but also to make sure I clear some space in my mind.

I thought about making contact with my therapist, Dr Rene, on the ride here but I know I have come so far since I last attended therapy and I got myself out of the paralysis in less than 2 minutes using everything I have learnt over the years. A message pings on my phone as I run on the treadmill and I realise it's 07:00 already.

**Gina -** "How the fuck did I miss a nightmare? I miss all the good stuff. Hope you're okay Mol. I'm grabbing coffees from Maureen's on my way in, who wants one?"

**Sally -** "*holds up hand* is the pope catholic Gee? Don't ask stupid questions. Extra coffee shot for me please, some inconsiderate individuals woke me from my slumber last night."

**Mollie -** "I've had 3 coffees already and I'm on a 10 km treadmill run. I think I should stick to water for a few hours. And Sal, I'm sorry about last night. I'll let you eat my cream cake at today's meeting, I'm totally trying a new health kick to try slim down before Max comes back."

**Gina -** "Girl I hope you know you're already hot stuff!"

I laugh, hitting stop and jumping off the treadmill, heading over to do some weight training before I finish and head into the showers. I am so glad I got up this morning, I needed this session to relax my mind enough for my busy day today.

There is only me inside the gym this early which has given me the chance to fatigue myself, without looking like an eccentric pigeon that's totally lost the plot on a Friday morning. I finish up my round on the weights, glancing at the clock on the wall which now reads 07:30am. Grabbing my towel, I decide I should get myself ready for work.

Speed walking towards the changing area, I turn the corner at speed, face-planting straight into a sleek, chiseled chest. Caught off guard, I almost fall flat on my ass as a pair of massive muscular arms latch onto me. I stare up wondering who my saviour is only to meet the eyes of Joey Kincaid, my brother Gray's best friend. I bounce back almost losing my footing and let out a little gasp, quickly clutching at my headphones and pulling them out of my ears.

"Woah! What's the rush?" Joey laugh shouts at me, a smirk rolling at the corner of his mouth.

"Hell Joey! You almost gave me a freakin' heart attack!" I exclaim, taking a step back and rebalancing myself. Joey continues to hold onto my arms and I wonder for a beat why he hasn't let me go yet.

"Mol, you're the one acting like you're on roller-skates, needing to be somewhere yesterday." Joey replies, his tone calm and soothing, eating at your mind, like a smooth hot chocolate on a winters night.

I hesitate on my response, not really sure on how to reply to him and it's as if he reads my mind.

"You had a nightmare didn't you?" Joey questions, his eyes soaring into my soul.

My breath catches and my cheeks flush rose. "I.. er…" I let out a breath I didn't even know I was holding, reminding myself who I was standing in front of. Theres no way he would see through my bullshit excuses on why I had spent the last 2 hours at the gym in the middle of the week, because in all honesty, I am not a gym girl, and he's known me almost as long as I've been alive.

"When did they start back up? Where is Max? Shouldn't he have returned home by now? Are you on your own at home?" Joey reels off, too quickly to even put in an answer in between the questions he is firing.

"Joey slow down, I'm fine! Yes, I had a nightmare but I dealt with it as I always do. That's not why I'm here anyway, I've decided I need to make an effort to look attractive again for when Max returns, so he doesn't come back to a girlfriend that resembles 'Fiona' from Shrek. I'm doing this for me, it's a good thing," I say in a reassuring tone, hoping that Joey will understand and lay off the twenty Q's.

Besides, it wasn't a total lie at all. I am here to knock off the pounds and soak up the super sexy fitness girl vibes.

Joey looks at me, concern lacing his eyes and I know he doesn't fully believe me, although he desperately wants to.

"You know you don't need to change a thing for that ungrateful douchebag right? He should fucking count his blessings he has a women like you, Mol." Joey says, accenting his words in a way that honestly seems like he means every word.

"Joey, play nice man, I'm doing this for me. It's a good thing, don't make it a negative." I widen my eyes like puppy dogs, curling my bottom lip to sweeten him back up. The corner of his lip twitches and I know I have him. "Gotcha Joey!" I say, flashing a deep smile. Joey's posture relaxes as his shoulders drop and he returns a wide smile to me.

"You're like my own little sister Mol. I just give a shit that you don't feel like you owe him anything. Just because he can't pull his head out of his ass long enough to realise he needs to return home to you, permanently, and that you are worth it. You're worth an ocean Mol and he's constantly just giving you puddles. Don't forget that. Please." Joey responds, his tone pleading with me. His eyes meet mine and I inhale trying to slow my pulse down, hoping he hasn't noticed the change in my breathing. Why am I reacting this way to Joey? He's Gray's best mate, my 'adopted' brother for all intents and purposes. Compose yourself Mollie, *for fucks sake!*

"Joey, that's not what's happening. You know he has 1 tour left, he even said he would be home for my birthday."

"And then what Mol? He goes back again? Have you even told him you're having nightmares again?" Joey exclaims, raising his voice slightly, his shoulders tense.

"I'm not 'having nightmares again' Joey, I had one. I'm stressed at work, it was accidental. I got this, stop worrying." I shoot back quickly, trying to douse the fire before it's lit back up again. I do not have time for this shit today.

Joey sighs, rubbing his hands down his face. "Make sure you tell Gray, Mol. Before I get to him first, you know he needs to hear it from you first." Joey exhales and with that strides past me and into the gym.

What the fuck just happened.

****

I finish showering and drying my hair in the gym. I head to the office, swinging by Maureen's Cafe for a camomile tea, before pushing through the doors in to the foyer. I exhale when I see Gray stood there, arms folded, face like fucking thunder.

I do not need this shit today.

"Gray, to what do I owe the pleasure of this unannounced and clearly cheerful visit?" I say, sarcastically towards my brother who is clearly acting like he has a chip on his god damn shoulder.

"Joey called." Gray states, his tone a clear matter of fact.

*Fucking great.*

"And? Do I need to reiterate the same shit I just told him or has he done that for me, so I can spare myself the wasted breath?" I say, continuing the sarcasm that's oozing from my pores.

"You're funny. Why are you keeping things from me Mollie? You know what Dr Rene said, you need support networks. You need people to speak to. You need family!" Gray states, almost shouting at this point.

"Gray will you keep your voice down. This is my workplace. You can't just come in here and demand I divulge my life details all because you want to play big fucking brother seven years too late." I wince as the last words to leave my mouth, knowing that was a little harsh, but being thoroughly done with this whole 'over-protective' situation.

Thanks for giving me time to tell him Joey.

I waltz past Gray and head towards the lift, pressing the button to call the lift to take me up to my offices on the 10th floor. Gray begins to follow, his scowl deepening, his eyes so deep in anger, I'm about 90% sure he's 5 minutes away from either spontaneous combustion or having a fucking aneurism.

The lift doors ping open and I step in, holding my palm up to Gray to stop him from getting in. "Not today, Gray. I'm not keeping anything from you, I just haven't had chance to let you know. I'm sorry for what I just said, it was a low blow, but I have a lot on. Today is a big day. Please. Just not right now. Later? My house 6pm?" I plead, sorrow leaking out of my every fibre.

Gray eyes me suspiciously but nods. "Fine." And the lift doors close me in.

I sigh, glancing at my watch and it reads 08:40am, 20 minutes before my meeting. The lift doors ping open at level 10 and Gina stands there with a sympathetic look painted on her face. I stand up straight, initiate full boss girl mode and stride out the lift. "No time for crying today Gee, game face only do you hear me." I announce to Gina, sipping on my camomile tea, imagining the calming vibes I should definitely be feeling.

Gina nods swiftly "Sonja called up from reception, I thought you'd need…"

I place my hand up in front of her face. "Gina. Not. Today!" I whisper shout so we don't attract attention but enough to make sure she gets my vibes, before turning and striding towards my office, smile in place. Gina follows me, scurrying behind. Sally is sat in front of my office desk when I enter and Gina quickly shakes her head 'no', eyes wide, signalling to Sally to keep her mouth shut.

My office is a spacious room, my desk central. The walls are a shaded sage green, neutral and calming throughout. There are a number of plants situated and a reading corner on the far left. I take a seat at my desk, spinning to face the large windows which line the outer edges of the room, looking over NYC and Central Park. I never get over this view. Being a British born girl and being from the countryside, the vast differences between the city life and the calming of the greenery is just spectacular to me.

"Riley Austin's PA is coming in today for a meeting about the release of the next book. As usual, Riley can't even be bothered to grace us with her actual presence but expects the earth from our perspective." Sally borks, interrupting my trail of thought as I look out at Central Park.

I swivel on my chair, turning towards her, a grin tugging at my lips.

She shrugs "Well you don't want to talk about that-which-must-not-be-spoke-about, so I thought, best crack on with the goods." She states, very matter-of-factly.

We continue to start the day on the more pressing issues, Riley Austin. A pretentious, self-righteous author that is so fucking arrogant, that she doesn't even fucking turn up to our office for meetings, which benefit her and her book releases. She is our largest paying client at MR Publications and for that reason, we accept her terms and conditions, and just do our jobs. Her PA, Cilla, is a force to be reckoned with and she gives us hell on earth whenever she turns up to the office, hence the total shit show we're all scrambling to put together for today. Cilla will not budge until we have everything Riley *fucking* Austin requests down to a T.

"We're in for a long day girls, sip your coffees and put on your business faces. Cilla-zilla is on route and it's about to get wild."

We all take a sip out of our drinks in unison before holding them into the air, and screeching "Girl Power!" As per our usual routine to psych ourselves up, before laughing like the honest, care free, bunch of assholes we truly are.

****

The day continues to be an utter shit show. Failure after failure in meeting the wishes of Riley *'fucking'* Austin. I sometimes wonder how the fuck I've built this business up from nothing, seen as all we seem to get is a variety of bad luck situations. I stand from my chair, pack up my items into my bag, feeling like the weight of the world is on my shoulders.

I look up, startled to find Gina leaning against my office door.

"What did Gray want?" Gina asks apologetically.

"The usual, to yell at me for not keeping him in the loop as soon as I fart." I reply, slumping back down in my chair.

"You know he feels bad Mollie, for past times, he doesn't mean to be intrusive," Gina says, striding through my office door and sitting on the seats at the foot of my desk.

"He's treating me like I need bubble wrap because he's guilty about our parents, the backpacking, everything. I get it Gee, but it has been seven years already. The shit in my life doesn't have to involve him and his incessant need to smother me. What happened, happened. We can't change that now. I've done my time healing Gee, I just need to move on." I sigh, defeated.

Gina looks at me, her face a mirror of the grimace on my own. She knows the struggles I've faced, overcoming everything in my past, but that's just what it is. It's my past. We can't change it, we can only build from it and be the new version of myself.

I sigh again, "Come on Gee, it's Gin-o'clock, let's fuck off," I grin as I throw the rest of my belongings in my bag and stand from the desk. Gina smiles back at me, "Damn right it is after that fucking day." We laugh together, before leaving the office for the night.

# Chapter 2

## Therapy
## Three years ago
## Session 156 - Final Session

I sit in Dr Rene's therapy room for my final therapy session. It's a surreal feeling of both loss and accomplishment.

Dr Rene enters the room, followed by Florence, her assistant, who brings us fresh pastries and camomile tea into all of our sessions.

"You've made it Mollie. How do you feel about today?" Dr Rene says, as she takes a seat, her voice as smooth and calming as always.

"Honestly?" I begin, taking a minute to think about how to explain my feelings, "I'm a little nervous, but ultimately, I am proud of myself, for getting here." I reply, not really knowing how to explore my emotions at the moment.

"You've changed your hair colour since your last session." Dr Rene states.

"Yes. I felt that I needed to start my new era with a statement. What better way to make a statement than a change in hair colour." I respond nonchalantly, brushing the ends of my now deep brunette hair which once blossomed a deep Auburn.

Today is my last session with Dr Rene after a little over three years of work together and I know just how far I have come throughout these three years. It hasn't been easy for me or for Dr Rene.

I glance around the room that I have spent so much of my time in, once a week, maybe even twice some weeks, for the last few years. I take in all the reasons I had to be here three years ago and how simple things like the sage colour on the walls always made me feel safe and calm, even when I usually felt lost when I walked through these doors.

I look around at the shelves with books stacked. Tonnes of information on how best to treat people like me. I stare at the plants which hang from the ceiling from macrame nets and remember the times where I would sit in this room, in silence, for entire sessions, looking at all the surroundings and knowing that despite not speaking, Dr Rene was always just there for me.

I make a note of how this room makes me feel safe now just as it did three whole years go. This session is for my final closure. To know how far I have come. To encourage me to continue to go on.

"I wanted today's session to be a recap on all the strategies we have learnt over the last three years, to remember where you were all those years ago and where you have built yourself to be now." Dr Rene says, startling me out of my thoughts.

Tears threaten to roll down my cheeks and I feel a lump forming in my throat. I feel emotional that I have spent so long relying on this person to help micro-manage my feelings and now it's coming to the end.

Who, in the right fucking mind, cries about leaving therapy. Someone who shouldn't be leaving therapy I think.

I start playing with the seam along my leggings, my eyes looking down. I don't think I can face looking her in the eye.

"Mollie, look at me." Dr Rene tells me firmly and I feel like I am rooted to the spot. I remember the times we have spent pushing me past these times, where I felt so out of control, like I am free-falling with no parachute. I eventually lift my head and look at Dr Rene in the eyes. She smiles softly at me and I feel myself mirroring her expression.

"Let's talk about your network, those you have around you. Tell me, who can you rely on?" Dr Rene asks.

I barely have to think before I answer "Gray, Joey, Gina, Sally and Sara." I state, without hesitation.

"And what techniques work best for you?" Dr Rene asks.

I think on this for a few moments, thinking of all the techniques we have used over the three years, to help me overcome all I have been through and how many times techniques have failed to support me quick enough to allow me to ground myself. I sit back and recap the ones that do work.

"Five Senses technique, breathing sequences and visualisation" I recall, the techniques embedded in my mind.

"Good, now remember that you haven't had a panic attack for six months, which is a great number to build on." She states, her tone reassuring, "So don't be afraid if you do relapse and have a nightmare or a panic attack. This is a new era of your life, and that is expected. Remember your techniques and that you can do this." Dr Rene encourages.

"Can I? Do I really have the skills to do this on my own? What am I supposed to do if things go wrong? I can't do this on my own." I start to breath rapid and I know I am on the brink of losing my shit. I close my eyes and breathe in deep, until I feel less jittery.

When I open my eyes, I am greeted with Dr Rene smiling at me from her chair. She lets out a small breathy laugh, reaching out to grasp my hand. "That is how I know you can do this Mollie, because it comes to you like it is second nature now, something natural. You know what your mind and body need to refocus you attention and ground yourself."

We spent the remaining 30 minutes of the session recapping my support techniques that I have developed for each different variety of fear I have. Mostly, my ultimate fear is feeling out of control when it comes to my own actions or outcomes. Over the years, I have struggled with nightmares, freeze reactions, spontaneous touching and panic attacks. I have worked so positively to build all of the skills up, that I know I have what it takes to go it alone.

It's just sad.

"I need to thank you for everything you have helped me with Dr Rene, honestly I think without you I'd be a shell of a person." I say, my voice quivering as I talk.

"Mollie, you've been here for three years now, you know you can call me Aria." She says, her smile beaming at me, "Everything you know now has come from you believing in yourself Mollie. You have earned this outcome, I am just your guide." Dr Rene states matter of factly.

I smile towards her knowing I have worked hard and knowing I have to take appreciation for the work I have done, but knowing that I could not have done it without her.

We finish the one hour session and it seems neither of us want to get up to end the session. The grandfather clock chimes a low smooth chime to signal the end of the session and my eyes fill with tears. Why am I so emotional about this?

I need therapy to get over the therapy.

Dr Rene stands first, being the professional, and I follow suit after her. She hands me her business card and reminds me that she will always be there to listen if I need support. I knew she would always remain close by after everything we have worked through together. I reach out and hug her, overstepping so many professional boundaries but it's welcomed and Dr Rene places her arm around my waist.

"You've got this Mollie."

I smile, "Don't forget to come and see me when you're ready to write a self-help book. I may be a new publishing company but we will one day conquer the world." We laugh together and I pick up my jacket and bag and head for the door.

"Thank you again, for everything Dr… Aria." I laugh, stuttering over her name.

Florence stands as I walk into the foyer and she shuffles to me pulling me into a warm embrace. I laugh and hug her back. "Go take on the world Mollie darling." Florence exclaims as she steps back and starts to shake my shoulder, then turning and grabbing a tissue from her desk.

Why is this so painful? I need to go now before I completely break down. We say our final goodbyes and I walk out of the office doors and down the steps.

I knew I would be emotional after this visit, so I asked Gray and Sally to meet me for coffee in the small cafe called Maureen's just down the street. I check my watch and it reads 13:05, 10 minutes before I scheduled them to join me. I decide to head over to the coffee shop and order for us.

I check both ways for cars and begin crossing the road. Just as I reach the other side, I notice a tall dark haired man out of the corner of my eye.

He is stood, back leaning on a tree that is stood in the centre of the path. He looks absolutely sensational, if I'm quite honest. He's wearing sunglasses, covering his eyes and his dark almost black hair is short but sleek styled with an edge. Despite not being able to see his eyes, I know he is looking at me.

I continue to walk towards the cafe, gliding behind the tree and the man. As I pass, I note his head clearly swivelling from left to right as I walk past, despite the fact he is facing the complete opposite way to me. I know his eyes follow me. Entering Maureen's, I place the order for Gray, Sally and I, before heading over to the seated cozy corner area. Taking out my phone I send a text to them both to find out where they are. I receive simultaneous responses with two minutes, which I think is eerily strange but I'm distracted by the gorgeous looking guy, who is still hovering over by the tree, although his face now seems fixed intensely in my direction.

The waitress places our coffees onto the table and I thank her just as Gray and Sally walk into Maureen's. I wave them over, sliding a quick glance towards the guy, who is still watching me from across the road.

"Hey Mol, how are you feeling?" Sally asks wrapping her arms around me, pulling my attention back to them.

"I'm okay, I feel a little lost right now." I respond, trying to ignore the penetrating stare from the guy across the road.

"I'm loving the new hair girl!" Sally states running her finger tips through the length and I smile.

"Thanks I felt like I needed a fresh slate you know. New hair, new me and all that jazz."

I notice the guy from street starts to make his way over towards the cafe, and I can feel the palms of my hands sweating. I start to tremble.

Who on earth is he?

And why do I feel like a naughty school girl?

He approaches our table and my heart is racing.

"Hi, I saw you crossing the road and you're just incredibly fucking beautiful. I felt like I had to introduce myself."

My mouth gapes and I can feel my cheeks blushing a crimson red. Glancing at Gray and Sally they're both sat staring, their mouths ajar and the shock evident on their faces just as it is mine.

He is even bigger in front of my eyes as I look up to meet his stare. He slides off his sunglasses and I am greeted with deep blue eyes shining back at me. If his face wasn't completely captivating, his eyes certainly do the job anyway.

He holds out his hand for me to shake and I place my hand inside his instinctively.

His smile widens and I can't help but imitate him, like I'm completely lost in the moment right in front of me.

Mesmerised by him.

He lifts my hand up and places a kiss on the tops of my fingers before announcing in the deepest most fucking incredible voice I think I've ever heard.

"Do you believe in fate? Because I think I was meant to meet you. My name is Max."

*Holy.*

*Fucking.*

*Hell.*

# Chapter 3

## Present Day

I wake up early. I can hear giggles and rustling coming from downstairs and I smile to myself knowing exactly who has broken into my house at 9am on a Saturday morning.

"Shhh! You're going to wake her." I hear Gina whisper shout to the others.

Gray's deep voice echos through my hall "Gina, your the loudest here and you're attempting to whisper."

A chorus of giggles erupt and I can hear Gina almost losing her shit at the others. I decide to remain in bed and wait for them to finish, so not to spoil the surprise they're creating.

I love my birthday.

It's the one day of the year that's mine to steal and be selfish on. It's the only day of the year I allow myself to think about how lucky I am to still be here, celebrating life.

I jump out of my day dream to a knock at the door.

"Come in." I shout and 5 of my favourite people pile through the door shouting "Happy Birthday!" in unison as they blow on party horns and pop confetti cannons in my general direction. They pile on my bed and we all burst out laughing together.

"I heard you all 15 minutes ago arguing like petulant children downstairs." I proclaim, a smile still broadcast across my face.

"It wasn't an argument," Gray protests, "Gina just can't understand how to whisper without shouting," he pushes Gina's shoulder playfully.

Gina mouths "Asshole" towards Gray and he smiles infectiously towards her. Gina pulls at my arms "Come on! Come see what we've done."

I smile and slide out of bed "Any signs of Max yet?" I ask hopeful. Gina's face drops and I already know the answer. I haven't heard from him since our last conversation 2 weeks ago, but that's not unusual for us. I smile again "It's fine, he said he would be here and there's still time." I say positively. Gina grabs my hand and squeezes, "Come on, we have so much fun things planned," she tugs my arm and we all follow downstairs.

I open the gifts from my friends and family and we finish breakfast together. The morning has been full of laughter and it's exactly what I needed after a few busy weeks at work.

Gray and Joey head out for the afternoon of 'guy-ing' around whilst us girls focus on looking birthday ready.

"So, we're getting ready and heading to Reggie's for bottomless brunch before the surprise later on right?" I ask the girls already knowing the answer.

"Of course. I'll head downstairs and grab us some pink gins now," Gina responds, ignoring the fact it is only 11AM and seeming just as excited as I am.

"It feels like forever since we really let loose Mol, your birthday came at just the right time." Sally says, and I know the feeling.

We usually meet for a couple of drinks and a gossip throughout the week but it's really has been a while since we let our hair down fully. I smile and nod in agreement, not helping that my mind is not completely focused on the celebrations ahead.

Sally notices my hesitation, taking my hands into hers, she smiles towards me, "Please stop thinking about Max, Mollie. Don't let him not turning up spoil your day. He can be such a fucking asshole." She almost seems like she's pleading with me.

I sigh. I know she's right. It's not unusual for Max to not turn up when I expect him to and it's certainly not unusual that I don't hear from him for long periods of time.

The room remains quiet for a beat.

"I guess, I just really thought he'd be here this time." I respond, a small smile etching at my lips.

"We're not doing this today Mollie. Today is for fun, frolicking and flaming tequilas!" Sally shakes my shoulder and I can't help but laugh. She's right, I am not here to dwell today.

Gina returns with our gins and puts on some music. "Jesus, who died in here?" She jokes, sensing the seriousness circling their air. We laugh together and I know today is going to be amazing, with or without Max here.

We start to get ready and Gina picks out our outfits. She collaborates a sleek black fitting dress and some sparkling heels for me to wear and I know that little number is hot.

I head into the shower, taking out my hair releasing my wild deep auburn waves down my back, the ends still tinted a slight dark brown, reminding me of how long it has been since I left therapy.

Taking off my clothes, I glance at myself in the mirror. The scars that blemish my skin, glistening in the mirror back at me. A persistent reminder of the times I have suffered, but also of the warrior that emerged as a result. I am a true reminder of all I have survived.

I decide that my day is nose diving and I need a pick me up, so I ask Alexa to play 'Becky Hill essentials playlist' to get the dancing vibes flowing and step into the shower.

I have always been a curvier girl, show casing the typical 'mom-bod'. I've always just embraced my body shape, well that and the fact that I have always sucked at dieting. Let's face it, food is life. It's never really bothered me on the whole but I'm not sure if I've let myself go more recently or whether I'm just feeling insecure about the whole Max scenario.

I really thought he'd show today and that is totally messing with my mind.

I finish up washing my hair and body, before stepping out and wrapping my hair up and my body with a towel. I step back into my bedroom and join Gina and Sally who are both stood in their bra and knickers, dancing around the room. We spend the start of the afternoon laughing and getting ourselves ready to paint the town red. I decide to accent my deep green eyes with a smokey eye look and I slip on my dress.

Gray and Joey arrive back at my house at 1pm to collect us. I slide my feet into my heels. Gina has been the bartender, so it's safe to say we are on our merry way to 'drunks-ville'. Locking my door we jump into Joey's Range Rover and make our way into NYC.

We arrive at Reggie's and my favourite waiter, Charlie, is at the door ready to greet us.

"Girls, you look hot!" Charlie says, bumping hips with each of us as we stride through the door. "I have your favourite booth ready, and as always Mollie darling, your first Porn Star Martini is on the house. #BirthdayPerks!"

Charlie walks us to our booth and we all pile in, girls on one side and boys on the other.

I check my phone and spot a message from Max has come through.

**Max -** "Happy Birthday Babe."

Is that it?

He's supposed to fucking be here and he sends birthday fucking wishes, no apologies, no fucking explanations, no anything.

What an asshole.

I put my phone back into my bag without even responding. I have no words to say without completely losing my shit, and I refuse to let this ruin my day. Charlie returns with our drinks, I smile graciously, holding my glass into the air to 'cheers' with my nearest and dearest.

"Forever Young!" I chant, as we clank glasses and everybody repeats in unison after me.

We continue sharing tales of our weeks at work with each other, laughing and joking. This is my definitely my happy place. Right here with these wonderful people surrounding me, I am so grateful to have all of these beautiful humans with me.

The afternoon continues and Charlie brings us cocktail after cocktail. We are already merry and everyone is ready for some dancing.

"So what's the rest of the days plans?" I ask, knowing Gina has definitely booked a surprise for the day. Gina smirks at me knowingly. She glances at the watch on her wrist.

"Perfect timing to ask actually, Mol. Let's head out of here, our ride should be waiting." She hunches her shoulders up and down quickly, as a small, excited squeal leaves her lips, her smile infectious.

We all stand and Joey links my arm as we walk between the tables and out on to the street.

"You look sensational tonight Mollie, not a day over 21." Joey whispers into my ear.

I turn to look at him, as he stares into my somewhat alcohol glazed eyes. "Oh Joey, you too are a delicious slab of man-meat yourself," I respond, patting his chest with my free hand, and adjusting his collar so it sits properly. Gina laughs at my quirks and as we stand on the street a black sleek limousine arrives.

"You're carriage awaits you Cinderella," Gina exclaims opening her arms towards the car.

I laugh, "This is amazing!" I squeal "was an Uber not sufficient enough to get to the next destination Gee?" I say, a little sarcasm lacing my voice but my happiness beaming through all the same.

"Not on the 21st+4 birthdays girl big day" She states, as if this is a matter of fact and I can't help but laugh.

We all climb into the back of the limousine and pop open the champagne. The driver proceeds to navigate the streets of NYC.

"So where are we going G?" I ask again, acting a little impatient.

"You will soon see my sexy sunbeam," She replies, and I know she is totally on her way to drunk town and I'm not really sure she can even remember the plans herself.

The driver seems to be making a series of right hand turns, for around about 30 minutes and at this point I am so fucking confused, that I am sure we're just driving round in one big square. I'm not sure if it's just the alcohol fog clouding my sense of direction so we continue to listen to dance classics and I can feel myself fully unwinding. Gina opens the sun roof and stands up, pulling my arms up to join her outside of the roof. Sally creeps up outside the sunroof with us, despite the gap being questionable and we're all pretty much sardined in.

I love it.

As I turn around to face the direction we're travelling, I realise I was right. We start to approach the front of Reggie's Bar again and I know we have been driving around in squares for 30 minutes. However there is now a group of 30+ of my nearest and dearest stood outside holding a banner up.

***HAPPY 21st(+4) BIRTHDAY MOLLIE***

"What the fuck Gina?" I laugh out loud, "Why the hell have we just drove round in a limo for 30 minutes?" I ask, although I have to admit, my smile is beaming across my face. I couldn't be happier right now.

"Why the fuck not girl! Besides we had to get everything set up. Come on, let's go get shit-faced and dance until our feet bleed," she smiles back at me before dropping back through the sun roof. I look at Sally.

"You heard her, let's go get shit-faced!" Sally repeats, as she slides back through the sunroof gap herself.

I really do have the best friends a girl could ask for.

We get out of the limo and head into Reggie's bar, all of my nearest and dearest surround me. The music is thumping and I just know that tonight, is definitely about to get messy.

****

I stagger through my door tripping and falling flat on my face. I roll over, a giggle bursting out of my throat. Joey jumps out of the Uber, jogging up my front porch steps. He grasps my hands pulling me to sit up.

"Joey I'm fine, the door got stuck and when it fell away, I fell away." I wave my hands about in the air like that was going to help describe how the door was there, and then it wasn't, "Ask me tomorrow when the alcohol has wore off and I'll probably tell you something different. But right now, I need my bed." I say, still giggling at the fact I've just took on my front door and the door freakin' won.

Joey sighs, "Be careful Mollie, I can stay and make sure your okay if you like," Joey says, his voice is so calming, it literally makes my toes tingle.

"I'm honestly perfectly fine. Go home, the Uber is gonna leave if you don't hurry." I reply just as Gray shouts from outside to hurry Joey up.

Joey scowls at me, but obliges "Lock your door immediately after I leave Mollie." He says, so much seriousness in his voice.

"Yeah, yeah, I know. I'm not completely incapacitated Joey," I sass back. Joey smiles and pulls me up, bidding me a good night and closing my front door as he leaves.

It's just after 3AM and I have had the best night. I hold myself up using the sideboard and lock my door just as Joey ordered. Grabbing myself a drink from the kitchen and check my phone for any more messages from Max.

Still nothing.

*Asshole.*

Kicking off my shoes at the foot of the stairs I carefully climb them, balancing my drink in one hand and my phone in the other. Walking into my bedroom, with no hands spare I leave the lights off and stride across the room placing my phone and drink on the table beside my bed. I take myself into the en-suite and begin to take off my make-up.

My ears are ringing from the music in the club and I re-live moments in my mind giggling to myself. I have had such an amazing day and night with my closest people and I loved that even Sara was able to make it to the evening for some full on party girl time. It's the best feeling having all of my girls close by, it was just what I needed after Max was a no show.

I take off my clothes, staying in my black lace bra and thong set I picked out in the hopes of Max's return. Climbing into bed I pick up my kindle and small reading light and decide to wind down to make sure I avoid any possibilities of a nightmare ruining this blissful day. I continue reading my favourite T. L. Swan book calming my mind, easing myself into my slumber. I reach a spicy scene in my book and I can't help but squeeze my thighs together as pressure builds in my sex.

Hell, I'd kill for Max to be home, despite the fact he's a fucking asshole for not showing up. I try to continue to read as the scene unfolds and I am panting, my sex now throbbing wet. I have not been fucked in so long and it is evident in the way my body is reacting to this scene. That and the alcohol is clearly leading me astray.

I place my kindle on the bed and decide to try and satiate myself, giving into my bodies need for pleasure. Running my finger tips from my right hand down my skin to the tip of my underwear. I push my hand beneath the lace and trail down towards my sex. Rubbing and circling my fingers over my clit and through the slick wetness of my sex. I spend some time working myself in further, using my thumb to massage my clit while brushing my fingertips through my wet heat. I picture Max and how full he would make me feel inside, the thought causing my walls to tighten on instinct.

Dipping my fingers inside my sex, I let out a breathy moan at the soft and sensual feeling my fingers are giving me. I continue a slow rhythm, pushing my fingers in an out of my sex whilst circling my clit. Licking my fingers on my left hand, I begin to massage my taut nipples, pinching them and circling, touching my senses, I can feel my climax building.

My hand continues to slowly pump inside my sex, my legs widening giving myself full access. I curl my fingers inside my sex and start working my G-spot. I feel my orgasm building and my breath is hitching, panting. I decide to reach for my vibrator from my nightstand, placing this on my clit, turning on a low level vibration.

My hand continues to work flicking the tips of my fingers inside me, as I know my orgasm is close to peaking. I intensify the vibration stimulating my clit, and my fingers start pumping faster. The sound of my wet sex fills my silent room and I know I am close to coming undone. I push my vibrator up one more setting and curl my fingers inside my sex. I cry out in ecstasy as I come hard, my legs snapping shut as the walls of my sex squeeze my fingers tightly. My breathing is rapid and I keep my vibrator pressed against my clit, as I bring myself back down to earth.

"You are fucking sensational when you orgasm," A deep voice purrs from the corner of my room and I fucking scream throwing the vibrator towards the sound of the voice.

I hear a thud as it make contact with whatever just spoke to me in the corner.

"Fucking hell Mollie, what the fuck!" I hear the voice fire out and I realise it's Max's voice I am hearing from the corner of the room. I reach out to turn on my bedside lamp.

"What the fuck are you doing sat in the corner of my room in the dark?" I screech back, "And why the fuck is your dick in your hands?" I add, fully shocked. Am I fucking imagining this shit?

"I arrived around midnight and you weren't home yet. I figured you wouldn't be long so I decided to chill over here waiting to surprise you, clearly I fell asleep waiting and then when I woke up, you were in full flow and I'm not gonna lie, it was fucking hot Mollie." Max responds nonchalantly, like it's the most normal fucking thing to do, sitting in a dark corner and watching someone masturbate, while you sit with your dick in your hands.

He rubs his head where there appears to be a red mark and a small lump, obviously where the vibrator had managed to make contact with his head, at least I had a great shot.

"Why didn't you stop me? Join me? Fucking anything but the creep in the corner?" I exclaim.

"I did join you, hence why my dick is in my hands," Max states, like it's a matter of fact, totally normal, not fucking creepy behaviour.

I flop back down on my pillow. Between the alcohol, the orgasm cloud and the adrenaline from Max's appearance, I don't know if I'm floating or falling.

Max takes off his army t-shirt and combat pants. His dog-tags hanging round his neck lying on his perfectly toned pecks. He walks over to the bed, climbing in besides me.

"Don't be mad at me baby. I'm sorry I missed today, I was delayed on my flight in," Max says, his lip curling out in a sad face expression. He strokes my cheek, continuing down my neck to my collarbone. "I hope you wore this sexy number for my benefit not anyone else's?" He asks, hopeful that I'll just drop the whole missing my birthday shenanigans.

"Max, I get that sometimes inevitable things happen which stop you from communicating with me, but today you managed to message Happy Birthday to me, so how could you not have just added 'flight delayed sorry' into that. Why do I have to feel like you just don't give a fuck?" I respond, deciding not to let this slide.

"I know, I'm sorry. I didn't know how long I'd have signal for, I thought it would be best for me to at least say Happy Birthday, so you knew I was alive and I hadn't forgotten. I promise I was typing another message and the comms dropped out." Max states, still stroking me along my collar bones.

I sigh, feeling so torn by the fact I have missed him and I should be grateful he's here, not grumpy that he wasn't here when I expected him to be.

Max starts nipping at my ear lobe and I know he's trying to distract me away from his 'assholery' with sex. I can't bring myself to say no to him, it's been so long since I felt him inside me, I need him just as much as he needs me. I may have already come once but my bodies reaction to his large muscles pressed against me and his touch along my skin, has my sex dripping wet again ready for him.

He runs his calloused fingers along my breasts, unpicking the front hook of my bra, releasing my them. He dips down, sucking softly on my nipple as his mouth surrounds it, a breathy moan escaping me. My back arches and I can feel my insides tighten as I'm almost gagging for him to be inside of me.

I look into his eyes, reaching my hand down to grab his erection, stroking him up and down sensually, the pre-ejeculation tipping the edge of his cock as I run my hands across the head and use this to lubricate his shaft.

"I've worked myself in, so you can just fill me up and fuck me into tomorrow." I breath into his ear as he reaches between my legs. Max feels the slick wetness between my lips, before he rolls on top of me. He reaches into my nightstand, rolling a condom onto his length before lining up at the entrance of my sex, stroking the head of his cock along my dripping wet lips. He bends down taking my nipple between his lips again biting and sucking, the sensation like fuel to the already deep burning fire at my core.

"Do you want hot and hard, or soft and sensual baby?" He asks, a devilish smirk pulling at his lips.

"I want you… to fuck me… into tomorrow Max," I respond flatly, instantly knowing I want my fucking brains splattered on my headboard. It has been far too long for soppy love making, that shit can wait for tomorrow.

"As you wish," Max responds, biting down hard on my nipple, before lining himself at the entrance to my sex, and slamming home hard. The moan bursts out from inside me, as the pain and pleasure mixed takes over my senses.

Max works at piston pace, the sound of our arousal hitting together, satisfying in so many ways. He remains looking down towards our bodies connected, watching his dick slide into me repeatedly. We continue to fuck, hot and hard like I asked for, my orgasm is on the brink but not quite enough to send me over the edge.

Max grunts, continuing to look down towards our sex meeting, before he slows into long deep thrusts. He folds over on top of me and I know he's finished.

He didn't even wait for me to finish.

His breath is laboured and he sits up kissing my forehead before heading into the en-suite bathroom. I watch as he walks away. He closes the bathroom door behind him.

I search for my underwear around my bedroom and I can hear the sounds of splashing, slap like noises in the bathroom. My face wrinkles not really sure what I can hear so I assume he's decided to wash himself off following our sex session.

After 20 minutes he returns into the bedroom with a towel around his waist, still not making eye contact with me.

"Is everything okay Max?" I ask, not sure what's happening and why the mood changed.

"Yeah, I erm, I need to pack," Max replies.

"What do you mean you need to pack? You just got back like half an hour ago?" I reply, annoyance on my voice.

"I know, I only had a brief stop over here, I persuaded my commanding officer to place the layover here so I would get to see you but my next flight out is at 6:00AM," Max responds, his voice is flat, seemingly with no emotions.

I stare at him blankly.

*Is he fucking serious right now?*

"Did you not think to say something when you arrived back? Before you got into my bed to fuck me and then decide you can't stay?" My voice trembling as I feel myself getting angrier about the fact he thinks this is normal fucking behaviour.

Max remains quiet, going into his draws and collecting new pairs of combats and matching military grade T-shirts to pack in his duffle bag.

"Are you not even going to reply to me? Max you can't be serious right now, when are you going to realise you need to come home for longer than 5 minutes? We can't carry on like this." I exclaim, my voice is raising, I know I am close to losing my shit with him.

"Mollie, you know the score, I go where I am needed. I have six months of my tour left and then I'm back for good."

"Six months? You said two months almost two months ago. We've been together almost three years now and you seem to be getting further away from coming home for good it seems!" I'm shouting, really starting to lose all sense of self control.

"I need to finish my mission Mollie. I can't just abandon it midway through," Max continues to pack some clothes and I note that he has still not made eye contact with me, not during sex, not after.

"Why won't you look at me?" I ask directly, my tone so sharp as I feel the venom creeping up from my throat.

"I'm packing Mollie, don't be so sensitive, it's not about you all the time"

I see red at his down right audacity to call me fucking sensitive.

"Sensitive? Max you didn't look at me when you were fucking me either. Why won't you look at me?" I can feel my whole body trembling with anger.

Max stands, picking up his rucksack, and placing this on his shoulder before turning and looking directly in my eyes.

"Are you happy now?" He says, as his eyes burn into me.

He's fully clothed and ready to go. I glance at the clock which reads 5AM remembering he has to be at the airport for 6AM.

"I'm sorry Mollie. I'll be in touch," he blows me a kiss and before I can object he's left the bedroom and I hear the front door slam.

*I'll be in fucking touch.*

Spoken like I'm not his fucking partner of three years.

Shock fills my every pore. I stand at the foot of my bed, it takes a full five minutes for me to realise my jaw is still open and I am just stood here aimlessly lost in what has just happened.

I walk round to my side of the bed and jump inside, deciding that I need to sleep to compartmentalise this shit show. Lying my head on my pillow, my mind is racing but I drift myself into a restless sleep.

****

I wake up to a faint buzzing sound, rolling over grabbing my phone from the nightstand. I see a series of text messages and look at the time, 10:20AM. I open the messages and see what I've been missing.

**Gina** - Who the fuck did I see leaving your house at 5AM Mollie? You did not bag Joey Kincaid did you? OMG he is sexy so if you did, I do not hold it against you. #MaxWho?

**Sally** - Dirty girl! But Joey is fire! #HotAsFuck

**Sally** - We need to know all the details Mollie.

**Gina** - She'll still be asleep in dire need of 'sexual healing'. Imagine that I sang that.

**Sally** - Well she has around 20 minutes before I come pounding on her bedroom door for all the details.

**Gina** - Mollie, hurry up or were coming for you!

I smirk to myself before the reality of how intense last night was, knowing I need to speak to my girls about everything. I place my phone onto the bedside table and hop out, heading to the en-suite to get ready for the day.

Turning on the shower, I close the door to let it warm up. Glancing at myself in the mirror I see the evidence that last night really did happen on my body. Marks from Max's mouth, present all over my body.

Last night was so strange. I was unsure if I dreamt it, but looking at myself now I know it actually existed. The marks, the tenderness of my breasts and sex tell me I most certainly did not imagine it. I just can't get my head around the whole ordeal. I turn to jump into the shower and my eye catches sight of something in the bin. I notice an empty bottle of lubricant is placed inside the bin alongside the condom from last nights sex with Max.

As I reach for the lubricant bottle, it dawns on me that we didn't use lube. Picking up the condom, I notice something peculiar. There is no come inside it.

I search for a tear, a rip of some sort. Not concerned around birth control, as I am on the pill, but just curious as to why there wouldn't be evidence of semen in there.

There are no rips, no tears.

Reality sinks in.

He fucking pretended to come.

And then he had a wank to finish himself off.

*What the fuck.*

# Chapter 4

## Therapy
## Three years ago
## Session 144

I look outside the windows of the room. It's a sunny day today in NYC, which always puts me in a good mood. I sit waiting on the large cream sofa. There is definitely something about this room that always makes me feel safe.

I have spent what is quickly approaching three years, pouring out my soul to Dr Rene inside these four walls and the journey has definitely been a sad affair of bittersweet happiness and tragic sorrows.

The door opens and I jump, startled by the interruption to my thoughts. Florence enters, placing a warm latte and a caramel biscuit down on the coffee table in front of me. I smile at her graciously as she lets me know Dr Rene will be with me in a couple of minutes. I nod to acknowledge her and I take myself back into my own thoughts again.

I have 12 more sessions before Dr Rene thinks I will have everything I need to conquer life outside of therapy. If I'm honest, the thought is terrifying me, but it is somewhat wholesome.

Dr Rene enters the room with a smile as bright as Christmas itself .

"Mollie, welcome, I'm sorry I was delayed." She announces before taking a seat in her arm chair across from me. I want to respond to her but it's as though the words just can't leave my lips.

As if she is in my mind, Dr Rene smiles sympathetically towards me. “What’s on your mind Mollie?” She asks curiously, knowing all of my tell tale signs.

My eyes leave hers and I return to glancing at the vast greenery of Central Park, which covers acres of ground below the windows. I go to speak and my words just won’t leave my mouth. Closing my lips, I inhale a deep breath and close my eyes tight.

Dr Rene waits, as patient as always for me to build myself up to speaking out loud. I return my gaze towards Dr Rene.

“We have 12 sessions left.” I whisper.

She nods at me. “We do, is this bothering you?” She asks

I shake my head, gesturing no. I know I can cope outside of these sessions. I know my friends and family are always there to pick me up if I need grounding.

“It doesn’t bother me, no. I just…“ I hesitate, trying to pick out the words I need to justify these feelings I have. “What happens if I meet them again?” I spit out.

Dr Rene closes her note book, unfolding her legs. “What do you think would be the right thing to do if you saw them again?” She bounces back at me. “Would you recognise them?”

I take a moment to think again, glancing back out of the long floor to ceiling window. Most of the organisations men wore hoodies and bandannas over their faces to cover their identities. But not Melvin, their leader. He didn’t hide anything about himself to me. I know the answer that I should say so I decide to give that one.

“I’d phone the police. Tell them I have found them.” I respond.

Dr Rene smiles, “And what would you really want to do instead of that?”

I scoff out loud, my smile pasting my lips and leaving just as quick as it came.

"I'd want revenge." I say deadpan, looking down at my fingers.

It's almost been three years since I started therapy with Dr Rene. But today is unique as it marks three years to the date since I was found.

Alive, albeit barely.

No amount of therapy I feel will ever allow me to forget the shit I went through and the thought that the people responsible are still at large, that's what turns my stomach. I can feel the bile rising up my throat as I recall the memories in my mind, seeing the light peer in through the sliding metal door. At this point I had been abandoned. I had escaped and managed to get myself to a cold and damp warehouse just on the outskirts of London. I was told I'd been there on my own for at least three days. But the reality was that I'd been somewhere between there and hell for eighteen long months.

I had managed to slip past their defences, before everything was a mess of men searching for me. I had no idea where I was, I'd called the police but when I realised the hoods were searching for me, I ran and found a derelict warehouse, hiding from them. The exhaustion led to me passing out.

When I woke, I had been found. It had been three days though.

The organisation knew I had made contact with the police and they made sure there wasn't a trace of their existence surrounding me or within the local area that I had been kept in. Not a DNA sample, not even a fucking strand of hair. They just upped and left.

I still have no idea who they were or why they chose me.

"Mollie" Dr Rene says calmly.

I jump again at the interruption, realising that I am absent today.

"You're seemingly quieter than usual Mollie. Can we explore this further?" Dr Rene asks, although I know this isn't an actual question.

I nod towards her, "It's today." I say, my voice is barely above a whisper.

"I know it is today." She confirms back at me. Her face never falters but I know she's known me long enough now to sympathise more than she lets on.

Today's date is the anniversary, of day I was released from captivity. Or I should say escaped. Today is when I found a safe place to hide and hoped that someone, somewhere, would find me.

"But we have twelve sessions left so let's look at some of the reasons that you won't be here with me next year Mollie." Dr Rene redirects the session and I know she's been tactful in changing my outlook.

We talk about the usual mantra which I have built on to ensure I can navigate my life, without therapy. I have made a start on building my publishing empire and my friends are in this with me so I know everybody is so close by.

"I think, it's the change that I'm struggling with," I say, knowing that consistency has been the pinnacle of my healing.

"This is always a change which you will struggle to navigate Mollie, but you have built on the micro-steps that have developed and shaped you into the woman you are today. You have suffered great loss, more than you should have for a young woman, but you are a survivor." Dr Rene shares and I know that she believes in my success after this process.

"I think, I struggle more with this day because I lost so much at the same time that I also gained everything. I don't understand how to feel so elevated but also crushed." I respond, feeling as torn and raw as the first day I was found.

Dr Rene opens her notebook again and starts to scribe notes, presumably my reactions to today's session.

"Reality and truth can wind a person Mollie, and that reaction is perfectly normal."

"Normal?" I mock "How is it normal to feel nothing but happiness when you have finally been freed, despite discovering your parents are dead. They died. Well, they were killed by the same people I was a fucking slave to. Because I couldn't just listen and follow the rules." My voice sharp and anger seems to be shining through my pores.

"How can I claim to be a good person when the day my brother told me our parents were not at my bedside in the hospital was because they had died on the search for me, and all I could think and feel was that I was just glad that it wasn't me." I look down, knowing I've lost my temper and attempt to refocus myself.

Dr Rene states firmly "Mollie, you know that you were not to blame for something that happened while you were not here."

"But it is my fault. Because I was the reason they were searching. I am the reason they died because Melvin fucking knew where they were and I just didn't listen to what I was supposed to do. Fuck, I am the reason for multiple people dying in the organisation. I am the reason they were taken and I am the reason they died." I declare, swiping the tears falling from my eyes and returning my gaze to the greenery.

"We have worked through this Mollie. You are feeling vulnerable and you are trying to convince yourself that you need me to be able to go through day to day. But you don't. You did not have a nightmare leading up to todays session and that is a milestone. You have control and you are not losing control Mollie." Dr Rene asserts and I know that what she is telling me is right deep down.

I stay quiet and Dr Rene allows me to gather my thoughts and compose my emotions.

"Emotions are good Mollie. It shows your good intentions. Somebody with good intentions, despite having a past which has had a period of extreme upset and trauma, still strives to be the best version of herself. You must remember your resilience and the steps we have taken to help you when you feel that your control is slipping." Dr Rene reminds me.

We have spent so long building on methods to support my worries and work through these moments, where I feel out of control.

"I'm sorry." I sigh, feeling a little defeated after todays session.

"Don't apologise for feeling, Mollie." Dr Rene conquers and I smile up at her.

I decide the session has gotten a little heavy and I opt to use one of my learnt techniques and cue the word to ask for a 10 minute breather.

"Beach mode." I say, turning my eyes to the windows and taking in the view before closing my eyes to focus on my breathing.

When I open my eyes, Dr Rene is writing in her note book and I turn my head back to face her.

"Great use of your methods, Mollie. You are in control, this is your life," Dr Rene closes her notebook and places her pen on the top of this.

I nod in response and glance at the clock realising we're five minutes over time. I gasp, placing my hand over my lips.

"I'm so sorry, Dr Rene. I didn't realise when I called out 'Beach' that we would run over." I feel the sense of dread glazing over me for infringing on her end of day. I am the last session in for today and I can't help but feel a guilty twinge in the pit of my stomach.

"No need to apologise, Mollie. I was late in to session remember," her smile is wide and genuine and it fills me with a small dose of serotonin.

I stand, gathering my belongings and head out of the room.

"See you next week Doc."

# Chapter 5

## Present Day

"Wait a minute." Sally proclaims, finger held out, wagging it in my direction. "Let me get this fucking straight." She pauses again and I swear, it's just for dramatic effect.

"So, the guy who we saw leaving here at 5am, was none other than 'no-show Max'. Who turned up, like a fucking silent assassin in the night. Tugged his teeny weeny in silence, while you saw to your sad lonely sorry self." Her head is wagging at me, along with her finger, outrage written on her face.

"And then, he got up like king-fucking-ding. Dipped his love stick, didn't give you the long awaited orgasm you actually deserved." She continues, at this point she is pacing the room.

"And then he abandoned the fucking mission. And proclaimed he had to leave because he couldn't abandon the mission. But not before making some questionable slip and slide noises, by himself, in the bathroom," Again she pauses for dramatic effect, still waggling her finger and shaking her head.

"And this morning, after said abandonment, you discover he didn't even fucking orgasm himself. He fully faked the situation and lubed his pathetic love stick up, to whack a solo one out in the bathroom after leaving you high and dry!" Sally finishes, her pitch so high I don't even know how we can still hear her.

Gina remains sat at the end of my bed, her jaw on the floor. I sigh, and nod at the reality that this shit actually happened to me.

True to Sally's word after 20 minutes her and Gee came bounding across the grass, still in their pyjamas, and Sally even brought her duvet. We managed to get Sara on FaceTime and that's when I divulged the extent of the shit show that unfolded last night.

"Was the sex at least good?" Sara asks, the bottom left side of her lip pulling down at the side.

"What fucking sex is good when you don't even have time to show that you've enjoyed it Sara." Sally answers before I can even open my mouth.

I snort, "Gee, you can have sex without finishing you know." I say, not really convincing myself that means anything, but part of me feels the need to defend Max. "I had already finished myself off before we had sex so maybe he just thought that was fair game."

"Oh fuck off, Mollie. A man who doesn't give a shit about satisfying you is not worth the time in your vagina. I know damn well men like Gray or Joey would…" Sally starts ranting before pausing and I hold my hand up to interject.

"Sally, do not finish that sentence about how well my brother has managed to satisfy woman's needs. I do not need that image in my head when I'm already feeling delicate and quite frankly on the verge of PTSD."

"We need more drinks." Gina announces, clearly picking her jaw back up off the floor.

"When will he be back Mol?" Sara asks, and I feel the sorrow lacing her voice.

"Who knows?" I say, flopping myself back on the bed.

"We need more drinks" Gina repeats, as if no one heard her the first time and not that we ignored her.

"Fuck it. We need drinks," Sally says, jumping up and walking into my wardrobe to pull out some clothes.

"I gotta go girls, my flight is in 30 minutes so it's boarding time. I'll catch up with you all soon," Sara proclaims.

We all jump back onto the bed on either side of Sally. "We will Sara, love you girl. Text us when you land safely."

We all bid our fair wells and Gina slings the iPad back on my bed.

"Right, fuck it, we're going Reggie's, you're going to tell the boys everything you know and we'll get a male perspective on the situ. Get dressed. I'll score us an Uber. You have twenty minutes Mollie." Gina says as she pulls Sally up and before I realise it, she's already exited my bedroom and is half way down the stairs.

I guess it wouldn't be the worst idea to ask the guys what they think. I jump out of bed and get myself dressed. The twenty minutes pass by in a flash and before I know it, we're all in an Uber and heading into NYC.

****

We're sat in the booth at Reggie's and eating some lunch. Joey and Gray have joined us and I've caught them up on last nights issues.

"Nah Mollie, that is odd fucking behaviour," Joey scoffs, shaking his head.

"So, I'm not just being over sensitive?" I reply, not wanting to come across as the needed girlfriend.

"Mollie you're not the fucking issue here. He is. Do not justify shitty actions because you think you're too intense wanting your boyfriend, of almost three years might we add, to give you some fucking time and effort." Gray says. "He spent a fucking year pursuing you, following you round whenever he was near us to persuade you to even give the sad sorry loser a chance and here you are, almost three years on and living the life you told him you weren't interested in for this very reason." Gray proclaims as Sally raises her arms in a Hail-Mary gesture.

I don't even know how the fuck I've got in this position with Max, where I am not pining for him while he seems to become less frequent in my life. At first, he was so tentative, despite the intimidation I felt when he approached me in the cafe, when I'd left my final therapy session. He was swooney, and he pursued me for a little bit before I finally agreed that I'd commit to being with a military man. I just didn't need to be abandoned at that point in my life but eventually, it just seemed to work for us.

"I don't know what the fuck is happening, but I know I need to speak with him about this whole situation because I am not getting any younger." I finalise, leaning back in the booth, not really feeling hungry any more. Everyone seems to be giving me that irritating sad, sorry look which drowns me further. I feel like I did when I first started therapy and everybody treated me as if they thought if they said too much or touched me too hard, I'd break into a million pieces.

I am not that girl anymore.

"I'll deal with it. I'm not taking this fucking shit anymore." I say, dropping the money for my food on the table. "I've got work to do before tomorrow, I'll see you girls tomorrow."

I hug each of them, before collecting my jacket and bag and heading out onto the city street.

****

I head into the office, Monday's are always chaotic, as it is in most jobs when you're catching up with the weekend. Everybody gets the Monday blues. Today, I certainly have the Monday blues more than usual.

Following my birthday weekend, I should feel elated. Like I'm floating on water, but instead I feel a little lost. But more than anything, I'm so fucking angry.

I sit on my office chair and spin around to face the greenery of central park. I picked this office because of the view and the ability to remind me of how far I have come. The view always calms my thoughts when they become too loud, just as they did when I was in therapy.

After leaving Reggie's yesterday, I treated myself to an oatmeal and lavender bath and I thought out every logical reason there could be for Max faking an orgasm. The outcome of that process was not positive, with thoughts that I'm just not attractive to him anymore, but that doesn't make sense because he was giving me all the vibes whilst he jerked off in the corner, like a fucking ninja.

I pick up my phone and decide I need to go through this properly with Max. I have so many unanswered questions and I need to know what the fuck is happening. I compose a message, typing and deleting and typing again, not really sure what I want to say without seeming like a lunatic with the 'oh hey babe, nice to see you at the weekend. Any insight why you faked your orgasm, had a wank on your own time, then fucked off?' vibes.

I settle for plain and simple.

**Mollie -** We need to talk.

I place my phone down, focusing on my laptop and start trawling through my emails. I come across one from 'Cilla-Zilla' just as Gina and Sally pour into my office. Sally places a caramel latte on my desk and they both slump down into the chairs at the front of my desk.

"I feel like I could sleep forever," Gina announces, rolling her head back and letting out a whine.

"It's been a busy weekend, but there is no rest for the wicked Gee, have you seen Cilla's email?" I bounce back.

"I have, Riley's team now want market research into masturbation, what the fuck is that all about?" Sally states and Gina scoffs almost snorting her coffee straight through her nostrils.

"Jesus fucking christ, why? Can Riley not just fucking explore for herself and be satisfied with the results?" Gina exclaims and we all giggle in unison.

'The email from Cilla states that Riley is expanding from sex books to creating an app platform for discussing masturbation techniques, likes and dislike, including finding 'mutual masturbation friends', whatever the fuck that means," I recall the email out loud.

Gina's face is a picture, her jaw is slack and I never thought I'd see the day that she is left speechless.

"Do we have the budget for this?" I ask Sally, refocussing on the business element.

"I'm going to run numbers back to them because we're not covering this if they want to expand, that's more than we're contracted to do." Sally responds.

"Mutual. Masturbation. Friends." Gina echos in a delayed response and we all set off in fits of laughter again. This is the reason I built a business with my best friends.

****

We spent the start of the week looking into research for masturbation forums. To give Riley Austin her due, there doesn't seem to be a platform for this type of situation, probably because it's a little on the 'taboo' side but we did find that people are more than keen to be involved. The process has been a quick turnaround and Riley, or should I say the voice of Riley - Cilla, has managed to pilot an app for trial. The app went live this morning and we have been ensuring that this works smoothly, supporting an additional external team during the day.

When 5pm finally hits, myself and the girls gather in my office for our end of day showdown.

"We're going to have to download this app you know," Sally says, a look of utter disgrace on her face. "I cannot face Cilla when she finds out we don't want to be an actual part of this, which she definitely will find out. Even if we don't tell her. It's like a sixth sense." She continues.

We all agree, pressing to download the app onto our phones and create our accounts.

"Why is it asking me how I flick my clit? Does Riley want me to draw a fucking map too?" Gina scoffs whilst she continues to fill out the form.

"Where does it say that?" Sally gasps, starting to rapidly scroll.

"Well, it doesn't actually say those words Sal, but you get me. Why does it need to know what my preferences are in my nether regions? Can a girl not just wing it?" Gina states and I chuckle at her.

"It's meant to help other people know what you're good at G. What you've discovered works so you can help others, you know." I widen my eyes, pointing my hands towards my crotch before making a flicking motion and rolling my eyes to the back of my head and giving them the best orgasm climax face I can muster up.

We all burst into laughter hysterically. Just as Gray walks into my office.

"Gray! What a surprise, what are you doing here?" I say, the interruption unusual.

"The news? I guess you haven't seen it?" Gray responds, his voice cautious, almost seeming wary of my reaction.

"No?" I say, my answer more of a question as concern grows inside my stomach, picking up the remote to my office television, I flick it on.

The news channel fills the screen as the headline rolls along the bottom of the screen on a repeat cycle. I read it, before freezing solid to my seat.

**‘Notorious Tourist Trafficking Gang members spotted throughout NYC'**

I’m rooted to the spot. This can’t be true, this city is huge and not full of the types of tourists they look for.

Have they altered their plans?

Are they looking for me?

I can feel my breathing become rapid and shallow and I realise that my brother and my friends are trying to coax my attention back to them. I have no idea how long I have been fixated on the screen.

I snap my eyes over to my brothers, holding back the tears that are threatening to fall.

“I’m here, Mollie. Nothing will happen to you. I’ve come to take you and the girls home.”

“I’m fine.” I plaster a smile on my face, knowing I can’t panic him. He is already over protective and I just don’t need it. “I don’t even live in the city. We don’t live in the city and we always travel from office to home in a car. We’re fine, we're all fine.” I splutter, not sure who I’m actually trying to convince, them or myself. Gray’s eyes look at me sympathetically and that’s exactly how I feel.

Pathetic.

“Don’t look at me like I’m fragile. All of you, stop it.” I stand from my desk and grab my things. “Let’s go home then, if you’re chaperoning us,” I announce and head to the door of my office.

We each jump inside Gray’s car and I know I need a distraction from everything.

“We have to finish this app set up girls, I am not hearing Cilla yell at us tomorrow, it's just not worth the ear ache.”

I pull out my phone along with Sally and Gina as we continue our individual set ups on the app. The page pops up to enter a user name and we each take a moment to think of a masturbation related pun for our names. We decide not to share our names with each other, so not to die of embarrassment if we actually use the app. Giggling to myself, I type in my chosen name into the app.

**Username: BerryBean**

Opting to reference my deep auburn red hair. I fill out the remaining boxes with my preferences before setting my phone back in my bag.

We arrive at our little Cul-de-sac and Gray tries to insist I either stay at Gina and Sally's house, or I allow him to stay with me.

"Gray, I'm a big girl, I had my therapy and I am set to conquer the world. If I have a nightmare I'll survive it, I have my techniques and I know what I am doing." I open the car door and step outside. "I love you big bro, but you smother me sometimes." I finish as I slam the door shut behind me and round the car to his side.

Gray sighs, turning to yell at me out of his window, "Okay fine. But contact me if you need me Mollie, promise me?"

"I will. I promise."

I give him a quick hug through the window, before walking up the path to my home. I pour myself a gin and lemonade and I head into the bathroom, flipping on the shower.

A ping sounds from my phone and I sigh awaiting the overdramatic and unsolicited texts of worry from everybody who knows an ounce of history about me.

Instead, I see a notification from the 'Mutual Masturbation Friends' app. I find a message from Username: ClitHero. I slide the app open, my curiosity peaked.

**ClitHero:** Hi BerryBean. I like your profile, wanna exchange tips?

I gasp. What the fuck? This has got to be Gina or Sally fucking messing with me, they must have seen my name whilst we were in Gray's car, the fucking fuckers. I place my phone back down on the sink unit and jump into the shower, leaving the message on 'read'.

Finishing up my night time routine, I hop onto my bed as my phone pings again. I pick it up and check the notifications again.

**ClitHero -** I'm sorry, I didn't mean to sound forward. We can get to know each other before we talk tips if you like?

They're really fucking trying this shit on. I close the app and grab my iPad, instantly bring up FaceTime, to call the group. Gina and Sally pick up while Sara rejects the call, which isn't unusual.

"Which one of you two fuckers is ClitHero? I'm not falling for this shit, so you can screenshot me and have humiliating ammo for future endeavours." I say sharply.

"What the fuck are you going on about?" Gina says, her face seeming genuinely confused.

"That means it's you Sally. Confess your sins, asshole."

"I haven't done anything but pour myself a wine, so keep your allegations to yourself, thank you very much," Sally states, shaking her wine glass at me.

I scowl, one of these fuckers is lying and I will find out.

"Which one of you class clowns is ClitHero?"

Gina bursts out laughing "ClitHero? Like, Clit - Hero?" She can barely contain her laughter.

"What's each of your names on this app? It's one of you I know it is!" my voice is practically screeching at this point.

"Can you just explain? I thought we were keeping our names a secret so we can't spy on each others user activity?" Sally says, her face equally looking just as confused.

"So did I Sally, but it appears one of you untrustworthy fuckers scouted my user name and now you're trying to trick me!" I exclaim, continuing to increase in pitch.

"It's not me," Sally shakes her hand as though she's waving a little white flag.

Gina is still creased laughing "Wait, wait, wait, you actually have a message on the app? The 'Mutual Masturbation Friends' app?" She continues to laugh, actual tears streaming from her eyes.

"It's you, isn't it? You're ClitHero?" Gina folds over laughing more and I am getting irate.

"Are you doing this as some kind of distraction technique because it won't work G." I proclaim, at this point I'm fucking pouting into the camera. Gina finally finishes wiping the tears of joy from her face and takes a breath to speak.

"It's not me. I swear to you it's not me." She opens the app on her phone and shares her username with me as I spot 'MasterBlaster' is spread across the top of her screen and I chuckle out loud.

"Sally, it's you then."

Sally picks up her phone and opens the app displaying her user name at me, ThePenetrator spread across the screen. Gina cracks again and begins howling for the second time.

"Well, you've created a separate account. I know it's you guys come on just confess."

They simultaneously respond "It's not us Mollie!" Before laughing their heads off again.

"What does the messages say?" Gina asks when she finally finishes her giggle fest.

I sip my gin and read the 2 messages out that I have received from ClitHero.

"You have to answer back Mollie!" Sally declares, giggles still erupting from the pair of them.

"No, I fucking don't!" I announce returning my phone to the bedside table.

"You do. Come on, this could be hilarious! What if it's Cilla?" Gina states, as her and Sally crease over laughing again.

"You two are fucking arseholes. Maybe I should reply to ClitHero because clearly, I need new best friends." I deadpan, shaking my head and dropping it back onto my headboard. "I'm going to bed, you two are unhinged," I state before they both burst out laughing again. Flipping them the bird, I press the red button to end our call.

I turn on the TV and the news fills my screen again. The headline continues to circle and I feel the dread swirling in the bottom of my stomach. Sipping my gin and lemonade, I pick up my phone and browse the MMF app again. Opening messages, I select the message from ClitHero. Thinking for a moment I decide, what's the worst outcome for messaging this person back. Maybe she could have some good tips that I am just dying to know about. I spend most of my time at home alone anyway. I finish my gin and place my glass back down on the side before tapping out a message.

**BerryBean -** Sorry, I was in the shower when I saw your message. Getting to know each other seems a good idea before diving into all the gossip. Hope to hear from you soon.

*Hope to hear from you soon.*

Who the hell do I think I am messaging? A long lost penpal? I shake my head and close my phone. Turning off the TV and my bedside lamp, I decide to call it a night.

****

*I'm strolling down the beach, admiring the vast amount of stars across the night sky. My friend, Felix, is walking alongside me. He offered to walk me home tonight, well back to the hostel after the white party, as Gina and Sally wanted to continue their night. We are currently visiting the West coast of Bulgaria on our trip around the world. Striding along the beach, the sky is clear and I start to point out the constellations in the sky that I recognise. Turning around, I realise that Felix has gone.*

*"Felix?" I shout, glancing around the empty beach*

*How long have I been walking alone? Where the fuck is he?*

*"Felix?" I shout again, louder this time. Panic clenches in my chest. What if he's fallen in the sea and I haven't noticed?*

*"FELIX!" I shout at the top of my lungs.*

*A bag is slung over my head, blackening my vision and a pair of strong arms lock around me. I scream before a deep husky voice whisper shouts into my ear, "Shut your pretty fucking mouth, slut." A cloth is placed over my mouth as I struggle in his arms, my shoulders trying to break from his grip.*

*No, no, no. This can't be happening to me. No! The cloth stays firmly pressed to my face and I feel myself relaxing. My mind is screaming to fight but my body is sleeping. Fucking come on Mollie, fight.*

*But I can't.*

*I can't do anything.*

****

I wake up, my body is trembling and I quickly realise I am post nightmare. I can't move my arms or legs and I can feel the tears rolling down my cheeks. I knew this was going to happen after hearing the news yesterday but the reality is painful. I count through my routines and complete each grounding element until I start to feel my arms become part of my body again. Placing my hands on my face, I wipe away my tears. I need to go and see Dr Rene sooner rather than later. I haven't had a dream about Felix since I started in therapy but it spurs me to make a mental note to head to Felix's memorial plot for a visit soon, I haven't been to visit for some time. I glance at the clock as it reads 5:05am. I know I'm not going to make it back to sleep after this, so I decide to go ahead and work it out at the gym. I pull myself out of bed, grabbing my phone and head downstairs to make myself a coffee.

Whilst the coffee brews I sit at the kitchen island and look at my phone notifications. There is a new notification from MMF app. Opening the app, I head to messages.

**ClitHero -** Glad you chose to respond. Your name is intriguing. Does it give away some secrets?

I smirk at my phone, deciding to shoot a quick response back.

**BerryBean -** Of course there is a hidden secret in my name. What about yours, are you a real Clit hero?

I press send as my coffee maker finishes brewing. Pouring the coffee, the phone pings on the work top. I pick it up and look at the response.

**ClitHero -** I most definitely am by definition a Clit Hero. Early response today Berry, are you usually an early riser or is this just flick your bean time?

I gasp, a giggle bursting from me. This girl is ruthless and a little flirty. I ponder on the response, wondering if I should be truthful on why I'm awake so early or if I should just pretend. I take some time, hesitating on my response before deciding that maybe I could tell this complete stranger the truth and that way, I wouldn't need to worry everybody else with my woes. I tap a message back out.

**BerryBean -** I wish it was bean flicking time. Unfortunately, I suffer from severe nightmares and therefore, this results in me being wide awake at 5am.

A response pings back instantly.

**ClitHero -** Maybe you really do need to flick your bean. You know, relax a little.

I snort a laugh, the girls got a point. We continue to chat for some time and I completely forget my plans to go to the gym. I glance at the clock and realise it's now 07:00am.

Fuck!

I start to rush, getting myself dressed for work. A town car pulls up outside my house at 08:00 and I can see Gina and Sally making their way across the grass verge from their house. I shoot ClitHero one last message, letting her know I'm on route to work as I grab my belongings and head out of my house to get into the car.

Once we get to work, we immediately start business with Cilla. She's reported back from Riley that the apps launch was a complete hit with over one million users registering within the first 24 hours. Who knew people would be so into discussing their masturbation preferences.

"Maybe we should branch into web branding" Sally suggests, her face stoic and appearing completely serious in her suggestion.

"I guess I'm not completely opposed to this, but we're already at capacity right now Sal, we'd need an official plan in place and possibly some additional funding, but sure run the numbers and start the motions, I can't see why we can't expand further." I respond as Sally's face splits into a smile and she heads back over into her own office.

The day continues and it's certainly a busy one. I occasionally have chance to respond to 'ClitHero', and to be honest, it's been nice to have someone to talk to outside of those who are known to overcrowd me. The app is supposed to be talking about techniques but to be honest ninety percent of the conversation has been on other completely random topics, with the odd innuendo insinuated. I laugh at the incoming message

**ClitHero -** I hope you manage some sensational bean bashing in your office. You know you're tempted to spread those legs and work yourself into a frenzy. Happy Flicking.

I lean back in my chair, laughing at the message. This girl is something else.

"Am I interrupting you?" Gray's voice calls into my office and I jump out of my skin.

"Holy shit, Gray!" I shout placing my hand on my chest, calming my nerves back down through deep breaths.

"Sorry! I didn't realise you hadn't heard me come in. Who has you smiling like that? Has Max finally pulled his finger out of his arse and responded to you?"

Max.

Fuck me, I forgot he existed for a minute. Well, almost week actually. He hasn't responded though, so who gives a fuck.

"No, it's not Max. I haven't heard from him. It's a friend." I say hesitantly.

"A friend? That your smiling like that for?" Gray eyes me suspiciously. "Who is he?"

"She, is a friend on an app. It's a work thing." I bite back.

"And what's her name?" He quirks back, his tone patronising, as though he doesn't believe me.

I hesitate. I can't exactly say fucking ClitHero can I, for fucks sake.

Gina bursts into the office.

"Who is she texting Gina? I've just walked in and she shit herself, like I've caught her out on a dirty little secret." Gray interjects before Gina can speak.

Gina's head rotates slowly in my direction, her jaw drops a little slack in shock. "Are you sexting with ClitHero?" She squeals.

*Fucking hell.*

"Clit. Hero? What the actual fuck?" Gray looks like he doesn't know where to put his face.

"I am not sexting! I am just chatting with her."

"How do you even know that she is a she?" Gina asks, attempting to run behind my desk to glimpse at the messages sent between us. I lock my phone and place this under my bum on the chair.

"I just know okay." I state, "Leave me alone and go and do some work."

Gina laughs, dropping some documents on my desk that she had originally come into the office to deliver, before flipping me the middle finger "Bye Gray," She waves at him and exits my office.

"What do you want, Gray?" I ask, seeming exhausted.

"I came to check in with you. How are you? You didn't message about any nightmares. Does that mean you managed to keep a clear mind?" He asks, concern evident in his features.

"Yeah, I've had no nightmares. All is good." I lie. I know I shouldn't be lying but I just can't deal with anymore drama. I have work to do and if I tell him now he will just make a fuss and never leave.

He doesn't look convinced but he takes my word for it before departing my office. I will tell them all eventually I just need to feel normal again for just a few days. I'll just call Dr Rene when I have 5 minutes for a catch up. It'll be fine.

****

I walk in through my front door, reading some of the messages on this MMF App. Some of the messages I've received are just creepy, so I choose to ignore these ones. I spot a message waiting from ClitHero again, a smile creeping in at the message received.

**ClitHero -** So, did you manage to flick your bean before work this morning?

I laugh at the choice of words again and tap out a response.

**BerryBean -** I've definitely been too busy to flick beans, haven't even had chance to cook beans let alone flick them. But I'm sure I'll try your techniques when I get the chance.

I enter the kitchen and place my bag onto the counter when a message pings back at me.

**ClitHero -** Don't wait too long. Your bean will thank you.

I let out a giggle and place my phone onto the counter. Opening the fridge and grabbing the wine bottle. I turn to pour some wine into my glass, just as a figure catches my eye. Jumping at the sight of a 6ft 4 Max in combats, whose expression looks quite literally murderous. I swear he lets out a fucking growl at me, his pupils near black.

His deep voice growls at me, "Who the fuck are you messaging with a smile like that?"

# Chapter 6

## Therapy
## Three Years Ago
## Session 132

"Mollie, Happy New Year! You're looking great today, how are you feeling?" Dr Rene asks. She's chirpy today, but I guess people get like this when a new era approaches.

"I'm great. I have great news to share." I exclaim. I'm so excited to tell her my new year plans.

She smiles, "Share away," she probes.

"Well, over the Christmas break, I've decided that I want to build my own empire. Of course with my girls involved, by my side. But I've started the process of creating my own publishing company." I say, barely keeping the smile off my face.

I feel good today. At the moment, I honestly feel like a weight has been lifted recently and I don't have so much baring down on my shoulders.

"That's great news, it's not an easy feat to start a company Mollie, but that said if anyone can, you can do anything you put your mind to."

I knew Dr Rene would be happy for me. When I told Gray, all he wanted to do was point out how I needed to focus on my mental health, blah blah blah. My brow furrows and I barely notice that I've turned to gaze out of the windows.

"Mollie? What's on your mind?"

I snap my head towards Dr Rene again.

"My brother, he doesn't think it's a good idea. He thinks I should be focusing all my energy on my mental health and 'getting better' and 'back to the old me'." I sigh, "But, I don't think the 'old me' exists anymore." I say truthfully.

Dr Rene nods, "You're bound to change Mollie. That's part of the healing process. Have you told Gray about your feelings?"

I play with my fingers, counting them in sequences.

"No," I admit honestly, "It's not an easy task, admitting to those who loved the person you were before all of this, that you don't ever think you'll be that person again." I turn my gaze back out over Central Park, the greenery calming my nerves.

"Of course not. But it could allow you the growth you need." She responds and I know she's right. She's always right. I continue to look outside the window, counting the trees up to the lake.

"I want to discuss your most recent panic attack Mollie, but first, we need to finish your final hypnotherapy session."

I nod and turn, placing my legs up on the sofa and laying my head on the cushion behind me.

Staring at the ceiling I listen to Dr Rene as she counts me down into my unconsciousness.

"Focus on my voice Mollie. We are in a safe space. You are feeling drowsy, 10, 9 , 8, your eyes are feeling heavy, 7, 6, 5, your breathing is slowing, in, out, in, out, 4- 3- 2-, you are asleep 1."

Eyes closed, my body is heavy as I lie on the sofa, immobilised.

*I'm standing in an abyss of blackness. My hair is blowing lightly as I look around the empty space.*

*It's a strange sensation being here. It's like an out of body experience where my body is here, but my mind is floating.*

"Mollie, what happened when you were found?"

*I hear Dr Rene's voice echo into the blackness as it ripples around me and I can feel my body falling before I land on the cold concrete floor.*

*I sit myself up off the floor, with my knees raised and my arms wrapped around them tightly. There is a dripping noise to my left. It's constant.*

*Drip. Drip. Drip.*

*My clothes are wet, but I'm not shivering. I think I'm numb to it now but I'm not sure how long I've been here at this point.*

*My face is swollen over my right eye and I'm not sure if my head is bleeding, but there's a definite throb.*

*How did I end up here? I've been here before. I recognise the smell, but I know I'm not in the room I'd been gifted by Melvin previously.*

*I got a little mouthy with one of the men after he spoke to me and some of the other girls like absolute horse shit. I've just about had enough of their fucking bullshit.*

*They're nothing but scum.*

*Pawns in a much bigger operation, although they absolutely think they're untouchable. I know my status here is a captive, but I also know when Melvin catches the state of me, what they have done to me, he won't let them get away with it.*

*I rack my brain to form some coherent thoughts but the fucking throbbing is so distracting. It's so dark in here.*

*I use my hands to feel around my head, finding a lump that feels wet, indicating that my head is split open. I run my fingers around it finding jagged edges of what must be a break in my skin before bringing these to my nose and sniffing.*

*Blood.*

*I can tell the distinct metallic smell along my fingertips. It's deep, and I'm going to need treatment for it sooner rather than later, but who knows when someone will be back for me. Just as the thought crosses my mind, the manhole grid opens above me. My whole body stiffens in response and tears threaten my eyes.*

*One of the men climbs down the ladder, jumping off the last step and splashing his boots in the water below.*

*I school my face, determined that I will not let these fucking arseholes into my emotions.*

*I glance up, there's another man perched in a squat above the manhole, his face is covered by a black bandanna, and his eyes are covered by sunglasses. Complete cover up, just like they all are.*

*What is his purpose? Is he here to just fucking watch me take another beating?*

*The other man strides over towards me, his face on full display, clearly zero fucks given if I know who he is or not. Probably because he know's I'm never getting out of here. It takes everything in me to not flinch. I sit up, snarling at him as he chuckles at me. Squatting down he brings his face right up to mine. He can't be more than a centimetre away from me, I can smell everything he last ate on his breath and it makes my stomach growl.*

*"Hungry darling?" He spits, his saliva coating my cheek. I remain stoic. Determination not to flinch pumping through my veins like fuel. After all, my stubbornness is what got me in this hole, in the first place.*

*"Not speaking darling? Maybe you should shut your fucking face more often. You wouldn't get yourself in these predicaments would you, if you had just shut the fuck up in the first place," he snarls, his accent a broad London accent and I wonder if that is where I am being kept.*

*I remain silent. Refusing to give this prick an ounce of my time.*

*"Fair enough, pretty one." He slurs as he runs his large calloused thumb across my swollen eye socket, applying the slightest of pressure to cause me pain. But I don't flinch. "Boss wants you for dinner darling. You're coming with me."*

*He wretches my arm up, and my stomach sinks as I clamber to my feet.*

*"I'd say ladies first, but your a fucking disgrace so fuck you." He spits at me and walks ahead, up the ladders.*

*What a delightful man.*

*I follow behind him and wonder silently if there's anything around me I could use to take this fucking waste of oxygen out.*

*He starts climbing the ladder, his arse crack poking out the top of his pants, and it just adds to the fucking ambience doesn't it. I glance down to avoid the view just as something catches my eye.*

*My wide eyes peer back up and I have to curb my excitement as I spot the fat fuckers keys dangling from his arse pocket.*

*The plan was always for me to escape tonight. I had spoken at length with the girls about how we were going to plan it out. That included getting myself beaten for being mouthy, in the hopes that Melvin would find out and request my presence, while the other two seduce the other men.*

*It's working like a charm.*

*Here we are, the plan is unveiling, with no real knowledge on how I would get out of the complex and now, as I stare at his fat ass climbing up each step, the keys that line his back pocket continue to edge further and further out.*

*I hurry to clamber up the ladder closer to him so I can try and catch the keys as they fall without too much noise. My heart is racing and I feel myself trembling at the possibility that this could just fucking work.*

*I will not fuck this up.*

*The masked guy still remains above his head and I'm not sure how much he can see, but I am desperate and I will try anything at this point.*

*Even if it gets me killed.*

*The keys are dangling from his pocket as he reaches the top step.*

*"Fucking help me you useless twat!" he scolds the guy on the outside of the manhole. The guy hoists his body and the momentum causes the keys to slide out and drop.*

*I catch them, muffling the sound in my jumper. I glance up rapidly to see if they noticed the noise but the creep is making so much noise climbing out of the hole, that I think it's gone unnoticed.*

*I tuck the keys between my breasts and continue to climb up the ladder. I can feel my pulse in every limb and I know I need to be clever about this.*

*Climbing out of the hole and each man grabs an arm. The masked man places a black bandanna around my eyes as a blindfold, and I am grateful as he seems to be a little gentler than the other guy who came into the hole. They both simultaneously pull me along. My senses are clinging onto where I am whilst blindfolded, trying to decipher my surroundings.*

*As they pull me along I notice the floor is cobbled beneath my feet, I can feel the changing of the stones as we stride across. There is a smell of peony and blossom in the air and I figure there must be some trees around, so I am definitely outside.*

*"Boss wants you showered and dressed darling. Lucky you, you might get a good fuck tonight." He sniggers as he holds his face close to mine again.*

*And if that wasn't enough motivation to make a fucking run for it, I don't know what else would be.*

*He pushes my arm into a building and we ascend the stairs where I am placed into a room.*

*The blindfold is pulled from my face as I look around and take in my surroundings. I'm back in my own room, which houses a small bathroom. On the side is an assortment of toiletries including a razor and a long red dress is hung on a nail sticking out from the wall.*

*I pick up the razor and there's a clear pubic hair  stuck out of the blades. I suppress the need to gag.*

*"Boss expects you clean, shaven and presentable. You have 30 minutes." He sneers, his blackened yellow teeth lining his mouth, like old crooked gravestones. "I'll be waiting here for you precious."*

*I turn around and decide to execute the plan.*

*"I think the boss would like all three of his girls to satisfy him tonight, don't you think that would be the best treat." I pull my mouth into a seductive smile, spinning the lengths of my auburn hair through my fingers.*

*The guy grabs onto his dick, clearly turned on by my words which makes me want to gag but I'll be damned if I stop this act.*

*"Maybe you should check with him, and then collect Morgan and Verity." I suggest, "Or maybe, he would like it to be a surprise, you could get bonus points for thinking outside the box. Imagine that, impressing the boss with this idea. I promise I won't tell him it was me." I smile sweetly at this complete fucking air head of a man, as I see the cogs working incredibly slowly in his pea head.*

*"I'll go and get the other girls ready. Fucking get ready." He announces. "And this was my fucking idea not yours? Got it?" He declares.*

*"Oh absolutely, I won't say a word."*

*"No, you fucking won't or I'll fucking kill you!" the big ass dope says to me, like I'd feel threatened by him when I've clearly already proven how much of a fucking idiot he is. Not that he's aware.*

*I played my part and acted terrified about his threat. He sneers at me before leaving me in my room and locking the door.*

*I rack my brain for a way to get out unnoticed. I can't keep hold of these keys for much longer before they notice that they're missing. Pacing the bathroom, trying to think of a solution.*

*Outside the bathroom, I can hear an altercation. The window is boarded shut, but that doesn't mean I can't hear what is happening.*

*"Lenny! Fuck! Lenny get down here!" I hear shouting from outside the bathroom. Lenny. That must be creeps name. I press my ear to the bathroom door and I can hear the men scurrying across the gravel.*

*I know the plan has begun.*

*It's now or never.*

*I throw open the door careful not to slam it. I scan the area around me. There seems to be no one around. I look around noticing small cabins dotted about and grids lining the streets.*

*What the fuck is this place.*

*Sucking a deep breath, knowing that picking a direction and running is all I have. I've mapped out in my mind the steps and locations of where I think things should be located, but I can't be completely certain about that.*

*I slide the door shut and lock this again, hoping that will buy me extra time if they think I'm showering. I start making my way across the complex, it's evidence that everybody is responding to whatever the fuck is happening elsewhere, what ever chaos Morgan and Verity have managed to create. I head to the back of the complex and locate the fence line. Spotting a gate, I tug on the handle and to my surprise it opens. Peering my head outside the fence, I scan around before stepping outside. The back of the complex backs onto an alleyway which is lined with bins. The floors are cobbled and I struggle to cover ground fast, my footing uneven.*

*Freedom is just moments away. I have no idea which way to go, looking left and right I close my eyes and inhale.*

*Lucky left? Fuck it.*

*I turn left and start running along the alleyway. Looking for an insight to which way I should go. I reach the end of the alley to a set of tall black gates. Pulling on them, they're locked. I pull out the keys from my cleavage and scramble for the right key.*

*It takes a few attempts but I find the key, the lock clicks open and I pull the gate just as a large hand pushes the gate back shut.*

*I flinch, my heart sinking.*

*No, no, no!*

*I turn my head and the masked man stands a foot away.*

*Tears brim my eyes. I was so close.*

*He tilts his head sideways.*

*"Please." I beg. My reserve completely fractured. I know if I return with him, I am dead.*

*"Please just let me leave." I sob.*

*The man remains silent. But he hesitates.*

*He lifts his hand off the gate and raises the number five with his fingers before pointing out the gate.*

*"Five? Minutes? And then you'll tell them I'm gone?" I respond, my voice barely a whisper.*

*He nods before turning and walking away.*

*I gasp for breath.*

*Fuck.*

*Shit.*

*Pull yourself together Mollie.*

*I run.*

*I run and run through the streets that I now recognise to be the streets of London. I reach a telephone box and dial for the police as I sink down the glass walls of the phone box. As I begin to hear the police responding over the line a voice pulls me back to reality.*

*"Fucking find her! The boss will fucking kill us."*

*It's Lenny.*

*The scurry of feet running instills a fear in me. I search through the glass of the phone box, knowing I can't stay here or I'll be found.*

*"Hello, is anybody there?" The operator says over the line. And I say the only thing I can think of saying as quiet as possible.*

*"Help me, please help me." I drop the phone and decide to keep running.*

*Finding a warehouse that looks to be abandoned, I rush inside and tuck myself behind the wall, hidden the best I can be. Relief fills me when the sound of sirens fill the air. Exhaustion takes over my body as I sit there waiting to be found. I pass out as a result, the realisation comforts me.*

*It's over.*

"3 - 2 - 1 - Mollie, you're back in the room."

I snap my eyes open. Fatigue running thick through my body, I can feel that I spent a lot of that session tense in my unconscious.

"Well done, Mollie, that was a deep hypno-session." Dr Rene reassures me as I nod, still coming around.

"I want to explore the real emotions you felt at the time, which you suppressed Mollie. I think naming those emotions will help you to recognise and compartmentalise what happened and allow you to develop further on these."

We spend the rest of the session analysing my emotions during, before and after in relation to what happened to me. Although, Dr Rene knows a lot of elements to my story, she only finds out the full extent of what happened when we go into hypnotherapy sessions and I speak fluently from the memories I've suppressed.

She never falters on her demeanour during session, her knowing that I need strength and stability at the forefront of our sessions, but I do know that at times my stories affect her deeply.

"Finally, I want to round up the reasons your brother may feel so protective over you now, following what happened." Dr Rene states and I again turn to the view of central park before glancing at the clock, noting it's five minutes before the end of session,

"Gray feels guilt. Guilt for what happened to me. Guilt and blame for what happened to Mum and Dad." I inhale a shakier breath.

"And how does what happened to your mum and dad link to you?" Dr Rene asks.

"Because while he was searching for me, he thinks he pissed off the men that took me that much, that they killed them. Gray feels responsible for that."

"Do you blame Gray?" Dr Rene asks and I genuinely take a moment to think about the question.

"None of this is Gray's fault. The only people to blame are the men who did all of this."

"Try and relay that message to Gray. It may help to rebuild your relationship." I nod as Dr Rene closes her book.

"You did great today Mollie." Her smile is wide towards me.

Really?

Because I feel fucking terrible.

# Chapter 7

## Present Day

"Holy fucking shit, Max!" I screech, managing to keep the wine bottle in my hand.

Max grabs at my phone and repeats his question at me. "Who the fuck are you messaging Mollie?"

I go to grab my phone back out of his hands, but he turns and strides across the kitchen.

"What the fuck is this shit? Mutual masturbation, are you for real Mollie?" Max sneers at me, like he's disgusted.

"Oh fuck off, you're never here so I have to meet a need somehow. Besides that's a work project."

"You're a publishing company Mollie, not a sex line." Max gripes, he is really piercing my fucking nerves right now.

"Max, give me my phone back, have some respect. I'm chatting to other females online about tips and techniques they use, so, you know. I can try new things."

Max sniggers. "You're unreal. Use a vibrator like a normal person Mollie." He slides my phone across the kitchen island before walking out of the kitchen and up the stairs.

I throw a text to the girls group chat.

**Mollie -** Max is back. Attitude like a stubborn arsehole pile. May need back up. Will keep in touch.

I head upstairs, taking a minute before I stride through the bedroom door. Don't lose your shit Mollie, he's rarely home and we don't have time for arguments when he is home. I push the door open and I am greeted with the muscles that line his torso.

He really does provide the best distractions in the form of eye candy.

"Max..." I murmur quietly, my eyes tracing his torso, meeting the trail down into his pants. He leans on the door frame to the en-suite, his arm muscles bulging. I tiptoe across the room towards him. Reaching him, I glide my hands across the muscles on his shoulders, sliding them down his back and round to the abs across his torso. I lean into him placing my cheek onto his back and running my finger tips along the tip of his trousers.

"Baby..." I breathe "talk to me"

Max lowers his arms, spinning to face me. His deep blue eyes peer down at me as he places his forehead on mine. My breath hitches before running his jawline down to my ear lobe, sucking this between his teeth.

"Have you been a naughty girl while I've been away my little Mollie-bird?" He whispers, and I feel my knees weaken.

"No baby, never" I gasp back. He thrusts his fingers into my hair, tugging my head back and running the tip of his tongue along my jaw before placing a soft kiss on my collar bone.

I need a release for this pent up frustration between us, but my mind is screaming at me to talk to him about what happened last week.

He rips open my shirt, my buttons exploding across the room, his eyes roam down to my breasts, before placing the tips of his thumbs and pushing beneath my bra, caressing my nipples in smooth strokes.

"Max, we need to talk..." I gasp out as pleasure builds up and I feel the heat escalating between my legs.

Max drops to his knees his hands roaming to my behind, unzipping my pencil skirt and letting this fall to the floor beneath me. He places kisses along the edges of my thong and my head falls back, edging towards the need for release, my whole thought process being left behind.

"We can talk later, it's time for me to show this tight little pussy just how much of a naughty girl it is." He looks up at me, his eyes awestruck, while he slides my panties down my legs. I pick my feet up for him to remove them and he places my legs wider apart before bringing his face closer to my centre and inhaling my scent.

"I can smell your desperation for me Mollie." He declares, and I know I am already dripping, I am that wet for him. He slips out his tongue and runs it along my folds. A gasp escapes my lips at the intimate touch, my legs buckling slightly as my hand fall to grasp his hair.

He picks up my leg, placing it on his shoulder and allowing him further access to my sex. I am gasping for more touch and I resonate that our chat can absolutely wait until after.

He sucks my clit into his mouth and I moan in appreciation, grasping at his hair to keep my balance. He rises off his knees his arms under my thighs, lifting me and carrying me to the bed. He lies me down on the covers before running his eyes along my the length of my body. My breaths are shallow, and I swallow in anticipation of his next move.

"When are you going to learn that naughty girls don't get nice things Mollie?" Max whispers, taking my nipple and sucking this into his mouth. I gulp taking in his serious facial features as he stares up at me, his eyes dark and unreadable.

He pushes himself up and walks over to the bathroom, entering and slamming the door behind him, locking it.

I push up on my elbow my jaw dropping. He cannot be serious right now.

What the fuck.

Again.

How have I got myself in this situation, again?

I hear the shower turn on and the realisation hits deep that he genuinely is not coming back. I clamber off the bed and pick up my underwear and clothing. He ripped a fucking good shirt for that shit show. Grabbing my phone off the night stand I head downstairs and decide tonight calls for a stiff fucking drink. I check my messages and see some from the girls chat.

**Sally -** What? He's just turned up without a word that he's returning? Has he said why he hasn't been in touch?

**Gina -** What a douche-canoe. Fuck him off girl. Actually no wait, find out why he did some freaky shit last week and then fuck him off…. I need to know the deets.

**Sally -** He did it because he's a poor sorry excuse of a man? What more do you need to know?

**Gina -** True. But still, closure is everything and you could not close unless you knew the facts, right?

I laugh at the messages and send a quick response back to the group.

**Mollie -** Things got fucking weirder. I'll be round for a Gin in an hour. I need to talk to him about last week, this week. Fucking life. Pour a strong one. Chin, chin motherfuckers.

I pour myself a pink gin and lemonade and proceed to check the rest of my notifications. Opening the MMF app I see a message from ClitHero. I open app and navigate to the messages, discovering a message from 'me' or should we say, a message that Max has sent through. Anger rises and I can feel the heat in my cheeks as I grind down on my teeth.

Fucking asshole.

Opening the message I read.

**BerryBean -** Don't message my fucking girl again.

**ClitHero -** I think, 'your girl' isn't satisfied with you if she's on a masturbation platform. I'm not the issue, it's you.

I gasp. Hell, I'm so glad Max has not seen the response from the chat. I decide now isn't the time to put a response back and I place my phone on the counter. I ask Alexa to play Owl City and sit waiting for Max to head into the kitchen. I sip my gin and think of everything I need to say in my head, not entirely sure how I'm going to approach the whole situation at this point. I sigh and taking another sip of Gin as a message pings from Gina.

**Gina -** I'll turn the ice machine on. See you soon Queen.

I put my phone back down just as Max enters the kitchen. I watch a he strolls across the tiles and grabs a beer out of the fridge.

"I messaged you after last week. You didn't respond," I start off, figuring I'm best starting from the top. Max doesn't respond to me and proceeds to open his beer, before taking a sip and heading into the living room. I slide off my kitchen stool and follow him into the living room.

"Max don't just shut me off. We need to talk!"

"Why Mollie? Are you going to tell me you've found someone else? That you're finally done putting up with me serving my country? That it's *time I come home,"* He states, mocking my voice.

Who is this guy? I feel like I don't even know him anymore.

"It's not about me wanting to end this Max, why would you even suggest that?"

He scoffs a dark laugh "You tell me then, messaging others while I'm away on tour."

"Max, what are you going on about? I am part of a forum for work related purposes. It's a platform for females who want to share tips on how they pleasure themselves. Yes, I am messaging somebody and yes that person makes me laugh, but as a friend Max. I haven't even met her." I start to justify the stupidity of his allegations.

"You have no idea who it is on the other end Mollie. But enlighten me then, what do you possibly have to talk about?" He's short and sarcastic. I want to fucking punch him.

"What happened last week? Why did you hide in the dark in the bedroom? Why did you not let me orgasm? Why did you not orgasm?" I reel off quickly as a laugh escapes his lips and he turns and walks away from me.

"Max, don't fucking walk away. This isn't okay. We need to talk and figure out what the fuck is going on because I just seem to be waiting for you to fucking decide if I am worth staying home for." I grab his hand as he strides away and he snatches this from my grip.

"I can't leave Mollie. Don't you get it? I have a duty, I have a job to do. I can't just fucking leave because it doesn't suit your agenda anymore." He shouts back at me and I flinch. His eyes soften as if realising the impact of his actions on my body.

"Answer my questions Max. Why?"

He looks down at his feet before walking away and heading upstairs. I hesitate on whether to follow him and after a minute I decide that I need to know what is going on.

Heading up the stairs, I enter the bedroom. Max has started packing his rucksack again and has got himself dressed back in his combats.

He's running.

Again.

I fold my arms. "Is this your answer? To run away and leave all this animosity sitting in the air?" I fire at him. At this point I'm almost nuclear with anger. Who the fuck treats someone like this.

Max remains silent and continues packing his shit.

"Max. Answer my fucking questions!" My voice is a shunt now.

His anger peaks and he picks up his rucksack throwing it across the bedroom.

"Why did I creep in? Why did I not wait for you to fucking come? Why did I not finish myself?" He repeats, almost spitting venom, his anger is palpable.

"I didn't do any of those because you are a fucking mess Mollie. You come with baggage and you ooze 'pathetic' from every fucking pore. I couldn't finish and for that reason, you weren't being satisfied either."

My face falls.

I feel like I've been stabbed in my chest. I don't understand what has changed between us.

"You don't mean that Max. You're angry, I don't know why, but you are and you're trying to hurt me and…"

"Fuck off psychoanalysing me, Mollie. You have no fucking idea."

He picks up his belongings that he threw across the floor before exiting the bedroom.

I hear the front door slam and I don't even have the words. My phone pings in my hand and I glance down.

**Gina -** Just seen him leave. Are you okay?

**Sally -** Is it finally over?

**Gina -** Mollie?

**Sally** - Maybe we should go round?

**Gina** - Mollie?

**Gina** - Grab your shit. Let's go Sal.

I stare into my phone, grateful of the girls I have so close to me. I hear my door open and close downstairs, the sound of footsteps jogging up to join me. The girls enter my bedroom and I remain stood in the same spot, the shock invading all of my body as I stand rooted to the spot.

****

After a full three hour interrogation from the girls and a few Long Island iced teas, we are far from in a fit state to continue the evening.

"We need to go to bed, it's a Thursday and we're all tanked." I slur my words.

Gina is flopped onto my bed, in a fit of giggles, while Sally seems to be staring out of my bedroom window at the moon, harping on about space and other possibilities.

"I think we'll just sleep here Sal, what do you say?" Gina announces while pulling my duvet covers over herself.

*Thanks for asking G.*

Sally turns and makes her way over to the bed, tucking herself in to the covers next to Gina. At least they came over in their pyjamas. I sigh and resign to the fact that this is happening, I check my phone as I slide into bed next to the girls. I check the app, feeling so embarrassed about what Max had wrote. I decide to shoot over a message to apologise.

**BerryBean -** I'm sorry about my partners reaction. He can be so irrational at times, despite me trying to explain that we're just girlfriends chatting. I hope to speak to you again soon.

I flick over to my messaging app and my finger hovers over Max's name. I know I shouldn't send a message first again, but my heart is so conflicted. I don't even know if we're still together. I decide to leave it for tonight, locking my phone and placing it on the night stand. I snuggle in with my girls, knowing I'll sleep well tonight with them here.

****

My phone ringing on the side table rouses me from my slumber. I hastily grab it wondering if Max is trying to get in touch. The Caller ID unknown, I hesitate for a moment before answering.

"Hello?"

"Who fucking calls someone this early?" Gina moans from the side of me. I swat her in a silencing gesture and listen intently to the person on the phone.

"Good morning Mollie, my name is Detective Russ Palmer, one of the officers dedicated to the case surrounding your disappearance some time ago." A deep husky voice speaks. My heart is beating rapidly and I can feel the lump forming in my throat.

"Oh Hey, hi, hello, wha… what can I help you with?" I stumble on my words and I know I need to breathe to calm myself down.

"I just wanted to see if you could pay a visit into the station today?" He asks, and I can sense he's nervous through the phone.

"What is this about? I don't have much scope today. Can we not just speak over the phone?" My heart is racing. I don't have a good feeling about any of this.

The officer seems to stutter on the line, the hesitation making my stomach sink and my mind race. Dread fills me as I wonder if something happened to Max when he left here last night? Time feels like it is at a stand still and I just need him to tell me now.

"Please." I prompt, filling the space.

The officer sighs, "We have reason to believe that some of the gang members in relation to your case attempted to infiltrate your neighbourhood last night, Mollie." He resides. "I just wanted to make you aware and let you know that we have officers patrolling around your home as a precaution. There is nothing to worry about, we have everything under control. I just wanted you to be aware."

Silence fills the line as the worry floods my veins. They can't be so close to me. How have they found out where I live? They haven't found me in all these years, why now?

"Mollie, are you still there?" The detectives voice sounds through the receiver, but I can't bring any words to leave my mouth.

"Mollie? Whats happened?" I hear Gina say, the concern evident in her voice. Sally hitches up on her arms before placing a hand onto my shoulder, but I am frozen. My breathing is rapid as I struggle to get enough oxygen into my lungs.

I feel fucking sick to my stomach.

They're here.

They've come for me.

# Chapter 8

## Therapy
## Four Years Ago
## Session 120

"Mollie, welcome," Dr Rene greets me, her smile broad and welcoming as I walk through the door and into the therapy room.

My smile meets hers, and despite everything that's been happening, I am feeling rather optimistic today.

"That looks like a positive face today Mollie, it's great to see. Do you have a reason or are you just feeling good?" Dr Rene asks.

I gaze out the large window at central park, my smile still spread across my face. "I don't know, I just feel good today," I say turning back to face Dr Rene.

"That's good, I'm glad you're feeling well."

It's unusual that I'm having a good day, since I have not had a good week. I know Dr Rene is going to bring it up and part of me wishes she wouldn't. It will definitely bring my mood down.

"Is there anything you want to bring up today Mollie? Before we get to unpicking your week?" She asks, the smile still stretched across her face.

*Great.*

"Erm, no? Denial has always been my best trait, right?" I laugh awkwardly.

Do you think I could just leave now?

"So, we need to touch on what has happened this last week. I know you're reluctant to talk about this, I can see it in your eyes, Mollie. You're considering running out like you used to, but you have grown since then Mollie. You have learnt to discuss what has happened, to overcome. So please remember this." Dr Rene tells me and I nod back at her, knowing that I am bigger than running from my problems now.

"Now, tell me what happened?" She asks.

I look up towards the ceiling, thinking of the best way to get my words out. Taking a deep breath I begin.

"I had a panic attack again. It kind of took me by surprise. I've been working really hard on keeping myself positive, working on managing myself and keeping control." I start speaking, my hands are clammy and my heart is beating rapid. All of my senses are responding and I wonder if I'm going to have a panic attack again just retelling the events. I take a breath, glancing out of the window and finding my solitude in the greenery.

"There was a report," I pause, taking in some breaths before I continue, " A sighting of the gang, and I lost it." I continue, my hands have started shaking and I begin my routine finger tapping to try and ground myself.

"You didn't lose it Mollie. You had a reaction based on your past trauma. That is okay. You need to accept that it is okay to have an emotional reaction to something that triggers your trauma." Dr Rene interjects and I know she is trying to help me level myself, by justifying my reactions positively.

I nod, I know what she is saying is right, but every time I fall into a panic attack, I feel like I have failed myself again. Will I ever not need therapy? Am I always going to be so fucked up?

I continue to explain. "I was watching the news and when they mentioned that the gang were at large and roaming the city, I felt like I couldn't breath. I felt like I was there again. I could smell it. I could smell the environment, I could taste the blood in my mouth. I could feel the pain in bones." I explain, my eyes start to fill with tears. I find it so hard to return back to these emotions. Taking in a deep breath, I continue, tapping my fingers on my palms to remain grounded, but it's okay, I know Dr Rene will just sit and wait for me to be ready.

"I started to panic that they were close to me. That I was going to end up taken again. My mind was trying to rationalise, but I couldn't." I say, turning again to face out towards the greenery.

"Did you try and call someone?" Dr Rene asks.

I nod.

"What happened with that then?" She continues.

Continuing to stare out into the greenery, I take a deep breath and continue. "They didn't answer. None of them. I tried to call them all. Twice. No one was there. I was alone."

"You are never alone Mollie, you must always remember that. Just because someone isn't available doesn't mean you are alone." I know that makes sense. It really does, but in the moment the concept just vanishes.

We spend some time talking about how I can help myself and what I can do if I ever feel alone in the future. I have to admit I feel better after speaking with Dr Rene. We talked about my reaction to the information I receive when it comes to my past and she gave me some really positive and helpful techniques to help me to move past these, especially when there isn't anybody around to support me.

"So, let's do a quick overview Mollie. Let's recap what you said were your biggest fears?" Dr Rene asks.

"Being taken again, being so close to the people who did this to me, and my friends or family being taken by them." I relay back to Dr Rene.

"And what techniques have we learnt to use to help you to refocus?" She continues.

"Breathing exercises, positive talk, keeping myself active," I respond, just a few of the suggestions we have talked about during this session.

"Great work today, Mollie. I feel like we have definitely turned a corner in your recovery. Remember, only you are responsible for choosing your own outcomes. You are in control of your life." Dr Rene concludes. I take a deep breath and in all honesty I'm glad I chose to stay and I didn't run away from my problems.

I definitely feel better for it.

# Chapter 9

## Present Day

It's close to the end of my day in work. My head has been aching since the phone call I received from the police this morning. I can't think straight and I just need some quiet time. I gather my things before the end of the day and hurry towards the doors, with the aim of avoiding each and every person who will inevitably overcrowd my space come 5pm.

The lift reaches ground floor and I go to step out, catching a glimpse of Gray and Joey pacing the lobby in the corner of my eye. They're standing right by reception, clearly waiting to ambush me when I finish.

*Fuck this overprotective shit.*

I glance towards the building receptionist, Sonja, widening my eyes and gesturing my head towards Gray and Joey. I hold a finger up to my lips, making a shushing expression. She grabs their attention quickly, averting their eyes from my direction and I quietly sneak over to the front door. Sonja gives me a curt nod and smirks as she pretends that there is absolutely nothing to see here.

I exit the building, my breathing is rapid.

You'd think I was completing the great escape or mission impossible or some shit. I think up a plan, there's no way I can go to Reggie's and they wouldn't turn up there within the hour. I glance up and down 7th Avenue, before deciding to hail a cab.

Climbing in, I think on for a moment, turning to look towards my office building for a brief moment.

"Take me to a quiet, Irish bar please," I request, before sitting back inside the cab. The driver nods and we set off down the busy streets of New York City.

I reach an Irish bar called 'O'Reilly's'. I've already had 16 missed called from Gray and a few texts from the girls, but I did make sure to leave them a note saying I just needed some space and that I'm okay. I sit myself on a stool at the front of the bar, just as a friendly bartender approaches me.

"Good Evening Miss, haven't seen you in here before, what can I get you?" His accent is a thick, rich Irish and it provides me with some home comforts I didn't even know I needed.

A warm smile stretches across my cheeks, "I'll have an Irish whiskey please." The faint British accent resonating from my voice, one that I thought had long gone after all these years living in New York.

The bartender places my drink on the bar "Would you like a tab opening miss?" He asks.

"That would be a great idea," I respond taking a sip of the amber liquid.

"My names Cam, shout me if you need anything else." He says, flashing a smile, before continuing to do his job. I pick up my phone, glancing at the missed calls.

I now have 30 missed calls from Gray. Shaking my head, I open my messages from the girls.

**Gina -** Mollie, where did you head out to? We will come find you…

**Sally -** We all like a drink Mollie, come on girl, let us join you!

**Gina -** You're not at Reggie's….

**Gina -** Mollie? Where are you? Why are you hiding from us?

**Sally -** Gray is besides himself Mollie, you can't go missing when you've just heard that there have been sightings. Please just text us back.

**Sally -** Gray is about to go nuclear Mollie. Just give us a text so we know you're okay and he might chill the fuck out for 5 minutes.

A sense of guilt floods through my veins and I decide to drop a text back to Sally.

**Mollie -** I'm fine. I'm not at Reggie's because I knew you'd try and interject. I'm somewhere safe, just let me have some time. Please.

I've no sooner sent the message and put my phone on the bar before Gray's name lights my screen as he calls me for the 31st time. I sigh and press reject. He has no boundaries.

A text pings through.

**Sally -** Thanks Mol. I'm working on Gray! Keep us updated girl. We love you.

I smile, knowing how much hard work my brother can be. I'm surprised he's not put me on his 'find my friends' app yet so he can fully commence stalker duties. Glancing at my phone again I take note of the home screen photo of me and Max from the start of our relationship. My chest tightens and for the first time in a while, I feel something other than anger towards him.

I feel hurt.

My eyes begin to well up and I swat my tears away determined not to allow myself to physically feel this way. I decide to avert my thoughts away from Max for now, knowing inside that I'm not prepared for the outcome of that shit show yet.

I glance around the bar, taking in the environment. The walls are a dark mahogany, covered with signed sports shirts and memorabilia from varying Irish football teams. There are photos of the people with famous Irish stars who have clearly visited the bar when they were in NYC. I recognise one of the guys in the photo to be the bartender, Cam. I wonder to myself how I have never known about this bar before now.

Thinking back over my recovery, I go back to the times when spending time in a bar alone was never an option, without fear crippling me and panic setting in. The thought makes me smile at just how far I have come since the past and for a moment, I feel proud of myself.

"That's a pretty smile you have," a sultry deep voice says to the side of me, and I jump in fright, turning to see what can only be described as one of the most delicious looking males I have ever laid my eyes on.

The shock seems to stick to my face and he lets out a chuckle while I pick my jaw back up off the floor, reminding myself that it's rude to stare.

"I didn't mean to startle you. My names Rian. You looked a little lonely over here, so I wondered if you wanted to join me for a game of pool?" He holds his arms are up in the air, waving them comically, as if he's surrendering himself to me.

"I'm ok here, thanks." I respond, my lack of trust is palpable.

"I promise I won't bite. Just one game. Loosen up a little," he encourages, his smile is cheeky, made of all things fucking sexual.

I let out a breath, glancing again at the photo of me and Max on my phone screen.

*Fuck it.*

"Fine. But I'm taking the first shot," I jump down off my chair, grabbing my belongings, before walking towards the pool table with as much swagger as I can muster up.

*What am I doing?*

Fuck it. Theres no time for thinking now.

"You never shared your name with me?" His deep voice low as he lays out the pool balls.

I hesitate a little before announcing myself.

"My names Hallie," I lie.

I don't even know why I felt I had to lie to him, but for tonight, Hallie it is.

"Well,… Hallie… Off you go, take your shot," Rian says, seeming to hesitate on my name, as though he can completely see through my lies. I play my shot, spreading the balls out wide, without potting anything and take a step back, leaning against the wall. I watch as Rian takes his shot and for a moment, I take in the man that's stood in front of me. He looks to be around 6ft5, broad shoulders and chest, his body evident that he works out well. He has tanned peach skin, which symbolises that he isn't usually so bronzed, but that he's sporting a tan. What stands out the most to me are his eyes. They're the most mesmerising emerald green eyes, that appear to shine. It's captivating.

"It is your turn again… Hallie." Rian chimes and I startle out of my daze, realising I've been fully engrossed in him for far too long.

How embarrassing.

I give off a quick smile, trying to seem like I'm totally playing it cool, before I line myself up and playing my shot.

We play pool for what seems like five minutes, but actually, it's been four hours. It's now 9:30pm and we have chatted about almost everything you could possibly think about, without giving away a single ounce of our personal lives. It's strange to me, how easy I feel around a guy I've just met, and there's definitely a part of me that feels like I know him better than I know Max right now.

"I should head out." I announce and Rian folds out his bottom lip at his displeasure for my departure. I elicit a small giggle. "I've had a great time. This was just what I needed tonight. Thank you," I continue.

"No problem… Hallie," Rian responds again, hesitation on my fake name. He has to know I've completely bullshitted him.

I pick up my phone and glance at the entourage of messages from Sally and Gray. Seems he didn't calm down much after all.

I put my coat on smiling back at Rian. "Maybe I'll see you in here again sometime?" I suggest.

Am I fucking flirting?

Jesus Christ Mollie, pull yourself together. You haven't even told him your actual name.

"Maybe… Hallie," Rian says, smirking and I know he's onto me.

I hand over my card to pay the tab and then make my way to the door, waving over at the bar tender who gives me a broad smile, just as my phone starts buzzing in my hands.

Fuck off Gray, I'm coming.

Glancing at the screen, I freeze on the spot.

Max.

My hands start shaking and I tremble slightly.

"Are you okay?" Rian calls over as he starts walking towards me.

I place my phone to my ear. "Hello?"

"What the fuck do you think you're doing Mollie?"

"Excuse me?"

"Don't treat me like I'm thick Mollie. What the fuck are you doing with another man?"

"I'm not."

*Fuck.*

"I'm not *with* another man Max. I'm jus…"

He cuts me off "Don't fucking lie to me, Mollie! Answer your FaceTime now."

The phone buzzes on my cheek. I close my eyes and inhale deeply before swiping the green button.

Max's face takes up the screen. He looks angry as his features are contorted into lines across his forehead and nose, and for the first time in our relationship, I feel a sense of fear towards him.

"Show me where the fuck you are, Mollie? I know you're not home!" Max spits, I can feel his aggression through the phone.

I slide my gaze up and I can see Rian looking at me from across the room. I position the phone and scan the camera to look around the now busy Irish bar, before returning it back to my face.

"Are you happy now?" I retort sarcastically.

"Who were you with Mollie?"

"What makes you so fucking sure I was in here with someone?"

"None of your fucking business how I know, Mollie. I want to know who he was," his attitude is venomous and I sigh, resonating that there is no point in lying to him.

"I came here alone," I respond with a sigh.

Max tries to interject and I cut him off repeating myself louder "I came here alone, Max. I have had a shitty few days, believe it or not, no help from you. I was sat, having a drink and gathering my thoughts when a guy in the bar asked if I fancied a game of pool." I roll my eyes and glance away from the phone trying to hold my own anger levels together.

"The answer should have been no, Mollie. You belong to me, not some bar wanker. Just me, Mollie!" Max shouts to me. He is really furious about this.

"Max, I am hardly yours, let's be honest. Last time we interacted I'm sure your words to me were, that I am, what did you say again Max, ahh yes 'a fucking mess' and that I 'ooze pathetic from every fucking pore'. So do excuse me if I don't believe that I 'belong to you'. Goodbye Max." I press the red button before he can respond, my anger levels are rising and I am in no place to unleash all of the baggage surrounding me.

I glance up to Rian standing in front of me. "Are you okay?" He asks gently.

"Perfectly fine. Extremely embarrassed." I respond before giving a small smile and exiting the bar.

I decide to walk myself to Reggie's from the Irish bar. After catching up on my texts, it appears the group are still there and although I know I'm going to  have to face Gray's fury, I need my girls. The walk will help to settle my nerves down a little. I make my way along the side streets of NYC. The city is always chaotic, no matter what the time is, it truly is the city that never sleeps. I cross over the street and from the corner of my eye I swear I can see a dark figure following me.

I pick up my pace, continuing to glance over my should as I walk. The streets are busy, so I feel safer and I know it's likely just the demons in my mind trying to haunt me. I keep my eyes on the path ahead and continue on my way to Reggie's.

Turning to cross the street again, I definitely catch a glimpse of a hooded figure behind me. My heart starts to pound and I take in deep breaths. I close my eyes and inhale deep continuing at pace down the streets.

*Not today, Satan.*

As I continue to pick up the pace, the figure behind me also picks up pace. Panic floods through me and I realise quite quickly how fucking stupid it was for me to go to another bar alone.

I quickly keep navigating the pedestrians in the street, ducking and diving around. I can see the sign for Reggie's a few blocks down, so I continue to pick up pace, almost sprinting at this point. The figure behind continues to chase me down and I start feeling nauseous. I'm almost at the front of Reggie's, spotting Joey outside on the phone.

Thank Fuck.

I reach the doors, bumping straight into Joey. He startles, almost dropping his phone.

"Shit, Mollie!" Joey shouts before ending the call he was on without hesitation.

I gasp for breath, sweat lining my forehead, the evidence clear that I've ran… no, sprinted for at least the last five blocks.

Joey grasps my arms, holding me up into place in front of him. I turn my head, checking behind me for the figure I know was following me. This is not in my mind, right?

"You need to speak to me Mollie, what the fuck is happening?" Joey says and I realise I haven't spoken in the two minutes since I reached him.

"I felt like someone was following me." I said, still breathy as I haven't quite refilled my lungs.

Joey's eyes shoot up scanning the area for anyone that looks suspicious. Wrapping his arm around my shoulder, he pulls me towards the door and into Reggie's, his eyes never leaving behind us.

We walk along the bar to the back, where our usual table is located. Gray's eyes meeting Joey's, followed by mine and immediately the over protective brother expression plasters on his face. But this time, I think I'm grateful for it.

I manage to sit down, just as I start to explain what has happened, a man dressed in black jeans and a black hoodie approaches the table. I flinch, panic coursing through me.

Joey and Gray stand up creating a human barrier in front of me.

"Who the fuck are you and why are you following my fucking sister?" Gray exclaims, squaring straight up in the face of the stranger.

He pulls down the hoodie from his head.

Shit, it's Rian!

"Oh my god! Rian!" I shout, loud enough to catch my brothers attention. Pushing between Gray and Joey, I stand in front of Rian.

"Jesus, Mollie. Are you some kind of track star or something?" He says, although he is not seeming as exasperated as I was five minutes prior. Confusion covers my face, he knows my real name, he must have heard Max call me Mollie.

"What? That was you behind me? You were chasing me?" I say, trying to keep my tone level and not seem like I'm almost mid-panic attack.

"I wasn't chasing you. Oh shit, you thought I was chasing you? No. No! You left your card. I ran out of the bar to catch up to you and you just started running. I tried to keep up but, shit you're fast, and I assumed that you were clearly worried, so I stopped running and started walking. I've seen you in this bar a few times with your friends, so I chanced this is where you were heading," Rian answers, his eyes drifting to his pocket where he pulls out my bank card and holds it out towards me. A shy smile crossing his face, as his jaw flexes tight.

My hand floats over my mouth in an attempt to hide my shock and well, stupidity.

"I'm so sorry Rian. Thank you for bringing it back to me. It's…" I hesitate, trying to not seem like a total fucking loser, "It's complicated, I guess." I respond nonchalantly, looking at the floor.

"It's fine. Nothing personal remember, I hope you'll visit the bar again soon." He says his smile stretching over his beautifully chiseled face. He waves the card at me again, and I realise I haven't actually taken the fucking thing out of his hands. What the fuck are you doing Mollie?

I hear Gina and Sally sniggering behind me and honestly I wish the ground would swallow me up.

I take the card, embarrassment flooding my cheeks a wonderful crimson colour.

"Thanks again." I say sheepish.

Rian smiles and nods, he gives a small salute towards the group, before giving me a cheeky wink and heading back out of the bar.

I fan myself, suddenly aware that I am fucking hot right now. I start to gather my belongings, trying to abort this scene before it can get any fucking worse for me.

I should have known better, as Gina snatches everything I pick up back out of my hands and tugs me back down to sit.

"Oh, hell fucking no. You do not get to fuck off to another bar unannounced, run in here like a maniac, only for one of the sexiest male specimens I have ever laid my eyes on, to walk into the bar to return your fucking bank card!" Sally exclaims, while Gina sits back down behind her, giving all the "mmmhmmm's" in agreement. Gray shoots a look towards Sally, clearly unhappy about the sexy male comment.

I stare at my friends and I know there's absolutely no chance I'll get out of this shit. I sit myself in the booth and get comfortable, while I explain everything from the phone call in the morning, to the bar and Max's call.

"So, he has someone watching you?" Gina whisper shouts, looking around for anyone who has potential stalker vibes or looks suspicious.

"Well, it would seem that way," I say, equally scanning the same surroundings, looking for someone who looks like they could be watching me.

"No way, he's not that creepy. Maybe someone he just knew was in the bar and they've messaged him. It's not that cynical. It can't be." Gray answers, "And besides, if he does have someone following you, is that the worst situation? Having someone who is secretly keeping you safe," he adds.

"Gray, you cannot be serious. That violates my privacy on so many levels." I respond without hesitating.

"I get it Mol, but while the creeps who took you are being sighted in NYC, maybe he's done it as some kind of additional protection. Maybe it's not a negative. Maybe this is him showing you he still cares," he says.

I never thought I'd see the day that Gray approved of something Max did. It's a miracle and really, it makes me think twice about the whole situation.

I sit quiet for some time and consider what Gray's been saying. Maybe he is right. Maybe Max is making sure I am protected.

I just wish he had told me.

# Chapter 10

## Therapy
## Four Years Ago
## Session 108

I'm sitting in the waiting room, ready for my session with Dr Rene, browsing the walls as I always do before my time slot arrives. Over the last couple of years, the changes in the décor of this room have only enhanced the 'chilled out' vibes I feel while I'm in here. The walls are sage green, and there are plants hanging from the ceiling. The photo frames lining the walls contain inspirational quotes that I read each time I come to a session. Not that they ever change, but I just enjoy the reminder at times. The floor-length windows bring me just as much peace as the colour on the walls and it's crazy to think, I feel at home here.

"Dr Rene is ready for you now, Mollie." Florence calls from her desk in the corner.

The interruption startles me slightly from my daydream, but I give Florence a curt smile and stand to head into the room.

"Mollie, welcome. Take a seat." Dr Rene greets me.

I sit down on the sofa, as always taking in the vast greenery outside. No matter how many sessions we've had, or how many times I've sat in this room, it's always somewhat uncomfortable when we start one of my sessions. I never really know how to feel, or what to think. My mind stays in the past here, while I build on and work towards a future.

"So, today Mollie, we're going to look at developing a 'coping family' and then we'll move on to some hypnotherapy, relaxation and reflection," Dr Rene begins explaining, "Do you have any ideas on how you think this could work, which won't make you feel like others are controlling you?" she asks.

I'm glad she considered that element because the thought of someone else having the majority control in my life scares me more than it should.

"I think that, if I can choose those closest to me, and set the boundaries, so that they don't interfere unless I ask them to. Maybe that could work?" I answer honestly.

"That's a great suggestion. Who would you pick?" Dr Rene continues.

Every time this question is asked in sessions, I don't even have to spare a thought into it as my answer comes almost immediately.

"Sally, Gina, Gray and Joey." I begin, "They are my closest people, the people I trust with absolutely everything." I say with the most confidence and certainty I've ever had.

"That sounds like a positive choice. I'd have recommended the same circle of friends for you." She reassures, and that somehow makes me feel even happier.

"So let's move on to working through some memories which cause you issues. I'm going to start with relaxation, as usual, and then when we're in the moment, you'll hopefully will be able to talk to me about any particular times where you felt unsafe."

I nod. These parts of the sessions always trigger anxiety in me. I know it's easier for her to understand the trauma if I open up about it, but it is the most difficult part.

"Are you ready Mollie?" Dr Rene asks.

Glancing out the window, I nod and release a breath. "I'm ready."

"Can you tell me about a time that you felt truly scared during your time in captivity?" Dr Rene asks.

My hands begin to tremble as I recall the past events. I close my eyes and begin telling my story.

*When I had been there for some time, it felt more and more like I was a part of their team. Like each day that passed by, I blended a little more. It was like this was now my new forever, if I ever wanted a life to live. I was treated to special things if I was good and did as I was told. These rewards would vary, depending on how good I had been or what task I had satisfied 'the great Melvin' with and could be anything from extra food, fresh clothing, or a hot shower. Those were the most common types of treat.*

*But I do remember one occasion, it's embedded in my memory, like a mark for my sins. A forever blemish to my moral and ethical values. On one occasion, I had been so 'good', that they upgraded my room. I was given a 'luxury' room, which basically meant I was above ground instead of in the grids below, and I had a mattress to sleep on, with a bathroom inside my room.*

*The small, shed-like box, although it was disgustingly filthy, was certainly better than being below ground, on the concrete, wet floors, with the rats running around.*

*I had been completing my tasks, like they had told me to and honestly, I started to become good at it. I became numb to what was right or wrong, and a big part of me just wanted to die so it would all be over. The other half of me was terrified for the people I loved.*

*Melvin had given me this 'nice' room, and he had even took the opportunity to hang pictures of my family along the walls. Pictures that had been taken by his hitmen, who were evidently trailing my family and friends closely. New photos continued to appear daily, reminding me that they were always following them and if I made one wrong move, I risked their lives.*

*I remember on one occasion when I was escorted back to my room, the door was ajar slightly as we arrived. I tried to push back towards the guy taking me to my room but he just grabbed onto my arm and shoved me forward towards the door. My pulse was thumping, and I just remember a smell assaulting my nose as I reached the room. The smell of sweat and salt laced my nostrils, as I placed my hand on the door hesitant to push it open.*

*The guy behind me shoved me forward a second time and I fell through the door with haste. In my room stood a man, his face covered with a bandanna but he was otherwise completely fucking naked. He definitely wasn't a picture to look at, overweight with a beer gut while his legs were particularly skinny. I looked him up and down, as he let out a chuckle. I remember him taunting me*

*"Like what you see darling?" He questioned as he took his own dick into his hand. It's at that point I noticed he had a belt in his other hand, wrapped around his hand with some length hanging down. My hands carried on trembling and my breathing was erratic.*

*Is this it?*

*Is this the time they finally rape me?*

*I had done everything they had asked of me. I hadn't disobeyed them. I remember thinking, why was he here waiting for me, when I had been so good. Panic started rising in my veins and he began to laugh at me.*

*"Let me tell you exactly what is going to happen princess," he said, his voice creepy and sadistic sounding, full of conviction. "I need a little entertainment to watch and you are just the solution darling," he slurred.*

*"No!" I shout back at him instinctively, just as the belt in his hand is whipped across my face. I hadn't even had time to brace myself. I feel the sting on my cheek as if it was happening to me right now. My cheek was so sore, but I did not falter.*

*"You will do as your told darling, or I will whip you black and blue until you pass the fuck out!" he threatened, shouting at me as the spit from his words coats my face.*

*But I couldn't. I couldn't let them have me that way. To expose me sexually. That would have taken the final piece of me and I might as well of died right here and now if that was the case.*

*So I refused.*

*And I took my beatings.*

*He whipped me with the belt 58 times, and the worst part was he got off on it. Tugging on his tiny shrimp dick while he struck me over and over again.*

*I lay on the floor, in a ball while he assaulted me. Until someone from outside came in and with a loud commend echoed around us, "Enough!"*

*He argued the toss though, shouting back at the other guy, "Who the fuck are you to interfere in my business?"*

*But there was one set of words that did stop him.*

*"Melvin said, that's enough."*

"Did that happen to you often Mollie?" Dr Rene asks, pulling me from deep within my memory.

"A few times, yes. I think it was always the same guy, although I never saw any of their faces. I was always rescued, if that's what you can call it, by one of the other guys. I'm not sure if it was the same guy, though I like to believe it was. That there was someone with an ounce of ethical moral within those walls." I finish.

"Possibly Mollie, and I guess that thought brings you some comfort, which is okay." Dr Rene reassures me.

"I have to check my doors now." I say, my eyes looking up and meeting Dr Rene's gaze. "I have to check them over and over before I leave. Somewhat obsessive behaviour I guess." I share with Dr Rene before glancing towards the clock and noting it's the end of our session. Dr Rene smiles at me as she notes the time too.

"It is time to finish Mollie, and you did so well today. It's okay to need to check your safety. But we can work on the obsession part of things as we continue through sessions." She smiles back at me.

I smile towards her, although, no where near as beaming as she is to me. She really has no idea of the real fears I hold for locking my door when I leave my home.

I am terrified.

# Chapter 11

## Present Day

I flick over to my messaging app, my finger hovering over Max's name. I know my head is telling me I shouldn't send a message first again, but my heart is so conflicted. I don't even know if we're still together at this point. After some mind torment, I decide to leave it be, for the hundredth time, locking my phone. The feeling of being so defeated by the whole situation overwhelming my thoughts.

My phone buzzes on the side and I reach for it in a haste, far too quickly for anyones liking, hoping it's finally a message from Max. What the fuck has happened to me. I'm supposed to be a strong independent women, not someone who pines for communication. Glancing at my phone, I quickly realise it's not Max.

**Joey** - Just checking in. Are you good?

I smile at seeing Joey's name on my phone. He's such a good guy, even if he can be just as much of an overbearing asshole as my brother is. My smile wavers a little but remains stuck to my face as I type out a quick message back.

**Mollie** - Yeah, I guess. I just feel in limbo. I'll be good though.

The conflict between my feelings almost makes me feel a little dizzy. I place my phone on the bed as it immediately buzzes back with another message from Joey. He's eager tonight.

**Joey -** I get it mate, but ignore what Gray thinks. Max has always been a dodgy bastard, Mollie. Trust your gut. Besides, that guy from the other bar was totally c-ute.

My smile spreads even wider across my face now. He's such an idiot. Placing my phone on the bed, I start to take off my make-up. It's been a long ass day and I am beat. Tomorrow is going to be even busier with organising the final plans for our charity event this weekend and I definitely need my beauty sleep to focus on this. Each year, my company hosts a charity event that intends to collect funds to support victims of exploitation and trafficking. The funds go towards helping families to try to locate and reunite with their loved ones, who are missing or the victims who have survived.

Victims.

People, like me.

****

I arrive at work the next morning, still nothing from Max. I'm still undecided on whether to reach out to him myself, feeling a little empty and the panic is starting to rise the longer I leave everything unanswered. Despite his flaws, Max has always been there for me, from the moment I finished therapy. I sit and question whether I have unintentionally become dependent on him? But no, I don't believe that. In fact, I refuse to believe I've come all this way because he was by my side. He's barely even present and when he is, he's got one foot back out of the door.

"Mollie?" Sally calls, standing at my door, bringing me out of my own thought spiral. I glance up and paint a smile on my face.

"Don't fucking bother pretending to me Mollie. I'm your best friend."

She's right, there is absolutely no one on this earth that knows me better than her. My face flaws, as a tear lets slip down my cheek. I swipe it away, quicker than it appeared.

Sally's eyes widen at the sight of me crying. It is definitely a rare occurrence.

"I'm fine Sal. Honestly I don't have time to fall to pieces right now." I continue with my painted smile, blotting the tears that manage to escape. She slides into my office closing the door behind her quickly. Most probably to stop anyone else from seeing the impending melt down that she thinks is seconds away from happening.

"Mollie, please." She begs, "You can feel this if you need to. You don't have to keep putting your feelings in a box and pretending you have to be the strongest person. It's okay to not be okay for at least once in your life."

"I don't think I can stop this, even if I wanted to Sal." I breathe out between sobs.

I am really falling to pieces here.

Shit.

Sally walks across the room towards me, reaching out and pulling me into her arms. "You've got this Mollie. You need to cut him off by the fucking testicles, and leave him out to dry. He does not get to do this to you. You have worked too fucking hard to be brought down by that pathetic excuse for a man. He doesn't even have a big dick." She exclaims and I snort a laugh, pretty sure that snot has flown right out of my nose and everything.

Releasing me, she holds onto my shoulders. "You have us. You will always have us. You know I don't like to interfere or tell you what to do. But it's time Mollie. Please move on, for your own sake sweetie."

I nod at her, still not able to form words, but the tears seem to have slowed down, at least for the moment.

"Right." She announces, back into business mode as if I haven't just fallen apart. "I have interesting news. As you know, we have a charity event to run through the plans for, however this year we have some big hit sponsors for the event," she begins and I can see her excitement building, "one of those sponsors is none other than Riley Austin herself." My eyes widen towards Sally.

"No fucking way!" I exclaim.

"Yes fucking way. And, she has already RSVP'd to the event. She is coming. In the flesh!" Sally continues, her voice almost a screech.

"No fucking way! We're finally going to meet her?"

"In the flesh girl!" Sally waggles her finger at me.

I am speechless. We have never met Riley before, just her bitch of an assistant. This news has definitely cheered my day up.

We continue through the day, finalising the plans and helping those that need support to attend. The event itself is a black tie event, although we know that not all of the families we help are able to afford attire that is suitable, so each family receives an invite from us as a company to send them over to our studio room to borrow something suitable if they need to.

"I think that's almost everything done. Two days and counting!" I beam a smile as I speak to Sally and Gina while we sit inside my office, the end of the day nearing.

"Now that's sorted, have you decided what you want to do about Max?" Gina asks. I can tell she's hesitant, and I know Sally must have filled her in on my brief episode earlier in the day.

I spin on my chair to stare out of my office window at Central Park, the vast greenery providing me with that grounding feeling.

Finally, I spin back around to look back towards my girls, before I release a pent up breath.

"I need to end it."

****

We have somehow made it to Reggie's bar after work and I can't deny that I feel much better for having some down time. Gray and Joey have joined us girls as usual, although we are definitely airing on the side of sensible tonight with only a couple of drinks on the go, accompanied by some food.

Struggling to eat my food, I'm unable to shake this feeling of sickness that is in the pit of my stomach. I still haven't spoken to Max, but I know I need to end things, I can't just do that over text. It's not fair after all this time, but equally who knows when I'll next see him, if ever. I decide to take a trip to the toilets to freshen up and attempt to call him.

I locate his name and hit the call button, releasing a breath I didn't even realise I was holding in. After two rings the phone cuts out. No fucking way did he red button me.

I hit call again. This time it rings once before cutting out again. I can feel the rage instantly rising in me. Who does he think he is?

A third time I hit call. This time it rings 3 times and I have some hope that maybe he's considering picking up but that hope soon gets up and fucks off, as I hear the beeps sound through the phone to let me know he rejected the call, again.

I decide to call a fourth time. Not because I'm desperate or foolish. No, this time I'm calling with the hope that this cunt rejects me again, and I can tell his voicemail exactly what a complete and utter fucking douchebag I think he is. The phone instantly goes to voicemail, meaning he's either turned it off, or blocked me.

Motherfucker.

I wait for the beep, readying myself for the onslaught of my unspoken emotions, somewhat thankful inside for this gift of yet more rejection from him to push me to absolute certainty that I am doing the right thing. The beep sounds and I start my speech.

"Max, it's me, Mollie." I laugh. "It's funny, you know. You, rejecting my calls 'cause, I thought we were adults. In an adult relationship. Guess that's me and not you. Listen, I didn't want to do this over message or voicemail or whatever but you seem to not want to give me any other choice."

I take a breath and steady myself. Staring into the mirror of the bathroom to find the remaining strength in myself to continue.

"Max, I'm done. We're…" I hesitate for a beat… "We're done, Max. I'll have your things shipped to your base camp."

I hang up the phone, placing it back into my bag. Looking into the mirror again, I fix my hair and scowl at myself. I know I've done the right thing. I leave the bathroom and return to my friends in the bar.

"Are you okay Mollie? You were gone for a while" Gray asks as I seat myself back at the table.

"Yeah, I err… I tried to call Max." I say before starting to pick at the food on my plate.

"Why?" Joey asks. His tone nonchalant, like he's bored of the situation.

"Because I wanted to end things. I felt I needed to speak to him and maybe we could have met up and I could have ended things face to face. I know you guys think he's a dick and he absolutely is, I completely agree with you but…." I say.

"Damn right we do." Sally interjects.

"…But, we have been together a long time. It deserved more than just a text."

"You're a bigger person than I am Mol. That creature doesn't deserve an ounce more of your breath in his direction." Joey says, although he hasn't once looked up from his food, he just keeps shovelling it in.

"Well, it didn't matter anyway because he rejected my call. Not once, not twice, but four times." I say, a little hesitantly because I know they'll all judge me for calling the guy 4 times.

They all just stare at me, mouths a gape. Even Joey has stopped eating.

"I know, you're thinking why the fuck did she call him four times. I actually called him 3 times, but then the fourth was purely to leave him a voicemail telling him what a wanker I really think he is."

Sally snorts a laugh. "I wish you'd have invited me to the toilet rejection party. Sounds like a hoot." She states, giggling to herself.

"So I did. I ended it." I finish.

"You ended it?" Gray repeats back to me. Everyones faces are still appearing shocked.

It's giving anxiety. Hell, do they think I shouldn't have ended it?

"Yeah, I left him a voicemail. I didn't call him a wanker. But I did tell him that we are supposed to be adults, in an adult relationship and that clearly he wasn't. And I said I was done and that we were done"

Shocked faces continue before broad smiles take over. "Hallelujah! Fuck me Mollie, yes! About fucking time!" Sally says, standing on the booth seat and climbing over the other side of the table to reach me. "I am so proud of you girl. This is it. This is your time to shine." She says, bringing me in for a hug and planting a kiss on my forehead.

"Does this mean I finally have a chance with you?" Joey states winking at me.

"Fuck off Joey, that's my fucking sister." Gray scowls at him, before turning back to me "I'm proud of you, for standing up for yourself Mollie." He says, wrapping his arm around my shoulder, although I'm pretty sure he's just done that to cop a feel of Sally's tits on the other side of me. I wish they would just come out with it already.

"Has he tried to contact you back since you left the voicemail?" Gina asks. I hadn't even thought to check my phone again. Reaching into my bag, I pull out my phone, illuminating the screen.

Nothing.

"Nope, but that's not unusual is it." I roll my eyes and place my phone back into my bag. "Now, let's carry on with our night. I feel free!" I say, the first genuine smile spreading across my face

****

Gray pulls into our quiet little street. The girls and I are definitely a little more merry then we should be, but after the whole ending-shit-with-Max situation, the night felt almost like a celebration of my freedom.

I step out the car, blowing kisses to my nearest and dearest as I make my way up the path and towards my front door. I'm laughing for the first time in so long, I feel light and free. The night has taken a real twist from sadness and sorrow, to feeling like a weight has been lifted from my shoulders.

Turning half way to my door, giving them all another wave before tripping slightly over my own feet. Joey jumps out the car and scurries towards me quickly, shouting over, "Are you sure you don't need any help Mollie?"

"Get the fuck in the car Joey." Gray exclaims and starts to get out the car himself.

"I am fine, you bunch of over protective assholes. Now fuck off." I say, smiling back at them.

Turning back around, I reach into my bag pulling out my house keys. Holding them up I go to push my key into the lock when I notice the door is slightly ajar.

What the fuck.

I take a step back. Fear overtaking my veins as my heart plummets into my stomach.

"Mollie?" Gray shouts, as I start walking backwards away from my door.

"Mollie, what's up? What's happened?" Gray shouts again as he gets himself fully out the car.

I turn to face them. Not wanting to admit the words out loud, knowing admitting it out loud will make everything real. A moment passes and Gray starts to make his way over to me.

Grabbing my shoulders he shakes me slightly. "Mollie?" He shouts, "Mollie, talk to me, what is it?"

I gasp a breath, as the fear surrounds me, flooding my body and stilling me on the spot. Gasping in a breath, my eyes meet Gray's.

"I think someone is in my house."

# Chapter 12

## Therapy
## Four Years Ago
## Session 96

"So, I've been figuring out a plan for your panic episodes this week Mollie, I have spoken with some other professionals and we have all agreed that you may benefit from using what's called a 'compression hug', have you heard of this technique before?" Dr Rene asks me during our session.

We've been in session for 30 minutes already, talking about the levels of my panic attacks, when I am able to bring these back myself, and when I struggle to, although these seem to be becoming less frequent, there are times where I cannot pull myself out of the panic.

"No, I've never heard of it." I respond, sitting back against the chair, quite interested in this suggestion.

"Well, a compression hug is a deep pressure therapy which can involve the use of heavy items such as weighted blankets or clothing, but can also factor in general pressures from someone wrapping their arms around your entire body. The aim is to help you to feel calm and grounded." Dr Rene tells me. I feel like this could be a good match for me. "I'd like you to tell your support network about this, and then if necessary ask them to use it when supporting you. Hopefully this will help with bringing you back around in the cases where you are in a deep panic"

I nod, feeling quite hopeful about this technique.

"Okay, let us move on, you've told me before that you were made to complete tasks while captive, can we explore this more?" Dr Rene asks.

I nod, remembering back to my past, I start to recall what happened.

*I think I had been there for quite some time at this point. The days just seemed to be merging into one, and I had definitely lost count by this point. I slept in what seemed to be a basement. The walls were concrete and the room pitch black, unless they opened the grid above me. I started off tied to a wall, but as time went on, I started to just be able to roam around in the dark, my hands and feet still connected together by a long chain, like I was some kind of prison inmate, but I had the freedom to roam the space down there, not that I could see anything. I don't know what changed to make that happen, I just know that it was different now, compared to at the start.*

*They hadn't really bothered to do much to me and to my surprise, nobody had tried to rape me. At this point I'm not entirely sure why I'm still here. Why I'm still alive. The grid opens up and light beams down at me through the hole. Food and water was dropped through the hatch and onto the floor in a basket.*

*"Eat" a deep husky voice growls at me. "You will need your energy today sweetheart" I remember the guy said, his accent was a thick London accent. The grid slams shut and I was once again back in the dark.*

*"How do you expect me to eat if I can't fucking see anything asshole?" I muttered, quietly and to myself, so not to anger anyone. Although I hadn't been touched sexually, there have been many occasions when I have been physically hurt and part of me felt that this was only a matter of time before the worst happened.*

*I walked forward, aiming ahead of myself and hoping I'm going towards the basket. After a few steps, I fall to my knees, feeling around the floor for the basket.*

*I never used to eat the food they gave me but it got to the point where I was so hungry. At the time, I thought I might have died here anyway, so what did I have to lose if they were poisoning me. I was already dying from starvation. From that day on, I decided to just keep eating the food provided. Every day was the same meal, repeated throughout the day. I got 2 meals a day, lunch time and evening and it usually contained a ham sandwich, a bottle of water, and some ready salted crisps.*

*I found the basket and felt around for my sandwich. I noticed in the basket there were four items inside, instead of three. I picked up the unfamiliar item, feeling it and assessing what it could be. I remember thinking it was rectangle in shape and was in a wrapper of some kind. I peeled back the wrapper and sniffed the item.*

*Chocolate.*

*I hesitate for a moment, wondering why they would be giving me a chocolate bar. I placed it back into the basket and picked up my sandwich, eating this and my crisps, while I pondered on why I would have been given a chocolate bar today.*

*After some time, I opted not to eat the chocolate bar, feeling uncertain about the situation. The grid hatch opens again and a man started to climb down the ladder. My heart began to race. It's never a good sign when they come down into here for me.*

*"I haven't done anything. I haven't tried to escape. Why are you coming in here?" I sputtered to him, my voice jittery and laced with fear. I don't even try and hide it any more.*

*"The boss wants to see you," the deep voice repeats as he grabs me on my arm and lead me to the ladders. I climbed up without hesitation knowing if I don't listen I'll just end up being beaten.*

*Once at the top of the ladder, they placed a bag over my head. The usual practice when transporting me from my below level cage to another part of where ever the fuck I was located.*

*I was pushed to sit in a buggy and I remember feeling the sensation that we were moving, feeling the increase of air on my arms and legs signalling faster movement.*

*I'm pulled from the buggy before being lead through a doorway, and up some stairs. The room smelt musky and old, with a strong potent smell of sweat lingering. The bag was removed from my head and I find that I am stood in front of a guy who I assume to be the boss, otherwise known as Melvin. He was the only one in the room that quite happily showed his face. The rest of his gang were all dressed the same. Black hoodies and snoods which cover 90% of their faces, just leaving their eyes exposed.*

*"Mollie, dear" His voice purred towards me as I felt goose bumps scatter along my skin.*

*I stood stoic, not uttering a word back towards him.*

*"No need to be quiet. Did you enjoy your chocolate bar?" Melvin asks me, his confidence that he runs the show was ever apparent.*

*I continued to look forward towards him. "I...I didn't eat it." I responded, my words stuttering.*

*"Why not? That was a treat, from me to you" His large toothy grin exposed his front top 6 teeth as a solid gold band.*

*"It was different. I don't understand why I got chocolate today." I responded, and I remember feeling somewhat braver than I should have been on this day.*

*"Well, Mollie. You have been here for some time now." He began, rubbing the palms of his hands together and leaned over to his desk. "And now, it's time you start completing some important tasks for me"*

*"What do you mean tasks?" I asked.*

*Melvin sniggers, and I remember seeing spit flying out of his mouth and spraying across the dark wood desk that his arms were resting on.*

*"Well, darling, you are my property now. Whether you like it or not, you belong to me. As everyone in this organisation stands, you have a role to fulfil." He started to explain to me.*

*Chills ran down my spine and I remember the feeling of being full with dread. I can't help these monsters. I won't do it. I remain silent, staring at Melvin as he leans back on his chair.*

*"You, Mollie, have a very important job indeed. You will be allowed out of your pit hole, with a chaperone of course and you will bring me what I need." He stated, his voice laced with malice and deception. He smiled his disgusting gold tooth grin at me.*

*"Don't look so fearful, Mollie. They won't be your choice. You will be taken to whoever we have in mind, and you will recruit them, whether that's by force, or willingly."*

*"No," I said instantly, my words were short and static to emphasise my point. Melvin laughed again, deep and dirty, from the gut.*

*"Oh Mollie, you think you have a say. The answer is yes. Because if it's not yes, you best believe your family and your friends will die, one by one until it is a yes. Are we in agreement yet?"*

*"Fuck off, no. Leave my family out of this. Do what ever you fucking want with me but leave them alone." I continued to shout, enunciating my words to try and mask the fear I was feeling.*

*"Mollie, you don't tell me what I can and cannot do. You see, you just hit the nail on the head didn't you darling. You couldn't care less what we do to you. But you do care about those around you. Have a think, and I'll see you soon? But remember. Every day you wait to give me my answer, I will take someone from you."*

*Before I have the chance to respond, the bag is thrown back over my head and I was being dragged backwards by my arms. Once back at the grid, I was slung back down into the hole and the grid hatch was slammed shut, leaving me in the pitched black.*

*Two more days passed by. No food or water arrived for me in those two days and I was glad that I had saved some water over my time in here. That was when the grid finally opened and one of Melvin's guys pulled me out again, bagged my head as usual and took me on the buggy. I knew exactly where I was going.*

*To Melvin.*

*Once we reached the destination, I was dragged out of the buggy and hauled up the stairs to his office.*

*"Mollie," I heard his voice, seemingly cheerful. "I have something for you." He said, his voice changed to more of a sadistic tone.*

*The guys behind me pushed my shoulders down so I was forced to sit on a chair on the opposite side of Melvin's desk.*

*Photos were laid out in front of me, a car wreck. I lean in, scanning the photos. They felt familiar.*

*"What is this?" I asked Melvin, conviction lining my words with more confidence that I actually had.*

*"This, Mollie, is what you have caused for yourself."*

*"A car crash, how have I caused a car crash when I'm sat in my grid?" I said, somehow finding a sarcastic tone.*

*Melvin sniggers "Do you not recognise this vehicle Mollie?" I look down again scanning the photos before I caught a glimpse of the registration plate. My face drops and I'm pretty sure my heart stopped fucking beating for a moment.*

*That's my parents car.*

*"I warned you Mollie, and now they're gone. Who will be next?" Melvin threatens.*

*Tears pooled inside my eye lids and my heart felt as if it was being ripped in two. My poor mum and dad.*

*I remember letting out a sob.*

*"You know how to stop this, Mollie." Melvin announces, leaning back in his chair.*

*I raise my eyes to meet his, I felt the hatred shining through and I hoped he could fucking see just how much I hated him. But I had no choice. Is it going to be Gray next? Gina, Sally or Joey? My shoulders sagged and I knew I had no choice.*

*"Fine. I'll do it" I told him, dropping my chin and wringing my hands together.*

*"Excellent choice, Mollie." Melvin grinned at me, spinning around on his chair. The pleasure smug across his face.*

*He placed two photos of two beautiful girls on the desk in front of me.*

*"Their names are Morgan and Verity. You will bring them to me" My heart sunk down to the pit of my stomach.*

*Fuck.*

# Chapter 13

## Present Day

I am frozen to the spot. Fear is starting to overtake me and I can feel my panic attack coming on. Gray and Joey are out of the car and have reached me within seconds, and while Gray heads over to me. I can see Joey in my peripheral, heading through my front door, his hands clasping hold of a baseball bat over his shoulder.

Gina and Sally have made their way over to me. Sally places both of her hands onto my shoulders, she's talking to me but I can't hear the words coming out of her mouth. The sound is muffled, as I continue to stare at my front door, frozen to the spot.

I briefly catch Gina telling Gray to go search the house with Joey and bile rises up into my throat. This is it, my worst fear. They're coming for me, or worse they're coming for my family like they have threatened to do so, many times before.

I can feel myself shaking.

Joey exits from my house and it attracts my attention, my eyes shooting over to his direction. I notice that my breathing is erratic and suddenly I'm feeling light headed. I can't get any words out of my mouth. I almost feel like I am in one of my nightmares, like I'm paralysed in the moment.

Joey picks up my right hand as I look down at it, he loops around latching onto the left side of me, eventually standing with my back pressed against his chest. His hand remains linked with mine, wrapping tightly and flush against my chest. He applies pressure to me.

A compression hug.

I feel myself melt into him and my breathing starts to settle down. Leaning in to my ear I can hear his voice, “No one is in there, Mollie. There is no damage, nothing seems out of place.” He whispers into my ear. “Everything is okay. Just keep breathing.” He starts a rhythmic tap with my hands across my chest, like a metronome helping me to regulate my breathing to the beat.

I feel so, I don’t know how to explain it, I guess I feel safe?

I feel safe. Stood here, in Joey’s arms, I feel like nothing, not one thing in this world, could harm me. I feel safe.

Gray exits my house and Joey releases his hold on me, like I’m a hot potato. Luckily, I feel grounded enough to function again.

“Nothing seems out of place, Mollie. Maybe it was Max? I mean you did end things with him? Maybe he came to speak to you?” Gray suggests, but I feel like he is just saying things to calm me down. “His things are still here though.” Gray states, matter of factly.

“Okay, let's just think about this rationally and stop running to conclusions.” Sally states, waving her hands in the air. “Mollie, are you sure you closed your door to begin with?” She asks, looking at me sympathetically. I think on this for a minute.

There is no way I left my door open. I am not like that, not now, not after everything.

“Yes Sal, I didn't leave it open. That’s not me, I can’t.” I respond, my voice seeming panicked.

“I know babe, but it's odd don’t you think?” Sally responds, again her voice seeming sorrowful, like she’s speaking to someone who has completely lost it. “You haven’t exactly been on top form recently. You’ve been a little irrational at times.” She tells me, and I can tell she is trying to remaining platonic and calming.

"Irrational? I have not been irrational!" I defend myself, although I know I haven't been totally in the right mindset.

"No Mol, please don't take it that way, I just mean…" She pauses and sighs, rubbing her eyes. "I just mean, there is a lot going on, there are sightings of people who did horrible, horrible things to you and that can cause us, well you, to be elsewhere in your head space." She continues. I know she's right, and I know she doesn't mean to insult me, despite the fact that I am insulted.

I consider the possibility for a moment. Have I left the door open? I really don't know but I guess if nothing has moved, then that's all I have to go off, other than the idea that Max is still in New York and he turned up here looking for me.

"Tomorrow, we install new cameras. I can't believe you haven't replaced the old ones when they broke." Joey lectures me as he slinks his left arm back around my shoulders and walks me towards the door. "One step at a time Mollie, let's go inside."

Once inside, after a lap of the house checking in all the rooms, I can see and feel that nothing is out of place and I start to feel a little more settled.

Without even mentioning anything, my friends start to unpack the spare duvets and pull out mattresses. I don't even have to ask them to stay over, they just are. I honestly have the best bunch of friends anyone could ask for.

"You guys don't have to stay you know, I'm a big girl now I can handle this." I say, guilt filling me up inside that they're all just putting their lives on hold for me.

"Non-sense Mollie. Remember, this is how we cope. Note that I said we," Sally announces, with absolute certainty in her voice. "We are your coping network and we are here to stay." She smiles a wide grin that warms me from the inside.

My bedroom is big but there is literally no room to move with the two mattresses placed on the floor. Sally and Gina, grab some pyjamas from my drawers and decide to jump into bed with me, while Joey and Gray take the mattresses on the floor.

"You guys are amazing." I say, as I climb into bed. "Honestly, I love you all so much."

There is a chorus of goodnights as I settle my head on my pillow. Glancing one last time at my phone, nothing from Max. Not that I expected it. He's such a self righteous asshole at the best of times. I start to close my eyes, feeling safe with my family. I know this would have gone entirely different if they had just left me to be alone, although I don't want to admit it, this whole situation is freaking me out. I decide to put the thought to the back of my mind and drop off into a deep sleep.

****

The following morning we all get up, ready to start the day. I'm feeling good, I didn't have a nightmare last night, which part of me felt like I might do after my panic attack, but knowing everyone was around me definitely gave me that warm comforting feeling I needed to settle down. It's Friday today, the day before the charity ball and we have the finishing touches to complete to make sure everything runs perfectly.

A small part of me feels a little odd today, after I ended things with Max yesterday. I'm not sure what the feeling is inside me, whether it's sadness, happiness, relief or regret. I just feel, incomplete. I know I need to clear my head, as my mind can't be focused on other things today. I need to get myself together.

Sally opens my bedroom door "Are you ready?" She announces, "Gray has said he will drop us off at the office if we can go now."

I plant a smile on my face hoping she doesn't sense that I feel off. "Yeah sure, let's go," I say, grabbing my bag. Sally looks me up and down and I just continue to smile at her, striding past and out of the bedroom.

Not today, Satan.

We get to the office and step out of Gray's car. "Catch you later girls." He calls before revving his engine and screeching off down the street.

Such an asshole.

Once we make it up to our floor, we all take a seat in my office. Meryl has already prepared our favourite morning drinks and has placed all the relevant paperwork into our usual seating arrangements. She is such a beautiful person.

We sit for what feels like forever, discussing the final touches needed to finish off the charity ball, which is set to happen tomorrow. Once we have organised everything, we opt to take a journey to the venue to check over the final preparations and making sure everything looks perfect. As we arrive at the venue, my smile spreads wide as I look up at the sign above the door.

**MR Publications presents:**
***'New Beginnings Ball'***
**on behalf of the TVF Charity**

I always feel somewhat overwhelmed when the ball comes around and I start to remember just how far I have come since everything that is in my past. From starting my own business, to investing and supporting the 'Trafficking Victims and Families charity'. I continue to stare up at the sign, feeling uncertain from last nights events. I just can't seem to shake this feeling.

"Mollie, come on!" Sally shouts, startling me back into reality and I hurry across the golden carpet to catch up as we walk through the main doors, into the venue. We check over the decor, with only a few minor errors and amendments, but otherwise, everything is looking incredible.

We decide to work from the venue for the remainder of the afternoon since all of the work we are doing today, is solely focused on the event tomorrow. We all take a seat at one of the tall bar tables and Gina flips open her laptop.

"So we have three major investors in this years event. I'll be receiving confirmation this afternoon for you to add them into your speech, Mollie." Gina reels off the key information to prepare me for the following day. We continue to crack on with our work and planning through the afternoon. At this point we have each had four coffees and we're all working at super speed with caffeine lining our veins.

"Shit! You can't be serious!" Gina exclaims.

"About what?" I query, the look of shock on Gina's face giving me chills.

"No-fucking-way." Gina gasps out her shock again.

"Spit it out women. What the fuck are you leaving us in the dark for?" Sally shouts, her patience clearly less than mine.

"I've got the investors list," Gina replies.

"And why are we making a holy scene about this?" Sally chimes in, before I can.

"You're not going to believe who is on the list. This one you are going to just die about." She bursts out.

"Go on, enlighten me." I laugh out loud.

She takes a breath, staring at Sally and me while we wait in suspense. "Fucking spit it out Gina!" Sally pushes the haste, banging her hand on the table.

"Riley. Fucking. Austin." Gina emphasises in a slow bold statement.

"Oh my hell. So she's RSVP'd and is the key investor. What have we done to deserve all the love?" Sally chimes, sniggering at her own sarcasm.

"Do you think she will actually attend the ball? Like, do you think we will actually finally meet her?" I ask, the excitement clearly evident in my voice. Why is this such a hot topic? Are we really this sad?

"The email doesn't state whether she will be attending but she did send back confirmation in the original emails chain. The other investors on the list state 'in attendance' following their names." Gina informs us and we all deflate a little.

"Who the fuck invests money into something and doesn't bother to attend the event?" Sally says, clearly unimpressed.

"I can't say I'd be surprised that she didn't attend to be honest. I'd be more surprised if she did." We all break into a laugh, "But let's make sure she's on the guest list, just incase." I quip back. "Does it say how much each person has invested Gina?" I ask, curiosity peaking inside me.

"Yeah," She says, looking up from her laptop and straight into my eyes. "She's the highest investor. She has invested $500,000."

"You're joking?"

"I wish I was, but no. Riley Austin is this years charity ball investor of the year."

****

The day has finally arrived. I'm still not feeling myself, following Thursday night but I just don't have the time to have a breakdown, not today anyway. I still haven't heard anything from Max after I ended things and I can't deny that I'm feeling a little guilty with how I handled the situation. Maybe I did act irrationally. Maybe I should make contact with him and ask to speak to him. What if he hasn't even got the message.

Sally and Gina knock on my door. I open it and paste a smile on my face and welcoming them in.

"I do hope you have food in Mol, I am starving this morning." Sally quips and lucky for her, I have prepared us breakfast and Prosecco.

"Of course I have Sal, food is life!" I reply and we all laugh.

We get ourselves fed and watered, before each of us have a shower and get ourselves ready to head out for our hair and beauty appointments in the city. Gray and Joey have said they will take us into the city, so we decide to sit around the kitchen island having one final minutes rest and a cheeky Prosecco while we wait.

"Hate to bring a downer on the day but have you heard anything from Max?" Sally asks, her tone is sensitive and cautious, like she senses I'm on the edge.

"No," I sigh, frustrated with the whole situation. I don't even know why I'm disappointed.

"Have you tried to contact him again?" Gina adds.

I sigh again "No, for once I've just left it be" I say.

"That's so good, Mol. He's not worth it and it's definitely time to walk away now," Sally says, her voice is sympathetic.

"I know, but part of me wonders if he's even got the message. I don't even know whether his still in America or whether he's gone back overseas." I respond, the sag in my shoulders apparent.

"He has to have gotten it Mollie. He's just too much of a dick to rise to the occasion and fight for you." Gina chimes in and I try hard to agree with her, although I can't help but have this sinking feeling of loneliness.

A knock sounds at my front door and we all shoot our gazes towards it, as Gray and Joey let themselves in.

"Ready ladies?" Joey asks us all and we each beam a smile back.

"Absolutely! Let's get this show on the road!" I paste the smile back on my face and return our mood to happy and excited for the rest of the day to unfold. We head out to Gray's car and off to our appointments.

****

It's now 6:00pm as we all arrive at the venue, dressed in our best clobber and ready to have a good time, for a great cause.

My auburn hair is pinned into a curly up do, with my make up a soft natural look. I opted to wear a floor length black sequin dress, which is low cut to show off some cleavage. Honestly, I feel like a million dollars in the flesh and it has certainly picked up my mood.

Joey links his arm through mine, as we walk across the golden carpet at the entrance. Cameras from the local journalists in the city snapping shots of the guests as we walk. This is the first event I've hosted in the last three years, that Max hasn't walked the carpet with me, so we know that's going to be a hot topic of discussion. Lucky for me, Joey is known to be one of my closest friends and I'm hopeful there won't be any speculation around his kind gesture.

We stride across the carpet and Joey leans into my ear, whispering gently "You look incredible tonight Mol."

A smile spreads across my face at his words. I pull him sideways towards me, squeezing his arm "Thanks Joey, if I'm honest, I feel great." I say, my excitement palpable "You look amazing too, Mr Kincaid," I say and throw him a cheeky wink. He smiles back towards me and before the conversation can continue, we are interrupted by the start up of music and the influx of guests beginning to enter the room. I unhook my arm from his, and position myself towards the doors, ready to greet as many guests as possible. Tonight is going to be a good night, I can feel it in my bones. I smile towards Sally and Gina, flagging them over to stand at the doors with me. Gray and Joey head deeper into the room and the night is definitely starting off well. The first people through the door are my girls, Morgan and Verity, both victims of trauma.

"Girls, I'm so glad you made it!" I greet, hugging each of them and encouraging them to take a free drink from the waiters. "We will have a catch up later, I promise," I say as they carry on into the room. The flow of people arriving continues and the night already feels like a hit.

The drinks have been flowing for a few hours and the night is absolutely pumping. I completed my speech, thanking all those involved and started the bidding raffle for further funds to be raised.

"Still no sign of Riley, have you guys had a glimpse?" Sally asks as we take a rare moment together.

"No, I've spotted Cilla but she told me it was 'not of my concern' where Riley was. She's such a fucking dick," Gina quips and we all crack a laugh.

Out of the corner of my eye I spot a familiar face.

"What the fuck is he doing here?" I gasp.

"Who?" Sal and Gina chant together.

"Rian, you know the guy from the random bar I went to not long ago." I say, craning my neck to look through the crowd towards him.

"Oh, that guy who chased after you, looks like fucking sex on fire?" Sally blurts out, also now scanning the crowd to try and spot him.

"Yes, that guy. I wonder how he made it to the guest list." I state, not really interested in the reason why if I'm totally honest.

"Go, Go! You need to chat with him, you know you want to." Sally coos, wiggling her eyebrows at me before pushing my shoulder in his direction.

"Sal, no, he hasn't even spotted me! What if he can't even remember who I am?" I say in a rush, a little bit of excitement lacing my voice. What the hell is this? Am I blushing?

"I think he has already spotted you," Gina states as she takes a sip of her mojito. "Hottie on route," She finalises.

I turn and notice Rian walking towards me, all 6ft 5 inches of him, a sly smile tugging at his lips. He is literally squashed into the suit he's wearing, it almost looks painted onto his body it's that snug and he looks absolutely divine.

"Hallie," he says and for a minute confusion laces my features, before realisation hits me like a freight train.

Fuck! I told him my fucking name was Hallie.

"Ah yes, well no, actually not Hallie." I say, feeling slightly awkward.

"I never thought it was, Mollie." He replies, his voice is rich and smooth, making my insides into putty.

"How did you know?" I ask, feeling a little silly now.

"Mollie, you are a beautiful and successful business women with many hands, in many pots. Of course you were easy to recognise." He says and I smily shyly.

I giggle, "Don't, you'll make me blush." I say. Am I flirting? What is going on with me?

He continues to talk to me but my attention wavers, as I take note that he smells absolutely incredible. The mixture of citrus, spice and wood fills the air around me and I am lost to this.

"Are you okay Mollie?" He asks.

Shit, have I just been zoned out.

"Ahh yes, so sorry, I'm just exhausted from everything," I wave my hand in the air to gesture the party planning, as I try and recover myself.

Fuck, Fuck, Fuck!

"I can see it's been a busy night to plan, but an incredible one at that." He says, and a sense of pride fills me up.

"What brings you here? Are you part of the family network?" I ask, curiosity taking over.

"No, not as such, I just choose a variety of charities each year which I feel are good causes and like to get involved a little."

"That's good of you, it's such a good cause and…" I pause, feeling my phone vibrating in my clutch bag under my arm.

I take it out and see the name across the screen.

Max.

I stare at it for a moment. I really should just ignore it. The phone continues to ring and a text message pops up across the top.

**Max -** Don't you fucking dare ignore me.

My eyes shoot up scanning the room.

What the fuck, is he here?

"I'm so sorry Rian, I need to take this, but I will catch up with you soon." I say, touching my hand on his shoulder and pressing a kiss onto his cheek.

His hand places onto my elbow and strokes down my arm to my finger tips.

"Until we meet again, Mollie Rutter." he says, his voice melting in my ears. What is this man? My heart flutters for a beat, before I catch a glimpse of Max standing on the other side of the balcony.

Stepping away from Rian, I pick up the phone that is still vibrating in my hand, pressing green and placing the phone to my ear.

"Max…" I say, my voice quivering and my heart is racing right now.

"We are not over, Mollie. Not unless I fucking say we are." He states. His tone firm and commanding, although somewhat caressing.

I pause, not really sure how to respond.

"I'll see you in the upstairs bathroom, Mollie. We need to talk." He says before the phone cuts out and I watch him make his way through the crowd to the staircase. I stand and think for a moment. Do I really want to go upstairs with him? Is he mad at me? I hesitate on the spot briefly before deciding that I need to see this through. I need to end this, face to face, tonight.

I enter the upper floor bathroom and walk into the centre of the room, looking for Max.

"Max?" I call out just as I hear the lock click on the bathroom door. Startled slightly, I turn around to see him stood there in his tux. He looks furious and my heart starts to pound in my chest. Neither of us choose to say anything as we just continue to stare at each other, waiting for the other one to start talking.

"I guess, after you had everything to say last week, you now suddenly have nothing to say?" Max starts, his voice so laced with ferocity, I start to tremble slightly.

"I said what I needed to say last week, Max." I still myself, enunciating my words, to make sure I'm not showing the weakness I feel.

"You can't just decide to end things on a whim, Mollie. We've been together for years, not weeks!" Max shouts.

"What does it matter, Max? You're never here? You've spent months avoiding me, avoiding us and everything here. I'm done with it." I say, maintaining my cool and trying to voice everything before I chicken out.

"You knew I was a military man when we met, Mollie. Fuck! Why is that now a sudden problem?" He takes off his jacket, uncoupling his bow tie and unbuttons his shirt, removing this leaving himself shirtless as he walks over to the circular sink unit. He runs his hands through his hair as his biceps flex with the motion.

His body on display has my own instinctively reacting to the sight. My heart beat is erratic as I feel myself becoming more and more turned on, the more I look at him, his muscles flexing and tensing.

*What the fuck is wrong with you Mollie? Pull yourself together, he's an asshole.*

He uses the water to splash across his face before leaning his arms out stretched onto the sink, his face looking down.

"Max," I say softly. "I'm sorry that I ended it on a voicemail. But this hasn't been working for months. You know this, you're just not concerned about me or us anymore. You never want to be home. Fuck, even the last time we had sex, you finished yourself off and left me high and dry." I say, my heart is still racing and I can't take my eyes off him despite this tumultuous love-hate feeling I have for him.

"You know I still want you, Mollie." Max declares and I can't help but spit out a laugh.

"Is that a joke? Max you put me down all the time, you never want to be home, when you are home it is for literal moments and there is no thought for me or us ever." I say, my anger increasing slightly as we continue, "Can you be honest with me, is there someone else, Max?" I ask spontaneously. I haven't really thought about the possibility of this until now.

"You have to be joking, Mollie?" He says, snapping his head up towards me, his eyes so intense I feel like they're burning a hole through me. "I have just stood there, watching you in that fucking dress, looking beyond incredible, while you flirt with another man, the same man I caught you entertaining not long ago, mere days after you end things with me. And you want to accuse me of having someone else?" He sounds genuinely hurt by my allegation.

His words take me aback slightly and I stutter trying to get my words out. He stands upright, his bare torso exposed to me, his muscles flexing and my eyes drift down him. My mouth is dry and I lick my lips while I drink the sight of him in.

Max starts walking towards me slowly, and my pulse quickens, the sight of him turning me on so much, the throbbing between my legs intensifies. I can feel myself, slick and wet, aching for relief. I back up until I'm pressed against the wall, Max's right arm props himself up on the wall. He stand inches in front of me, his aroma surrounding me, turning me on further.

Picking up my right hand, he interlocks our fingers before guiding my hand down to the engorged erection in his pants. I gasp, a small moan leaving my lips as my centre clenches, my body reacting to his, knowing I have missed this sultry side of him.

He leans in to my ear and whispers to me, “Does my cock tell you that I don’t want you, Mollie?” His voice is a purr in my ear as he strokes my hand along his length beneath his pants, up and down. My breath hitches and I go to move my other hand towards myself, feeling the need to relieve the ache pulsing inside.

“Not this time Mollie, I’d like to remind you just how much I want you,” he whispers into my ear before reaching around the back of my dress and tugging the zip down. The dress falls to the floor exposing me, without a bra in place, my breasts out and my nipples growing harder as the cold air breezes across them.

I squeeze my legs tighter, the ache almost vibrating inside me, I feel sure I’m so turned on, I could come on the spot. Max takes my nipple into his mouth as I gasp, my hands lacing through his hair as he lifts me up into his arms, carrying me over to the vanity unit and sitting me down on the edge as his tongue continues to assault my nipple. He slides my panties to the side, admiring the glistening view of my wet pussy as he starts gliding his fingers across my flesh and I can’t help but gasp, letting out a breathy moan. His thumb begins circling my clit, varying the pressure to keep me on edge, while is hand starts to work me around my vulva, caressing and sliding through the wetness that is dripping from me, the throbbing intensifying with every stroke of his hand.

“More,” I cry out, my hand reaching for his pants as I unhook them and expose his large erection, taking it into my hand, I start to pump my fist up and down his shaft slowly. Max lets out a deep growl as he continues to tend to me, he pushes two of his fingers sharp and deep inside me, pumping them as I match him with my own pace.

I am on the brink, my insides tensing with every pump of his hand. Max brings his mouth to mine, biting my lip as I pant. "You are mine, Mollie, do you hear me," He bites out and I nod, a complete and utter puddle of mercy. He removes his fingers and I wimpier at the loss of contact for a second before he slides me towards the edge of the unit. Releasing his cock from my hand he lines himself up at my entrance, sliding the tip of his cock through my wet folds and I gasp, the ache to have him fill me almost sending me over the edge.

He looks at me, straight into my eyes "I love you, Mollie. Always remember that," and then he slams into me, filling me deep, his rhythm quick just as my body wants. I scream out, my moans filling the bathroom as he grunts along with me, our wetness combined, the sweat coating each of us. I reach for him, grabbing his chin with my hand and pulling his face closer to me, the need to kiss him unfathomable. Our lips connect and I can feel myself on the brink of release.

Our lips part and I let out a moan "I'm going to come," I say and Max's thrusts become more ferocious.

"Come for me baby," he says, and it's enough to send me crashing into euphoria, my walls clenching around his cock, as my body trembles. Max follows me straight over the edge and we both collapse, our breaths rapid and bodies spent.

Our breathing slows, and our heart rates begin to settle. Max lifts his forehead from mine and I spend a moment trying to gain some clarity from his eye contact.

"Well, that was…" he pauses, placing a snigger in-between, "that was definitely not my intention, but fucking hell, that was incredible." He dabs kisses down my chest and I feel a little less vulnerable for it.

A smile tugs at my lips "Yes," I answer "Very unexpected." He peels himself off me, his cock pulling out, the feeling of being unexpectedly empty. I stand, turning to look at myself in the mirror. My make-up is somewhat still standing and my hair has a slight 'just fucked' look about it.

"I'll definitely have to give this a fix," I say, pointing at my hair, and we both smile.

I pick up my dress and place it back on "can you zip me back up?" I ask Max and he reaches out tugging my zip to the top. Searching for myself in the mirror I make some adjustments to my hair grabbing some pins from my bag and patch my face back together with some powder. Spritzing myself with perfume to mask the smell of sex. I feel ready enough to return to the ball.

"I can't believe we've been gone for so long." I say to Max, a sly smile tugging at my lips.

Max hasn't bothered to put his bow tie back on and has left his shirt buttons uncoupled at the top.

We exit the bathroom and make our way back towards the staircase. "We still have a lot to talk about Max, sex doesn't just fix everything that was wrong before." I say as we descend the stairs back towards the ball room. The room is still full and it seems our absence may have gone unnoticed. Apart from with Sally, who is glaring at me from the balcony bar across the room.

Max sniggers leaning into my ear he says above the music, "Mollie, you ended things, not me. As you said, we're done. I just wanted you to remember what you walked away from." He pulls back and reality starts to put coherent thoughts together as I feel like my soul is leaving my body, and my pulse quickening.

"What does that mean?" I say, trying to remain strong, when I can feel myself shattering into pieces.

With a wink and a smirk he says, "Catch you soon. Enjoy your freedom, Mollie." He spins around and walking away across the ballroom floor.

Fucking hell.

How could I have been so fucking stupid to fall for his charms? I feel the panic rising in my chest and I glance around trying to spot my people. I remember that Sally was at the balcony bar and I glance over, her eyes are still on me. My face must tell it all because she sighs and her shoulders sag as she gestures for me to head over to her.

I glide across the dance floor and when I reach Sally, Gina is sat there and to my surprise, Sara is here.

"Oh Mollie, what have you done?" Sally says, but despite her obvious disappointment in me she pulls me in for a hug.

Sara leans her head on my shoulder. "Missed you Moll-bear," she says, as she squeezes me. "Come on let's catch up and get fucking mortal," Sara adds, which brings a smile to my face despite my eyes glazing over with tears that I am trying my hardest to keep at bay.

"I was so stupid girls. But I can't go into it now. We just need to get through tonight and I'll tell all tomorrow. Get me some fucking alcohol." I say fanning my eyes to stop the tears from falling.

Gina holds her arm in the air and a waiter approaches. She orders me a Long Island Iced Tea for a strong hit, and we carry on the evening as if nothing has happened.

****

We arrive home in the town cars I had arranged for us and climb out. The night was a real hit and we raised so much money for TVF Charity, which is exactly what we do this night for.

"We can come and stay over at yours if you want Mollie? Or you can stay at ours?" Sally suggests.

I immediately shake my head no, "Honestly guys, I'm fine, I'm exhausted and I just need some time to process what happened tonight." I say defeat showing in the sag of my shoulders.

"Okay, but we're just across the lawn if you need us." Gina says. I smile, giving a small wave and turning back towards my house.

Once in my house I close and lock the door, leaning against it for a brief moment. I grab myself a glass of water and head up the stairs to get ready for bed.

Heading into the en-suite, I grab my make up wipes to take off my party face and start to remove the pins holding in my curly up do. Looking at myself in the mirror, I feel entirely different from how I had earlier when I looked in the mirror. The defeat is heavy in my features and I'm saddened that the hot flush still stains my cheeks. I think some part of me expected to come back home and find him here waiting for me.

But that is not the case.

Deciding not to dwell any more, I open my toiletries bag to place the clips back inside before heading into my bedroom. I always feel sentimental after attending the charity events and seeing all of the people who have been affected by these horrific trafficking organisations. I feel so lucky to have escaped and been given this opportunity to live and help others to find their families or overcome their sufferings.

I head over to my bed and scurry underneath, searching around I pull out the shoe box which contains the photos of my family that Melvin had given to me as bait when I was captured, keeping me motivated and on side. Rubbing on the lid, a tear fills my eye as an overwhelming sense of happiness and dread overcomes me. No one knows I keep this box. Not even Max and he has lived here. This is something I kept for myself. I'm not even sure why. I lift the lid slightly and start shuffling the photos around in the box, seeing a glimpse of everyone who is important to me as they went about their lives.

Something catches my eye and I open the box fully. Inside there is a small envelope which is titled, '**Mollie**'. Confusion lines my features and I flip this over, scanning the back, noticing the envelope is not sealed. Opening it up, I find pictures.

Recent pictures.

Pictures of me from over the last few weeks.

I pull out a piece of paper, unfolding it.

My face falls.

No, no, no.

This can't be happening.

I read the note, once, twice, three times.

***Hello Mollie,***
***Long time no see.***
***We're closer than you realise.***
***And now we've been inside your house.***
***We are coming for you.***
***Catch you soon.***

I can't breath.

The panic floods through my veins and I can't find any words inside me. I stumble back dropping onto the bedroom floor. Gasping for breath, the attack is hitting me hard.

They've been here. They have been in my house. I knew it. I knew I hadn't left the door open.

I can't think. I can't find my phone.

Gasping for breath, the panic is overtaking me.

I can't stop it this time.

I'm lay on the floor, my face pressed against the sleek wood as I try and grasp my breath. I still can't breathe, the pain in my chest so intense it feels like it could crack.

All coherent thoughts are gone and I feel completely lost to this attack. Lying frozen on the floor, paralysis overtaking and my eyes start to leak tears. In this moment, I honestly feel like I could die on this spot. I hear a noise downstairs, the clicking of the front door opening and bile rises to my already restricted airways.

No, this can't be happening. I can feel myself shaking, my muscles spasming and I wonder if I might dip so low as to end up fitting. I don't know what to do to fix this. Footsteps sound rising up the stairs and I continue to cry, unable to move from the spot I'm lay in. The bedroom door creaks open and I see boots coming through the door.

That's the last thing I see before I'm gone completely. Blackness darkening my vision and my subconscious sending me into a darkness of its own to protect me.

# Chapter 14

## Therapy
## Five Years Ago
## Session 72

"Your eyes are feeling heavy Mollie. You're slowly falling deeper. 3…2…1… and you are in a deep sleep. It's just me and you Mollie, tell me where you've gone." Dr Rene lulls to me, while I lie with my eyes closed.

Feeling sleepy, I feel my mind taking me away from the therapy room and into the cascade of my sub-conscious as the memory rolls through my mind.

*I'm standing outside of a bar, in the city of London, I can see the London Eye and Big Ben. It's a cold evening, with frost making the floor glisten, while my breath steams as it leaves my mouth. The season tells me that it's certainly winter time. I scan the area to try and find any evidence of what the date is but I can't seem to find anything which can help me at this point, although I know that I have to have been captured for around a year now, as it was last winter I decided to go somewhere hot for a break away.*

*I run my hands along my body, feeling the ridges of the straps situated all along my body. Of course they wouldn't just let me out of their torture chambers to walk around London, free as a bird. That would definitely be wishful thinking. No, instead they have strapped me with explosives, which could be used to blow me, and likely a large portion of London up, should I try to escape.*

*Melvin laughed when they were strapping me up, I can still hear his voice spitting the words out, as his gold tooth grin smiled at me.*

*"There is enough gun powder here to put Guy Fawkes to shame, Mollie dear. So I suggest you behave yourself. Unless you want to blow up half of London," He sniggered and spit shoots from his mouth, speckling across my face.*

*"Come the fuck on, Mollie." A voice snaps me back to reality as it buzzes through my earpiece, I am shocked that the voice is a female. I remember where I am and sigh, concluding that I literally have no other option but to do this, otherwise half of fucking London are at risk of blowing the fuck up.*

*I walk up into the bar where I've been told that Morgan Holt and Verity Platt are located. I scan the bar trying to pull out the faces of the girls I have been given photos of to find and recruit. It's not long before I spot them sat at the bar.*

*Taking a deep breath, I head over to the bar and take the stool next to them. My hands are trembling and I know I need to pull myself together. I order a Pink Gin and Lemonade from the bar, asking for some snacks, the thought of having something more than a sandwich to each giving me incredible vibes. I sit back and start to plan how to introduce myself.*

*It's not long before I find myself chatting away to both girls. They're American, step-sisters that have come to London for the holidays. Guilt laces my throat as I lie to them about who I am and where I come from although before I realised it, I gave them my actual name.*

*I learnt almost everything about those girls that someone could in one night. I learnt they were both 23, and their parents met when they were 12. I learnt about their blended families, and how they were both studying in University to be Doctors but they had opted to take a few weeks off over Christmas before their final exams started.*

*The guilt started to eat me up inside and I decided I needed some space to calm my nerves. I stood, telling them I was just nipping to the ladies room and that I would be back.*

*"Where the fuck do you think your going?" The voice questioned in my ear.*

*"I just need a fucking minute." I snapped back, knowing I look like a fucking mad women to the people I am passing but I can't fathom the fuck to give.*

*I burst through the toilet door and immediately slam into the cubicle, throwing up the contents of my stomach, before slouching down the cubicle wall into a heap on the floor as I begin to sob.*

*"Can you hurry the fuck up and finish what you're supposed to be doing before I put a fucking bullet in your brothers skull," the voice rings in my ear.*

*I feel so lost. Nothing I do at this point achieves anything positive.*

*If I walk out of here, they could blow me and half of London up.*

*If I delay any longer they could kill Gray.*

*If I go out there, I have to steal the lives of the two beautiful girls, who are incredible, kind, giving human beings.*

*"You have 5 fucking seconds to make a choice Mollie." The voice in my ear announces.*

*I find the courage to stand up, and exit the toilet after checking myself out in the mirror. Returning to the bar, I greet Morgan and Verity again.*

*"Hey, sorry about that I was desperate." I say, the fakest smile plastered across my face.*

*"Oh I bet you are after all those drinks," She jokes and I fake a laugh along with her.*

*"Hey, my friends band are playing a gig in a bar not too far from here, it's actually why I'm out tonight. Do you fancy tagging*

*along with me? It'll be a great night." I say enthusiastic, although my heart is pounding and my hands are trembling.*

*"Yeah, that sounds awesome!" Morgan replies and I point to the doors at the front.*

*"After you," I say and they take off towards the front of the bar. I place my hands into my coat pocket to try and mask the shaking.*

*Once outside I declare, "It's this way, just a 5 minute walk." They link arms with me and we start along the Thames riverbank.*

*"Take a left when you see the alley on the corner in 20 yards Mollie," the voice in my ear says and I close my eyes tight as I walk, dropping my head and letting out a breath.*

*"Are you okay Mollie?" Verity asks catching me off guard. My eyes shoot up and I must look petrified because the look on both of their faces says they know something is off.*

*"Yeah, all good, just err..." I hesitate, "Just feeling a little iffy." I rub my tummy for dramatic effect, hoping I've managed to sell the tale and turn off down the alley. They continue to follow and my breathing starts getting more erratic.*

*Out of the darkness the hooded figures appear, slinging bags over Morgan and Verity's head as they cover their mouths with cloth that I assume has chloroform on.*

*They let out a scream before there's a deathly silence.*

*"Well done, Mollie." The creepy female voice in my ear congratulates me. I drop down on to the ground, my breathing erratic, I feel like I can't take in enough oxygen. My chest tightens and there's an intense pain inside, still gasping for breath, I can't breathe and my eyes start to sparkle.*

*I think I'm going to pass out.*

# Chapter 15

## Present Day

I wake up, gasping for air, I feel my surroundings before opening my eyes and peering around the room.

I'm lay in my own bed, my pyjamas are on, and a hot coffee has been placed at my bedside.

What the fuck.

Was that a nightmare? Did I dream all of that last night?

I step out of bed, confusion filling me, kneeling down I pull the box out from under my bed.

Wait. A hot coffee? Who the fuck made that?

"Mollie," a voice startles me.

"Shit! Fuck!" I drop the box, before turning and looking up at the one and only, Max.

"Sorry, I didn't mean to startle you." He announces, holding his hands in the air as if to surrender. My face must be a picture of 'what the fucking fuck' because that's how I feel.

"I know, you're confused. I'm sorry." He announces, running his hands through his hair as his muscles flex and I find myself ogling at him, even though I want to hate him.

"What are you doing here, Max? What happened last night?" I ask, a little more harsh than I should have.

"I came here, after the event. I felt awful about what I said at the ball, after what happened between us, so I went back to the ball and Morgan said you had left already, so I got a cab and I came here." He begins, his voice seeming sorrowful. "When I got here, I knocked but there was no answer so, I let myself in thinking maybe you had gone to sleep already, and when I got upstairs you were on the floor, shaking, you sounded like you couldn't breathe. I rolled you on to your side and ran over to get Sally," He finishes, worry lining his face.

"You got Sally? Why?" I ask softly.

"I didn't know what was happening to you, Mollie, you looked like you were dying!" He exclaimed, and he genuinely seems hurt. "She got here and said it were just having a panic attack. She asked me to pick you up and put you into bed. She got you changed out of your dress and then she told me to just let you rest." He continues "So that's what I did."

"And where did you sleep?" I ask, like that's the important factor right now.

"I slept in my spot next to you." He says, like he's not just violated my privacy.

"Your spot? Max when was the last night you fucking slept in this bed, for the whole night?" Not holding back my frustrations towards him.

"I was worried Mollie! You seemed..." he pauses for a moment, "You seemed lifeless. Fucking dead!"

"Oh and you suddenly give a fuck? Get fucking real, Max" I shout, my annoyance entirely readable now.

"Of course I give a fuck, Mollie, you're my girlfriend. You have been for three fucking years."

I laugh "Girlfriend? Funny that because you were so fucking sure it was over last night after you got your dick wet and fucking left me!" I am fully raging now, remembering how he made me feel last night, everything floods back in, raw and fresh.

"Mollie, come on, I said I'm sorry."

"You're Sorry?" I laugh out loud "Oh well, fuck me sideways Max, let me just bow the fuck down to you again shall I? In fact let me just take these pants off, lie on the bed and spread my legs to give you a pretty little pussy show, is that what you want Max, babe?" the sarcasm seeping from within me.

Max drops his head, staring at the floor in defeat.

"I put the photos in the kitchen and the note. I think you should hire someone, a body guard or something." Max says, again seeming like he gives a toss about anything other than himself.

"I'm done with this conversation, Max. Get out of my house, last night was a mistake." I say, grabbing my towel and heading into the en-suite, locking the door behind me.

I press my back against the door, taking in deep breaths trying to keep myself calm. Knowing that last night was all real and not a nightmare is putting me back on the edge. I need to keep myself grounded and not lose control.

I hear a slight bang on the opposite side of the door and I sense that Max is on the opposite side.

"I'm going, Mollie. But please know that I am sorry, for everything. I'm trying though. Please know I'm trying," he says and I can feel my heart shattering. I suddenly feel alone, and I know he's left without even leaving the bathroom. A text comes through on my phone, as I turn on the shower.

**Sally** - Just seen Max leaving. Will come over in 10.

I smile. She knows me well enough to know I need my closest people around me right now. My shoulders relax a little as I slide into the shower knowing my girls have always got my back.

****

Monday comes around quicker than I'd have liked. I did enjoy the ball, despite how the night ended overall. I have given some serious consideration to Max's idea of hiring a body guard but after speaking with Sally and Gray, we decided it was best that I make sure I don't travel anywhere alone right now. Most of Sunday was spent updating the police on the break in at my house and what I had found the following week.

The photos from my box were taken for forensic testing but I know the organisation well, and I know there won't be an ounce of evidence leading to them.

I decide that a gym session is just what I need to refocus my mind and to help me to release some of the anxiousness I'm feeling of late. Joey picks me up from my house and we head to the gym together.

"Do you want to talk about Saturday night?" He probes as we both head into the gym. I side eye him before sliding my AirPods into my ears and striding away and towards the treadmills.

"I guess that's a no!" I hear Joey shout, as he stops at the weights and we both continue our work outs solo.

I run on the treadmill for going on an hour and my legs are close to buckling beneath me. Joey appears on my right and it startles me to almost trip, just as he presses the red stop button in the centre of the treadmill.

"That's enough running, Mollie, you're going to burn yourself out." Joey says, his voice a command rather than a request, as he watches the sweat beading down between my breasts. What has got into him lately?

"I'm fine Joey." I argue, I don't know why I always want to oppose him lately. Maybe I'm just sick of men trying to control my life.

"No Mollie, you're not fine. You're trying to run away from your issues. Maybe you should consider giving Aria a call and scheduling a session to chat with her?" He questions, concern evident in his expression as his eyes seem sympathetic.

"I'm fine Joey!" I say, my voice rising slightly as the irritation builds up inside me. He sighs, and shakes his head at me.

"Come on, we have to go, it's 8:15." He prompts me. I glance at my watch, shocked at the time. Heading over into the female changing room, I quickly shower and when I exit, Joey is waiting at the front door for me.

"Ready?" He asks, gesturing his hand towards the door.

"As I'll ever be," I smile back and we head out of the gym towards Joey's car.

We pull up at my office building and Sally is waiting at the door for me. I'm already fed up of this 'Mollie-goes-no-where-alone' bullshit.

I step out of Joey's SUV and close the door, turning towards Sally. "I'm pretty sure I can walk from the car to the office in broad fucking daylight, Sally." My sass palpable and I glare at her. She rolls her eyes, flipping the bird at me and shakes a tray of disposable cups from Maureen's in my direction.

"Hurry the fuck up will you." She shouts back and it brings a smile to my face.

I lean into the car window, "Thank you for this morning Joey, same time tomorrow?" I give a hopeful smile towards Joey as I lean through the car window.

"Sure, I'll pick you up at 6:30 tomorrow morning." He smiles back at me "Have a nice day Mollie." I lean back off the window and he speeds off down the streets of NYC.

Turning towards Sally, she exaggerates staring at her watch and shakes her head at me. I laugh and head over towards her.

"What do we have planned today, Sal?" I ask as we both stride across the marble floor, giving a cute wave towards Sonja as we head for the lift.

"Well, we have quite a relaxed morning, and coffee scheduled at 11:45 in Maureen's with Morgan and Verity." Sally begins as she hands me the paper tray of drinks and pulls out her diary. "Then we have a meeting scheduled with Riley Austin's team this afternoon." She says, slight hesitation in her voice as she knows I could do without attitude from Cilla after this weekend.

"A great start to the week." I deadpan.

"I know, it's last minute scheduled. I believe it was only put in the calendar this morning." Sally responds.

"That's never a good sign."

The morning goes by quickly and before we know it, it's time for our coffee meet with Morgan and Verity. Sally is joining but Gina has hung back to prepare for the meeting with Riley's team this afternoon.

I'm honestly so excited to see these girls and see how they're feeling, with everything going on at the minute. We walk into Maureen's and spot the girls sat in the cozy corner that we usually meet in whenever we get the chance. I order a Camomile tea to try and keep my nerves settled and we head over to the corner. The girls bounce up from their seats and we each share hugs and hellos.

"It's been so long, I'm so sorry I didn't get chance to spend time with you guys at the ball on Saturday night, it was just so chaotic." I say, sitting and taking a sip of my tea.

"Chaotic is definitely what I'd describe your night as. I saw you scrambling into the second floor bathroom with Mr tall-dark-and-handsome." Morgan coo's at me, giving a cheeky wink in my direction.

I feel my cheeks flush red as the memory replays in my mind and the embarrassment of being caught out fills me.

"Oh, it wasn't like that," I begin, before smirking slightly, "well, it wasn't supposed to be like that." I laugh, picking my cup up to hide behind this.

Sally rolls her eyes besides me, "He's still a cock, Mollie." She quips, evident that she is not Max's biggest fan. We all chuckle and the conversation continues.

"So, how are you girls feeling about everything? With the organisation seeming to be being sighted in NYC?" I ask, my face falling and a veil of seriousness  appearing over my face.

"It's frightening for sure." Verity responds, looking down at her hands, her body tensing at the reminder.

"We're just trying to make sure we're not really out at night and if we are, we are making sure that it's not just us two." Morgan adds.

"Have you had any contact made with them?" I ask, curious if it's just me they've tried to link in with, or if they know that Morgan and Verity are also in New York.

"No, we've not heard anything, they don't seem to be aware that we're here in the city we don't think." Verity says, "Have you had anything?"

I sit back, thinking momentarily whether I want to share what is happening to me. As useful as it is, I don't want them to worry or panic. Looking over at Sally, she gives a curt nod and I know she agrees that in order to keep them as safe as possible, they need to know what's happening.

"It seems like I've been targeted."

"Targeted? By the organisation?" Verity snaps, louder than I wanted her to share.

I glance around the cafe to check if she caught anyone's attention, but it doesn't seem to have affected anyone that I notice.

"Keep your voice down, we don't know who we can trust or if I'm being followed," I say in a whisper shout. "On Thursday last week, we had been out for a little bit and when I got home, my front door was open." I begin explaining from the start.

"Nothing was out of place so we put it down to the potential that I just hadn't closed it when I left." I shrug my shoulders before looking down at my cup.

"Then, on Saturday after the ball, I got home and I always feel a little sentimental after the event, so I went under my bed and pulled out my photograph box where I keep all of the pictures that the organisation had threatened me with whilst I was captive." I continue, both Morgan and Verity staring at me, their mouths agape.

"When I opened the box, there was an envelope," I pause, the memory rising my pulse slightly and I know I just need a minute to calm myself down. I pick up my tea and take a sip, a slight tremble in my hands appearing. Sally notices and she places her hand on my leg, giving it a reassuring squeeze. The physical contact grounds me and steadies my thoughts enough for me to continue.

"There was an envelope, and when I opened it, inside there were pictures of me inside, from every day recently," I say, my voice quaking slightly, "Photos of me leaving work, photos of me at the gym, photos of me in my bedroom getting changed."

"No. Fucking. Way." Morgan quips.

"Yeah, there was also a note, telling me that they're watching me and telling me that they're coming." I glance around the cafe again, searching for anyone who may be with the organisation and listening into the conversation, but I can't seem to pinpoint anyone.

"Do you think they'll come for us next?" Morgan asks, and I can hear the concern in her voice.

"I don't know, I guess if you've not felt like they're here already, that it may seem like they're not interested in you."

This seemed to reassure them both a little.

"Just, keep yourselves safe, please." I urge.

We carry on our lunch, enjoying some sandwiches and catching up on each others lives. For a while, I forget about the world around us.

The week rolls on, meeting after meeting. On the whole it's been a good week, we've signed some really good authors and business is looking up. It's just the news I needed when times have been so tough lately.

As usual, I look out the glass windows to wind down my day. The night sky has already rolled in, we're definitely late in the office today. I observe the vast darkness of central park with the beams of bright and red lights that line the edges like a picture frame. Sally enters my office and flops down on the sofa.

"Is the week done yet?" She announces, faining that she has fainted, her body sprawled across the sofa. I giggle at her dramatics.

"Almost Sal, almost."

Gina enters the office too, batting at Sally's legs to get her to move them off the end of the sofa. Sally does so and Gina sits down besides her.

"I have an idea." Gina announces which perks up the attention of both of us.

Sally tilts her head upwards, "I'm all ears Gina dear, hit me with your good intentions."

We all giggle and Gina continues "Well, tomorrow is an easy day, we have no scheduled meetings, and realistically, we could just bunk off for the day if the boss lets us," She shifts her gaze towards me, giving an exaggerated wink in my direction.

I scoff back at her "Continue…" I usher her on.

"Well, I think Mollie should take us along to that little Irish bar she wondered off to alone not so long ago and we can have some real hearty home-like laughs." Gina finishes. The smile across her face is infectious.

I'll be honest, that idea sounds incredible.

I haven't seen or spoken to Rian since randomly bumping into him at the ball, so it would be nice to maybe catch him around.

"I'm fucking sold, grab your bags girls, tonight is going to be wild." Sally states, jumping up from the couch with some new found energy.

"We can go for one drink. I'm telling you both, we are in work tomorrow, we have important meetings next week that we have to finalise some work for."

"Blah, blah, blah, Mollie, grab your coat and let's go already!" Sally calls as she's already striding up the corridor towards the lift.

When outside we holler for a cab and jump in. I ask the driver to take us to O'Reilly's Bar and he heads there, each of us brushing out our hair and topping up our make-up, so we look a little fresher than the 'tired from work' look.

We arrive at the bar, the green light outlining the name above the door. Exiting the cab I pay our fare and turn around, leading the girls in through the double doors. The place is just as I remembered, the feel of home sinking into my soul the minute we walk through the door.

We approach the bar and I instantly recognise the bartender, Cam. Sitting ourselves on the bar stools he approaches us "Ahh, you came back again," He says, wiping the bar in front of where we are sitting. I smile, it's humble and warming that he recognises me despite this bar being incredibly busy.

"Yes, my friend's decided they wanted a taste of the bar I snuck out to when they weren't looking." I laughed, and notice that Gina looks mesmerised by Cam.

"What can I get you ladies?" Cam asks, his Irish accent coarse and soothing.

Sally waits for Gina to respond but she seems to have lost the ability to speak. "Not a problem Gee, I'll start," she says nudging Gina on the shoulder and bringing her back out of her daze.

We laugh and order our drinks.

Once Cam places them onto the bar, we hold them in the air and clink them together, cheering to life and happiness.

"Have either of you been using this app Riley had us trialing?" Gina says, and I can see she's currently browsing the app.

"Not since Max found it and went ape shit at the person I was chatting with." I say, rolling my eyes as I pick out my phone from my bag

"He's an asshole Mollie. Log back on and fuck him off." Sally chimes in, as she pulls up her app and starts typing to someone.

I flick through my phone screen, locating the app and clicking it. As it loads I can see the notification number increasing on the inbox section.

Five unread messages.

I click on my inbox, my interest peaked as to whether this is all just the same person as before or if someone new has messaged. The screen loads up and I can see who the messages are from.

**Messages:**
**3 ClitHero**
**1 FoxyRide**
**1 SpeedSquirt**

I open the messages from the unknown accounts first, they contain a small hello, although SpeedSquirt also added that they'd like to 'finger blast me to the ISS'. Why do people send such random things to strangers? I finally click on ClitHero.

**ClitHero** - Morning, I hope you managed to shake off that asshole from your life and give yourself a good time. He definitely must have small dick syndrome. Hit me up when you see this so we can continue our chats.

**ClitHero** - Hmm, haven't heard from you today. I hope you're okay.

**ClitHero -** Ahhh BerryBean, I wish you had been brave enough to walk away from the toxicity. I'll be here when you're ready.

I read the last message and it takes my breath away.

Toxic.

This person doesn't know anything, but equally seems to know everything. I sit deciding whether to send any messages back or to just close the app and be done with it again.

Fuck it.

I can speak to who ever I want to. I am free.

**BerryBean -** Long time, no speak. Hope your life has been very orgasmic while I've been absent.

I hit send and laugh to myself. Who am I when I'm on this app? A message pings back almost instantly, which takes me by surprise.

**ClitHero -** Well, well, well, look whose back little bean flicker. I have to say, I've missed your insights.

I snigger, the message definitely cheering me up. I type back in a haste.

**BerryBean -** Well, the biggest question is, are you still a clit hero?

A response bounces back almost immediately.

**ClitHero -** Always. And I can be absolutely certain that I know you've been a naughty girl and flicked your bean, haven't you Berry?

My face flushes red, as if this is even an app. I can feel my cheeks flush as I cross my legs together trying to ease the ache between them.

**BerryBean** - I have done my fair share of flicking, I can't deny it. But right now I'm out in a cute little Irish bar in the city, I've had far too many whiskeys, and I'm all kinds of warm inside. We don't need to encourage me to be any more turned on than I am already.

**ClitHero** - Oh, you're naughty. You know you want to tuck away somewhere and relieve the ache I know you have. Those big Irish guys won't mind a wee show. I hope it's O'Reilly's, there's some real eye candy in there.

My face is so flush, I feel like I'm on fire from my core to my cheeks. I start fanning myself with my shirt and pop a response back.

**BerryBean** - Yes! O'Reilly's! But you're definitely right, the men in here are just beautiful. I should go, I'm out with my friends and I do not need to be this turned on. Catch you later. xox

I pop my phone back into my bag and take a large sip of my drink. Honestly, what has gotten into me. I turn to my friends and they're both engrossed in their own apps.

"That's enough phone time, put them away!" I announce, bopping each of their phones on the top.

They both oblige. "We are here for a good time together. So let's get to it." I say, standing and leaning against the bar, "Cam, pass me the cocktail menu please." I shout and Cam nods, picking up the menu and handing it to me.

"I do recommend the Irish Dancer, that's one of my favourites to make for you girls." He says, his accent always blows me back. Gina is still fucking besotted, every time he is near, she seems to stop breathing.

"Then it's settled. Three Irish Dancers is it." I say and hand the menu back. "Now let's get to dancing."

A few hours pass by and we are beyond merry. A DJ has appeared and started some Karaoke which we all dived on, I'm not sure how anyone remained in the bar with how awful we were singing. I take a moment to sit at the bar, sipping a drink of my fourth Irish Dancer cocktail, the smile is etched across my face. I pull out my phone from my bag and there's a few messages that have popped through whilst we have been busy enjoying ourselves. I quickly scan them.

**Gray -** Where are you girls at?

**Gray -** Mollie, don't fucking ignore me.

**Joey -** Can you answer your brother. He's irritating me because you haven't replied.

**Gray -** Where are you!!!!

I shake my head, such an overprotective asshole. I decide to pop them a message telling them where we are.

**Mollie -** Sorry, my phone has been in my bag, We're at the Irish bar I came to not long ago. O'Reilly's. Join us if you fancy it. xox

I go to place my phone back into my bag just as another message pings up, I assume it's Gray and pick up the phone to check his response.

**Max -** Mollie, Please can we talk. I need to see you. I'll come by our house on Saturday. Please see me. Please.

I sigh, I don't want him to put a dampener on my night. Although the ache in my chest starts up and I feel a little sorrow seeping in. I tuck the phone back into my purse and choose to respond another time.

"Hey stranger." A deep voice says seductively from behind me. I instantly recognise it.

"Rian." I say, spinning on the bar chair, a wide smile spreading across my cheeks. "Fancy seeing you here, are you stalking me? You seem to be appearing in many places that I go." I say, laughing as I twirl on the chair.

Geez, I am definitely well on my way to drunks-ville.

Rian's smile spreads across his face "How much have you had to drink already?" He questions, smirking towards me "Am I going to have to sack Cameron for intoxicating vulnerable women?" He says, although I can tell in his voice he's joking.

"Oh, do you think you have the power to do that?" I reply, I feel my cheeks flushing red.

Am I flirting? What has gotten into me?

Rian leans in close to my ear and I can smell the aftershave floating from him. He smells fucking edible.

"I know I have the power Mollie, since I am the one who owns the bar," he whispers, his voice sultry, making the hairs stand up on my arms.

"You own this place?" I retort back quickly, the shock evident on my face.

"Do I not come across like someone who could own a bar, Mollie?" My name on his lips literally turns my insides to mush. This has got to be the alcohol that's making me react this way.

Sally and Gina head on over to join us at the bar and it instantly tears us apart.

"Oh, here is the mystery man from the bar that also came to the ball, Rian is it?" She says, placing her hands on his chest before turning to me and giving me an exaggerated wink, like Rian can't see everything she is doing. "I have heard so much about you." She adds.

I hold my hand up to my eyebrows, this is not happening to me, the embarrassment is creeping up my face, I can feel myself completely crimson now.

"Ignore her Rian, she's definitely had one too many." Gina chimes in.

"Speak for your fucking self, go and holler at the bar guy you want to fuck so we can order some more cocktails." Sally gripes back and I can't hide my smile.

"You're friends are…" he pauses to think of a word to use, "Feisty," he finishes, a smile spread wide across his face that he has absolutely no way to hide.

"Well, Mollie, I best be on with sorting what I need to sort. But I think, I'll definitely have to see you soon. We can find out a little more about each other." He picks up my hand, bringing it to his lips and planting a kiss on the top.

I swear my mouth is hanging open. Rian slides on past me his hand brushing along the bottom of my back, sending jolts of electricity through my skin.

"Oh and Mollie," he turns back, whispering towards my ear. "You really shouldn't tell strangers on apps where you are." He winks at me and moved through the bar giving a high fives to his staff and customers.

What is that supposed to mean……

Oh Fuck.

ClitHero.

Rian.

Rian is ClitHero.

The words are stolen from inside me and I just watch him gliding around the bar, socialising with his customers.

"Stop eye fucking him, go and really fuck him," Sally suggests, bringing me back to reality.

Before I have chance to respond to her, Gray and Joey appear at the bar and we all get even more giddy. Sally calls over to Cam for another round of drinks and we head over to the pool table as a group. The night continues to flow, we really needed this night to let loose.

Joey heads over to me while I lean on the wall waiting for my turn in girls vs boys team pool games. "Whats happening in your head beautiful?" He asks, bumping his shoulder into mine "You've spent all night fixated on catching a glance of him, what's stopping you from getting your catch?" He asks.

"Max has text me." I respond.

He sighs at me, just as everyone does when they hear Max's name. "What did he have to say this time?" He asks.

"He just wants me to give him a chance to talk. He said he's coming over on Saturday." My gaze drops to my hands as I wring my fingers together.

"You don't have to let him you know."

"I know. I don't know what it is, but I feel like I owe it to him, and to me, to just hear him out." I say, my shoulders sagging slightly.

"And you're torn because you're interested in this guy here?" He asks, pointing towards Rian, whose eyes are burning into me.

"A little, I don't know what I feel for him, or Max, or anyone. I'm just a mess at the moment." I say, tears gathering in my eyes slightly. "I only know for certain that if it weren't for you guys, I wouldn't trust a single soul around me."

"I get that, you have a lot of reason to mistrust, Mollie. But you can't let that drive your whole life. That guy seems like he's decent, didn't he say he owns this place?" Joey reassures me.

I smile at him, "He owns a bar so that makes him decent?" I question, the humour thickening my voice.

"Hey, don't trust me, I'm absolutely tanked." Joey says shaking my shoulder, a wide smile splitting his face in half.

"Take your fucking turn asshole," Sally shouts over at Joey just as he flips her the bird.

"Come on, let's carry on with the night." I say, pushing back off the wall and walking back over to the pool table. I glance up again, feeling Rian's eyes on me as he leans on the bar wall. I wish I could just fucking put my trust in him and believe that he has genuinely good intentions. I just can't, and I don't know why.

****

Morning appears and I start to stir from my bed, having given the gym a miss this morning following last nights little tipple. I can hear my phone buzzing on the side table.

I pick it up, glancing at the name 'Sally' on my screen. I check out the time, 7:30am. What does she want? I'm not even late yet.

Sliding the button to answer I place the phone on my face.

"This better be good Sally, I definitely had another 45 minutes before I absolutely had to get up."

"Get up." She announces abruptly, "Get up. Get up. Get up! We have a meeting first thing with Riley's team."

I push up on my elbows, confusion edging my features as I contemplate what she's just said to me.

"What do you mean we have a meeting? There was nothing scheduled when we left yesterday?"

“I know, it’s last minute scheduled. I believe it was only put in the calendar this morning.” Sally responds.

“Fuck. That’s never a good sign.” I slide out of bed, trying to get my bearings but finding I’m just spinning on the spot.

“Me and Gina have already left for the office, but Gray is on his way for you, he’ll be about 20 minutes.”

“20 minutes, got it. See you there” I say before pressing the red button. I start to rush around, getting ready for what is inevitably going to be a fucking shit day.

Striding through the office, my heels clicking on the wooden floor. It’s 9:10am and Manhattan traffic has seriously done a number on me. I did not need this on a fucking Friday morning, especially when I’m slightly delicate following last nights ‘just one drink’ debacle.

I hand my coat and bag over to Meryl as she stands from her desk and reaches for these, our usual routine when I’m called into a meeting and running late.

“Great start to the day.” I deadpan, she gives a curt smile,

“They’re in the meeting room, Mollie.” She says as she heads into my office to place my coat and bag down. What an absolute gem she is.

Gina strides out of her office in a haste as I make my way towards the meeting room, “Mol…” she begins but I interject.

“Not now Gina, I’m already fucking late!”

“But…” she tries again.

“Gina,” I say spinning to face her, “Not. Now.” And I turn, my hand reaching the handle. I take in a deep breath and stride into the meeting room, game face firmly positioned on my face.

Striding into the room I begin speaking “I do apologise for my…” I look up and my eyes meet the most gorgeous set of emerald green eyes I’ve ever seen.

Theres only one person I know with green eyes so illuminated and captivating.

What the Fuck.

Glancing at Sally, I can see she also has the 'what the fuck' expression firmly planted on her face, given the 'cheese-grater' style smile that in reality, looks a tad psychotic. Cilla stands catching my attention.

"Mollie," She announces "It is with great privilege that I am finally able to introduce you to the individual behind it all."

I continue to stare at those deep emerald eyes.

"This, is Riley Austin." Cilla announces proudly.

He… not she, stands and outstretches his arm, flashing his beautiful smile as his on his cheeks.

"Don't worry Mollie, you can still call me Rian"

# Chapter 16

## Therapy
## Five Years Ago
## Session 50

"Your eyes are feeling heavy Mollie. You're slowly falling deeper. 3…2…1… and you are asleep. It's just me and you Mollie, tell me where you've gone." Dr Rene lulls to me, while I lie with my eyes closed, my memories becoming reality. I am taken away from the therapy room and into the cascade of my sub-conscious.

*I'm walking across the asphalt, I can feel the gravel crunching below my shoes. I've been given new shoes now I'm a recruit, which makes a difference from the cold wet shoes I have been wearing since I arrived here. The bag is still sung over my head, blocking out my view of the outside, despite the fact I am apparently a 'part of the team' now.*

*I arrive outside our destination and I am forced down inside the grid hole, and into the below chamber. The same assaulting smell of damp air and sewage assault my nostrils as I enter.*

*Today, I have been sent by Melvin, to speak to the new girls, Morgan and Verity about their roles within the organisation. It makes me feel so violently ill that Melvin has such a hold on each of us but each day I return back to my room, to new pictures of my family and friends, as they are watched daily.*

*It's heartbreaking that in some way, I do the tasks just so I can get more pictures. To know they're all just doing okay settles me somewhat.*

*"Mollie?" A voice questions from the darkness. "Is it you?" I hear again and I recognise that it's Morgan.*

*"Yes, it's me," I reply, reassuring her.*

*I hear a sigh of relief from both corners of the pit and it fills me with sorrow that it is my fault they're here in the first place. Guilt overwhelms me at every moment, that I am the reason they're here but I know that I didn't have any other choice in the matter.*

*My role now for Melvin, is to persuade them to comply to their roles. I don't know why Melvin thinks this is something I'd be best at but I can't help but feel relieved that I've not been sent back out to recruit.*

*Morgan and Verity have been here now for almost 3 months we think, despite the fact that we have no idea of time really. On the rare occasions I am taken outside, although I am still bagged to transport, I can smell the blossom beginning in the air. It's amazing how my senses have adapted, whilst being trapped here. My hearing seems to have improved and my sense of smell is definitely heightened.*

*I feel for the wall behind me, the room pitched black and I feel along it, stepping to the left until I reach the corner where Morgan is positioned. She takes my hand, although both of us still have handcuffs attached, hers looping through and connecting to the wall.*

*It took them both a while to open up to me when they arrived here. I remember it so vividly. At first they believed I was just captured with them, but Melvin's guys weren't about to let it slide that I was, in fact, the reason they were taken in the first place.*

*They didn't speak to me for over a month. I visited them every day. I pleaded with them to listen to me and to understand. It wasn't until they had their fair share of beatings that I think they finally understood what was happening around here, and the impossible position I had been put in.*

*"Listen to me Morgan." I whisper, "I'm not doing this anymore. I've wasted far too much time here already, and I'm not prepared to fucking die in here." I say, conviction in my voice.*

*"Oh my god! Yes, Mollie! What plan have you got?" She whisper shouts back at me.*

*"Why are you both whispering?" Verity calls in the dark across the other side of the room,*

*I shush her instantly, "Keep your voice down Verity, I'll come over and update you when I've finished here but we can't be heard." I reassure her.*

*I turn back to Morgan, although I can't see anything, so I could be staring at the wall for all I fucking know.*

*"I haven't worked out how, but it's not going to be an overnight thing. I need to build trust, I need to work on Melvin." I say, determination filling me and for the first time in such a long time, I feel elated.*

*"I will help. We can do this together. But you have to come back for us Mollie. Promise you'll come back for us." She whispers, I can hear the desperation in her voice.*

*"Absolutely, I'll be back for you. Once I'm out and I crack this shit show, I'll be back. I promise."*

*The grid opens and I flinch. "Mollie, times fucking up." The voice from above calls me.*

*"Tell Verity" I whisper quickly before making my way towards the light quickly so not to raise suspicion or concerns with Melvin's guys. I climb up the ladder and the bag is placed onto my head before Ive even surfaced above the grid.*

*Melvin's guy shoves me "Why so quiet today, Mollie?" He prods, shoving me in my shoulder again when I take a second to long to answer him.*

*"No reason, they just didn't want to talk. Maybe you finally fucking broke them enough." I spit back, anger lacing my voice.*

*I hear a snigger just before a boot connects with my shin, swiping me off my feet and face planting the floor. "Oops, how clumsy of me" the guy said as he spits on my back. "Get the fuck up and shut up!" he shouts.*

*I scramble back onto my feet, keeping my mouth shut this time. I need to try and keep myself out of trouble if I have any chance of working this plan properly.*

*We reach my room and Melvin's guy takes the bag off my head. I turn towards him, trying to get a good look into his eyes, but his hood is too low causing shadows to appear and stopping me from getting a clear view.*

*"Wait." I call just before he slams the door shut. "Tell Melvin I would like to see him." I say, praying this will work.*

*The guy sniggers again "And what makes you think he'll want to see you princess?" The guy quips back.*

*I smile and straighten my back "Oh that's above your pay grade sweetheart, just pass on the fucking message." I reply sarcastically, just as the door is slammed shut in my face.*

# Chapter 17

## Present Day

The meeting drawls on and I don't think I have spent any time invested in it. Instead I feel like I'm stuck in a daze and stuck in my own head. What the fuck has just happened?

I am shocked.

To my actual core.

He must have known all along that we were who we were, who I was, I have never felt so confused about something in all my life.

I keep glancing over at Sally who seems to be feigning the same facial expressions as I am, one of pure confusion. We've been sat in here now for over an hour, discussing business, like a bomb has not just been dropped and exploded all over this room.

"I think we have enough for today." Sally chimes in, reading my expression and knowing I am so done.

Riley, or Rian, which ever one he is stands. "Mollie, can we have a moment?" He asks tentatively.

Cilla glances between us and I can see in her face that she is confused. She isn't quite sure what's going on and I feel somewhat satisfied that she had no idea about this whole drama before we did. I glance over to Sally who seems wary, but I give her a curt nod to agree that I will be okay.

Everybody exits the room and I look up towards Riley or Rian. Who fucking knows what his name is.

"What can I help you with Mr Austin?" I retort, my voice giving no room for niceties.

“I thought that I’d be best explaining myself.” He replies, appearing a little apologetic in his tone. I scoff before my head can catch up with my attitude.

Yeah that is really professional, Mollie. Composing myself, I make eye contact with him.

“What is your real name?” I ask, my tone icy.

“I am Riley Austin,” he begins, taking a step towards me as I respond by taking a step backwards “My friends, they call me Rian, it’s short for Riley and Austin, like merged together.”

I guess that makes sense.

“When you met me at the bar, did you know who I was?” I ask

“No,” he clarifies and it somewhat fills me with reassurance. “I figured it out when we met at the ball. But I felt like I would be ruining any chances with you if I explained that I am in fact a multi-millionaire and I have been working with you for a long time.” He continues.

What he is saying makes logical sense. Although, I can’t help but just feel like I’ve been lied to.

“So, let's just line everything up.” I start, trying to get my ducks in a row so my head can make sense of what is actually happening. “You are Riley Austin, you own multiple businesses where you write sex books, sell beer, and help out poor trafficked individuals with your generous gifting.” I begin, my voice seeming a question but is definitely airing on the side of matter of fact.

“Well, yes those are all facts,” he responds.

“Why didn’t you tell me at the ball? Or at the bar last night when you revealed you were the person on the app that you manifested?” I continue, my voice appearing a little shouty now, as I get more and more frustrated with the situation.

"I don't really have an answer for that, neither time seemed appropriate." He replies. He is frustratingly calm and it's pissing me off more that I feel like I agree with him.

"But you felt it was appropriate to just turn up at my office on a Friday morning, when you knew we had all had a heavy night because you were there?" I snap, my temper rising slightly.

"After last night, I just needed you to know," The frustration appearing on his face. "I like who you are, Mollie Rutter."

I wait on his words for a moment, but I can't just get past this. The whole foundation of who we are has been built on a pyramid of lies. Trust is everything to me.

"Well, I need some time Rian… Riley… What do you even want me to call you?"

"Rian is fine." He nods reassuring me.

"Rian it is. Look, I need some time to process Rian. I'm not entirely just okay with this." I begin, I can't even look him in the face, "I'm just happy to remain professional in our work relationship and I'm more than happy to just continue working with Cilla as per the usual arrangement." I say, seeming to just be reeling off words now.

He sighs, the resolute evident in his demeanour. "I'll be in touch Mollie. Honestly, I didn't mean for you to be or get hurt by this."

I nod, feeling that he seems genuine and part of this is my own issues driving me to become more wary, but I have to listen to my instincts otherwise I'll never survive.

Rian leaves the meeting room and I perch myself on the long table. Sally and Gina enter the room, the looks of shock on both their faces.

"I tried to warn you Mollie, that's what I wanted to say when you were walking up to the room." Gina said.

"Gina. Stop. Let's just 'what-the-fucking-fuck' for a moment, please." Sally states, which brings a small smile to my face.

“What the fucking fuck!” I say throwing my hands in the air. I am honestly shocked.

“Do you think he’s fucking Cilla?” Sally asks, and it seems like a genuine question.

I roll my eyes. “Who gives a shit about who he is fucking, Sally? He has literally just blindsided us, me.” I say, starting to pace the length of the room.

“Fuck it, grab your shit girls, we’re going home.” I announce and the excitement on their faces is palpable and we all stride out of the meeting room to gather our belongings. Deciding to give the staff a personal day off too, full pay of course, we all grab our things and head down to the lobby.

“Where are we off to?” Gina asks as I hold my arm up to hail us a cab.

“Maureen’s. I need some coffee.”

“Can we not go to Reggie’s and get an espresso martini instead?” Sally questions, waggling her eyebrows up and down as I stare at her deadpan.

“Sally, it's 11am, and I am hanging out of my arse.” I say as the cab parks in front of me and I pull on the door handle. “It is not the time for hair of the dog.”

“Boring.” She announces as we all climb inside the cab.

We reach Maureen’s and get out of the cab heading inside. We seat ourselves in the cozy corner and a waitress heads over to take our orders. I reach into my bag and see a few messages which I need to look at. Gina and Sally get to chatting while I spend a moment reading them.

**Max -** Please message me back Mol. Just hear me out. I’ll come round tomorrow. I’m sorry. This can’t be the end of us. I’m sorry.

**Rian -** Don't stay mad at me for too long. You really are something unique, Mollie.

**Gray -** I hope you girls aren't too worse for wear this morning.

I sigh, thinking for a moment and deciding that I'm still too mad at Rian right now to want to listen to his excuses. I opt to drop some messages back.

***To Max***
**Mollie -** Okay, one chance Max. Tomorrow, 10am.

***To Gray***
**Mollie -** You have no idea the fucking morning we've had. Reggies after? We've already abandoned work.

After hitting send I focus my attention back to Gina and Sally. I dip back into the conversation they're mid flow in.

"We could look at flights to somewhere in Europe again?" Gina questions Sally.

"I guess yeah, but we would have to make sure Gray and Joey are free for Mollie to have nearby." Sally answers back.

I cringe inside, hating that they make plans based on me and my lack of ability to survive on my own.

"Yeah of course we do, but it could be a great opportunity, should we vibe city or beach?" Gina asks as she's tapping on her laptop.

"What are you guys talking about?" I ask even though I definitely got the gist of their plans.

"Just planning our next vacay holiday." Sally says, her smile filling her cheeks "We're thinking somewhere in Europe but we haven't decided on a city or a beach break yet."

I smile, although my smile doesn't reach far across my face. I hate that I can't travel with them but after everything that happened last time, I haven't been abroad or away with them since we went travelling and I was taken.

My mind whirls as I toy with the want to step outside my comforts, and knowing how I'm already spiralling knowing the organisation are so prominent nearby at current.

After 5 minutes, I realise that I have switched off from listening again and have been gazing out of the window, stuck inside my own thoughts.

"Why don't we plan a trip together?" I say before my mind takes over and thinks about what it is I'm actually suggesting.

"Together? Like you coming with us?" Gina asks, the shock in her voice.

"Yeah, I think we should do it next weekend." I say, what the fuck has come over me.

"Next weekend? Like as in we book now and leave next week?" Sally's shock absolutely evident in her voice.

"Yep. All of us, we can…" I think on for a moment, "I don't know, go to a retreat or something in the states, but somewhere that I have to get on a plane." I say, my voice sounding a lot more confident than I feel inside.

"Okay, well, let's ask the boys." Gina says, picking up her phone and dialling in Gray and Joey via FaceTime.

Both boys answer in unison and we all squash together to sit on the same side of the sofa.

"So boys," Gina announces, "Our girl Mollie here, has decided we should all take a trip, on a plane, for a holiday." Gina makes a point, accenting each statement and causing me to roll my eyes a little.

"Listen, I know you all think I've lost my fucking mind but I haven't. I really haven't." I start, "I just need to take back some control and I need to get out there again. I can't just stay in this city for the rest of my life." I insist. They all sit in silence, looking at me like I have three heads.

"Okay then." Joey finally says breaking the silence "When are we thinking?" He adds.

"Next weekend?" I suggest quickly, trying to assure that we get in there before I change my mind or have time to freak out.

I see Gray make eye contact with Sally, while her face resembles the infamous 'cheese grater psycho' smile we've all seen before. I roll my eyes, getting frustrated at everyones faces, acting like I'm just going completely insane.

"You know what. I'll make the plans, I'll pay for the trip, just turn up at my house on Friday at noon." I say, standing and grabbing my things to make an exit out of the coffee house.

"Mollie, wait! We're sorry." Gina says, her eyes sympathetic. "It's just strange for us all, you know. You haven't wanted to go anywhere in so long and now, of all times, when things are heating up in NYC with the organisation." She ends on a sigh and I get it. I understand why they think I've lost it, but surely they should just get on board and support me.

"I know but I also know that I need to do this." The urgency evident in my voice and my eyes plead with them all "I just need it." I look down towards my feet, feeling somewhat awkward.

"Then we do it." I hear Joey say. "We're going away to somewhere of your choice, Mollie. Book it and we will all be there," he smiles at me through the laptop screen and it brings a small smile to my face. Sometimes I feel like Joey understands me the most when I'm impulsive.

"Come on girls, let's get home, I need some sleep." I say turning to make my way to the counter to ask Maureen for some take away cups, "Bye boys!" I shout as I walk away.

Once we gather all of our things, we exit the coffee shop waving our goodbyes to Maureen and grab a cab back to the office building to collect my SUV from the carpark below and I drive us back home.

****

Back home, we all decide to spend the afternoon in our own houses. I spent an hour catching up on some sleep before deciding to fix myself a bath and trying to soak away the previous nights alcohol.

I head downstairs and start cooking a lasagne while I wait for the girls to arrive for us to plan our trip next weekend. I'm eerily excited while being perpetually terrified, all at the same time.

I pour myself a lemonade, leaving out the gin tonight, as my head is still feeling tender. My phone buzzes on the side and I reach over and pick it up.

**Max -** I can't wait to see you tomorrow.

I stare at my phone for a beat deciding whether to reply or leave him on read, when the front door flies open. Sally and Gina scurry in, both in their pyjamas and Gina carrying her laptop under her arm.

"Smells fucking delicious in here, what are you making us?" Sally sniffs up as she strides through the hallway into the kitchen and slumps her ass on a breakfast bar stool, closely followed by Gina.

"Lasagne and garlic bread," I reply before pouring and placing them each a glass of lemonade down.

"Thank fuck you've cooked because I am starving. If you hadn't I would definitely have been calling for a take out," Sally continues. Gina places her laptop down on the worktop and opens it up.

"So, where are we looking to go Mol?" She asks, hands posed, ready to start typing when I speak.

"How about..." I hold myself, teasing them with the suspense, my lips curl up at the sides and I continue, "Las Vegas."

"Fucking yes!" Sally jumps up standing on the stools footrest and pulling me into her arms for an embrace. I laugh knowing how much fun this trip is going to be. I just need to get there.

We spend the next three hours browsing hotels and flights to find the best last minute deals. We decide in the end, that if we're going Vegas, we're staying in the best of the best and we're flying like celebrities. Booking out the Penthouse in the largest casino hotel in Vegas and first class seats on our flight, I am definitely more than excited about this trip now.

We spend some time on FaceTime with Gray and Joey telling them the details of the plans and what time our flight leaves JFK. Once we've confirmed all the plans, we hang up the call and the girls start to set themselves up to sleep in my room.

"Listen, girls, if you're staying then I need you to be up and out by 10am." I say as I load up the dishwasher.

"10am!" Sally scoffs, "Why?"

"Well..." I hesitate knowing they're going to see their arses about me giving Max the time of day. I even contemplate whether I just make some shit up now, but I know in reality they'll likely see him arrive in the morning, so it's probably best I'm just honest.

The pair of them stare at me, their eyes intent and I swear they already know what I'm going to say.

"Well, Max has asked me if he can come round and if we can talk." I say, my voice reluctant to produce any sound.

"And why wasn't the answer instantly just fuck off Max." Sally says, her voice almost a shout.

"Well, I did ignore him for a while but, I don't know. I think I owe it to him, me, and our relationship to hear him out, see if there is anything left to salvage between us."

Sally rolls her eyes at me, which pisses me off more than it should. Gina just shrugs her shoulders at me and glances her eyes between me and Sally, whose own eyes continue to burn into me.

"Listen, I know he's been a fucking dick. I know this. And I'm not here to pretend he hasn't hurt me, or there isn't a lot he has to answer for." I fold my arms across my chest "But this is my choice and I need to do this."

Sally sighs again and it's making feel murdery. I want to punch her in the fucking throat.

"I don't agree, Mol. But you do you, I need a lie in so I'm heading home." She says, sliding off the stool. She heads over to me, pulling me into a hug. "Just don't let him take the piss out of your kindness, Mollie. Please."

I know she's right and I know she only cares about me. The guilt fills me for wanting to punch her moments ago. Gina scoots off of her chair and blows a kiss towards me. "Message any updates in the group tomorrow girl." She smiles and winks before her and Sally make their way for the door.

I head upstairs and tuck myself into bed, ready for the good nights sleep I need so Max doesn't manage to fool me twice tomorrow.

****

I've been up since the crack of dawn, my mind is whirling with everything I have to say to Max. I've tidied the house and had a bath. It's now 9:30am. I told Max to come at 10am, so I decide to make a cup of camomile tea and pick up my book while I wait, to try and help me destress.

The doorbell chimes and my heart skips a beat. I am full of all kinds of emotions this morning and I'm not sure which one I'll end up giving into. I'm angry for the most part, but I feel there's a part of me that's equally just hurt about everything that has happened. I stand up off the sofa and glance in the mirror to check how I look.

Opening the door, Max stands there with my favourite flowers posed in his hands and that fucking incredible smile across his face, his dimple popping out. I look him up and down, noting he's wearing a polo shirt and some dark grey combats. He smells like a floral wood spice. I take a minute to drink him in, and realise quite quickly that I need to pick my jaw up off the floor and actually say something.

"Hi," I bluster, like a besotted teenage girl.

*Pull yourself together women!*

"Good Morning, you look beautiful." He flashes his smile at me again and I feel my insides clenching and heat flooding through me.

"I got these for you, tulips, your favourite." He holds out the bouquet and I reach over and take them from him.

"Thank you. You really didn't have to," I say, taking the flowers and making my way into the kitchen to find a vase. Max follows me in shutting the door and following me through.

"I owe you a lot more than flowers, Mollie." His face drops and I can see the sorrow etched across his features. My heart is already melting and it takes all of my strength not to reach over, grab his face and tell him everything is going to be okay, that we're going to be okay.

"Lets go sit in the living room." I gesture towards the archway into the seating area, like he doesn't know where the living room is. It seems I have completely lost the plot.

"Do you want a drink? Tea? Coffee?" I ask, desperate to put some distance between us for just a few moments.

"Coffee, please." He replies, as he walks off to sit in the living room.

I make his coffee while fanning myself, I feel like I'm at least a hundred degrees. I need to stay focused, making sure I don't just give in to him. Not this time anyway. After a couple of minutes, his coffee is brewed and I take our drinks into the living room. I opt to sit on the chair adjacent to Max to avoid any possible close contact.

"Should I go first?" Max asks and I nod at him, my words trapped inside my throat.

"Okay, well, firstly I just need to say I'm sorry." He begins, his eyes are staring directly into mine and I can see those flecks of sky blue bouncing the light back at me. "There are no excuses that I can give you to justify the shit I've said and done, Mollie."

Well fuck me.

I've never seen him look so genuinely lost in a moment. It knocks the breath out of me slightly. I continue to just stare at him, my mouth agape but no words leaving them.

"Being away from you, is more difficult for me than I think you know or understand. My job it's…" he pauses, "It's eye opening. It's difficult to watch and be a part of. It's even harder that I can't share and explain to you what I do, or where I am, or why I can't always be around." He says and I can feel the torment eating him up. "It's not an excuse Mollie, but sometimes…" he waits a beat, his eyes staying locked in with mine. "Sometimes I just need you to understand that, without me explaining the situation over and over." He says and I nod along without even realising it. A sense of guilt fills me knowing how much I really do agree with him and everything he is saying to me.

"Being special-ops is both a privilege, whilst also being exhausting, physically and mentally. So I just need you to just trust that I will come home to you, when I can. I am yours and you are mine."

Honestly, I am melting into a puddle onto the fucking floor right now. When we met and he told me his job role, we agreed then that life would be hard at times, but we were both committed. Somewhere along the line, I guess that message got lost.

He edges closer to me, placing my hands into his. The touch of his skin sends my mind back in time to the ball, remembering his touch then and how it set me on fire. I can feel my cheeks flush crimson as we sit here.

"You are still mine, aren't you Mollie? Please tell me no one else has been with you? I don't think I can handle it" His voice is fragile and his eyes are glazed over, he looks about ready to burst the dam.

"There isn't anyone else, Max." I breathe out. His sigh of relief is palpable around the room, as he squeezes my hand.

"I couldn't handle that guy speaking to you at the ball, Mollie. When I saw you two together, I just wanted to rip you both away from each other" He continues and if I'm honest I think I would have acted the same if I had seen him with someone else when we were so fragile.

He turns to face me, his features strained and I know he is waiting for my response to him. I heave a sigh.

"You are not forgiven, Max…" I begin and his eyes shoot up at me, as his breath hitches, "…yet." I finish.

His head drops, sliding off the sofa as he falls to his knees in front of me.

"Fuck. Shit. Mollie my fucking heart stopped beating for a moment." He rushes out.

"Wait. Now it's my turn to speak." I announce, holding my hand out firmly in front of me to keep the space. "Get the fuck off the floor and pull yourself together, Max" I crass, setting my tone almost instantly. He slides himself back and sits himself back down on the sofa.

"You have treated me poorly. Job or no fucking job, I have accepted that we have limitations, I have accepted that our lives do not follow the traditional guidelines. But what I do not accept, is you picking me up and dropping me like we're not in this together. Like it's you and me, where and if I fit during that moment." My tone is feisty and sharp.

I continue on a roll before I lose my guts, "You have to make decisions WITH me Max. We need to look at what we both want from life, because I am not in this relationship to watch you fucking disappear, without consideration for me, us, our home or our future. Do you hear me?"

He nods, "Yes, babe. Anything, we can work shit out."

"Right. Well, as I said, you are certainly not forgiven but this is a fucking start. You owe me more. You are not living here for the time being, until you earn a fucking permanent place back in my life."

He nods again and I feel elated after that.

*Yes, girl! Don't fucking let him walk all over you.*

"I'd like to take you on a date. A real date. I've taken some time away from duty. I've been signed off for three months." He tells me, and the excitement literally fills me up. "So, Mollie Rutter, will you go on a date with me?" He coo's, his dimples popping at his smile and once again, I'm absolute putty to him.

"Yes, Max, we can go on a date." I smile back at him shyly.

"Are you free tonight? I can pick you up at 6?" He asks.

"Yes, I guess I am."

He stands, adjusting his clothings and picking up his phone and keys. "I'll pick you up at 6 then. Wear somethings fancy, we're going somewhere nice." He says, before placing a kiss on my cheek and making his way to the door.

I follow him and stand with the door ajar.

"Goodbye beautiful, see you later." He winks at me, as his dimples pop again.

Good-fucking-lord, my insides spasm in awe of his sex factor and I know that me and my vibrator definitely have a busy fucking afternoon scheduled today.

****

I spent a couple of hours letting off some of my pent up tension this afternoon, after feeling so caught up seeing Max. I then spent some time getting myself ready for my date night with Max this evening.

I don't think we ever really did the dating thing. We kind of just started moving forward quickly and before we knew it, we were staying together whenever we could and spent ninety percent of the time fucking like animals. I can't really remember when that ended.

But clearly it did.

I step out of the bath and hear a knock at the door downstairs before the door opens.

Fuck. He can't be here now, it's too early. I glance at the time which reads 5:00pm.

"Hello?" I call out, the anxiety rising in me.

"Only us, girl." I hear Sally shout and my body instantly relaxes, as I sigh a breath of relief.

"I'm upstairs, bring me a Gin and Lemonade." I call back, needing some relief to calm my nerves for tonight.

Sally appears first and I know she's left Gina playing mixology downstairs.

"Give us the details, girl. I've waited all fucking day for you to text us and you haven't." Sally announces as she bursts through the door and does a running dive onto my bed.

"I'm sorry, I've been, busy I guess," I say, my cheeks flushing at the memory of my vibrator session earlier.

"Busy… With what exactly?" Sally asks, raising her eye brows and eyeing in to my soul.

"Just busy, letting off steam," I say, a little giggle busting from me.

"Oh! I do not need any more details. I get the gist." Sally jibes.

"The gist of what?" Gina asks as she heads through my bedroom door with a tray of pink gin and lemonades with all the trimmings.

"That Mollie's afternoon has been…" she pauses to think on her words, "…buzzing with activity" she drawls out and we all burst out laughing.

"So, tell us what happened with Max?" Sally starts, her voice suddenly serious.

I take a deep breathe. Here we go.

"He was really…" I can't get my words out, trying to think of something that doesn't just give vibes that I've let him waltz back in without any fucking repercussions. "He came here with the right attitude. He was very apologetic. I laid into him about how much of an asshole he has been and he remained apologetic." I blurt out before I chicken out.

"So what? You've forgiven him and all is good?" Sally argues, I can see she's on the defence already.

"No, not at all, I've told him he isn't forgiven but I haven't shut the door for him to try."

"To try? How is he going to try then?" She asks, her tone a little more relaxed the previous.

"Well, he's picking me up in around 45 minutes and he's taking me on a date."

"A date? You guys have never dated. Like a real date?" Sally quips in.

"Yes, he told me to wear something fancy. So here I am. Can you guys just help me to get ready and be happy for me please?" I ask.

"Well, I can, but I can't speak for Sally." Gina adds. I forgot she was even here she's been so quiet.

"Fine. But he is not getting away with it Mollie. Not on my watch," Sally states, wagging her finger at me like she's my mother.

We spend the next 45 minutes getting me ready. Sally picked me out a floor length, figure hugging red dress, with off the shoulder straps and a slit that rides high up my thigh. My make up is flawless, thanks to Gina, my eyes pop with a gold shadow and my lips are a deep fire red, while my hair has scattered curls across my shoulders.

I feel fucking incredible.

"I'd definitely fuck you." Gina announces as I stand staring into the floor length mirror.

We all laugh and make our way down the stairs as there is a knock on the door.

It's 6:00pm on the dot.

I answer the door and Max is stood in an all black suit and shirt with his top button relaxed.

*Fuck he looks incredible.*

"You look absolutely breathtaking, Mollie." Max says, his eyes drink me up from floor to face. He swallows deep and I see his hand reaching down and adjusting his cock in his pants.

"I don't know how I'm going to hold myself together tonight, I'm definitely going to struggle keeping my hands to myself." He blows out a breath and holds out his hand to help me walk out of the door.

Sally and Gina follow us out, as Gina closes the door and Sally plasters her best scowl across her face.

"Girls," Max says, a smile spread across his face.

"You are not forgiven, Max Broderick." She points a long finger to his face. He leans back slightly so she doesn't actually make contact. He turns to look towards me his mouth edging to the sides. Gina just pats him on the shoulder, showing a small smile and follows Sally as they head back to their house.

"Shall we go?" Max says, bringing my hand to his mouth and placing a kiss on the top. I nod and he leads me to his black SUV, opening my door and sitting me in, before heading round to his own side.

We arrive in the city, at a fancy restaurant called 'La Rouge' which boarders fifth avenue and overlooks the greens of Central Park. Max exits his side of the car and circles round to open my door and help me out of my side. He throws the keys at the valet to park and places his hand on the small of my back, guiding me towards the front door.

"Broderick, for two" he announces to the maitre'd, who smiles graciously, picking up two menus and asking us to follow him through the restaurant.

"How on earth did you get a reservations for this place? It's usually booked up for months." I whisper into Max's ear as we walk.

"It's all about who you know in NYC, Mollie." He says as he nods and gives a casual salute towards one of the chefs in the kitchen.

We sit down on the first floor with a window view which overlooks the greenery in central park.

"This is amazing." I smile, my excitement evident.

"I'm glad you approve, beautiful. It could only be the best for you and I know how much the trees help you to relax." My heart skips a beat, knowing that he really put thought and effort in finding this place, with me in mind. His smile pops and honestly, I could take him to the bathroom right now and repeat the night at the ball without hesitation.

The night continues to go well and Max starts a role play, as if we haven't a clue who one another are. We laugh and pretend to pass information on to each other that we don't already know.

"Did you know…" He begins, leaning in across the table "There is a guy sat behind you, that has been eye fucking you all night and I'll be honest, it makes me fucking rock hard knowing you're here with me." He looks down towards my breasts and back up to my face as his smile pops his dimples. I feel the heat between my legs pooling and my cheeks reddening. A little giggle slips out from my lips, but I can't seem to form words I'm that flustered.

"I'm going to head for a bathroom break before my dick splits the seams of this ridiculously expensive suit." He stands, adjusting his crotch again before tilting my chin-up and placing a kiss on my cheek.

*Fucking hell, I am lit up from the inside out.*

I fan myself with the wine menu from the centre of the table and take a moment while Max has left to check my phone. I have a few messages and I take a quick glance at these. One message in particular takes my breath.

**Rian -** You look absolutely sensational. I hope your date appreciates what the fuck is sat in front of him because I'm close to coming over there and stealing you away from him.

My heart hitches. What the fuck?

I glance around the room and there he is. His eyes burning into me and suddenly I realise, he is the guy Max was referring to. I put my phone back into my bag, not replying to his message and take a large gulp of my wine to try and overcome the dry mouth I suddenly have. Max returns and it's as if he senses something is off with me.

"Are you okay? You seem tense?" He asks, his hand caressing me along my arm. I hesitate for a moment and decide if we're doing this we have to be honest with each other.

"The guy you mentioned that is eye fucking me before, is it the guy on the balcony level, in a white shirt?" I ask while keeping eye contact with him. He glances around my shoulder towards the guy in question.

“Yeah, do you know him?” A flare of anger seems to blaze through his eyes before he controls his temper, waiting for my answer.

“He’s the guy I was chatting to at the ball.” I say, my heart stuttering with panic, but knowing I need to be honest with him.

“Okay, has anything every happened between you?”

“No, no, nothing like that. I met him at a bar one day, and then it turns out that he was someone I’ve actually worked with him without knowing for a long time. It's long and complicated.”

“Tell me more.” He says, his tone less playful than before. I sigh and resolute to telling him everything that has happened with Rian, the bar, the app and him really being Riley Austin who we’ve worked with for a long time.

“Don’t you think that seems all a little strange?” He asks, giving a small glance behind me before looking back my way

“What do you mean?” My curiosity peaks.

“Well, he has put himself in to your life in several different ways without you knowing anything about him.” He says and I take a moment to think about what he’s saying.

“I’ve never really thought about it that way.” I say honestly, taking a sly glance over my shoulder to Rian who is still staring at me from the balcony. A chill runs over my skin.

“I don’t know, Mollie, it just creeps me out a little that he’s suddenly appeared in your life, at the exact time the organisation has made their way to NYC.”

I hadn’t even considered the coincidence of this. My phone pings in my bag and I glance at it.

**Rian -** I guess he’s trying to convince you I’m sent from hell. Don’t listen to him, Mollie. You look incredible. I’ll hope to see you soon.

I glance back over my shoulder to see that Rian has disappeared. I keep glancing around the bar picking out if I can see any hooded men lurking. My heart is racing and I start to panic.

"It's okay Mollie, I'm here. I've got you babe," Max says, squeezing my hand reassuringly. My head is a million miles away. I don't know what to believe anymore. Surely I've not been so naive.

It can't be anything to do with Rian.

Or can it?

# Chapter 18

## Therapy
## Five Years Ago
## Session 20

"Welcome Mollie." Dr Rene's calming voice brings me out of my daydream. I smile as she takes her seat in front of me. "Today, is our first hypnotherapy session. How are you feeling?" She continues.

"Nervous, I don't know what to expect I guess." I answer, wringing my fingers together. "I'm just worried about how I might feel after the session."

"That is completely understandable, Mollie. These sessions aren't designed for you to leave feeling vulnerable, but more about allowing you to leave feeling like you understand that your feelings are validated."

I know she is right, so I nod along with her, ready to get started with the session now.

"I want you to get yourself comfy, Mollie, put your feet up and lay your head back on the sofa. When you're ready, let me know and I'll explain more to you."

I nod and move myself into position, with my legs on the sofa and my head resting softly on the raised cushion. I feel sick with nerves.

"I want you to relax, close your eyes. And together we'll head into a deep sleep like sensation." Dr Rene starts, I focus on her voice as I shut my eyes, focusing on emptying my thoughts and waiting for my instructions.

"We're travelling deep into your mind Mollie. I want you to open up about what lead you to getting free of your entrapment."

I can hear her voice as I nod along and focus on the memories I feel surfacing in my mind.

"Deeper we travel… 3…2…1… We're ready to listen Mollie." I feel her voice bouncing around my mind as I lie here, feeling heavy and lifeless on the sofa.

"Tell me, Mollie. Tell me how you came to free yourself," and just like that, I am swept into my memory.

*A couple of days had past since I had been to see Morgan and Verity. The guys have been coming to visit me in my room. The one I was now privileged to have, but I had not been asked to visit Melvin. Worry filled me as I wondered if we had been heard talking, or whether Morgan had been caught when she had given Verity the message after I had left.*

*The door swings open and one of the hooded men enters my room. I sit, my legs tucked up surrounded by my arms while I sit on the mattress on the floor.*

*"Boss wants to see you," he announces as he approaches me, grabbing my arm and hoisting me up off the floor onto my feet.*

*"You could just ask me to get up." I say snatching my arm back from his grip.*

*"You could just shut the fuck up." He replies shoving my shoulder forward.*

*They bag my head as per usual, although I started tracking how many steps and counting how long we are on the caddy long before today, trying to create a map of the environment we are located in. The environment is big enough to need a caddy style transport but small enough to only ever be on the caddy for 40 seconds at a time, indicating it's something easily walk-able.*

*I track the route again and come up with the same numbers I have plotted the last few times I've been brought to see Melvin. So that tells me I haven't moved rooms or location.*

*We take the steps up to Melvin's room, and the bag is removed from my head. Turning towards my captor, I paste a smile across my face towards him despite only seeing eyes.*

*"Ever so kind of you to free me dear," I say sarcastically, however really using the opportunity to try and scan the environment behind him. He catches me and grabs onto my chin.*

*"Know your fucking place, bitch," he spits out.*

*I sneer at him, and turn to walk towards Melvin's room.*

*As I walk in, I note that Melvin sits at the top of the long dining table and with him are Morgan and Verity,*

*"Mollie, my best girl," He announces me as I enter the room. "You're looking a little dirty sweetheart, I'll be sure to allocate you some shower time, after all, you certainly deserve it." He says, flashing that gold toothed, crooked smile at me.*

*I stare, a little vacant, unsure of why or how this situation has come about.*

*"Please, sit Mollie darling. Sit with my new and beautiful team members." He gestures towards Morgan and Verity, my heart beating excessively fast. What have they done?*

*I turn my head towards them and silently try and signal to ask if they are okay. Morgan nods once and I turn my attention back to Melvin.*

*"To what do we owe the pleasure of being treated to this wonderful meal?" I make a sweeping gesture with my arm across the mountains of food which line the tables.*

*"Because my little starlight, you have done a wonderful job." He begins, holding his arms in the air, his golden smile widening further. "You have worked so hard and it has paid off. Morgan and Verity have decided they want permanent roles in the Organisation, just like you my little star." He announces and I shoot my eyes back towards Morgan and Verity who remain stoic and appearing in character.*

*"Oh, well, great," I say, taken aback slightly by the information.*

*"They have chosen a life of pleasure," he drawls out in what I assume he thinks sounds sexy, but in reality it's entirely undesirable. "These beautiful girls will be offering themselves up to my lovely men, as sexual desires." He announces and I freeze, my breath catching in my throat and my eyes shoot towards the girls.*

*What are they doing? Prostitution? This was not part of the plan.*

*I try and signal silently to Morgan but the look she gives me is one that tells me she will explain later on when we are not overlooked by anyone. I decide to bargain some items for us, playing along in the roles we seem to have acquired so far.*

*"So Melvin, other than this meal, what treats are we going to be graced with? I know deep down you're absolutely a generous man when it comes to good behaviours." I wink at him and my tone appears flirty.*

*He laughs "You have always had a little sass about you, Mollie. That's why I kept you."*

*I remain firm in my position towards him, awaiting his answer. He leans back in his chair and places his hands behind his head. Looking between me and the girls while he seems to be contemplating what he's willing to offer.*

*"I will give them rooms, like you." He announces.*

*"And you will give us all free access to shower time whenever we request it. They need to ensure they are clean for what you are requiring them to do." I declare, my face remaining fierce.*

*"You are cheeky, Mollie. But Fine, I agree." He replies "Now, let's eat."*

*We finish our meals and are escorted back to our rooms. They transport us all together this time and I note that both girls are now positioned in the rooms next to me. This could absolutely work in our favour.*

*As the night deepens and the amount and the frequency of the hooded men reduces, I take the opportunity to try and speak to Morgan who is in the room next to me, through the wall.*

*"Morgan?" I whisper shout, hoping she can hear me. But there seems to be no response. "Morgan?" I try again, losing hope slightly.*

*"Mollie?" A voice whispers questioningly through the wall.*

*"Yeah it's me, we need to be quick. What the fuck have you done?" I ask, short and sharp trying to reach the point.*

*"We decided we needed to help you to get out so you can get us out." She tells me and I sigh, knowing it's my fault they're here in the first place.*

*"How is you being fucking sex slaves a good idea in any sense?" I deadpan, terror rising up inside me for them.*

*"Because on the night you want to escape, we're going to willingly put on a show and tempt these guys into fucking us. Distraction by sex, it's genius to be honest," She says but I beg to differ, if I'm truthful.*

*"You can't do that Morgan. It's not fair."*

*"It's necessary to try and free us. If this doesn't work Mollie, we're as good as dead anyway. And if we didn't give it to them willingly they would absolutely take it from us anyway."*

*She right, it's now or never.*

*I sigh and change the focus of the conversation. "I've been counting the spacings and distances. I think I've managed to make a map of the compound." I whisper, keeping an open ear out for any activity outside of my door.*

*"When do you plan on doing it?" Morgan asks.*

*"Soon, tomorrow or the day after, I'll look at what maps I have and see if I can plan further. At some point I'll be blind*

*because there's only certain paths I've been down." I say back to Morgan. "I'll let you know when I'm done."*

*"You can do this Mollie." She cheers me on.*

*"I know. We need distraction, a way for me to escape, and then to know where I'm going. But I promise, if I make it out alive, I'll come back for you. I promise."*

*"I know, Mollie. I know you will. I'll let Verity know your plans."*

"You're feeling lighter in your sleep Mollie. You're waking up slowly. Listen to the sounds of the room, the fountain bubbling, the fan blowing," Dr Rene's voice stirs me as I begin to start blinking back into reality.

"How are you feeling Mollie?" Dr Rene asks.

"I feel, emotional. It was my fault they were there in the first place, yet they were so willing to help me."

"They also recognised that although it was you who brought them in, you were put into an impossible position and you had been doing all you can since that point to change the course you were all living."

I smile, although it does not reach far across my face.

"It all worked out, Mollie. You all got free."

"Not all of us, there were some girls who weren't so lucky." I respond quickly.

"And none of those are your responsibility, Mollie. You are a victim. Remember that." Dr Rene says.

I sigh looking out of the window, I know it's not my fault but I can't help but believe that it is.

# Chapter 19

## Present Day

We pull up outside my house in Max's SUV. Max exits his side of the car and heads around to my side to open the door for me. Taking my hand in his, he helps me scoot out of the tall vehicle and leads me up the path towards the front door.

As we reach the porch, Max tugs on my hand spinning me around to face him and scooping his other arm around the small of my back. The fire inside me ignites in response to him.

"I've had an amazing date night with you Mollie. I'd love to do it again, maybe a little more casual next time? Although, we can absolutely do this again if that's what you want?" His voice seeming wary and uncertain on what my reaction will be. He seems nervous.

I blush, "I'd love to do it again, and casual is absolutely fine."

His smile spreads wide across his face, popping his dimples which sends heat rising through my core.

"Are you free Monday? For lunch?" He asks, my hand still in his and his arm still securing me close to him.

"I'd love to." My smile widens, mimicking his.

"Can I kiss you goodnight?" Max asks in a whisper.

My heart hitches a beat as I breathe out, "Yes."

My eyes locking onto his before drifting down to his lips. He pulls me in closer, placing his lips on mine, soft and caressing. He deepens the pressures and we become engulfed in the moment. He slips his tongue in and electricity fires through my entire body. I feel like I am lit up. He pulls back, a growl leaving him, as I see him adjust his cock in his pants for the third time this evening.

He places his hand beneath my chin, as he runs his thumb along my lips, caressing the plump swelling that's rising. I suck in the tip, before using my tongue to stroke circles around the tip. I can see the fire blazing in his eyes.

"Mollie," He says, his tone a warning to the lack of restraint he is about to have.

I smile and give a small bite to the tip, before planting a kiss and taking a step back.

"You fucking ruin me, Mollie. I need to leave before there is no stopping me." He says, picking my hand up and planting a kiss on the top.

"I love you, babe. I've loved you since day one. I will fix this. I have to." Max reassures me. I am melting into a fucking puddle here.

He takes a step back, walking backwards down the path without breaking eye contact with me. I smile, blowing him a kiss and back up into my house before I beg him to fucking stay.

I feel incredible, desirable.

Happy.

I scurry up the stairs and head into my bedroom, the smile still beaming on my face. I call over to Alexa and ask her to play Kelly Clarkson - My life would suck without you. The music starts and I pull the zip on my dress down my back, shimmying it off. Starting to  dance to the music, picking up my hairbrush and singing along to the words at the top of my lungs. I glide around my room, in my matching red bra and thong.

I feel so alive.

Jumping onto my bed as we reach the chorus, I belt out, "Cause we beloooong, togetherrrr, nooow, yeahhhhh," shaking my bum. I jump and spin on the bed to face the door, continuing the song at the top of my voice, my eyes closed living for the moment. I take in a deep breath to continue, opening my eyes momentarily.

Holy. Fucking. Shit.

Max is stood, learning on the bedroom door frame, his arms folded, biceps bunched up making them look even more incredible.

"Max… Fuck… What are you doing here?" I pant out, a little breathless as I grab for my dressing gown from the ottoman and pull this up close to me, covering my almost naked self.

"Well, right now I'm enjoying the show, but I came back because you left your bag and phone in my car. I tried knocking but I could hear the music and well, I came upstairs to this." The smile lining his face is mischievous.

I'm still panting from all the fucking ass wiggling.

"Now, I held my restraint very well outside, Mollie. But this show, I definitely can't walk away from. Stop covering yourself up, you look fucking incredible."

My heart is pounding as his pushes off the door frame, striding over to me and taking the dressing gown from where I'm clasping it in front of me. He leans above me and I relax backwards onto my bed.

"You are so fucking beautiful, Mollie." He says as he nuzzles into my neck, running kisses up my jawline to my ear before biting down and sending sensations throughout my body. "I can tell that just like me, you are borderline losing control too, Mollie," He whispers in my ear.

He's absolutely not fucking wrong.

"Yes," I moan out, I swear I'm fucking almost there and he's not even touched me.

"I don't want to push this, us, you, Mollie. But I also need you more than you could ever imagine."

Oh fuck.

My breath is short, as the pressure builds inside me.

"So, I think I have an idea that helps both of us, without us crossing that line again just yet." He whispers nipping at my ear lobe again, before kissing me all the way to my lips, sucking in my lower lip and biting it. I am on fire, so fucking wet, I can feel it spreading down my thighs as I squeeze them together to try and elevate the throb.

"Are you interested in some fun, Mollie?" He asks, as he runs this hand down my body, touching my underwear, sliding his fingers down and in-between my legs to my sex, he slides my underwear to the side and runs his fingers along my slick wet heat. A moan leaves my mouth, as my hips buck at the contact.

"Fuck. You are so fucking wet, Mollie." He growls, I can see his restraint is wearing thin. "Do you want to have some fun?" He asks again and I nod, reaching down between my legs to try and relieve some of the ache.

"Move yourself up to the top of the bed, Mollie." He commands and I do exactly as I'm told, scurrying backwards up the bed.

Max unlatches his pants and walks to my bedside cabinet, pulling out my vibrator and placing it next to me along with my bullet toy.

My heart is pounding, I need this. This is fucking hot. Max announces, "Alexa, play 'Chris brown - Take you down'," as he tugs down his pants and boxers, his large cock springing free. The song begins and I can't take my eyes away from Max.

He rounds the end of the bed and climbs on top, positioning himself on his knees at the bottom, his engorged cock in his hands and he gently strokes up and down to help relieve himself a little.

Leaning over the top of me, he starts kissing my lips as he continues to slowly tug on his cock before stopping. Sliding my underwear down, he tosses it across the room.

He dips his head down between my legs and I can feel his breath brushing against my heat.

*Fuck. Fuck. Fuck!*

He sucks onto my clit, before licking me completely up the centre of my opening. My eyes fucking roll and I am almost a goner.

He picks up my bullet, turning it on and placing it in my hand.

"I want to watch you play with yourself, Mollie. When you're close, I want you to fuck yourself until we come together." He says, his voice is commanding and raspy.

I nod and place the bullet onto my clit, the sensation sending stars across my vision. I keep my eyes on Max, who starts to tug on his cock, the pre-cum beading at the top. Max dips his fingers to my sex, running them along my wetness to coat his fingers before using this and spreading it onto his own cock for lubrication. I grab my vibrator, the tension between my legs becoming unbearable. I turn it on and crack up the setting to an intense buzz before placing it at my entrance. My eyes meet Max's as he looks down, his hand continuing to slide up and down his cock, watching me as I slide the vibrator around my entrance, his gaze intense. My eyes rolls back as I push it in deep, a moan bursting from my lips. I begin to pump the vibrator in and out, the sound of my wetness filling the room. Max increases his speed, his grunts becoming louder as we both head to the edge. Our eyes meet as the intensity burns between us, and I know I'm on the edge.

"Fuck babe, I'm close, are you with me?" He grunts out.

"Yeah, I'm there. I'm ready."

Max edges closer, locking our free hands together, he arches over the top of me, as I tug his interlocked hand up to caress my breasts with me.

My moans become louder as I build the pace faster and faster, matching Max in rhythm, readying myself to go over the edge.

Our eyes meet and that's all it takes to send us tumbling over the edge together. My sex clenches around the vibrator in pulses, just as Max's seed covers my body, his grunts echoing his release.

Fucking hell, I think that's one of the sexiest thing I've ever done.

"Fuck Mollie. Fuck!" Max groans as he slumps down to the side of me, planting a deep kiss on my lips. Our bodies slick with sweat.

"That was…" I pause, finding the words I want to use, "That was fucking unreal."

"I agree. We need to get you cleaned up." He rolls me so my ass is pressed against his dick and peppers my neck and shoulders with kisses.

"Yes, I don't think your cum makes a good moisturiser." I say sarcastically back, drawing a giggle from his throat. He stands up, off the side of the bed, taking my hands and pulling me up with him.

"Come on, let's get you cleaned up." He holds my hand guiding me around the bed and into the ensuite.

Max turns on the shower before standing at my back and unhooking my bra, sliding the straps down my shoulders. I stand facing the floor length mirror with him pressed close against my back. His hands stroking my arms as he peppers kisses along my neck and shoulder line.

He tugs the shower door open and I step in and under the splash of water, Max following me in and turning me to face him, the water streaming over our bodies.

He picks up the body pouffe and body wash, squeezing this onto the pouffe before starting to circle this along my body cleaning the mess that's splashed across my stomach.

Turning back around, he presses my back against his front, he moves the pouffe across my stomach, edging towards my sex. He picks up my left leg in his hand, before guiding the pouffe in between my legs to clean my swollen sex, the sensitivity still high. My head drops back onto his shoulder and he plants a kiss on my lips.

I turn to face him, pressing my back against the shower wall. His cock hard again and pulsing from the contact between us. I pour soap into my hands and run my hand up and down his length, rubbing my thumb around the tip. He hisses as he presses his arms either side of my head to steady himself.

"I thought I'd lost this, Mollie." He breathes out. "I know I haven't got it back completely. But even just a little bit is more than what I expected."

"Love isn't meant to be easy, Max." I whisper back as I reach back down his shaft and smear soap further down, caressing his balls as I clean him.

His breath hitches "Fuck. Mollie I'm going to end up coming again."

He tilts my head up to look at him, "Let me wash your hair, we have plenty of time for more orgasms another time." I laugh with him as he spins me around, starting to apply shampoo first and then  conditioner to my hair, brushing this carefully.

This is a side of Max I haven't seen for what feels like forever. I thought this version had long gone. I'm definitely glad to have him back.

We finish in the shower and step out, Max wraps a towel around me before sorting himself out and we make our way back into the bedroom.

"Well, all that was unexpected. I thought I'd done well to walk away outside." He announced, a smile tugging at his lips and that to die for smile, which got us in this ungodly situation in the first place popping out.

"Put that smile away before we end up knee deep in trouble again" I can't help the smile spreading, as I pull on my silky shorts and vest pyjamas. Max laughs with me. "You can stay here you know, it's late and I don't want you to feel like you have to leave" I suggest.

Max laughs, walking back over to me, he tilts my chin up, meeting my gaze with his. “I’m not pushing my luck that far yet, I’m happy to give you the space you need. But I’ll message you and we can make plans for Monday’s lunch date?” He says, it is more of a question than a statement, his voice so calm and cool that I can’t help but feel so settled and content.

I smile up at him and nod in agreement.

He dresses himself in some of his shorts and a t-shirt out of his wardrobe and gathers his other belongings before we head down the stairs and on to the front door. He places soft kiss on my forehead.

“I’ve had the most amazing night Mollie.” He says and again starts to back up the path before turning around and walking towards his SUV.

I can’t help the smile spreading across my face as I watch Max beginning to walk away, just as something catches my attention to the right and I spot the sights of a fleeing Graham leaving Sally and Gina’s house. Max glances over at the movement too before turning back and raising his eyebrows at me. I shake my head and shrug my shoulders. Gray doesn’t seem to notice us in the cul-de-sac as he jumps in his car and races away.

I watch for a moment longer as Max gets into his car. Giving me a wave and a wink he sets off and I close the door.

Tonight has been so surreal.

It’s been like a blast from the past, having the old Max back. The guy I fell completely in love with still exists in him, I just hope he’s here to stay. I glance at the time and spot it’s 02:15am, deciding it's absolutely time for bed I take myself upstairs and tuck myself in before decide to drop Max a text.

**Mollie -** Tonight has been sensational. I feel like the man I fell in love with has come back to see me. I hope he’s here to stay.

**Max -** If I have anything to say about it, he's definitely here to stay. You're my everything Mollie. I love you.

I smile at this last message and put my phone on charge feeling ready to get myself some good sleep.

****

Monday morning rolls around quick after a lazy Sunday. I feel like it's been the best weekend I've had in a long time.

I feel whole again.

I came to work early this morning, beating Sally and Gina into the building and sit in my office taking in the view as usual when I arrive early. At 08:30am Meryl knocks on my office door.

"I didn't realise you were coming in early, Mollie. I'd have made the effort to come in and join you," she announces, "Would you like a latte making?" She offers.

"Meryl, you don't have to come in early, you're already here half an hour before your official start time now," I laugh, "but yes, a latte would be incredible, thank you." I smile warmly as she heads off to collect the drinks.

I've spent the morning blocking out our calendars from Friday to Monday now we've decided to head to Vegas for a long weekend. Some things need rescheduling but I am definitely enjoying the decision to go on a trip.

"You're early today." I hear Sally call as she stumbles into my office with all of her belongings.

"I just felt ready this morning, I've had an amazing weekend and I'm excited for the trip this weekend coming." I reply, a smile spread across my face.

"You never did message to tell us about your date. Hang on let me shout Gina." She scurries to the door and bellows "Gina!"

down the corridor. Thirty-seconds later, Gina heads into my office and sits on the sofas in the corner next to Sally.

"So go on, we're listening." Sally says, her face seeming less than enthusiastic which instantly makes me not want to share the story. I already know she's going to ruin it.

"Well, he took me to La Rouge, we had an amazing window seat. We ate and had a nice date. Then he took me home." I say, keeping it brief.

"And what? He just left? Because I'm certain I saw his car still outside your house at 01:00am?" Sally jibes back at me.

A smile tugs at my lips, "Well, he did leave but then he came back because I had left my phone in his car, he caught me singing and dancing in my underwear and then things got a little heated, without us actually having sex." I say, the smile clear on my face as the memory replays in my mind.

"I definitely just assumed he wanted to fuck and leave again," Sally quips at me, my face instantly dropping at her negativity.

"No, he was really kind and genuine. He was like the old Max you know, the guy I first met."

"Hmm, shame he's really just a fucking asshole." Sally snipes again, her tone dulcet and her attitude is really starting to piss me off.

"He sounds like he's at least making the effort, Mollie." Gina chimes in, which brings a small smile back to my face. Sally scoffs next to her.

"You're absolutely fucking delusional if you think he's a reformed character." She fumes, seeming more irritated that Gina has stepped in to support me.

"Look Sally, I know he's done wrong, but can you just give him the chance to make things right? For me?" I plead, trying to ease the tension just a little.

"I don't trust him Mollie. He hurt you. He hurt you deep and I don't think he is worthy of you." She pushes and I understand her vibe, it's just irritating when I've had such a good weekend and I just want them to be happy for me.

"Let's move on, we need to chat about the plans for Vegas."

"Yessss!" Gina hollers from the corner.

"Fine, but you know I'm not impressed." Sally states as a matter of fact.

"Sally, maybe I should ask you why you were awake, looking at my business at 01:00am. I don't think you'll want to answer that question." I deadpan, hoping to tear her away from the subject, since she was in fact 'secretly' fucking my brother and that's how she knows Max was at mine.

I am successful and she swiftly changes the subject.

We video call in Gray and Joey to discuss the details of the flight times, what hotel we are staying in and what we all want to do while we're in Vegas. It's the consensus that we all want to mix sight seeing and pleasure so we decide that all activities we can do as a whole group.

"This is going to be fucking incredible." Joey beams with enthusiasm as they chat to us through the video call.

"I'm so excited! My first trip with my bestest people." I hesitate a moment realising that Max isn't on this trip with us. "Hey, how would you guys feel about me inviting Max?" I ask sheepishly.

"Max? Is he back on the scene?" Gray asks, looking confused and I now know that he has absolutely no idea that we saw him leaving Sally's on Saturday night.

"Yes, he is." Sally deadpans to the camera, "She went on one date and fucked him like all is fucking forgiven." She says, the irritation clear in her tone.

"Woah, I do not need that information!" Gray shouts.

"I did not fuck him! I already told you this. Don't be a dick Sally. Other than Sally, who would mind if I extended the invite out?" I ask turning my back slightly to Sally. She can piss off, she's irritating me today. The group all agree that they wouldn't mind if he came and Sally sighed, standing up and declaring she was gone, before leaving my office.

"What's that about?" Gray asks.

"Same old, Sally doesn't agree that I should be giving Max a second chance to prove himself to me but she's hardly one to give out relationship advice when she hasn't been in one since she was in high school." I snipe, the annoyance clear in my tone.

"I'm sure it'll all work out Mollie, she just needs to come around to it again, she's only looking out for you. In her own way." Gina sympathises while rubbing her hand up and down my back.

I know this, but it's still infuriating.

"Anyway, boys we have work to do. Catch up with you later," I announce and hang up the call.

Gina returns to her own office and I take a second to glance at my phone. I have two messages.

**Max -** I'll pick you up at 12:00noon x

**Rian -** You can't ignore me forever, Mollie.

I ignore Rian's message as I have with all the others and shoot a quick text back to Max.

**Mollie -** Looking forward to it. x

I set my phone away and continue the morning's work, cracking down on some important deadlines.

Lunch time came around quickly and I get a buzz to my phone from the reception desk downstairs.

"Sonja, how can I help?"

“There’s a Mr-Tall-Dark-and-Handsome filling almost the entire reception area with his muscles here. He says he’s here for you.”

I giggle, “Yes, Max. Tell him I’ll be down in a moment.”

“I might tell him you’re too busy but I’m free if I’m perfectly honest.” I laugh with her.

“I best hurry up before you steal my man,” I quip and put down the phone.

I close down my laptop and check myself out in the mirror located in my office, making sure my make-up isn’t smudged and my hair looks reasonable. I top up my lipstick and head out the office.

“I’ll be back around 1:30/2pm Meryl, feel free to treat yourself to an extended lunch hour, you’ve earned it,” I say smiling at her and head to the lift.

As I reach the lobby, Max is waiting just outside of the lifts. His face lights up when he see’s me and I stride over to him. Picking up my hand, he places a kiss on it.

“You can give me a real kiss you know” I hint at him.

“Oh can I…” his eyebrows rise and he moves his hand to tilt my chin upwards, placing a soft, but longing kiss on my lips.

He pulls away and a wide smile spreads across my face. “Where are you whisking me away to today, Mr Incredible?” I coo, up at him as we walk together, his arm around my shoulder.

“Wherever you want.”

****

Thursday rolls around faster than expected and the end of the day is looming close. The week went by fast but today seems to have completely dragged out.  I’ve put it down to the excitement for our trip tomorrow. I can’t deny that I am totally fucking shitting myself but I have the best people around me so I know deep down, I’ll be okay.

Sally and Gina have come into my office to wrap up some final pieces of work before we all depart the place tomorrow. We've given the whole office a long weekend on us to help promote wellbeing and work life balance, so we are just sending out client emails to ensure they are aware of the situation.

"Have you guys packed?" I ask the girls while we're all typing away and shooting off emails.

"Almost," Gina replies still typing away.

"Yeah, I'm pretty much done, what about you?" Sally adds.

"I've not even started yet. Max is coming round later though so we can pack together."

"Ergh, I still cannot believe you asked him to come." Sally blurts and rolls her eyes at me like I'm the irrational one.

"Don't start, Sally. Can you just be nice for at least this one trip."

"Yeah, I'll be nice enough on the trip, but that doesn't start until tomorrow. So for now, you get the less than impressed version of me." She wags her finger at mc and I return a sarcastic smile back at her.

I let out a heavy sigh and swing round on my chair to face out the window. It's dark now so the usual greens are a deep black colour surrounded by the heavy bright lights of the flowing traffic.

"What about Rian?" Sally cuts in. "Why have you just wrote him off because he didn't tell whole truth, but you've forgiven Max for what I think is much fucking worse?"

"I don't trust Rian. I knew Max before he had the patch where he became different. I knew the real Max that I met 3 years ago." I snap back almost instantly, my anger rising inside, fed up of the argument at this point. "Rian lied from the start. Everything has been so suspicious about him, it just doesn't add up. I have a bad feeling about him."

"What do you mean it doesn't add up?" Sally questions.

"The fact he's inserted himself into my life, Sally. In multiple ways, without actually giving the game away. Don't you think that's a little suspicious?" I raise my voice as I speak, enunciating my anger.

"You can't be serious right now? This is definitely Max talking through you. What Mollie? Has Max told you that Rian is the big bad problem in your life. Un-fucking-believable!" Sally scoffs.

*Is she fucking serious right now?*

Rage floods me as my cheeks burn till there a crimson red. "It's not what Max has told me," I snipe back, although that isn't entirely true. "It's multiple factors that each add together. You know what Sally, I am sick of this argument with you." I stand and start packing my things into my bag and readying myself to leave the office. I need some space from her.

"Everyone but you can see it Mollie. He trapping you. Isolating you. And your fucking letting him" She jives back.

"Woah Sally, hang on a moment…" Gina interjects but I cut her up.

"Fuck off, Sally. Just fuck off. Don't offload your own pathetic miserable problems on me because you're lonely and my brother doesn't want to fuck you permanently. I'm fucking out of here." I grab my shit and walk out the office.

"Wait, Mollie! You're not supposed to be leaving alone!" Gina shouts but I continue to walk out the office before I say anything more that I'll regret.

Once I'm home, I pour myself a large pink gin and lemonade. I start gathering my things and add them to my suitcase. I am still furious and I need to calm myself down before Max arrives in a few moments to start packing. Taking a deep breath, I sip my gin as I browse through my phone. A message pings through from Gina.

**Gina -** Please let me know when you get home. I worry about you. Don't take Sally serious Mollie, she says all this because she cares and doesn't want to see you hurt. xox

I sigh, knowing Sally isn't malicious in her outbursts just that she can't help the need to tell you her thoughts, whether you want to hear them or not. I type a quick message back as I hear a knock at the door.

**Mollie -** I'm home.

I press the send button, not really wanting to start a long message back and rising my anger again, so I just ensure I've let her know I'm safe. Hearing a knock, I open the door to Max and he wraps his big arms around me pulling me in for an embrace. The tension I feel seems to melt away at his hug.

"You look like you needed that Mol, is everything okay?" Max asks as he walks inside the house.

I sigh before answering, "Yeah, Sally's giving me a hard time about you. But she'll get over it soon. Let's go pack." I respond, not leaving much room for that conversation to continue. I need to move away from it otherwise I'll fester on it and have a bad nights sleep. I'm already on the edge with this trip coming tomorrow, trying to ground myself before bedtime. I don't need any additional stress. We both head upstairs to fill our suitcases.

After a couple of hours packing, we're almost ready for our trip to Vegas. I asked Max to join us on Monday during lunch and he was excited to share this experience with us all. This will be our first trip on a flight together and out of the state since we met three years ago.

We have packed our individual suitcases with a variety of clothing for the trip. I've checked the weather forecast at least fifty times and concluded that even though it’s not too warm in NYC during October, it's warm enough for a mix of dresses, shorts and pants in Vegas which helps since we have only got cabin baggage to work with. I pack my backpack with some essential items.

“How are you feeling about the flight tomorrow?” Max asks, running his hand up and down my back, as I pack my items into my backpack.

“A little nervous,” I say continuing to stay focused on the task, “the flight is around 6 hours which is long really, probably should have started shorter but I’m ready. I’m so ready for a trip.”

“We’re all with you, don’t worry. Everything is going to be fine. The organisation appear to be in NYC anyway so surely leaving NYC is helpful at the moment.” He reassures me and I sigh, turning and placing my head on his shoulder.

Theres a knock that sounds at the door.

We both turn and stare at it, perplexed for a moment.

“Are you expecting someone?” Max asks, as we both continue to stare at the door.

The knocking starts again and I know it can’t be one of the group because they would have just walked straight through the door.

We head downstairs and I tentatively walk up and open the door. When I open it, two police officers stand at my door.

“Hello, can I help you?” I ask, skepticism filling me.

“Are you Mollie Rutter?” The officer on the left asks.

“Yes, that’s me. How can I help?” I ask again.

“We need you to come to the station with us.”

“Excuse me? Why? Whats happened?” I ask and Max closes in towards the door.

“There have been some disappearances in the city that we would like to clarify your whereabouts at the time.” The police officer announces casually, holding out his arm to gesture me towards his vehicle.

"My whereabouts? Am I being arrested?" I gasp, panic continuing to rise inside me, despite knowing I've done nothing wrong.

"Can I see some ID?" Max interjects, I can see the worry etching his features. I didn't even think to ask if they were legitimate. The officers pull out their badges and the holographic symbol is present making us realise that this situation is real.

Sally and Gina come out of their house, probably drawn by the flashing of red and blue lights coming off of the police vehicle.

"Am I being arrested?" I ask again, louder this time.

"Do I need to arrest you for you to get into my car or will you just come willingly?"

I look towards Max, as Sally and Gina reach us.

"What the hell is going on?" Sally asks.

"They're taking me to the station, I'm being questioned about some disappearances throughout the city."

"Disappearances? She's a fucking victim not a criminal." Sally defends me instantly and it warms my heart.

"Ma'am, we are just doing our job. I'm sure if Ms.Rutter has nothing to hide, she'll be home before you know it." The officer clasps my arm and pulls me towards the car.

"Sally, call Gray. Tell him what has happened."

The panic keeps rising inside me as I'm lead to the police car and situated inside.

But that's not the worst feeling.

No, the worst part is that they've started taking girls again.

And I'm being framed for it.

# Chapter 20

## Therapy
## Six Years Ago
## Session 1

I stand outside the large glass doors of the building, waiting for the right time to enter. Graham has decided that 6 months is enough time for me to sulk in my own sorrow before I need to get a grip and speak to someone about what I have been through.

I can't complain, he's given me time to try and overcome the demons myself but I just can't stop the nightmares from repeating, or the panic attacks from being so frequent.

It's no quality of life.

Gray has accompanied me here today to support me he says, but I am one hundred percent certain he has only come to make sure that I actually turn up and go inside. Deep down, I know I need this. Otherwise I'll just stay in the rut I've gotten myself stuck in.

"Are you ready to go inside Mollie?" Gray asks me, as I continue to admire the building. I turn and face the entrance to Central Park, still in awe of this beautiful city we chose to move to.

"I'm not sure, but I'll go in anyway." I reply, taking a deep breath and starting to walk towards the door. He follows me, shaking his head and I know I infuriate him. Well, the situation infuriates him. He feels so helpless when it comes to all of this. Maybe he's the one that needs therapy?

I head up to the second floor and I'm greeted by a big wooden door with '***Dr Rene - Hypnotherapy and CBT Clinical Psychologist***' printed at the side of it.

There is a little buzzer system and I press it quickly, deciding to do this before I chicken out and go back down the stairs.

A lady comes to the door, a welcoming smile placed on her face. She is the epitome of warm welcomes.

"You must be Mollie, welcome. Please come in and take a seat." She says, her tone full of soft notes, which makes everything seem down to earth. I wonder to myself if she is Dr Rene.

I turn back to look at Gray.

"I'm going to be waiting out here. I don't want to infringe too much on what I know could be your sanctuary." He says as he gestures for me to take a step into the room.

I hesitate but walk forward towards the sofa in the middle of the room, still no words leaving my lips.

"My name is Florence, I am Dr Rene's receptionist and personal assistant. Would you like me to get you anything to drink?" She asks and I just continue to stare at her, all doe eyed and lost. "Not to worry dear, I'll get you a camomile tea. It'll take the edge off those nerves of yours." She says and I smile, wringing my fingers together before sitting myself down and sandwiching them between my thighs to stop the temptation to fiddle.

She returns fairly quickly and hands me a beautiful china tea cup, which reminds me of home in England. I smile and manage to push out a 'Thank you' albeit extremely quiet.

"You are very welcome. Dr Rene won't be too long." She turns and strides off back to sit at the desk in the corner of the room.

I take notice of the room with its floor to ceiling windows. I like this look, it makes me feel, I don't know, free I guess. I wait around for a few minutes and a beautiful women exits the room to the side. Her hair is wrapped tightly in a bun on top of her head and she is dressed in a sage green formal dress.

"Mollie Rutter?" She asks with a question. "Please, come in and take a seat." She smiles, a warm and wide smile. My nerves cause a small hesitation but I eventually stand after a beat and walk into the room. The views of Central Park are incredible and it very much reminds me that we are so small in comparison to our surroundings.

"I'd like to start today with just some introductions and getting to know each other." She begins as she sits in the chair across from me. "So I am Dr Rene, I am a qualified hypnotherapist and clinical psychologist that specialises in cognitive behavioural therapy." She continues, although I have to say I am struggling to even hear her, not because she isn't speaking clearly, just that there is so much noise inside my head. My ears feel like they're screaming.

"I am a friendly face for you to rely on and while I know that we need to build on trust, I'd like to hope we can start positively." She says as I continue to stare out of the windows. My thoughts no where near the conversation in the room.

"Mollie?" I hear her say and it draws my attention back to her.

"Sorry." I say in almost a whisper.

"That's okay, Do you like the park?" She asks, glancing outside which entices me to turn and stare again.

"It seems so calm. Don't you think? The green, it feels like a cleansed palette wedged between the busy hustle and bustle of the city."

She smiles at me "I can see how it can make you feel that way." She says, her tone polite.

"So Mollie, would you like to share something with me about yourself?"

I think on for a moment, glancing down at my hands, as I notice I am wringing my fingers together again. I place my hands between my thighs again to try and stop myself from doing this.

"I'm Mollie. I moved here not long ago with my brother and our friends. We moved almost immediately after I was released from police custody, after everything that had happened."

"So, you've spent time in police custody?" Dr Rene asks, making notes in her little leather bound note book.

"Yes, after being in the compound and escaping, the British police spent time looking into me for my involvement in the trafficking and kidnapping of two girls who were also taken by the organisation." I say, surprising myself at how open I am being with this women.

There is just something about her. Her mannerisms, her body language, it's all so calming and soothing that I feel like I could just tell her anything and everything. I've never felt like that before.

"How did that make you feel?" She asks.

"I felt like I belonged there. In the police station. In the prison cells. Because I did bring them into the organisation, and I did cause them pain and trauma, things that they will never overcome. It will always stay with them and that's my fault." A tear falls down my cheek and I quickly swat it away, turning back to staring at the greenery of Central Park.

"Mollie, you know that isn't entirely the whole truth, is it? You were just as much a victim as those girls were." Dr Rene says in an attempt to reassure me.

I scoff. "I should have told Melvin where to stick his fucking task. I should have told him to just fucking kill me." I say, my voice lined with anger as I feel my throat contracting.

"Deep breaths, Mollie. You need to keep yourself as calm as possible." Dr Rene soothes.

I sit, staring outside taking in deep breaths deep into my lungs as tears continue to fall down my cheeks.

"I feel lost." I say, admitting this for the first time. "I feel so lost, in who I am, who I was, who I will be now." I say, as Dr Rene allows me a moment to speak my feelings.

"I feel like I should be locked away for my part, I feel I could kill the fucking bastards that took me to begin with. I feel angry, I feel lonely. I feel lost," the tears slowly become sobs and Dr Rene holds out a tissue box for me.

"Your feelings are validated, Mollie. Your feelings are a normal reaction to the situation you lived through. Remember that." She says, her voice floaty and calming, helping to relax me deeper. "What happened with the police findings?" Dr Rene asks as she continues.

"They dropped any and all charges against me, due to me being a victim myself."

"You have to take that on board, Mollie. You are a victim, not a criminal."

"I know this, but I just can't help but feel so fucking vile." I say, the sobs falling out of me so fast that I'm sure Gray will be able to hear me from outside the front door.

"Do you know who the girls are?" Dr Rene asks.

"Yes. Their names are Morgan and Verity. They helped me to escape."

"And what happened to them?"

"I escaped and I hid for a while but when I was found and taken to the police station, I told them what happened and where I had come from. They put together a full scale raid, they went to the complex and found Morgan and Verity. Along with 6 other girls who were kept in the below ground chambers. Although there were no obvious signs of who organised everything."

"Have you spoken to the girls since?"

"Yes, they were the ones who insisted to the police that I was not a criminal and they were not willing to testify or press charges against me." I say, dabbing my eyes with the tissue and continuing to stare out the window, not seeming to be able to make eye contact with Dr Rene.

"Do you feel like that helps you to feel better about the police dropping charges?"

"A little,"

"They forgive you for your input in anything they were involved in, Mollie. So we need to work on you, forgiving yourself."

I nod. I know this is about me and my feelings towards myself.

"During our sessions Mollie, we're going to explore your mind and your time in captivity through hypnosis, to try and help you overcome your trauma without having you re-live it. It will put your mind into a state of rest and relaxation, allowing us to really explore and overcome. Does that sound okay?" She asks and I nod, I know this is a necessity if I ever want to move on with my life.

We spend the rest of the session talking around the length of time I spent in captivity and the conditions of my stay. I feel like the time has passed by so quick. In my mind, attending therapy would just consist of me clock watching for an hour while some jumped-up-fucking-psycho-analyst made judgements on who I am as a person.

That is not the case at all.

We have talked about how each different element of my captivity made me feel, and at what point I felt completely lost and helpless. We touched on the loss of my parents and the guilt I feel around that and honestly, after everything we've talked about, I feel a little lighter.

"To finish the session Mollie, I'd like to summarise what we have discovered in three points for you to take away with you until next week."

I nod and this time, I turn my head to look at her. She smiles as if she's notice the change in me, my decision to positively interact with her, without just avoiding.

"Point one. You have been through some absolutely horrific times while captured and any decisions made during that time were not your fault."

"Point two. Morgan and Verity have forgiven you. So you should forgive yourself."

"And point three. You are a victim, not a criminal."

# Chapter 21

## Present Day

I sit inside the interrogation room at NYPD alone. The walls are a bleak grey, and I feel the cold throughout my bones. They sat me down in here and immediately departed the room, leaving me in here on my own without any further words.

I've been pacing around now for about an hour, breathing in deep to try and contain the panic attack I can feel sitting at the top of my lungs. Being in here makes me feel like a captive again.

I hear a deep and angry voice sounding from down the corridor. As it get closer, I recognise the voice as Gray.

"You are in violation of the law! Mollie is not a criminal, there is no evidence to suggest she is a criminal. She was cleared of all charges 3 years ago, so to list her as a potential suspect in a crime now is fucking criminal itself!" He booms, his voice stern and definitely in lawyer mode.

"Mr Rutter, we have only brought her in to ask if she has any knowledge on the matter."

"Don't give me that fucking bullshit. You do not lock a person in an interrogation cell, who is supposed to be helping you!" The lock clips and door flies open wide. Gray slides past the officer who has unlocked the door.

"Are you okay Mollie?" He says and I breathe out a sigh of relief as soon as he is here.

"Just about, I'm tense." I reply, gesturing to my chest giving him the signal that I'm close to having a panic attack.

"Come on, we're going to sit at an officers desk to answer their questions, considering you are not a fucking suspect!" His voice continues to be raised as he points his hand towards the door and gives a stern look towards the officer holding the door ajar. It's the officer who brought me into the station, so Gray must have known that it was him. As I round the door, a large plump man stands in the corridor outside.

"Ms. Rutter, my sincerest apologies for the misunderstanding that my officers seem to have gotten themselves in to. They were requested to visit you and ask for you to head into the station to help us. They were not supposed to drag you in, in the dead of the night, appearing like you were arrested." He announces as I stare vacantly at his face, I have no words left to say.

"You can fucking stick your sorry straight inside the compensation jar, asshole. You've just locked a vulnerable women, in an interrogation room on her own, when she has previously been a victim of captivity!" Gray seethes, I can see the veins bulging in his neck. He places an arm around my shoulder and walks me along the corridor to the front of the station.

It's there that I see Sally, Gina, Joey and Max all waiting for me. As soon as they see me they all rush towards me.

"Mollie, Fuck!" Sally says, throwing her arms around me. I instantly feel better knowing she's with me.

"I hope you're okay girl," Gina says as she turns her head to glare at the officer behind me.

Joey nods, patting my shoulder before making his way over to Gray to support him while he speaks to the detective.

I glance at Max over Sally's shoulder as we hug. He stands slightly away from the girls, with his hands pushed inside the front pockets of his jeans and gives me a sly smile. I let go of Sally, squeezing her shoulders and side step past her, towards Max. He opens his arms and pulls me in close to him.

"Are you okay?" He asks as he pulls back and glances over me, as if checking there are no marks or injuries to me.

"Yeah, I'm fine. I'm just a little shaken up. I could feel the panic attack rising inside me, but I think it was just the feeling of being trapped." I slump back into him, wrapping my arms around him and placing my head on his chest. He wraps his arms around me, securing me in an embrace and I feel the tension running out of my body like liquid.

"Mollie, I need you for a moment." Gray announces and I push off Max's chest. As my gaze meets his, I notice he's staring at the officer, his face contorted, seeming like a mixture of anger and worry. He quickly schools his expression, turning and facing me and putting on his best fake smile.

"Mollie!" Gray shouts me over again and I'm pulled away from the question I was just about to ask.

"I'll have to go over to him." I say and Max nods at me.

"I'll be waiting here for you." He says, rubbing his hands along my shoulders.

I turn and see Sally scowling in our direction. I roll my eyes at her as I walk past to Gray.

"Detective Palmer would like to ask for your assistance, to help them locate the Organisation. It is your choice whether you would like to, but as DC Palmer is explaining to me, it would mean that you have the potential to be used as bait." Gray says.

"No, no way." I snap back immediately, no thought even necessary.

Gray's head slowly turns back to the detective. "I told you she wouldn't put herself in that position again. I don't think you realised how fucking traumatised my sister is following this. She has had years of therapy."

I stand next to Gray, feeling more than vulnerable as he dishes out my deepest scars to the detective, like it is common knowledge. Elements of my ability to be so stoic and positive thrive off knowing that those around me do not know my past. Other than those who are closest to me. Feeling vulnerable I look down, wringing my fingers inside my hand and rocking on my feet.

“Well, there isn’t much I can do to change your mind I guess. It would be beneficial if we could have had you helping, Mollie. But equally, I understand your reasonings. Are you happy for us to contact you if we would like some help or information without the other elements?” The detective expresses and I feel a twinge of guilt about the situation.

“Yes, I guess that’s okay. We’re going out of the city for a few days but I will be back at the beginning of next week.”

He nods and turns back around to continue his conversation with Gray. I pat Gray on the arm, “Am I free to leave?” I ask, glancing between Gray and Detective Russo.

“Ah! Yes Mollie. So sorry for the confusion again.” Detective Palmer says and all I can do is muscle a fake smile back at him. I can feel myself getting more pissed about this whole situation now that my nerves have started to calm. There should be no confusion with how I ended up involved with the organisation.

“Come on guys, did any of you drive here or do we need to catch a cab?” I wave my arm at Sally, Gina and Max to follow me, which they do.

“I drove,” Max said, “I’m just parked over here.” He gestures down the street and me, Sally and Gina follow behind him, their arms linked either side of me.

The drive home is quiet with no one really wanting to spark up any conversation. The silence between the girls and Max is torture. Well, when I say the girls, I mean Sally. Gina keeps giving me the wide eye whenever I glance back as if to say, ‘awkward’.

We arrive home and there’s an unfamiliar car parked outside our houses.

“Who the fuck is that?” Sally says pushing open the door as soon as Max has put the car into park. We all file out and start looking around, searching for whatever Sally has noticed.

I glance over towards the steps up to Sally and Gina's door and spot a person sitting there, long dark, black-brown hair surrounding their face as they look down at their phone. Recognition hits me like a train.

"What are you doing here?" I immediately ask, the excitement reeling in my voice.

"Sara!" Sally shouts as she runs towards her with open arms. I turn, smiling at Max to share my excitement. His face seems distant as he stares across at Sara, his eyes wary.

"I'll wait inside for you." He says, his smile not quite reaching his dimples.

"Sure," I hesitate, as he turns and walks back into the house.

I turn back to Sara, her eyes locked on Max's back before she quickly shoots them to me.

"What's his problem?" Sara states, as she brings me in for a hug. I notice her eyes follow him intently.

"Oh I think it's just been a big night. He's already getting shit off Sally, he's probably wondering what the fuck is going to come from your mouth," she laughs with me and we all set off into Sally and Gina's house.

Once inside, Gina makes us all some pink gins, as usual and we sit on the sofa's under some cozy blankets.

"So, what are you doing here?" Sally asks as we are all given our drinks by Gina.

"I heard you guys had booked a trip and figured, what better way there is to surprise you all, than me coming to Vegas with you?" She says excitedly.

"Oh my god! This is amazing." I shout out in unison with a "Fucking yes!" from Sally and "This is going to be epic," from Gina.

We spend another hour catching up before we all decide it's late enough with it now being midnight and we should head to bed since, we all have a flight to catch in the morning.

"Right girls, I best go back home to Max. Sara, do you need a bed to sleep in? Or are you staying over here with Sally and Gee?" I offer as I put on my shoes.

"She can stay here. In the safe zone." Sally deadpans, clearly referencing about Max staying at mine. I sigh and head to the door.

"I'll see you guys tomorrow, I have limousines booked to take us all in one group to JFK for 10am. Flight leaves at 12. Be ready." I say, before opening the door and walking across the lawn to my house. Gina stands at the doorway to watch me cross and check I arrive at my destination, a whole 20 yards away, so I turn and wave at her as I reach my door.

I head inside and shout Max, as I lock the front door and place my keys on the side. There is no response so I start heading upstairs and walk into my bedroom. Still no signs of Max. Walking around the house, I start to worry that he's decided to leave or something, but just as the thought crosses my mind I spot him in the spare bedroom, fast asleep. Smiling to myself that he didn't just assume he would be sleeping alongside me, I pull the door shut and head to my bedroom.

I spot a note on my bedside table and my heart skips a beat for a moment, until I recognised Max's hand writing on the front. I open it.

***Didn't know how long you were going to be.***
***Hope you had a good time with the girls.***
***I'll be up at 8 to make us coffee.***
***I love you, Mollie.***
***xx***

My heart wants to burst as the smile spreads across my face. He really does seem to be making an effort this time and I feel a little relieved to have 'my Max' back.

I double check my suitcase to give myself some peace of mind and then begin to pin curl my hair so I can get up and get out tomorrow without thinking of what I'm planning on doing with it.

By the time I'm finished it's gone 01:00am and I am shattered. I decide to sneak into the spare bedroom and slide into bed next to Max. Snuggling in to him, I wrap my leg across his body before planting a kiss on his cheek. He remains asleep but wraps his arm around me, pulling me closer before we drift off to sleep together.

****

I rouse awake with Max's large frame leaning over me.

"Good morning, is there a reason you're hovering over me?" I ask playfully as I wrap my arms around his neck.

"I've just missed this beautiful view to wake up to in the morning." He says, a small smile tugging at his mouth. He plants a kiss on my forehead as I pull him closer to me. He rolls me over so I'm straddling him, my legs either side. His hands browse my body along my hips as I see his eyes roam my body. His cock is hard as it rubs my sex from beneath my seat. I start to grind myself on top of him, trying to release some of the tension that's coiled, making my sex slick and ready to take him. Max's eyes roll to the back of his head as a breathy gasps leaves my lips.

"Fuck Mollie, I can't tell you how much I need you this way again. But we need to get up before we miss this flight because we got carried away."

I let out a pretend cry but I know he's right. Leaning down I push my breasts into his face as I reach down and grab his length, stroking up and down through his boxer shorts. He tugs my t-shirt and bra down, my breasts falling out and engulfing his face. I hear a growl appear from Max as he is buried in my cleavage, peppering kisses along to my nipple. He sucks a nipple into his mouth and my sex clenches in response.

Fuck. We need to stop.

I pull myself back, covering my breasts back up as I climb off him. "Don't worry, it definitely won't be long." I say with a wink as I turn and head to my own room to get ready. As I leave, I hear a growl come from Max, which elicits a smile from me.

I have still got it.

We get ourselves showered and dressed, the rest of the morning has flown by and we're all ready and walking through JFK, heading to gate number 5 for the flight to Las Vegas. My nerves are in my throat and I'm starting to regret my decision to take a trip to anywhere.

The guys are keeping my head on and it's been great that Sara is now here to join us on this trip. These people really are the best bunch of humans I could ever ask for. I love them all so much, for all their help. We hand over our tickets and passports as we reach the gate and I continue to inhale deep breaths trying to keep my nerves a bay.

I don't know why the concept of flying triggers off this reaction inside me, because it's not the flying that was the root of the issue. I'm even glad to be getting out of the city with everything that's happening there right now. I guess it just triggers off my emotions.

Walking down the jet bridge, tugging my cabin case behind me, my arms are trembling. I can see Max, Sally and Gina all trying to talk to me but I can't hear the words they are saying for the pulse that's throbbing inside my ears.

Why am I panicking? It's just a flight.

I reach the door to the plane and my feet freeze on the spot. The air hostess looks startled by my reaction and I feel Max's hand graze the base of my spine attempting to encourage me to walk forwards.

"I can't do this." I whisper, so only Max can hear.

He turns to face me, looking straight into my eyes, the flecks of his blue eyes gleaming at me. Cupping my face between both of his hands he glides his thumbs caressing my cheek bones.

"You are so strong, Mollie. You have spent so long building yourself back up to being this incredible, independent, strong, beautiful women. You deserve this more than anyone." He says, his tone hushed so to not draw attention from others to his words. "You can do this." He finalises and I look down at my feet, willing them to move.

I gulp down some deep breaths, my trembles continuing and I can see Sally talking with the air hostess, likely giving her the information as to the hold up.

"We're all here for you Mollie." I hear Joey say as he rounds the walkway from behind me. I take a minute to the side of the jet bridge, sliding down the side and slumping to my ass, dropping my head in my hands. My heart rate feels like it could explode.

"Please just get on the plane. I just need a minute." I say as I take in some deep breaths.

A chorus of no's ring out from my best friends as they all refuse to get onto the plane without me.

Fuck!

Why am I like this?

Why am I ruining this trip?

My hands and legs tremble with the adrenaline pumping through me.

"Remember to breathe, Mollie." Max says.

My breathing gets more and more laboured as I can feel my panic attack coming on.

Fuck no. Not here.

My eyes look up at the group as tears fill them.

"I don't think I can do this."

# Chapter 22

## Present Day

I take Max's hand and nod at him before putting one foot in front of the other. I step onto the plane, greeted by the hostesses and pilots as a beautiful hostess smiles and shows us up the stair into first class.

"You booked us first class fucking tickets? You absolute legend," Sally jumps up excitedly before taking me into her arms in a bear hug.

"I figured it would be better if I panicked here, with just you guys rather than down there with everybody." I smile. "Now quickly, catch up," I say gesturing towards the gap between Sally and Joey who are following right behind the cabin hostess.

We reach the top deck and it is divine. The individual pods lining the pristine carpets. The hostess smiles as we all claim a pod each, I opt to pick a double pod and share the space with Max.

"My name is Lola, I'll be your hostess on top deck today. Anything you need I'll be happy to assist." She beams a smile at all of us. "It is just you 6 up here this morning," She finishes.

I glance around the cabin noting there are 10 possible pods within the section.

"Excuse me, Lola?" I ask, she turns towards me "Our friend is sat downstairs in economy, she added onto the flight without us realising, is there any chance we can bring her up here to join us? I'm happy to cover additional costs if necessary."

"I'll speak to the captain and let you know but I'm sure there won't be an issue." She scurries off and I glance up to see Joey staring as she walks away.

"Pick your jaw up off the floor Kincaid, you're drooling." I say, sarcasm oozing from me as a smile pinches at my lips.

"Shit. I'm busted," Joey laughs as a blush creeps up his cheeks. He actually looks like he's been caught red handed doing something he shouldn't.

"Do you like her?" I ask, genuinely curious for him

"She's fucking beautiful," he replies and I smile at him.

"Go for it Joey. You only live once." I say, bumping him on the shoulder before sitting down in my pod.

I take in a deep breath, exhaling slowly.

"Are you okay Mol?" Max asks, and I shoot my eyes up at him.

"I'm feeling much better, but still feel a little on edge. I think a drink will help to loosen me up."

The hostess returns and I hear her asking Gina where our friend is seated and what her name is. Gina provides the details and scurries off before returning a short moment after with Sara following behind.

I smile up at Sara, as she mouths a "thank you" at me before winking and blowing me a kiss.

It makes me so happy to have all my favourite people surrounding me. That itself helps to calm my nerves.

I put on a film, choosing to watch a romantic comedy to settle my nerves a little further. I feel the plane push back and the captain begins his start of flight speech over the speakers, introducing himself and the flight details putting our estimated time of arrival as 8:00pm Las Vegas time. The flight is predicted as six hours long from NYC to Las Vegas and surprisingly, my nerves aren't accelerating to panic attack stage. I can feel my pulse elevated but no where near freak out. Before we know it, we've taken off and are soaring into the skies.

I'm two films deep by mid-flight and I take a minute to think about everything before choosing another film to watch. I feel euphoric for this achievement, although there's a small part of me that thinks back to the amount of worry, panic and stress I am currently going through. I've relied on my friends to ground me on several occasions lately which hasn't happened this often in years. I glanced down the aisle at each of my friends that I can see, before spotting Joey with his best 'Come fuck me' face, flirting with the air hostess, Lola. Honestly, I don't blame him, she is fucking gorgeous. I hope he gets his happy ending one day.

"How are you feeling, Mollie?" Max's voice pulls me out of my day dream and I turn towards him.

"Still a little nervous." I say sheepish, although a smile does curl slightly at the side of my lips. "I think it's time that I look at going to see Dr Rene again, you know, with everything that's going on right now."

Max nods, "It's not a bad idea if it helps to keep you grounded with everything else."

I smile at him "Yeah, I agree."

"I have an idea for now though, it'll be a definite distraction for you," he whispers seductively and his face turns devious, his eyes glisten as he bites his bottom lip. My eyes drift from his face to his lips as I watch his tongue circle along his teeth. My insides start to hum, reacting to his teasing and I feel my nipples harden.

Fuck, my body just reacts to him these days.

He dips into his backpack pulling out some large clips before using these to place the blanket above us to make a tent like den.

"Max, stop, people will get suspicious." I gasp in a whispered giggle as I reach over to him.

"So let them," he grins, taking my bottom lip into his mouth and nipping this. "Close your curtain," he gestures to the curtain which lines the aisle and I nod at him and do as I'm told, as he does the same on his side.

"What are you going to do?" I whisper, my breath suspenseful.

"I'm planning on taking any and all of your worries away, Mollie." He says as he leans over the top of me. I sink down onto the double bed located in our pod as he dominates me, climbing on top, his arm muscles bulging and flexing.

"How do you suppose you'll be doing that?" I ask, my voice still whispering to try and reduce people hearing us.

He unties my pants tugging them down to my ankles before heading back up top. Running his fingers along my legs and up my thighs until he meets my wet heat at the centre. His fingers rubbing me over my thong and I slam my legs close as he touches my clit.

"Open your fucking legs, Mollie. I plan on taking those soaking wet panties off of that glistening pussy, and tasting you until you're gagging for release." He whispers into my ear and I release my legs. He continues to stroke my centre, a small whimper leaving my mouth, before I gasp as the circling stoking motion he repeats, intensifying in pressure.

"Quiet now, Mollie, we don't want to get in to trouble do we," he whispers into my ear before pushing up and removing his t-shirt so his bare chest is on show.

*Fuck.*

The ache between my legs is pulsing and I reach down to try and relieve some of the ache for myself, but Max swats my hand away.

"Patience, Mollie," He commands as he adjusts his cock in his sweatpants. The sight of his bulge is incredible and I reach over and stroke him on top of his pants. His eyes roll back at the contact and I feel fire ignite inside him.

He pulls my t-shirt over my head before unclipping my bra from the front clasp.

"Isn't that just a handy little contraption," He says as my breasts spring free. He takes my nipple into his mouth while he nips and squeezes the other in his fingers. Running his hand down from my nipple, across my stomach, his hand dips into my panties and he slides two of his fingers straight through my heat, massaging between my folds, coating his fingers in my arousal.

My breath becomes more unhinged, panting coming thick and fast as I feel the pulse in my pussy throbbing.

"Shhhh, Mollie, someone might hear us," Max whispers while his face is a devilish smile. Removing his hands from my panties , he slides one of his fingers deep into his mouth, sucking my taste into his mouth.

"You taste incredible Mollie," he says as he rubs the other finger across my lips. I part them, dipping my tongue out and tasting myself on his fingers. He sucks in a breath, his restraint at the end of his will power as I lick and suck in his finger tight, before releasing it and circling my tongue along the top. His eyes close as he gathers his restraint and adjusts his length in his joggers.

He rips the centre of my panties so my pussy is visible, slapping my clit, I jolt as the pleasure electrifies my senses.

"Now Mollie, stay quiet like a good girl." He commands, dipping his head down, scattering kisses along my bikini line, trailing up my thighs. Using his hands he pushes my knees apart and spreads me wide before dipping his head low and inhaling my scent.

He places a kiss directly on my clit before sucking me in sharply. A gasp leaves my lips and I school myself, placing the corner of the pillow between my teeth.

His tongue slides up my slickness before sucking my clit in again and I am already on the edge of control, my walls contracting at every touch and I know I'm going to spill my come into his mouth at any moment.

He dips his tongue into my heat as he continues the assault between my legs, sucking and licking, caressing my folds as my legs tremble. My breaths are getting louder and I tap him.

"Please Max, I need your cock. Please." I beg as I see him tugging at his pants to give himself some relief.

"You will come for me like this, Mollie." He demands as he continues to fuck my pussy with his tongue.

"Let me suck you, Max. Let me relieve you too." I ask, and a growl resonates from his throat. He continues to suck on my clit as he removes his own pants.

He spins us around, sixty-nine style, so his back is flat on the bed and lowers me back down on to his face, his tongue beginning to lap my arousal again, sucking hard on my clit and darting in and out of my sex.

I stare at his erection as he continues to build my orgasm, joining him I start to lick around the head before taking him deep into my throat. He growls and I continue to lick up and down his length, sucking down on his head, the veins bulging and his length throbbing at the contact.

"Fuck!" He rasps from between my legs before latching on and sucking hard on my clit, I feel his fingers, two of them glide through the soaking slickness before he presses them deep inside me, my walls increasing in throbbing as he pumps me hard. I continue to suck on his cock, my pace increasing as we both build up to climax. My hand finds the base of his cock and I start to massage, the movements matching my mouth as I suck down deep.

Max pulls out his fingers and runs this along my ass spreading my juices across the entrance, a moan leaves me as I push back, the sensation to have him there overtaking me. He continues to suck on my clit before dipping his thumb into my sex, wetting this with my arousal before pushing it slowly but deep into my ass.

*Holy. Fucking. Hell.*

He pumps me in both holes, deep into my ass while curling his fingers inside my pussy, as his tongue continues to assault my clit and I am done. My walls clamp down and I come undone.

Sucking harder and swirling my tongue, I feel the hot salty liquid fire down my throat as Max meets his own release with me. We continue to suck, lick and pump each other as our releases come to an end. Max pulls his fingers out of me, a sense of emptiness fills me. Using his tongue, he licks me up around my sex, taking all of my arousal into his mouth. I swallow the hot semen that lines my throat and we both collapse, our bodies completely spent.

Max slides to the side as I lie down next to him. He runs his hands along my side as we both look at each other from top and tail.

“That was fun,” He announces as his fingers meet my nipple and he swirls them around it. I feel my body react to him again.

*Fuck my life, we've only just come woman!*

“Everyone definitely knows what we just did in here,” I say, embarrassment overtaking me, although there is definitely as smile tugging at my lips.

“But did it distract you?” Max asks, his smile joining mine.

“Oh it definitely distracted me.” I say, pushing myself up and leaning over him. My lips press against his as I kiss him. His hands cupping my jaw, as he pulls me in deeper into the kiss. Fuck, I am so lost in him again. My heart is beating rapidly, but this time, for all the right reasons.

A tap sounds from outside the curtain and I flinch, pulling at the covers up to cover myself.

“If you’ve quite finished doing whatever it is you're doing to my sister, lovely Lola here would like to know if you want any drinks.” Gray announces from outside and I feel my face flush crimson. Theres a chorus of giggles from the others and I feel mortified. Max just sits with a big fucking shit eating grin spread across his face. He picks up a wipe from his bag and wipes my arousal from his face, before slipping his head out of the curtain.

"I don't know what you're talking about, Gray, we were just sleeping." Max announces and I can hear the smile in his voice. "A Jack Daniels and coke for me and a pink gin and lemonade for the lady please." He asks the hostess before popping his head back into the den we've made for ourselves.

He takes out the wipes from his bag that he used to clean his face with and starts to clean me up, wiping my arousal off my legs.

"Do you have any spare underwear?" He asks, with no attempts to hide the smile on his face. His dimples popping out and he makes eye contact with me.

"Yes, they're in my case." I say as a matter of fact, pointing at my case which is tucked in the corner of the pod. He opens this, before picking out a new lace thongs. He looks at them, his eyebrows rising as he gives me 'come fuck me' eyes again.

I go to snatch them from his hand but he quickly retracts them. Placing them over my feet, he slides them up my legs. When he reaches my ass he pulls me into a seated position before picking me up and sitting me on his lap.

"I could literally spend all weekend like this with you, Mollie." He says as he inhales in to the crook of my neck.

"Me too," I breath out, pushing my breasts up against his bare chest.

I sit back slightly as he pulls at either side of my bra that hangs over my shoulder, and brings the clasps back together, securing the girls back into place. He graces each one with a kiss before picking me up off his lap and sitting me next to him.

Once he's fully dressed me, he gets himself cleaned up and suitable before removing the blanket roof he made. The lights assault my eyes from being in the dark for so long. I glance over and Sara is eyeing me warily, with Sally right by her side. The pair of them with their judgemental eyes. Gina on the other hand has a big grin on her face while she puts her thumb in the air and winks at me. I smile shyly and decide to start up a conversation to change the topic.

"Whats the plan for when we arrive then? It'll be late, do we want to head out for a few drinks or is everyone feeling beat from travelling?"

"I'm happy to just chill in our room tonight personally, we have a sight seeing day tomorrow and none of us can be trusted to have one drink and go to bed." Gray answers back and everybody mumbles in agreement.

"Okay, I agree, I just thought I'd check." I say before I return to my cozy pod and pick a final film to see the end of the flight in.

The plane wheels hit the ground in Las Vegas and the sun is long gone making way for the stars to shine brightly across the clear sky. I have butterflies swirling in my stomach although I feel refreshed after that mid-air sex session.

We gather our bags and exit the plane first. I see Joey slip a piece of paper into Lola's hand and I smile at him, no doubt that he's just given her his number. He's such a flirt. We head straight through the airport after passport control, heading out the doors to meet the chauffeur here to collect us and take us to the hotel.

We all arrive at the hotel and I check us in, asking for several key cards to our room, the penthouse, so we can all come and go if we feel like it. The penthouse, located at the top of the hotel, with views spanning the whole width of Las Vegas, we can see for miles through the floor to ceiling panoramic windows that line every edge of the room.

"This is spectacular," Gina proclaims as we each file in. We decide to get straight to picking our bedrooms, although with there being 10 to choose from there is no need to scramble, each room has a unique feature which makes them individually appealing. The group collaboratively decide that I should get the best room in the penthouse, with 180 panoramic views of Las Vegas through the  floor to ceiling windows and a big spacious en-suite.

I seek out Max as he starts to look through the catalogue of bedrooms.

"Max," I say, reaching for his hand and locking my fingers with his. He looks down at my hand, startled slightly at the contact before moving his eyes to look at me. Worry etches his face.

"Is everything okay?" He asks with haste.

"Yes, oh sorry, I didn't mean to startle you." I reply quickly and give a big smile to reassure him, "I just wanted to find you before you found a room."

"Why?" He asks, his facing looking somewhat confused.

"I just, erm, I just wanted to ask you if you might want to share my bed with me this weekend?" I ask, feeling like a school girl, giddy but nervous.

"With you? Share a room?" The shock on his face is palpable.

"Yes, unless you don't want to?" I say, the smile dropping from my face so fast and my heart rushing with worry.

"Oh no, god no, of course I want to Mollie. Fuck. I just didn't expect it," he takes my hand and places a kiss on the back. A Smile spreads across my face as I turn around and lead the way back to our bedroom.

****

Saturday night rolls in and we're all finally ready to go see what Vegas nightlife is all about. We've spent the day sight seeing, first heading down the Las Vegas strip, before visiting the

Hoover Dam and taking a helicopter trip over the Grand Canyon. It's been incredible.

We head down to the lobby and towards a restaurant on the strip that we made reservations for earlier in the day. We've all made the effort tonight, our outfits looking incredible. I chose to wear a little satin red number, that hugs my curves, cuts off mid thigh and accents my breasts. My hair is high up in a single plait pony that starts at to top of my head and my make up shows off a bright red lip with dark shaded eyes that bring out my icy blue eye colour.

I feel like the food we have eaten tonight is some of the best food I've ever tasted. Definitely a five star meal, the food was so incredible but does nothing for the bloat I'm facing in this dress.

I excuse myself to go and freshen up in the ladies room with Sally, Sara and Gina.

"You and Max seem to be on fire, Mollie." Gina states as we each polish up our make up in the mirror.

"Yeah, we're getting on really well. It's surreal if I'm honest." My smile spreads wide across my face without me even thinking about it. "The difference in him is incredible. I feel like I've finally got the Max I fell in love with back." I beam as I speak, feeling happier than I have in such a long time. That emotion is quickly squashed by Sally rolling her eyes at me and glancing towards Sara, some fucking shitty subliminal message passing between them.

"Right, you need to stop that," I wave my hand in a circle , floating it around Sally's face.

"Stop what? I'm just not falling for his bullshit again like you are," Sally says, her tone abrupt.

"You're boring me with this now, Sally. I get that you're not overjoyed by my choices but can't you just be happy for me? Can't you just accept the decision that I have made?" I argue with her, my irritation fully flaring now.

"I'm just not interested in the silly choice you have made."

"Silly choice? Sal, this is my life. Mine. Not yours, not Gina's, not Sara's, mine," my anger rife now, "so even though you don't like it, your job as my friend is to lump it, listen to me, be happy for me and be there for me if shit hits the fucking fan." My eyes start to water and I pluck at a tissue that's on the vanity unit in front of us and dab in the corners of my eyes, trying to keep my make up in tact.

"Sal, you're taking it a little too far." Gina defends me. "We should just go with what she chooses to do. If she's happy, we should just be happy. And if we're honest, he's really put the effort in so far." I smile and take her hand in mine giving it a little squeeze.

Sally looks at Sara, I guess looking for back up from her.

"I just don't think you should one hundred percent trust him, Mollie. I don't think you know it all." Sara announces and Sally grins smugly.

I roll my eyes back at them this time. "Sara, no offence but you're barely even here. All you know is what this one sided 'anti-Max' individual has sprouted to you."

"I know more than you think, but that's beside the point. Just take what we're saying into consideration." Sara says before turning and continuing her make-up.

"We just give a shit, Mollie, and I don't trust him. Period." Sally finalises and turns, continuing to fix her make-up.

"This trip isn't about me and Max. So from here on, you mind yours, and I'll mind mine." I say, irritation still lining my words. "And don't ruin the whole trip by actively trying to be an asshole to him at any and all given opportunities please." I say, picking up my bag and striding for the door, taking myself away from this conversation, again. I turn and nod at Gina and she gives me a sympathetic smile, before joining me in leaving the toilet.

"Just try to ignore her Mollie, she means well really, it's just how she's behaving about it." Gina says, wrapping her arm around my shoulder reassuringly.

"I know Gee, but she's being an asshole."

"I agree." We separate ways to sit back in our seats at the table. Max looks at me and immediately notices my eyes.

"Why have you been crying? Whats happened?" He asks defensively, like he's ready to take on the world for me.

"It's nothing, just a disagreement with Sally. Again." I reply fanning my eyes so not to start crying again.

"About me?" He questions and I nod.

"Don't worry about it. I'm sure she'll get over it soon." I say attempting to keep my voice level and firm.

Max lets out a defeated breath and nuzzles into my neck, inhaling my scent like it's a drug to him.

"Mollie, why are you crying?" Gray asks me across the table just as Sally and Sara take their places.

"Nothing, I'm good. Just a little emotional about everything that is all." I reply quickly, pasting a smile on my face.

"Are you giving her shit again?" Gray asks Sally outright and my face falls.

"Gray, I said I'm fine," I announce, my tone firm.

"I'm not giving her shit, she needs to remember what the fuck he's put her through because she's clearly got fucking amnesia or something."

"Sally!" Gina shouts as my mouth falls open. The whole table look between me and Sally and I feel so vulnerable.

"Stop. Stop it! This trip is supposed to be happy and a significant turning point in my fucking shitty history. Not a trip that makes me question all future fucking trips." I shout, anger flaring and I can feel my entire body reddening.

"Now if you all excuse me, I plan on going fucking dancing, doing some gambling and enjoying my night." I stand, tugging my bag off the chair arm and slinging it over my shoulder. "Join me and be happy. Or fuck off." I say before striding away without a care in the world.

Max and Gina stand with me and start to make their way out of the restaurant. I meet the waiter on the way out and pay for our meal before exiting and walking towards a dance club we spotted on our way from the hotel.

As we get to the club, I ask the bouncer for a private booth area. The idea of being so open in a nightclub away from home makes me feel uneasy, so being in the club but having our own area tucked away settles my nerves.

The bouncer shows us to a booth on the main club level and I tap my card to pay for the hire as we enter. Waitresses in next to no clothes swing round bringing us bottles of spirits and mixers on ice.

The music is pumping old school R'n'B and I am feeling the vibe. Gina starts mixing drinks as per her speciality and I decide to let loose and start dancing the night away.

I see Max sitting himself down next to Gina, they're talking but I'm not going there. Everything is too serious and I just need to feel free, if not just for this moment in time. I twirl around to the music and I see the rest of our group arrive. The bouncer looks at me to see if they can gain access and I nod at him, although I was tempted to fucking deny Sally.

Gina brings me my drink over and joins me as we rock our hips and vibe to the absolute hits that are playing. The DJ announces that he's going to slow it down for a beat and I feel Max's arms wrap around my waist, my back pressed against his front, as KCI and JoJo's - All My Life plays over the speakers. I arch my back, shaking my ass over his groin as he caresses my body. The chorus comes in and I hear him singing the words into my ear. My heart is about to burst as I rotate and to face him, wrapping my arms around his neck, I feel his hands cup my ass as we sway to the music. I am so happy right now. Nothing could ruin my mood. Not one single thing.

The drinks flow and the music is pumping through the night. At some point we lose Sara, Sally and Gray, but Me, Max, Joey and Gina are all staying strong.

I love these people so much.

After a couple of hours dancing and laughing, we decide to head back towards the hotel to go and have a little gamble at the hotel casino. Making our way back up the strip, we are all merry, the alcohol coating our veins. Gina is propped on Joey's back as he piggy backs her up the road, while Max just keeps me held upright so I don't trip.

We reach the little wedding chapel along the strip.

"Fuck, Mollie, you and Max should go get married. That'll fucking piss Sally off," Gina says, laughter bursting from her lips.

"Oh my fucking god, imagine her face." I reply, my laughter filling the air.

"You know I'd marry you in a heartbeat babe, but not here. You're worth so much more than a Vegas wedding."

I smile up at him and our lips lock together.

"Get a room," Gina and Joey say in chorus.

The wedding bells of the chapel start to ring out and we start to cheer for the happy couple about to leave the chapel.

"Ahh who said romance is dead," I announce as we see the door to the chapel opening.

A couple fall out of the door their faces locked together in a kiss, their hands roaming all over each others body.

"Jeez, look at them go. They're feisty," Gina says quietly so not to disturb their moment.

Max's eyes seem to zone into small slits, as if he's really into the borderline sex show across the street.

"Oh jeez Max, you can watch some porn if you really need to, come on let's go."

His stare continues to intensify. As we continue to walk forward, his pace lessening with every step.

"Mollie," he says after a beat.

"What's wrong with you?" I say, my smile fading.

Gina and Joey stop and turn around.

"Whats happening man?" Joey announces as he starts to walk back towards Max.

Pointing at the people who have just come out of the chapel, I turn to zone into what Max is pointing at just reality kicks me.

I hear Max's voice as I zone in on the happy couple.

"Mollie, I think that's Graham and Sally."

# Chapter 23

## Present Day

Last night ended in such a whirlwind of emotions. I honestly couldn't bring myself to approach Sally and Gray after we saw them leaving the chapel in a hot mess. I can't believe they would hide this. I can't believe they would leave me, well all of us, out of this massive life event for them.

I'm angry, sad, happy and bitter all at the same time. A knock sounds at the door and I look at the time, 11:00am, that should be the brunch I ordered to be sent up, predicting we would all be tender today.

I wrap a gown around myself, heading into the living area to the door and greet the waiter. Sliding the trolly through the door, thanking the waiter I hand him a tip before retreating back into the room.

I sigh, looking at all the food and not wanting to bother calling the others out with how I'm feeling. I have a spa afternoon planned from 2:00pm so I need to eat and get myself freshened up beforehand.

I opt it's best to call out announcing the arrival of food to extend the invite out everyone without having to see people. I start gathering some food items on a plate to take back into my room. Max joins me, wrapping his arm around my waist and planting a kiss on the side of my head.

"How are you feeling this morning?" He asks as he grabs a plate to start loading his own food choices.

"Not the best, I just need to get away from everybody for a little bit I think. I can't wait for my spa trip this afternoon." I say as I finish filling my plate and turn to walk towards the bedroom.

"Mollie, can we talk about last night?" Sally calls as I'm half way back to my bedroom.

I stop on the spot, still facing my bedroom, my pulse is thumping as the anger rises back up inside me. I am not ready for this conversation yet. I hear another door close and see Gina appearing from the corner of my eye. Assuming she's heard Sally's request, I glance her direction as she sends a sympathetic smile to me.

I sigh and turn around, looking directly at Sally.

"Which part of last night would you like to talk about Sally?" My attitude is in full flow, ready to give whatever she gives to me, straight back at her.

"About my feelings towards Max, I just wanted to say, that maybe I went a bit far. It's not my place to tell you what to do and although I don't agree with you, and I think you're making a huge mistake, I also know you need to make your own mistakes and I just need to be here for you to pick up the pieces when it inevitably goes wrong." She says, quickly as if she wants to get it all out before I interrupt her. My face warps into bemusement at her 'apology'.

I scoff. "Is that supposed to be an apology?" A sarcastic smile lines my face now "It seems more like a sorry, not sorry from where I'm standing. Did you genuinely get to this point yourself Sally? Or was this your HUSBANDS idea?" I enunciate the word husband to make my point clear.

Her face falls.

"My husband?" She laughs nervously but I can see she is startled that I know.

"Yes, your husband, my brother, one and the same." I shrug my shoulders, the sarcasm bursting from me.

Gray exits the bedroom, clearly having heard the commotion outside. That makes everyone in the living area now bar Sara, who seems to just be hiding.

"What's going on out here?" He says, pretending like he didn't just come out of Sally's room when we're all not supposed to know they are in a relationship, let alone fucking married.

"Ahh, and here is the groom himself." I snigger. "Welcome to the living room debate about who should have judgement on whose fucking life choices," I say.

The whole room stays silent, feeling my emotion riding the walls as my anger simmers to boiling point.

"I have had some fucking shitty things done to me in my life. Some real fucking low, deep, traumatic shit. But we all know that," I scoff, "yet what I saw last night, you two, walking out of that chapel, the bells ringing, having fucked off without giving a shit about any of us, not two thoughts about how this," I gesture in a triangle between Gray, Sally and myself, "Affects us all. Oh no, zero fucks given about that. Not a shit given about how you have lied for years about this shit, thinking we're all dumb and don't already know you sneak around." I shrug at them, as their faces fall like they thought they were actually fooling us all.

"Like I'm going to tell you 'oh no, don't be in love with each other and live your lives happy'," I mimic. "No, no, because I am not you, Sally. I wouldn't fucking do that to you. If you make each other happy, whether it's for now or forever, then fucking great. Because I want you both to be happy. That's clearly not reciprocated to me!" The hurt is evident in my voice now. Sally's face falls, her mouth gaping as if she's lost for words.

"Well, if you excuse me, I have my brunch to eat then an afternoon of being as far away from you fucking assholes as I can be. Happy fucking holiday," I finish, turning around walking off giving a casual air salute with my plate as I kick the bedroom door closed behind me.

****

After this morning, I left to enjoy my spa package. I've had such a nice afternoon. The spa is located in the basement of the hotel and I'm glad I thought beforehand to ask the hotel staff for some exclusive use of the facilities after my massage. It came at an obvious expense but I had decided when booking it that I definitely would need the tranquility to just unwind. I just didn't know exactly how much I would need it.

I enjoyed a full head to toe massage with hot lava shells for 90 blissful minutes, followed by an Indian head massage and a pedicure. I feel so calm and relaxed after this mornings situation-ship, that I could fully melt.

After I'd enjoyed my treatments, the spa facilities were empty just as I had asked for and I spent around an hour swimming in the pool, followed by some time in the steam room.

I decide to head into the thermal fire and ice room. I've never used one of these before but it definitely seems interesting. Putting my spa gown on the hooks outside the door, I enter. The room is hot, like a sauna, with and ice depositor centred in the middle of the room. Surrounding the ice there are mosaic tiled, recline shaped chairs. There is a tube which comes from the ceiling of the room which keeps dropping ice out of the spout into the pile as it melts in the heat.

I round the ice pile and sit myself on a reclining chair at the back of the room, swinging my legs up to rest and close my eyes as I take in the heat. Steam fills the room with a eucalyptus scent and I feel myself cleansing already.

This is invigorating at opening up your senses. I sit up, cupping some ice and bringing it over to chair and placing it on the arm. The room continues to repeatedly fill with heat and steam and I run the ice cubes along my skin to reduce my body temperature and allow it to become more bearable to withstand the heat. I hear the door open and close and my annoyance flares immediately. I paid for exclusivity for fucks sake.

I open my eyes and see Max. His muscles flexing as he stands in his swim shorts, his hair slick back, evident that he had just took a swim in the pool outside the room. The ice melts as it slides down my breasts and Max's eyes trail the length of my body, tracking the ice as it slides.

"You've been gone for too long, I missed you," he says, his voice a low rumble and his eyes still burning into me.

"I needed some space." I say, trying to act like his presence is pissing me off more than turning me on, but who the fuck am I kidding when he's stood there, muscles flexed and water dripping along his body.

"Am I welcome in your space if I promise you a good time?" He winks at me, his smile devilish as he runs his hands through his hair, flexing his biceps, his lips tugging a deep smile, and his dimples popping.

He fucking winked.

My insides coil, as the throbbing starts and I squeeze my legs together in attempt to ease some of the tension.

"That depends on what your idea of a good time is." I retort, a teasing tone lacing my voice. I'm ready to play this game if he is.

He walks around the ice pit, his movements slow and methodic as he approaches me, pitching himself over the chair, so he's towering over me.

Dominating me.

Taking a piece of ice he drops it on my chest. My head falls back at the touch of his fingers along my skin, while he slides the ice down.

His head dips down, his lips devouring the crease of my neck as I lift my arms and I run them over his back to his biceps, feeling his muscles beneath my finger tips. I let out a moan as he nips on my ear and my eyes flit open, taking in his body arched over mine.

“This is my idea of a good time Mollie.” He rasps in a whisper.

My eyes close as he moves away from me for a beat, before grabbing onto my bikini top and tugging at the string within my cleavage, the top barely keeping my breasts covered. He pulls sharp, snapping the string like it’s nothing but paper, following this with untying the bows at my hips and peeling the front of my bikini off. He peels the material of my top away, leaving me completely exposed, naked and vulnerable to him. He bites his lip, the fire blazing in his eyes evident as he adjusts his cock.

Despite the room being a stifling fire warm, my nipples are hard. I attempt to close my legs, the ache palpable between my thighs. Max tuts, pulling apart my knees and spreading me wide and bare for him. He skims his fingers through my heat, the touch electric as I gasp. He leans back down, grinding his rock hard cock along my sex.

Picking up another ice cube, he places this in his mouth, leaning down to my neck he moves his mouth and the cube along my skin, his lips brushing me softly until he reaches my breasts, taking one of my nipples in his mouth, sucking and nibbling, the cold contrast igniting my insides. My hands fly up to his hair as he assaults my nipples, he grabs another ice cube in his fingers, rubbing this on my other nipple.

A moan escapes my lips as he trails the ice cube along my skin and down towards my sex, before swirling this on my clit, in smooth circles.

Placing another ice cube in his mouth he moves down to my sex and sucks my clit hard, flicking and swirling his tongue and the ice cube together, the assault sending spasms straight to my sex. I see him pull out his cock, pumping this in his hands while I’m lost in the sensations he giving me. I am close to the edge as he flicks his tongue, licking and sucking. He grabs more ice as he continues the rhythmic lick and flick on my clit.

Placing ice at my entrance I feel him push them in with his thumb before sliding two fingers in and curling them, deeper and deeper with each pump, his rhythm picks up pace as he builds my orgasm sensationally. I can feel my legs starting to tremble as he continues to pump me, he pulls his mouth back, releasing his cock and using his other hand to continue to vibrate my clit. I am so close to the edge as he makes eye contact with me.

"Let yourself go Mollie, come all over my fucking hand," and that's all it takes as my walls clench and my arousal floods his fingers.

"That's a good girl," he praises, "but don't think we're finished just yet," he says, his fingers still pumping me as I ride out my orgasmic high.

I hitch my head up, opening my eyes to meet his gaze. His hand pulls out as he leans over my body, spotting kisses all over my skin. I lose control, pouncing up and rotating him so his back is to the chair. I spread my legs over him, sitting and grinding my pussy all over his cock, my arousal coating him.

He lets out a deep growl and I pick up his hands, bringing them up to massage my breasts as I dry fuck, or should I say very fucking wet fuck, his dick. Using my hand to grab onto his length, I run the head if his cock between my folds.

He hisses, the growl building in his throat. "Fuck. Mollie, you can't cock tease me like that," His eyes roll back as I continue the swirling grind of his cock around my entrance, dipping the head in slightly. "I fucking need to be inside you. Baby. Fuuuck!" He shouts, his restraint borderline none existent.

"So, be inside me, Max," I say, my voice seductive but convictive, dipping the tip of his cock inside my sex, edging him slowly.

His eyes blaze. "Don't fucking tease me, Mollie. Don't say what you don't mean, when I need you so fucking badly." He begs, his cock is pulsing as I rotate it along my arousal.

"I'm not fucking teasing," I whisper into his ear as I line him at my entrance and sit myself down, sinking him deep inside my walls.

Moans leave both of our lips, my head tipping back as the sensation hits me and I start to bounce on his cock, the wetness sounding all around us as I slide him to the tip of my sex, before thrusting him back deep inside me.

Max lets out a fierce, deep grunt as he picks me up from the chair to a standing position, his cock still buried deep inside me.

"Fuck. We need to take this where I can fucking show your pussy who fucking owns it," he states as he rounds the ice mountain and takes us through the door, the cold outside hitting me like a freight train, but Max notices as he grabs my dressing gown with one hand and slumps this across my shoulders, covering my nakedness and taking the edge off the cold.

He carries me to the private lift that takes us straight to the penthouse. We enter and he glides his keycard across the access button and presses the button for the pent.

Pushing me into the corner, he rests my ass on the hand rail while he plants kisses all along my neck to my mouth, his cock still inside me, as he rocks me slowly along his shaft. His tongue fills my mouth as we continue to fuck slowly while the lift rides up.

The lift beeps and he turns us together, our mouths staying connected as he strides our almost naked bodies across the living room, neither of us taking any notice to if anyone else is around, lost in this moment together.

Once in our bedroom, our kissing intensifies. He walks me back and rests my back against the floor to ceiling windows, tilting my knees higher up, so his cock angles deeper inside me, before slowly starting to fuck me, hard, deep thrusts into me as I'm pressed against the window.

The thrill of knowing how exposed we are, excites me beyond measures, whilst being so fucking high up that in reality no one can see us. My breasts bounce with his slow, deep thrusts as my climax begins to build again.

"I love you, Mollie." He whispers into my ear. "It's always been you. Don't ever forget that. Everything I do is for you, the good and the bad, don't ever forget," He continues as he buries his cock deep inside me.

"I love you too, Max," I say, slightly hesitant trying to take in his words, but lust and passion take over me and I need more of him.

"Max, I need you to own me. I need you to lay me down and fuck me, hard." I demand as I pant.

He picks me up off the window and carries me over to the bed, his cock still firmly routed deep inside me. As we stand at the foot of the bed. He removes himself from inside my sex and places me down on the bed, the emptiness making me feel lost.

I lie back on the bed, my whole body on display as he walks around. He gathers a pillow, placing this underneath my ass, as he kneels at my sex, picking up my legs and resting these on his shoulders, he lines himself up.

"Fuck. You are incredible." He moans out as his eyes devour my body. "Are you ready for me?" He asks, rubbing his head all over my slick sex as he glides his cock through my folds.

"Yes," I moan out, as he slams home. He fucks me, hard and deep as my orgasm builds. Bringing his mouth to my nipple, my leg still on his shoulder, intensifying how deep he is as my legs start to tremble.

"Fuck, Max! I'm going to come. Ah, fuck!" I gasp, my sex pulses, the sensation fills me as my walls slam down, coming hot and hard, heat rising as my orgasm floods out all over him. The tightness of my insides clamping down on his dick, milking every ounce of him as he comes undone with me. He continues to pump me his pace slowing as his own release fills me up, my walls feeling every throb of his hard cock as it spills inside me.

He lays down beside me, releasing my leg as we lie next to each other. I can feel both of our hearts pounding, our breathing is laboured. Running my hands through his hair, I smile at him just as a smile tugs at his lips.

"You really are my favourite human, Mollie Rutter." He says before pulling me into his chest and covering us both up with the duvet. Our bodies so exhausted that we almost instantly fall into a deep sleep.

****

We ordered room service for the Sunday evening, opting to remain in the room for the night. After our afternoon shag fest, I definitely feel like a cosy night with Max is all I need to finish the weekend away.

Sally hasn't spoken to me since I yelled at her earlier. I've seen her slumping around the penthouse during the evening, but her Gina and Sara all opted to go out again tonight. Gina begged me to go out with them too but I just wasn't up for pretending everything is okay with Sal. It wasn't my finest moment shouting at her and letting all of my feelings out, but what I said was very real. If I'm honest I'm finding it hard to have regrets for what I said.

The afternoon and evening with Max has been amazing. We have laughed and watched a couple of films whilst cozied up in bed, so I'm definitely feeling content. Max is fast asleep but I'm struggling to sleep after our post-sex nap time earlier. It's now 1:00am at the current and Sally, Gina and Sara are still out. I consider texting them and seeing where they've got to but decide I can't be bothered getting myself ready for a night out in Vegas at this ungodly hour. I decide to check with reception whether I can head to the spa downstairs for a swim.

I speak to the concierge on the front desk who stated the spa is not open for access to the guests but with me being in the Penthouse they were happy to make an exception. I smile and gather my swimwear and towel, writing a note for Max before leaving him in his slumber. As I exit my bedroom and catch Gray sat in the living room area, a whiskey in his hand.

"Where are you going?" He asks, his voice calm but a little slurry, so I know he's had a few whiskey's.

"I'm just going to the spa, for a swim." I say, a little sheepish knowing I've yelled at his new 'wife' today.

Fuck. I don't think I'll ever get used to that.

"It's deeper than you realise, Mollie, you know, me and Sally. It isn't what you think, but it's not the time to go into that now. Go and swim. I'll be coming to check on you if you're not back in an hour." He says, before standing and heading over to the liquor cabinet to top his whiskey up. I decide not to press for more information from him since he's already half cut and head to the penthouse lift down to the spa.

Once changed into my swim wear, I sink into the pool. The water is cool but refreshing. I spend some time doing laps in the pool. I've always enjoyed a swim, so I make a mental note to look into local pools when I get back to NYC.

Perching myself on the side of the pool I reach over for my phone. I hit the socials and see some posts from the girls doing shots. They look like they've had a great night out and a little regret stirs inside me. I need to make things right with Sally, sooner rather than later.

I continue scrolling just as something catches my eye. My gaze shoots up into the corner of the large pool area, certain I've seen something move. I zone my eyes in, trying to make out anything but I can't be certain it is anything. My heart rate has instantly peaked and I have to focus hard to maintain my breathing.

It's just in your head Mollie. Calm the fuck down. Placing my phone back down on the side, I push up on my arms and spin myself to sit on the side of the pool. I start tapping my fingers on the side of the pool to settle myself down, just as I shoot my head up a second time, I definitely saw someone this time. I have no doubt about it.

"Who is there?" I demand, trying to keep my voice steady and seem like I'm not completely losing my shit inside. "Max, is that you? This isn't funny," I say sharply.

No one answers and I know it definitely can't be someone I know. They wouldn't do this to me.

"If you're so fucking hard show yourself." I demand, while gathering my belongings. Looking around me at all points. I note the lift access on my left hand side and decide I need to make a break for it. I startle at a noise to the right of me which gains my attention.

Fuck.

I start walking backwards, the room having a dark ambiance already making my vision difficult. I see a figure in the far right corner as I walk backwards. Zoning my eyes in on the area, I make out the details of a hooded figure standing in the corner.

Fuck.

No fucking way.

Panic rises and I think I could be sick. I back myself up keeping the figure in my sights but also trying to see if this person is alone or if I can make out any others.

If they know I'm trying to leave, they'll definitely grab me quick, so I decide to elicit conversation to who ever is out there.

"Did Melvin send you to collect me? Could that asshole not come and find me himself?" I let out a snigger, building my walls to make me seem braver than I feel.

I reach the lift wall and press the button. The lift pings as the doors spring open.

"Do me a favour and pass this message on for me," I take a step back into the lift, "tell him I told him to go fuck himself," I swipe my keycard and push the button for the penthouse just as the figure starts to run towards me.

Fuck!

The doors start to close as I see him approach.

Fuck! Fuck! Fuck!

Come on, hurry up and shut!

# Chapter 24

## Present Day

The lift pings open in to the penthouse suite and I burst out of the doors. Gray is still sat in the living area as I scramble, dropping my items all across the floor before I plummet down in a heap myself, scrambling backwards and away from the lift.

"Fuck! Mollie, what the fuck has happened?" Gray shouts as he jumps up from the chairs he's been sat in all night.

"There was someone there, in the spa. A hooded person, man, figure!" I blurt out as I collapse on the floor and watch intensely making sure the lift doors close.

"What? What do you mean there was a hooded man there?" Gray shouts the question at me.

"I mean, I saw someone. I heard them first and I thought I was just being stupid but I definitely saw them moving. And then when the lift opened and I stepped in they started running towards me. I thought they were going to get in the lift before the door could shut." I say, my breaths laboured and I'm panting, the panic attack edging closer.

Max exits the bedroom in a rush, he must have heard my frantic voice. "Mollie! What's happened? Are you okay?"

Just in that moment the lift next to the one I've just appeared out of pings open, as Sally, Gina and Sara appear from the main lobby, their laughter filling the room for a brief moment before their faces fall at the sight of me in my bikini, sprawled across the living room floor. Gina scurries over to me at the same time Max reaches me, the pair of them tending to me.

"Mollie," Gray's voice asserts "You need to tell me more. We need to go to the security room. This is not okay!"

"I don't know more than what I've told you! The receptionist told me the spa isn't available to anyone at this time of night but they allow exceptions for penthouse guests." I reply, "I was swimming and they were just there."

"Who was where?" Gina asks me as she strokes my back. At this point everyone is in the living room questioning me about the events.

"I saw a hooded figure," I say, my voice shakes and my breath labours slightly again.

"Are you sure that's what you saw? Have you been drinking tonight?" Sally asks and my face falls.

"Don't patronise me like I'm fucking crazy or question if I've been drinking and hallucinating. I know what I saw." The anger rising in my voice while I respond to her. All the guilt suddenly leaving me for the argument we've gotten ourselves into.

Who the fuck does she think she is questioning what I saw?

"Get dressed, Mollie, we're going to speak to reception and asking to see the security footage. I want answers to how someone has been allowed to get into an area for just the penthouse." Gray demands as he stands from his chair, suddenly seeming like the alcohol he's consumed has had no affect on his behaviours. Max helps me to my feet as him and Gina escort me to my room. Sally stands there for a moment before taking herself off to her own room. Things between us have never been like this before and it adds to my worry inside.

We head down to the hotel lobby to speak to reception and hopefully we can get to the bottom of what has just happened to me. Gray, Max and Joey all accompany me downstairs while Gina tucked herself into bed, a little too drunk for all this seriousness.

The receptionists are really accommodating, and we head into the security room with the night manager after I explain what has happened to me. They are more than apologetic, stating they do not understand how someone other than penthouse access could have gotten into the Spa.

Once we're seated in the security room, the officer starts to look through the footage of the pool area of the spa. I see myself swimming and tell them to stop as we start to watch me leaning out of the pool. My heart is racing at the thought of reliving this moment as you see me look up and start to search around the room.

"Is there any sound?" I ask so we can hear anything I was listening for. The guy nods and shows me how to turn the volume up. You can hear my voice as I question the sounds I can hear. But there doesn't seem to be any other sounds picked up on the speaker. The video continues and you see me lock eyes on something in the corner.

"Is there a camera that shows the angle I am looking at?" I ask and the security officer pans out to 4 separate camera angle choices. I click the option that shows my back, knowing that will show them what I am looking at.

But there is nothing apparent on the camera.

I point and say, "He's there I know he is, zoom in." My voice a little frantic as we watch me panicking and scurrying into the lift. Another camera angle showing the lift, but there's nothing there. No one is making any noise other than me screaming.

There is nobody on the video.

What the fuck.

****

The rest of the night was spent discussing my mental capacity when we arrived back into the penthouse at 4:00am. Gray spent his time lecturing me about the need for me to see Dr Rene, which he is right about and I had already made this decision, but now he's suggested it I just want to avoid and refuse. We had a couple of hours sleep before needing to get ourselves up to catch our flight back to NYC.

The nerves were still swirling inside me as we made our way through the airport terminal at Las Vegas airport but I felt much better than I had leaving NYC. It could be the fact we're heading home to familiar turf, but I think deep down I just cannot wait to leave this trip behind. So much has happened in just this one weekend, I don't really know where we all go from here.

We all stride off the plane and straight through customs as we land back in NYC. Max and I walk together, his arm draped across my shoulder as we pull our bags along. I am glad that I did the trip, it gave me some well needed confidence to leave my familiarities again.

We reach the town car and all climb in. The ride home is silent, just as it has been since yesterday morning. Sally and Gray are sat on opposite sides of the car, not even making eye contact, so I'm guessing there's definitely trouble in paradise.

Sara changed her flight and decided to re-route back to NYC with us. Not sure why, but it gives us some time to chat I guess before she goes away again for a long period of time. I'm not sure how I feel about parting ways without fixing all this tension between our group.

The town car drops us each at our homes, ending with our little cul-de-sac last. The five of us pile out the car, grabbing our bags. Sally shoots straight off into her house with Sara following closely, while Gina brings me in for a hug.

"I'll speak to her. You were right yesterday, just wrong in how you delivered it, girl. But you know that," She says, squeezing me tight.

I nod, I know what I said was a bit much but everything just got on top of me. Max takes my bag and heads into the house as I follow behind him. We immediately get to unpacking and I know Max can sense the tension in me. Gliding over he starts to rub my shoulders and back in circular motions. It feels incredible.

"Thank you." I say, turning to give him a small smile. He leans in, his hand reaching to tilt my chin up towards him. His soft lips meet mine, as he presses a deep kiss into me. I melt towards him, leaning into the kiss as our lips move in sync with each other. I feel his tongue slip along my lip to nudge its way through and heat pools inside me. Deepening the kiss, Max hoists me into his arms, as I wrap my legs around him, our tongues tangling as the passion between us builds.

Max heads towards the ensuite, balancing me in his arms as we mouth fuck, our tongues exploring each other tentatively. I nip on his lip and a growl leaves Max, as a smile tugs at mine.

"We're going to get in the shower to freshen up, but whilst there Mollie, you can be certain I'm going to bury my dick deep inside you." He rasps towards me. I feel my sex pulse in response, the tense feeling coiling inside me, as a small moan leaves my lips.

Once in the bathroom, he places me down on the vanity unit. Tugging on my t-shirt, pulling this over my head and removes my bra. My breasts bounce with the speed he is undressing me, just as he slides down my pants and underwear, exposing my slick wet heat. He picks up my feet and places them on the vanity unit, my knees bent tight. Removing his t-shirt and pants, his hard cock pulsing with need as his eyes devour me. I sit on the vanity, so exposed with my legs spread wide, my sex on full display to him as I feel my wetness pooling.

"You're glistening for me, Mollie." Max growls as he drops to his knees, right in front of my sex. I feel my muscles tense tight in anticipation for him, in any way he'll give it to me. His calloused fingers run down my sex, circling my entrance before he leans in and takes my clit into his mouth. His tongue circles my slit as he sucks and swirls around it. I lean back resting my back on the mirror as his mouth fucks my sex. His hand still circling my entrance, he slips one finger in, slow and sensual he glides through my slits, his mouth continuing to devour my clit.

His pace picks up as he places a second finger inside me. My breaths become pants, as my legs fall open wider, needing more of him. He stands, the loss of contact on my clit enticing a small wimpier from me as Max lets out a chuckle.

"Patience, Mollie," his sultry voice purrs, his mouth covered in the glisten of my arousal. He dips down, sucking in my nipple as his hand pumps me deep into my sex. Moving up to my mouth and I devour him, the taste of my arousal coating his skin, my tongue exploring his lips, taking in the taste of myself.

Max steps back, opening the drawer of the vanity where I keep my sex toys, I eye him suspiciously.

"Lucky guess," he smiles up at me, with a sly wink and I know he's definitely pre-planned this. Reaching in pulls my butt plug vibrator out. His eyebrows raise as he turns to me "I think we need to have some extra fun this time, Mollie," his deep voice purrs to me as my sex clenches in response.

Fuck yes!

Lining the toy on his palm, alongside his fingers he pushes them deep into my sex together. The intrusion only heightening the tension coiling inside me further. Holding the toy in place inside of me he slides out his fingers, gliding them down to my ass, repeating the motions to ensure my arousal has coated me. My breathy pants becoming deeper as the tension fills me and the need to be filled excites me.

Max runs his thumb along my clit as he swirls the toy inside my sex, before taking the plug out and directing it down to the entrance of my ass, rubbing my clit he slowly starts to push the toy in.

"Relax Mollie baby," he purrs and I let out of breath in response. The tightness fighting against the push from Max. He continues to work my clit and dips his hand deep into my sex, curling his fingers as he works for me to relax. My body responds to him as the plug is fully inserted, Max presses the on button to entice the vibrations.

Fuck. The feeling is incredible, I feel my sex throbbing in response and I know I could come from this alone.

"Patience Mollie, don't come without me." Max says, his voice a command as I pant. He takes his cock in his hands, the pre-come beading at the tip as he circles this around his head.

"Are you ready to take us both baby?" He says as he leans in close and nibbles on my ear.

"Yes, fuck yes! I need you to fuck me, Max"

A deep chuckle leaves his lips as he lines himself up at my sleek sex, the arousal pooling more now than before. He runs his head through my sex, before pushing his cock deep into me. I moan loud as the sensations overtake me, he continues to pump me slow and deep before leaning down and picking me up. He walks us towards the shower, his dick still deep inside me as the vibrator in my ass buzzes. Stepping into the shower he turns on the stream of water as he leans my back against the wall. I gasp at the cold contact of the wall, but that is short lived as Max starts to pump his cock inside me, his rhythm still low, but deep and punishing. My breathing is laboured as the pleasure fills me.

"I need you faster, Max. I need you to fuck me deep and fast," I manage to breath out.

Max reaches around to my ass, clicking the vibrator up two settings so the speed is more intense. A gasps leaves me as the vibrations fill me and my sex clamps around his length in response.

"Are you ready baby?" He asks, kissing my lips as the water coats out bodies. I nod a response, not sure I have any words left at this point and Max adjusts his arms, hooking them under my knees to bring them up higher and elicits a deeper angle inside me. He starts pumping me faster, the angle deep and fucking incredible as he fucks. The sound of sex filling the echo of the shower as a moan escapes me every pump he gives, his rhythm, deep and punishing. Tingles fill my sex as I feel myself on the edge of my climax.

"I'm going to come, Max," I wail out, my climax hitting me like a freight train, my walls clamp down on his cock deep inside me as he continues to pump me hard. A growl escapes him as his pace quickens even more, chasing his own release. Grunting I can feel the telltale pulses of his cock spilling inside me. His rhythm slows as he enjoys his climax.

He reaches around me, "Relax again for me baby," he says as he pulls out the vibrator, turning this off and tossing it to the side. Releasing my legs one at a time and placing on the floor, he tilts my head up, leaning his arm on the wall beside my head.

"I fucking love you, Mollie." He says before learning and placing a deep kiss on my lips and finishing with "and I love fucking you".

We both laugh at his cheesiness and continue to shower ourselves together. We finally finish up and get ourselves out, dressed and dry. Max continues to be tentative, scattering me with kisses as we unpack our cases. A little into the afternoon, I decide to drop the group a message to get this shit sorted sooner rather than later.

**Mollie -** Hi all, can we meet at Reggies 6:00pm? We need to fix all of this shit.

For a while no one messages back and worry starts to overtake me as I feel my whole support network is falling apart. I remember making a mental 'note to self' for me to reach out to Aria when I got home and book myself in with her so I shoot an email over to her.

*Hi Aria (Dr Rene),*

*It's Mollie Rutter from a few years back. I was just wondering if there was a possibility I could book a session or two with you? There is a lot going on right now and I just need some reassurance and support from a familiar face.*

*Let me know.*

*Kind Regards*

*Mollie.*

I snuggle down into Max as we lay on the sofa together, feeling like a little weight has been lifted now I've make contact with Dr Rene.

My phone pings and I grab it quickly to see who has messaged. Disappointment instantly fills me when I see it's no one I expect but in fact it's Rian.

**Rian -** Hope you enjoyed your trip. I have some business I'd like to schedule so drop me a line this week so we can discuss.

"Why is he messaging you still?" Max says, I can hear the jealously spiked with anger in his tone, although he's making a conscious effort not to lose his shit.

"I have no idea. I keep ignoring him but he just continues. It's hard for me, having to work with him on some contracts," I reply honestly.

"Hmm, I don't like him Mollie. He really creeps me out," he says, "why wouldn't he just take the hint and move on? Why is he still trying? It's weird Mollie." He reinforces.

It is weird. I do agree with him on that.

My phone pings again and I glance over to it spotting Sally's name on the front.

**Sally -** Okay, I agree. We all need to talk. See you later.

The relief I feel is incredible. I turn to Max and see him smiling having read the message over my shoulder.

****

The whole group arrive at Reggies at 6:00pm sharp. We sit down in our usual booth, the fit snug with the two extras added to the group but we make it work.

We all grab some drinks and order food before sitting in silence for a beat.

"I'll start should I?" I say to break the tension. Gina smiles at me and gives me a thumbs up, encouraging me to go on.

"I shouldn't have said everything I wanted to say, the way that I did." I begin, "But I don't plan on sitting here and apologising for the whole situation because what I did say was raw but truthful." My eyes glance down as my fingers wring together on my lap.

Max takes my hand and gives it a squeeze, distracting me for a beat. My eyes glide up to meet his and a smile overcomes my features as I meet his dimples smile gazing back at me.

"I think, this weekend should have been incredible. It should have symbolised a massive milestone for me, but instead, the night was stolen with negativity towards me and Max, our choices, which should have just been put aside for at least one night." I continue, and I notice Sally face fall as she looks down.

"I agree." Gina starts. "Sally, this weekend wasn't for you to voice your opinions on Max. You've already made it clear a multitude of times. Mollie is well aware of your feelings about him. It wasn't the time for you to hound down." She continues, giving me a small smile in reassurance, which I reciprocate. "I don't know whether it was you feeling like you had more of a voice, with Sara being in agreement with you or what, but you were out of line this weekend. Period," her tone is harsh, which takes me aback somewhat at how defensive she is being for me, although I am definitely grateful.

"I'm sorry Mollie. I'm just struggling to see you put yourself in a situation with someone that stripped you down so bare, you lost yourself." Sally begins, reaching over the table, holding her hand out for me to put mine in hers.

I hesitate, not really wanting to just yet, but offering her a small smile as my head tilts. She lets out a breath.

"My intentions are whole, Mollie. And I am sorry Max but I just don't fully trust you. I have watched her soul get crushed the last few months, hell even years, while you've been god knows fucking where, turning up and treating her like shit as and when you want to. It's been hard, you know?" She directs her voice towards Max now.

For a moment there is silence before Max takes his eyes away from me and meets Sally's gaze.

"I know I've been a shitty person over the last year and I'm not about to sit here and explain my emotional state to you guys, but I have spoke to Mollie about everything. She is the only person that matters in this. I have laid my soul bare for her and she has chosen to listen and give me a chance." Max says, his voice trembling slightly, the struggle to open himself to his vulnerabilities visible in his demeanour.

"And I appreciate you so much Sally. You are the fire that keeps my girl warm while I've not been here. You keep her safe from the chaos. You are a true best friend." He leans back as he compliments her and I see her face soften towards him, taking in his words. "But you have to let her fly sometimes, Sally. I've made my intentions clear and I don't plan on losing her just yet."

She appears to back down slightly and starts to nod in agreement "Fine. I'll back off a little. But you are far from forgiven Maxwell." She calls him by his full name and it triggers us all into a laughter.

"Right, now that shits over with," Gina interjects, pointing her fingers between Sally and Gray, "How the fuck did you two end up fucking married?"

The pair of them glance towards each other and at the same time say, "That is not a conversation for tonight." Before Sally calls the waiter over and Gray sparks up a new conversation with the lads. I look towards Gina as we exchange a curious gaze together. We will get to the bottom of this one day.

The night flows on, the drinks are heady and our group is back to being happy and care free. As the night draws to a close, we all start to wrap up our final drinks.

"So Sara, when are you heading back?" I ask, nonchalantly.

"I have a red eye flight in a few hours." She smiles sweetly at me. "I've been meaning to tell you guys, I've based myself permanently in London for a while. I've been putting it off, you know, with everything that happened to you in London Mollie, but I am excited to have a new permanent place to stay for a while." She says, a smile spread wide across her face.

"No, don't be silly, that's amazing." I reassure her, feeling so happy for her. "Do you have any plans made for your birthday in December?" I ask Sara, her birthday is in the bridge between Christmas and new year.

"I know, I'm so busy at the moment so I'm not really sure when I'll find time to head back to NYC to see you guys. I thought I best share the news now while I can. It'll probably be in the new year now by the time I can get back here." Her mouth dips into a sad expression, as she tilts her head sideways slightly. "But we can celebrate then, we will definitely plan something."

We all agree and start to make our way out of the bar. Walking down the sidewalk to the nearest subway station for Sara to make her way to JFK. We give our kisses and hugs to Sara as she departs our group, and we head back over to Max who has parked outside Reggies. Sliding into Max's SUV with Gina and Sally, we make our way back to our homes.

"I have an idea for Sara's birthday." I announce as I turn and face Sally and Gina the back of the car "Why don't we plan a surprise visit to her in London?"

"London?" Max, Sally and Gina all say in unison, shock lining each and every one of their faces.

"Yes, in London," I deadpan, "I don't have to avoid the place just because it holds some shit memories for me. I am British after all." I say, my voice assertive, trying to get across my strength.

"That's a big step Mollie, like a real big step." Gina says, worry etching her face.

"How is it? What difference is it to being in the city right now? The organisation are clearly around NYC and I'm here. What difference would it make if I was in London. Hell, I know they were in fucking Vegas watching me anyway despite all of you thinking I'm fucking losing my mind." I say, sarcasm filling the car.

"I see your point. But it worries me Mollie. You're barely holding it together in NYC right now. I'm sorry to say it." Sally states and it's not entirely untrue despite the fact I don't want to hear it.

"I know, and I've contacted Dr Rene about it. But come on girls just consider it. The three of us, surprising her, she'll be so excited." I bounce in my seat, the excitement filling me.

"I'll think about it." Sally says as she side eyes Gina.

"Yes! That's all I'm asking." I say and turn back to face the front.

Max stays silent, his eyes strained in on the road as he refuses to make eye contact with me, which tells me he's not happy with my idea. I decide to leave him to simmer on it, not allowing him to swallow my good mood. Tonight has been a good night and I won't be torn down from my high.

We arrive back in the cul-de-sac and Max parks his SUV in my driveway. Giving the girls a quick hug we part ways and I head into the house. I find Max leaning on the kitchen island, his head slumped down in his hands. He still hasn't said a word to me since I suggested the trip to London to the girls, so I decide to raise the issue.

"What's your problem with the London trip?" I say directly.

"I don't have a problem," he answers back, his tone short and snappy.

"Well, can you tell that little slice of information to your face and attitude please? Because I don't think the memo reached them." I sass back at him. He's being such a fun sponge.

"I just don't think it's the best idea Mollie. You're struggling here in. NYC, you are borderline panic attacks on the daily and you want to put yourself in a position where you make yourself vulnerable. You barely managed to step foot on to the flight to Vegas, how on earth do you plan to survive getting on a plane to London," He blurts out like it's been caged up inside him, waiting to be unleashed.

"Ahh, so we do have a problem." I say, rolling my eyes and heading over to pour us both a lemonade.

"I don't have a problem. I worry about you, Mollie. I worry for your safety, for your mental state. I worry!" He says as his voice is slightly raised, accenting his words to put his point across.

My attitude softens slightly as I empathise with his worry. I walk over to him, placing his lemonade down on the kitchen counter and hug him from behind.

"And I appreciate your worry. But you need to take your own advise that you gave to Sally and let me fly."

He sighs "I just don't think I can get onboard with it Mollie. Not right now, maybe see Dr Rene and have some sessions, think on it for a while. Just give it time" he says and despite my disappointment, a smile overtakes my face knowing he's only concerned about me.

"Okay my love, I will see Dr Rene. I will think about everything very clearly before I make any crazy decisions." I say as I turn him towards me and plant a kiss on his lips.

His phone begins to ring and he pulls this out of his pocket glancing at the screen. I don't catch the name on the screen before he stands and announces he needs to take the call and exits the kitchen.

I decide to sit browsing the socials while I wait for him to finish his conversation. After a few minutes, I can hear the tone of his voice sharpening as he speaks in to the phone in the other room. Is he shouting? My attention peaks and I decide to edge closer to him to check if he is okay.

As I reach the door, I hear snippets of the conversation, only from Max's perspective, and I freeze to listen.

***"No, No you can't just fucking demand me back."***

***"I won't do it."***

***"Things have changed, I've changed. I've made up my mind and I pick to stay here with her."***

***"Because, I do, I've already fucked up enough because of all this shit you've had me doing"***

***"Fuck off"***

***"No, fuck off."***

***"I said no! I'll be back in service for my final stretch in a few weeks. Then I'm done sneaking around and lying about everything."***

***"Because I can't keep doing it. I don't want to."***

***"That's my final decision, I'll send in my letter of resignation when I next report for duty."***

A knock on the front door startles me and I drop the glass in my hand smashing it all over the floor. Max jumps at the interruption, swinging round in my direction as his gaze meets mine, caught red handed as I spy on him through the ajar door.

Fuck.

"I'm going. Bye" Max presses the red button and strides to the door, as I turn and make my way to the front door to answer whoever has knocked.

"Mollie, what happened? Were you spying on me?" Max asks as I reach the door.

"No, I err, I came to bring your lemonade and then there was a knock at the door and it startled me. I wasn't listening. Well, I was but I didn't hear much. Some, but not much," I turn and prise the door open.

No one is stood there. I step out looking around either side and find myself stepping on an item that's been placed on the door mat.

I lean down picking it up and turning it over.

"Have you ordered me something?"

"Babe, it's 1:00am, there's no delivery drivers out and about now." Max sniggers as he responds to me.

I turn over the small box, a tag dangling off it. Picking it up, I read the inscription.

**Mollie,**
**A small peace offering,**
**To warm your inner Brit.**
**I hope you speak to me again soon.**
**Rian.**

"It's from Rian." I gasp.

"Rian? Is delivering you a parcel, to your house at 1:00am?" Max scoffs, his face laced with confusion.

"I guess so, yeah." I shrug, not really knowing what to say.

I open the box and inside is a Links London charm bracelet with a number of charms already positioned.

"Why the fuck is he buying you jewellery?" Max snaps, I can hear the anger palpable in his voice.

"I don't know." I say, my mind a whirl of thoughts.

"Were you guys something? Have you slept with him?" Max fires questions at me and panic fills his expressions.

"No! Oh god no, Max. Fuck! Honestly it was just some harmless flirting occasionally."

"So why the fuck is he hand delivering items to your house in the dead of the night? How the fuck does he know where you live?" Max shouts at me.

And it hits me.

How does he know where I live?

I turn to Max, my expression haunted as I repeat Max's words back to him.

"How does he know where I live?"

# Chapter 25

## Present Day

It's Friday and the last week has been chaos. After receiving the gift in the dead of the night on Monday, Max has been working with Gray to look into Rian or Riley Austin, whatever his name is. Gray asked me if I wanted to file for a restraining order but I have to work with this guy, he's my biggest fucking client and as harsh as it sounds, I need to replace that source of income before I cut off my hand to spite my face.

But honestly, I think they're all being a little dramatic about everything. Since what happened to me happened, everyone is on full alert if someone strange looms in my path.

Thanks Giving is on Thursday next week which is exciting, as everyone is heading to my house for our usual Thanks Giving celebrations. This is one of my favourite holidays, being British we didn't celebrate this holiday until we moved here to New York over six years ago but I like to remind myself of what we have to be thankful for. It's humbling, especially in times like current when there are constant reminders around me of the danger I was put in and what I survived from.

I have a session with Dr Rene booked next Monday which I am looking forward to despite the worry inside me about what she might say. It's definitely over due and I can't wait to see her if I'm honest. I'm wrapping up the day, as 5:00pm nears on Friday afternoon. Meryl knocks on my office door and I greet her with a warm smile.

"Ma'am, I'm just about to leave, can I get you anything before I go?" She asks, so polite as always.

"It's Mollie," I remind her, "but no dear, I'm all sorted thank you. Have you got anything good planned for your weekend?" I ask quickly to fain a little interest in her life.

"Ah, I like to knit now I'm an elder, so just spending my time with the grandchildren and knitting some jumpers."

"Oh well that sounds lovely, enjoy yourself and I'll see you Monday."

She gives a small wave and departs my office.

I sit back and spin on my chair to face the windows. I've been thinking a lot about Felix this week. Despite only knowing him briefly when we met travelling, we grew a strong bond and I feel like I'm missing him this week. He would have been much less serious about the entire situation with Rian and my wishes to go to London. He would have made it laughable and encouraged me to enjoy myself, instead of things being such a serious topic. A smile crosses my lips and I decide I'll take a moment to visit his memorial stone this weekend.

"Girl, are you finished?" Gina calls to me from my office door.

"Yep, let's get out of here." I stand up and round my desk, heading out of the office for the week.

The weekend begins as Max and I wake up and get ourselves ready to head out. It's a cold November morning today in New York, the cloud cover is thick and white which indicates the potential for snow fall.

"We need to head to the farmers market and pick up the bits for Thanks Giving this week." I say as I butter my toast, "I've also ordered a turkey which needs to be picked up today." I continue with my speech. Max seems lost in his phone and I shake my head.

"Earth to Max! Come on, pay attention."

"I'm sorry babe. Just got a few messages flying through. The squad are hounding me about my return." He says, a sigh leaving his lips as he truly looks defeated.

"Hey, it's okay if you have to go back for a bit. I understand that you took a spontaneous leave of absence for this." I turn to face him as I bite down on my toast. He stands and starts stalking his way towards me, wrapping his arms around my waist and hoisting me onto the kitchen counter while he positions himself between my legs.

"No, I'm not going back until I said I was going to be back. I have three more weeks of me and you to get under my belt before I start my last stint." He grabs a sneaky bite of my toast as he finishes his sentence.

"Hey! That's mine!" I grumble playfully. I love mornings like this with him, feeling so free and so lost in the moments of lust and love. It's incredible.

"Would you mind if we stop by Felix's grave this morning?" I ask, a little sheepish. Max didn't know Felix as he was killed just as I was taken by the organisation, so sometimes it feels a bit of a tender subject asking him to come and visit some random guys grave with me. But he never moans about it.

"Sure, whatever makes you happy." He says as he takes the last swig of his coffee. "Are you ready to go?" He says as he picks his keys off the countertop.

"Sure," I say and we wrap up warm before exiting the house and jump into his SUV.

We reach the cemetery and I slide out of the car. We stopped at a small florist and picked up some flowers to lay at his headstone. Max steps out of the car with me, although he allows me space, staying a good 20 foot away from the grave.

"Hey Felix," I say, as I kneel down and place the flowers against the head stone. "It's been a while, I'm sorry I've not had chance to visit. Life is chaotic. I mean, you're probably up there watching me and all my crazy life choices right now. Stop judging me. And if you are watching, you probably know that they're back." I play with the edges of my coat trying to stop myself from wringing my fingers. I sit at the foot of his grave, it's a little unkept, clear that no one has visited him, possibly since I last did.

When the police contacted us to say that no one had recovered his body as it appeared he had no family, we only felt it was fitting that we arranged for him to be buried close by to us, so at least there would be someone there to visit him.

I spend some time pulling up the weeds and arranging the flowers I have just purchased, adding these to his grave to make the place look tidy. Then I sit for an hour, chatting to him and telling him the details of all the crazy things in my life.

Max remains stood back, keeping a watchful eye on me but never interrupting or asking if I was done. He just waited patiently for me to be done.

After an hour I stand, feeling a little more free now I've laid all the chaos out to Felix. But I always feel a deep sorrow that he lost his life in the process of me being taken. Dr Rene would be disappointed with me for saying that as we spent so long discussing how everything that happened to me was not for me to be blamed for, but the innate feeling remains.

We spend the rest of the afternoon picking up the turkey for thanks giving, along with the vegetables and trimmings. I decide to pick up a few decoration pieces to make my home look incredible.

As Sunday rolls around, we plan on starting the decorations and prepping some of the meal. The week is short in work and I have a session with Dr Rene tomorrow, which I'm both excited for and also terrified about. It feels like such a necessary next step, but also like a massive step back.

My phone buzzes and Max picks this up off the counter as I stand on the ladder hanging decorations from the ceiling.

"It's the police." He says as he holds it out for me to take.

"The police?" worry laces my voice as I take hold of the phone from Max. "Hello?" I say, the shake in my voice clear.

"Mollie, it's detective Russ Palmer from the NY police department," He begins, his voice broad New York American, snappy and decisive.

"Good Morning, What can I do for you?" I ask, worry filling about what they could say or tell me. Or worse, ask me.

"I know we spoke recently about you potentially helping us, and well, I'm here to ask if you'd reconsider your original answer around this?" He begins, trepidation apparent in his voice, he's definitely unsure on how I'm going to take his request. "Of course, I don't want to push you. But we really could use the help of someone who has been subjected to it previously. Someone who knows what we are dealing with."

Silence rings through the phone as I contemplate what it is that they are asking of me. My head and heart are completely torn between the decision to help or to keep myself as safe and as far away from this as possible.

"If you're still there," Detective Palmer begins and I realise I've not said anything for at least 2 minutes. "I didn't want to say this because I wanted you to make the decisions on your own merit Mollie, but," He pauses again and the suspense is choking me out.

"Fucking spit it out, Palmer" I say, the words bursting from my lips.

Shit.

Did I just swear at a police officer?

Max's face is a picture as he stares at me from across the room, waiting in suspense himself.

"The girls you trafficked into the organisation, Morgan and Verity," he begins.

Wow. Way to make a girl feel like shit.

"Yes, what about them? Are they okay?"

"They're okay. But they've received letters. Like you did, to their home. It's shaken them a little."

Why haven't they reached out to me?

Emotion overcomes me that I've spent my time away from them, while they've spent their time worried and scared.

"They've been told that they're coming for them. You know, the organisation. We've just asked them if they want to be taken into protective custody, but they don't think they're ready to just yet." I sigh as my heart is pulled towards helping my friends.

"Okay, fine. I'll help." I agree, with my heart in my mouth. I look at Max as his gaze turns sympathetic with what looks like a mixture of disappointment and fear, but maybe I'm confusing it. The call ends with me agreeing to meet with them the following day and I sit on the sofa with Max.

"So, you're helping the police now?" He jumps straight onto topic.

"They've targeting Morgan and Verity. I don't know, I just feel like I have to help. I can't just sit back."

"I know, Mollie. I just worry about you. It's not long before I head back on the last tour and my head is all over the show worrying about leaving you here." He grabs my hand and gives this a squeeze, "But you're brave Mollie. You're brave to help," he reassures me, taking me into his arms and squeezing me tight. "Come on, let's get ourselves in bed, it's a busy day for you tomorrow."

Monday rolls around after a poor nights sleep thinking and overthinking, I've spent the morning getting myself up early after I tossed over for the hundredth time that night and headed into the office early. The morning has been fairly smooth, with me spending time picking up my emails before my appointment with Dr Rene at 11:00am. I glance at the clock which reads 10:55am and decide I should make my way to her office.

Taking the lift to the floor below mine I step out in front of Dr Rene's door. Pressing the buzzer and not a moment later the door swings open, Florence stands with a broad smile on her face.

"Mollie!" She says excitedly. "I've been looking forward to seeing you. Which is silly really since we only work a floor apart, I could see you anytime really," She laughs.

"Florence, it's really good to see you" The smile that covers my face is the most genuine smile I've had in a long time.

I walk into the reception area, striding past Florence and take in the surrounds of the room. They haven't changed in all the years I've not been here.

I admire the view from the floor length windows, although not as good as my office windows on the floor above but the sole inspiration for my office location. They always did make me feel settled and calm. It still does to this day, and is a technique I frequent in practicing. Dr Rene's door opens and her smile widens.

"Mollie," She approaches me and brings me in for a hug.

"Aria," I say, bringing my arms around her shoulders to meet her embrace.

"I thought I might hear from you when I saw all the news about the Organisation in NYC," she says, her face full of sorrow for me.

"Yeah. It's not been a great time for me," I say, attempting a smile but my lip quivers in sorrow. I can feel myself losing emotional control and Dr Rene responds to me immediately, ushering me into her therapy room and closing the door.

I break down.

It's like someone opened the floodgates as tears cascade down my face, in uncontrollable streams.

I finally allow myself to feel, in the place that makes me feel the safest. And Dr Rene just lets me.

I sit and sob for a total of 15 minutes before I feel my tears dry up and I gather my breath. I gather the strength to meet the gaze of Dr Rene, who in all her beauty has sat there and waited for me to pull myself together.

"You've been holding that in for a while, Mollie." Dr Rene finally says as my eyes make contact with hers.

I nod, words still none coherent.

"Have you not felt like you could truly let go?" She asks, and it seems more curious than accusing.

I shake my head no.

"Can you explore that with me?" She asks and I glance out of the windows to gather up some courage.

"Building my empire and being the girl who is funny, care free, and sassy makes it hard to show another side of myself, you know." I begin, my voice still hitching from the tears I've just shed. "I am the strong one. I am the one who holds us all together," I say, my voice squeaky and high pitched at this point as I fight back another batch of tears from raining. "Or I was. Before this, before everything I was the one who was so fucking care free and happy and…" I pause as I struggle to say the words, "…and trusting. I trusted everyone and everything," the tears roll down my cheeks again.

"Mollie, you are still all of those things. Nothing is stopping you from being those things but your own feelings," she says, her voice firm and commanding.

I hate it when she's fucking right.

"So, what other than the Organisation returning, has brought you back to see me?"

"I'm losing control again, a lot more, panic attacks are flooding me frequently. At one point I had a panic attack which resulted in me passing out. Luckily, I was at home but I couldn't stop it. I couldn't get control again."

"Do you need control Mollie? Or can you use the people you have build it into your network, to control it for you?" She begins, her head tilts at me, "Isn't that why we created your support network?" She asks.

They're all great questions that I just don't have the answers to so I sit there, considering the questions instead.

"Does something stop you from confiding in those people Mollie?"

"Yes," I whisper, the words leaving my lips before I even think about what I've admitted to.

"Why?" She asks, her voice firm.

I hesitate on my answer, drawing in breath on several occasions to give my answer but stopping before I release the words. Dr Rene just sits, waiting for me to catch up with the answer she already knows.

"Because it's been three years, since the end of therapy Aria. Three fucking years. And it's been six years since I was released from them. And it's been nearly eight years since I was taken. I shouldn't need them. I shouldn't need to depend on them. I should be able to manage my own fucking emotions myself. I am an adult." I burst out, my voice rushed and strained, needing to finish everything that I have to say.

"Can you honestly say that before the last few months, you've needed them?" She asks and the question startles me into thinking back over the last three years.

I frown. Trying to recall a time in the last three years that I've needed them frequently.

I can't.

"Other than the occasional nightmare, but even then, I usually deal with them myself." I admit as a little pressure seems to float away from me.

"Have you ever thought that if you just cried once in a while, to those you have built around you, that maybe you wouldn't build to the panic attack or get stuck inside intense nightmares?"

The question hits me like a bus. I have never even considered the option of just crying. Showing emotion equally sends me into panic as I expose my own vulnerabilities that way.

"People would be able to see my weaknesses," I say in almost a whisper.

"Only the people you choose to."

And that sentence feels like an entirety in itself. It wouldn't make me seem weak and vulnerable to anyone who didn't know who I truly was as a person.

Dr Rene smiles at me as she can see me piece together the answers in my mind and I meet her gaze with a warm smile.

"You felt better today when you let out your emotions by crying, and Mollie, by all means you're welcome to come and visit me and pay for your time with me if you want this safe space to cry in. But in reality, trust the people with you."

I nod, knowing very well it's such a stupid concept to pay over $100 to come here and cry once a week so I can pull my shit together.

"I think, I need to visit London." I say, my eyes drawn to the greenery outside the windows, a telltale that I'm anxious.

"What is it that's making you feel that way?"

"I think, I need closure." My eyes snap back to Dr Rene and she's nodding at me.

Fuck. I didn't think she would agree so easily.

"You agree with me?" My voice comes across more shocked than I meant it to.

"Yes, Mollie. I think you live in fear about travelling and living your life. I think you consistently feel like you're going to be taken. When in reality, it's unlikely to happen again. Nobody is that unlucky," her smile broadens and I join her in a laugh.

“Yeah, I guess.” I say, feeling more confident about my decision to visit London. “I haven’t decided if I should go alone or with friends yet, what do you think I should do?”

“I think you should learn to walk before you can run Mollie. Going to London is one thing. Going to London alone is stupid.” She says quite frankly and a laugh bursts from my lips.

“That’s true,” I agree with her, the laughter still escaping me.

“Thank you for today.” I smile at her, warmness filling me and I feel so much better after sitting here.

“It’s no problem Mollie, anytime.”

****

Thanks Giving flew by and I feel like we are back in work so quick after such a short break. It was amazing being with everyone, and for once there were no arguments or snide comments made. In fact, I feel like I saw a turn in Sally, like she’s really decided to give Max a chance.

Sitting in my office, I feel a big smile spread across my face as I stare out into the vast greenery. Deciding it’s time to glance at my emails, I spin on my chair and startle as I see Gina and Sally at the foot of my desk.

“Fucking hell, can you guys not announce your presence instead of creeping up on me?” I clutch my chest as my heart pounds.

“Sorry, we only just got here as you spun around. But we have news. And you’re not going to like it.” Gina says, her lips tugging down showing the uncertainty in her.

I sigh loudly, “Hit me with it, what’s happening?”

“Well, we have a day out scheduled today.” Sally begins, her face displaying her cheese grater smile again as if to try and persuade me to remain positive.

“Spit it out, Sally.”

"We have a team building day planned with Riley Austin," she burst out of her mouth before sinking into the chair in front of my desk.

My face falls. "How the fuck has that got into our diaries? I'm not going. I refuse."

"I put it in the diary." Gina says as me and Sally swivel our faces in disdain. "Don't fucking start, the pair of you. He threatened to pull his contract. We cannot stay afloat if he pulls the contract. People would have lost their jobs. That is more important than your stupid, ridiculous disagreement and avoidance technique Mollie." She says, her voice stern, as if she's telling me off.

In fact, I think she is telling me off.

I blink back at her. "And you," she points directly at Sally. "You are the enabler. You are the women that feeds into her ridiculousness." Her breathing is rapid, as me and Sally just stare blankly at her.

"What are we doing?" I deadpan as I try and keep the disgust off my face, unimpressed with the need to do this but understanding why we have to go through with the shit show.

"That's the spirit," Gina smiles as she pulls up the itinerary. "Firstly, we have a rage room booked, followed by Axe throwing and then ending on food and cocktails."

"He's got to be taking the piss." I say, "A fucking rage room? Is he trying to be funny? Because he's fucking not." I roll my eyes, the ferocity coaxing my tone.

"He is a little bit funny." Sally retorts as her and Gina smirk.

"You're a pair of assholes." I say as I stand and gather my shit. "What time do I need to be ready? I'm going to have to go home and get changed now."

"No need to worry, I packed you a change of clothes," Gina exclaims, her face proud as punch.

"When the fuck did you do that? When have you been in my house?"

"I asked Max for some gym or casual wear so we could do some work activities. He was happy to help." She shrugs like she's some kind of genius plan maker. She hands me a bag of my clothes and I take this from her with a forceful tug.

"I'll be ready in 5 minutes."

We arrive at the rage room centre in downtown Manhattan. Outside is Rian, Cilla and another guy we've never seen before. I can't quite see his face but he leaves and gets back into the car besides Rian.

"You made it." Rian says, the shock that we've actually turned up clear on his face.

"Well, you summoned us." I say, my annoyance every bit readable.

"Ah, Mollie, I have missed your sense of humour." He says, a broad smile across his face.

What sense of humour? No one is laughing you, creep. I roll my eyes and Sally nudges me with her elbow.

"Play nice." She mouths quietly between her smile.

"This actually is why I decided we should do a rage room." Rian announces, "You know, to let off the steam your harbouring against me."

My anger is borderline at boiling point now, but I school my expression, placing a smile on my face as I reply.

"So kind of you to consider that, let's get this show on the road." And I stride past Rian and Cilla, into the building.

We spend the next hour smashing items to pieces, and I have to say, it irritates me that I do feel so much better after the session.

"I can already see you're less tense, Mollie." Rian smiles as we start out of the doors and back onto the streets of New York.

I have nothing to say back to him.

"We have the address of the next activity, so we'll meet you there." Gina cuts in trying to keep the happy go lucky vibes rolling.

"You can jump in my car, my driver will be round in a moment." He turns to glance up the street and I scowl at Gina making sure she knows there's not a cat in hells chance I'll be sharing a fucking car with him.

"No need, we have our own car parked locally so best to keep it close. Thanks though, really appreciate the offer," Gina announces, already heading off in the opposite direction. I scurry to catch up and we start walking up the street together.

"Fucking hell, I can't deny I feel so much better after that" I say as I exhale. "But the tension between us all is killing me."

"It's something else that's for sure. He's so fucking brazen." Sally quips as we hale a cab. "I can't believe you just fucking lied about us having a car so we could escape for a minute," Her laugh radiates around us and we all join her giggling.

The afternoon continues to fly by and if I'm honest, it's not the worst experience I've gotten myself involved in. The bar Rian chose is a block away from the office. We enjoy some food and drinks and not all that bad in company either. As we start to make our way back to the office, I see Rian jogging to catch me up.

"Mollie please," he begs, I glance at Sally and Gina.

"Maybe just give him a minute of your time," Sally whispers, and Gina nods along in agreement with her. I sigh in defeat as they back off to join Cilla behind us.

"Are you ever going to forgive me, Mollie?" Rian asks quietly as he catches up alongside me.

I sigh, trying to think of the words to say without letting him know me any more than he already does.

"Rian, before you met me, there was a lot that happened to me." I begin, feeling that maybe I owe him just a snippet to help him understand, "A lot of trauma, that I won't be getting into, but trust is absolutely everything to me, because I don't often give it away." My eyes meet his and I can see his eyes telling a story of regret.

"I didn't mean for it to be like this Mollie."

We round the corner to an overwhelming amount of police presence outside an office building.

"That's our building," Sally says as she catches up alongside me and we start to jog up the stretch.

We walk into the lobby and find Gray, Joey and Max all talking to the police officers.

"What's happening?" I ask as they all startle and immediate relief floods their faces.

"Fuck! You're here. Where the fuck have you been?" Max says as he pulls me into his arms tightly.

"What? What do you mean? We've just been on a work meeting out. Why? Why do you look like that Max?" I say, panic starting to rise as my heart beats faster.

His gaze looks between Gray and Joey as they all look defeated. Gray nods at Max, seeming to give him the go ahead to tell me.

"There has been an incident," Max begins, "in your office."

"What do you mean an incident?" Sally cuts in, worry filling her.

I start to look around the lobby as I see an incredible amount of police presence. The lift is cordoned off with crime scene tape and on the opposite side, there are groups of people being escorted from the building by police.

"Someone has been taken. Theres a note that's been sent to NYPD from the Organisation, telling them that they were going to be taking someone from this office building." Max continues, you can see the worry in his features and realisation hits me that they all thought it was us.

"Taken?" Sally repeats, the shock evident. "Who?"

But I stop taking in the conversation happening beside me as I glance around the lobby again. My heart beat pounding in my ears. Dizziness starting to overwhelm me as I try to keep myself together. I breathe deeper to keep the flow of oxygen and start tapping my fingers as I count.

But nothing could prepare me for what I see in that moment.

As I glance across the lobby, I notice a man, standing at the front of the office building, tall, skinny. His eyes locked onto me. I know that person.

That's when I see Rian approach him. He starts talking to him as I try and piece together why the man's face is so familiar.

Why do I know him?

I can feel Max tapping my shoulder but I can't remove my gaze as I fixate on him.

Then it hits me like a fucking baseball bat.

Felix.

The man I am looking at, is Felix.

How can it be? He's dead. I visited his fucking grave.

He is dead.

Max stands in front of me as I fold over, my body giving in, gasping for oxygen. He reaches out to catch me as I collapse, the fear in his eyes real. The panic attack taking over me and as I glance back at the door.

Felix is gone.

I can't breathe as I tremble on the floor, my limbs tensing and trembling while I fight for my breath. I see all my friends around me and then Dr Rene appears.

But I can't hear them.

And then, I can't see them as I give up and fade into the darkness.

# Chapter 26

## Present Day

I stir back into consciousness, my vision spinning as I try and understand where I am and what has happened. I see Gray and Max knelt down, their large frames towered above me.

I realise that I'm on the floor.

I turn my head slightly glancing around, taking in Sally who seems to be in a panic on the phone. My head is pounding and my hearing isn't there other than a loud ringing noise.

As my focus comes in more, my senses seem to regulate and I try to sit up.

"Woah, just take a minute Mollie, stay down." Gray says, "We're waiting on the EMT's to arrive and assess you."

What the fuck has happened.

"What happened?" I croak out, my voice feeling raw.

"You just started screaming, then you started shaking, it was like you were fitting. Then you dropped. Max leapt for you but he didn't manage to catch you in time. You hit your head pretty hard."

I reach behind my head to feel and meet Max's hand holding a cloth with pressure on the back of my head.

"You have a pretty nasty cut on the back of your head babe." He says, but his voice is calm, telling me I should be calm to.

"Why did I collapse?" I ask, confusion filling me as I'm not really sure what was happening beforehand.

"Lets just focus on getting you to hospital and into recovery. You're the most important person right now." Max says, a smile across his face, but I can see the worry etched into his features.

I nod and remain lying on the floor. Embarrassment creeps over me as I realise I'm lay on the floor of my office building, in front of everyone. I decide that's a worry for another time and try to relax back into Max's hand.

The EMTs arrive fairly quickly and the decision is made to take me into hospital as my head requires stitches and potential scans for anything internal. Everyone opts to join us, although only Max travels in the ambulance with me. When we arrive at the hospital, Gray, Sally Gina and Joey are all waiting in the emergency room. I am seen within no time at all, a junior doctor stitches my wound and I am taken quickly for an x-ray and CT scan to check for anything internal.

We wait in a private room for the neurosurgeon to visit me with the results of the scans they've taken and I take the opportunity to ask everyone what happened.

"Can someone put the pieces together for me? What happened before? How did I end up on the floor? I remember getting back from the team building day and then, everything is a little cloudy." I ask and they all just start to side eye each other, no one willing to give up the truth.

Fucking assholes.

"Stop acting like I'm fragile. You need to tell me what happened." I demand, annoyance filling me. Max sighs, and I glance over to him waiting for what he has to say to me.

"You got back from your day out. There was a lot of police outside the building and inside the lobby because someone has been taken from your offices, suspected by the organisation." He begins, his voice a little shaky as if he thinks I'm going to combust as soon as he passes me the information.

"Okay, and then what happened?" I say, my tone taking no prisoners.

"Well, then we told you what had happened, and you started to, you know, panic." Gray interjects into Max's conversation and my gaze swoops to him "and then, you were staring across the Lobby and you just started to scream"

"I started to scream?" Confusion laces my features, "What was I screaming?" They all share a look between themselves before Sally chimes in.

"You were screaming Felix's name."

And just like that, the memories fly back through my mind, of seeing Rian with Felix. I gasp as my hand flies up to my mouth, tugging at the IV's which are positioned in the backs of my hands.

*Seeing Felix.*

"I saw him, in the lobby, Felix. I saw him," I say in almost a shout as I sit myself upright.

"You saw him?" Gray says as confusion lines his features now. "Isn't he dead? We buried him Mollie? You visit his grave?"

"I. Saw. Him." I enunciate every single word as they leave my lips.

"He was talking to Rian. It was him. I know it was him,"

"Mollie, sweetie, you hit your head really hard. Maybe you just thought you saw someone that looks like him? You know, like a doppelgänger." Sally says, the smile on her face in that same psychotic, cheese grater style we all know too fucking well.

I steady my breathing for a moment, considering what she is saying. Maybe it wasn't Felix? Maybe he's just on my mind at the minute, with me visiting his grave and thanks giving just passing by.

I go to speak again just as a devilishly handsome doctor appears through my door. Sally Gina and me all gravitate towards each other.

"I'm sat right here, remember." Max deadpans at the side of me.

"Babe, I can look and appreciate as long I don't touch." I crass back as he rolls his eyes at me.

"Ms Rutter, I'm Dr Denton, the attending neurosurgeon, I've reviewed your scans and you look good to go. No cause for concern other than some minor concussion side effects." He smiles at me, his teeth the whitest and straightest I think I've ever seen. Gina is practically drooling.

"Thank you, Doctor." I say, as Gina keeps her eyes trained on his.

"No problem, I'll have the nurse bring in your discharge notes as soon as possible." He smiles although his attention seems to be taken slightly by Gina. He flashes her the cheekiest smile accompanied by a wink and I see her blush.

He leaves the room, and she turns back to us, realising she's not alone in the room.

"What happened to the bar guy you've been obsessed with for the last few weeks?" I ask her, laughing.

"Can't I just have them both?" She says seductively as she places her finger on her lip.

"You're all fucking dirty bitches," Joey announces, as he stands and gathers his belongings up. We all burst out laughing and I flinch a little at the pressure on my head.

The nurse comes into my room and removes the IV's from me, passing me my discharge notes as I get myself dressed.

"Let's get out of here." I say as I slide off the bed. Everybody stands and starts filing out of the room. My walking is laboured as the feeling of dizziness continues. My mind running around and around about whether I did see Felix or not, and even though I'm certain I did, my memories are still hazy.

"Are you okay?" Sally asks as she softly bumps my shoulder and walks along side me.

"Yeah," a small smile spreads across my face, "I think I may have to speak to Rian about who his driver is." I say, hoping that would give me the answers I need.

"I think that's a good place to start Mol." She wraps her arm around my shoulder and I lean my head down to rest on hers.

****

The weekend flies by and we are back in work once Monday arrives. I have a meeting with the police today, Morgan and Verity are joining. I expect them to arrive soon, glancing at the clock and it reads 10:30am.

My phone pings on the desk and I spin myself back around from staring out of the window expecting it to be a reply from Dr Rene after I messaged asking for another appointment.

I pick up my phone and my stomach plummets as I see the name **Rian** light up the screen. I do need to speak to him but there's something inside me that's telling me to keep him as far away from me as I can. I click to open the message.

**Rian -** I saw the commotion in the lobby the other day and believe you ended up in hospital. I hope you've made a recovery. Hope you catch up with me soon.

I glance at the message and sigh as I debate whether I go ahead and meet him myself or whether I just ask someone like Sally to do the dirty work for me. I decide to just get it over with and shoot a message back to him.

**Mollie -** Can you come to my office today. ASAP.

I shoot the message back and it hasn't been 30 seconds before an answer pings back.

**Rian -** Yes. I'll be there at 2:00pm.

I glance at the clock and see it is now 11:00am, so I opt to sort out a couple of hours work before I head out to pick up some lunch.

As I return back from lunch , Meryl is showing Rian into my office.

"Ah, Ms Rutter, Riley Austin is here just like you told me, I've put him in your office," I nod and thank Meryl as I stride down the corridor and through my office door, catching him as he glances through my book case.

"Quite a collection you have here," he says, making small talk.

"Yes, all of those are books I've published for authors." I retort, my tone firm, "But I've not invited you here for small talk." I say, getting straight to the point.

"Well, I never assumed you had Mollie." He smiles, "What can I do for you?" He asks as he takes a seat on the chairs in front of my desk.

"The man you were talking to when we got back to my lobby after the team building day," I say, conviction firm in my tone.

"Okay, what about him?" Rian asks, confusing spread across his face.

"Who is he?" I ask.

"He's my driver."

"Yes, I know that much, but what is his name? What do you know of him?" I ask, my tone a little accusatory now. Rian's face contorts with confusion but he obliges and answers my questions.

"It's Peter, he's my driver, he has been for around six years now. Why? What's the problem? Has he done something wrong?"

I hesitate not really trusting him enough to delve too far into my histories.

"It's a very long story, but basically, he looks like a friend of mine. Well, he's a dead ringer for him, excuse the pun." I start, "But that friend of mine died eight years ago."

"Dead? Well, how can it be him?" He questions.

"That is what I keep asking myself. But I'm telling you now Rian, that man is the exact carbon copy of my friend, who is fucking dead. I visit his fucking grave."

Rian stays silent, looking at me, I'm not sure if he thinks I've completely lost my mind or not.

"Well, I'll ask him? Or look into it? My guys do thorough checks before they employ anyone so I can't see it being him, Mollie. Just maybe a look-a-like."

"Yes, please, look into it. But maybe don't say anything to him yet?" I say, my voice firm.

"Okay, is there anything else?"

"No, that is all, for now. Thank you for coming.

****

I'm cooking dinner as the afternoon draws to a close and decide I need to tell Max about seeing Rian today and speaking to Dr Rene about the trip. I know he's not going to be happy and I've been avoiding this conversation for what feels like forever.

I turn down the hob, preparing myself to delve into the nitty gritty. My phone pings twice as it sits on the counter next to Max. He glances over before doing a double take.

Oh shit. I know from the double glance that he's seen something he didn't expect to see.

He slowly turns his head back to reading his magazine, but not without giving me what can only be described as 'the death stare' from across the kitchen.

Yep, timing is impeccable as always. Best not to sugar coat I guess.

"Who has messaged me?" I ask, tossing the food in the pan acting nonchalant.

"Sally and Rian." The sneer as he announces Rian's name is evident. Of course it's a double fuck up. Excellent.

“Oh, what do they say?” I continue, trying to stay level and calm as if unaffected and I have nothing to hide.

“Grab your phone and read them yourself.” He says, annoyance clear in his tone. Okay then, I round the counter and pick up my phone.

**Sally -** Looking for flights to London on the 27th December, should we get booked?

Ahh, the first fuck.

**Rian -** Thanks for seeing me today. I spoke to Peter, he says he has never been or known a Felix.

And the second fuck. I told him not to raise it with him. Why do men not fucking listen to simple instructions.

I sigh. Let's go then.

“Do you want to get the elephant in the room out now? Or are we just going to sit and simmer until you boil over?” I say, placing my phone on the counter.

“I have nothing to say, if you have nothing to share,” he deadpans.

Fucking awkward bastard.

“I do have things to share. I was just about to when you read those messages.”

He scoffs out loud, “Convenient,” he says, flipping the magazine pages a little more ferocious.

“Well, you can either believe me and we can crack on with the chat or you can just be an asshole.” I say, deciding to just go in all guns blazing.

“I’m an asshole? You’re the one whose lying to me,”

“Oh fuck off, Max, don’t be so fucking dramatic. I just haven’t got around to telling you yet”

"Well, you've been stood there for 20 minutes cooking in silence so why not tell me then? No suddenly you just want to tell me as soon as messages beep through on your phone." He scoffs back, his annoyance definite.

"I just didn't know how to say everything I needed to say, without getting this fucking reaction from you."

"What reaction? I'm reacting like this because you haven't told me you met up with another man, who quite clearly has feelings for you, and you've booked a trip to the place you were fucking abducted to without even giving me an incline to the thought of these plans. What Mollie? Were you just planning to let me go back to my tour and go to London and hope I wouldn't find out?"

His anger is evident and there are elements that I understand but he's absolutely overreacting to the whole situation.

"No Max, stop being so ridiculous. I haven't even got tickets booked yet."

His face turns beetroot red and I think he could quite literally explode.

"Ridiculous? You think my feelings are ridiculous. Nice one, Mollie." He stands from the kitchen counter and slugs towards the door before walking out of it.

My heart races. What the fuck? He said he had changed and here he is running as soon as the opportunity arises.

The door flies back open.

"I'm just going to say that I am coming back. But I need to gather my head space Mollie, before I say something I don't want to say to you. You've not been truthful to me, and I feel like you've hidden things. If this was the opposite way around you would absolutely not accept me calling you ridiculous." He says, matter of factly, "I'll be back." And then he strides back out of the front door.

I'm lost for words. But I also feel kind of relieved that he came back to tell me. Maybe he has grown as a person.

The following morning I get myself up and ready to leave for work. Max came home at around midnight and slept in the spare room. I'm not sure whether this was because he's still annoyed with me or whether he just didn't want to disturb me. Either way, I head out to work for the day, leaving him to sleep in. I drop him a text on my way  to the car.

**Mollie -** I'm sorry about last night. I should definitely have told you sooner, but I absolutely wasn't keeping things from you. I'll see you later and we can talk then. xx

Jumping into my car, I await Sally and Gina's arrival for our commute. Five minutes pass by and they hop into the car. I hit the accelerator and we set off into the city.

Parking my car in the spaces below ground, we jump straight in the lift up to the fourth floor. Entering the office, I greet Meryl and hand her my coat as I walk to my office door. Sitting on my desk I see a huge gift hamper. I glance at the tag and my face falls as I read the inscription.

**You were always my favourite Mollie.**
**Melvin x**

"Meryl, where did this come from?" I ask, quickly. She scurries into my office.

"Oh, Ms Rutter, I don't know, no one has come past me. I've been in for 30 minutes but I haven't been in your office yet," She says, her voice flustered as she seems to be panicking.

"Meryl, you're not in trouble, it's just important I find out who put these here. Can you ring down to security and ask them to check the CCTV for our floor?"

"What's happening?" Sally asks as she exits her office and makes her way towards mine.

I point at the hamper "Don't touch them, I need to phone detective Palmer." I say just as Meryl scurries out the office and begins to contact security. "Meryl, tell them it's urgent and a massive breech of security in the building." I am furious that they've gotten into the building again not a few days after they were in here and a girl was taken.

Sally and Gina walk into my office as I stand five feet away from my desk, staring at the delivery.

"What the fuck is that?" Sally asks as she heads to my desk.

"Stop!" I shout and she freezes on the spot. "It's a package, from Melvin." I say abruptly.

"What the fuck!" They both say in unison.

"What's in it?" Gina asks as she attempts to get a glimpse through the cellophane.

"I don't know! It wasn't my first thought when I saw a hamper from the guy who kidnapped me eight years ago if I'm honest, Gee" I say, sarcasm lining my voice.

She shrugs in response, "He could have sent you something good," she says as she takes a step towards the basket. My hand flies out and blocks her from taking any more steps closer.

"It's irrelevant, it's blood money that has bought anything in the hamper and I am not about to engage in his fucking games." I protest, "It could be a fucking Cartier bracelet embedded with diamonds and it would still be a fucking no."

Sally and Gina glance at each other before Sally chimes in, "Is it a Cartier bracelet? With diamonds? Say maybe for a wrist this big?" She points at her own wrist and I stare at her deadpan.

"You're both not funny." I say, keeping my tone firm and strict, like I'm telling them off for being petulant children. They totally are fucking funny but I'm not about to admit that to them. The intercom rings on my desk and I round this pressing to hear.

"Yes, Meryl?" I announce.

"Detective Palmer is here to see you, with Morgan and Verity." She says over the speaker.

"Thanks Meryl, send them in" I say.

"Wasting no time this morning is detective Palmer." Sally chimes in a moment before the three of them stride into my office. Detective Palmer enters my office and immediately starts to take photos of the hamper as he circles my desk.

"Interesting, very interesting," He mutters under his breath as he surveys the item.

"What is?" Sally interjects loudly, which makes us all jump slightly.

"It's interesting that Mollie received a much larger hamper than these other two lovely ladies." He announces and my head swivels to Morgan and Verity. "You must be his favourite." He finishes as I turn back to his voice, just as his eyes look towards me without so much as lifting his head, rimming the tops of his eye sockets and making me feel eerily.

"You both got a hamper?" I ask them, my heart pounding for them. They both nod at me.

"We've got a few notes over the last few weeks, threats to take us, threats to kill you, threats that if we don't bring you to him that he'll kill our families." Morgan starts and I can hear the quake in her voice.

"We've decided that we're going to take the offer to go into protective custody, our families will also be placed into protective care but not with us. We can stick together though." Verity continues and my heart sinks for them.

"Mollie, I'll offer the same to you again." Detective Palmer starts "If you would like to go into protective custody, then I can arrange that for you and your friends." He says.

I scoff, "Fucking hell Palmer, I'm a publisher, with my own business that is literally my fucking name." My irritation every so present in my words "There is no hiding for me. If I hide, I give up everything I've ever worked for." I say, before slumping down in my chair.

I wish it was as easy as walking away from who I am and starting again but it's just not. Maybe I should have done that when I escaped eight years ago, made a new identity and pretend the person who was locked away for all that time didn't exist anymore. Like she died in captivity. Sally rubs my shoulders from behind as I stare out into the vast.

"Morgan and Verity have nominated you to know their new identities. You to be their confident." Detective Palmer says. "I'll hand deliver their details when we know who they are."

With that, he scoops up the hamper and him, Morgan and Verity head to exit my office. I stand and take the girls into my arms for a hug.

"You guys are so brave. So, so brave." I whisper to them, as a tear streams down my cheek. And then they leave, heading out of the office following the police officers who escorted them here.

I sigh escapes me as my eyes start to well in sadness and frustration.

"I feel responsible." I whisper as I slump down onto the sofa, the tears rolling down my cheeks. "If I had just said no to Melvin all them years ago, they wouldn't be here now, changing their lives because of a situation they were put in."

I swat away my tears as they fall uncontrollably.

“No Mollie, but it’s unlikely any of us would have been.” She says as she takes me into her arms and holds me tight. I lean my head into her.

“I just need a minute here, okay?” I ask as Gina sits behind me on the sofa and my head remains rested on Sally’s shoulder.

“As long as you need, sweetie.” Sally says, her hand stroking the lengths of my hair.

We sit in silence and when I glance at the clock, 30 minutes have passed by. The tears are no longer streaming down my cheeks. I sit up boldly and decide to continue the day.

“Right, we have a trip to London to arrange.” I say just as a knock sounds at my office door. I glance at myself in the mirror, checking I have no mascara leakage across my face. Other than the slight swelling on my cheeks, I don’t look too bad.

“Come in,” I shout towards the door, straightening myself out. Max walks in, his hand holding a bunch of tulips.

“Am I interrupting?” He says, his face seeming worried when he notices my swollen eyes.

“No, no just Morgan and Verity are being put into protective custody, Melvin dropped a hamper on my desk, and I’m just feeling guilty about everything.” I reel off like it’s casual chit chat.

Max’s face flushes and I know he’s curious as to whether I’ve told Sally and Gina about our argument last night.

“Sounds like you had a rocky morning,” he says placing the tulips on my desk and pulling me into his arms for an embrace. I wrap my arms around him and breathe in his scent. It feels like the scent of home as it fills my lungs and makes me feel safe. Max plants a kiss on my head as he holds onto me tightly. I pull back and look him up and down. He’s wearing gym clothes and I can tell he’s on his way to the gym not from the gym as he doesn’t have any signs of a work out sweat on him.

"What are you doing here? Other than delivering flowers," I say, picking up the tulips and inhaling the smell.

"I came to apologise. I was a bit of a dick last night, I overreacted and I'm sorry I left the house instead of talking it through with you."

Wow. I was not expecting that.

"I want to ask you on a date, on Friday night before I deploy on Saturday. Me and you, some pasta, your favourite alcohol? Maybe Don Antonios?"

My heart swells as I feel him really trying for me.

"Yes, of course I'd love to." I smile at him and I feel like all my worries from the last 30 minutes have melted from existence. He takes my hand and kissed the top.

"I'll make the reservations. I love you Mollie, see you at home later" he turns and waves towards Sally and Gina as he departs my office. I lean back on my desk, all kinds of flustered now.

"Alright, I'll admit it. He's fucking trying." Sally says and I turn towards her, my smile widening even further.

"She's finally admitted it," Gina cheers as we all start to laugh.

"Well, that's all I'm saying. Now, where were we? Ah yes, planning London baby!" Sally jives as we all sit on the sofa and Gina takes out her laptop to get searching. Despite everything happening right now, I feel great.

Later on that day, as I arrive home, the smell floating through the house as I realise Max is cooking some food for us.

"Hey," I shout as I walk in the door.

"Hey babe, in the kitchen," he says before he continues singing along to 'I'm walking on sunshine' by Katrina and the Waves.

I walk through the kitchen door and my heart is about to burst as I see him grooving and dancing as he tosses our food in the pan, wearing nothing but an apron.

He turns down the stove as he spins around and begins to approach me, pulling me into a jig as we float around the kitchen, spinning and circling, as he serenades me. Laughter bursts from inside me. I don't think I've ever seen him so care free and fun.

"What has gotten into you?" I ask as we continue to dance around. He stops and spins me on the spot, continuing to sing along to the song.

Just as the song comes to the end he tosses me backwards in his arms and plants a kiss on my lips.

"Max!" I giggle like a naughty school girl, my cheeks blushing.

"I'm making fajitas, my love and I've made the best decision of my life. But I need your help," he says as he returns me back upright and heads back to the stove, turning the heat up and continuing with the meal prep.

"Oh yeah, and what decision would that be?" I say, pouring myself a lemonade and taking a seat on the breakfast island stools.

"Ahh Mollie, the best decision I could ever make, is you." He says, the confidence in his voice radiates through the kitchen.

"Me?" I ask confused, not really understanding what he's saying.

"Yes baby, you. I'm resigning from the forces. I need you to help me scope my letter of resignation, so I can hand it to my sergeant when I arrive back on tour." He says, his eyes focused on the food and not really on me or my reaction. He's calm, cool and it's evident that this decision doesn't cause him any form anxiety. In fact, I think he seems less anxious than he usually does.

"Have you taken something to relax yourself?" I ask, the confusing lining my face, although I remain playful with my words. He joins me and laughs.

"No babe, I'm not high, well, other than high on you, and me, us and our future. But the answer to your question is no, I've not taken anything to relax me." He reassures and he lines the chicken peppers and onions on the wraps. "I choose you, Mollie. I choose us. I've done my fucking around, almost losing you and us. I'm done and I'm coming home to you."

My heart could burst as every single fibre of my being fills with desire for this man. I didn't think I could ever love or want him more than I already did before now. But this is something else entirely as I feel everything from the past three years fix itself in an instance.

"Well, we best get writing that letter then," I smile as I lean up on my tip toes and sink a kiss into his lips.

****

Friday comes around quickly again after a busy week I work. Christmas deadlines are coming thick and fast and I definitely have that Friday feeling. I've been on cloud nine all week, as I've waited for date night to come around. We spent the rest of the week building on his resignation letter ready for Max to take with him when he departs tomorrow.

It's a strange feeling really, because usually before he leaves for tour I feel sorrow and loss impending. But this time I feel joy and happiness.

I left work early and treated myself to my hair, make-up and nails done for tonight. I ordered the perfect outfit in the week, a burgundy velvet one shoulder jump suit so opted for my hair to be styled around the opposite side to the shoulder piece.

"Are you ready babe?" Max calls up the stairs as I glance over myself in the mirror.

"Yeah, I'm coming" I say back, grabbing my clutch bag and heading down the stairs. Max greets me at the bottom step as he takes my hand and spins me around, pulling me in close to him. He inhales my scent.

"You look incredible Mollie," he says as he begins to pepper my neck with kisses.

"You look incredible too, Mr Broderick, but I do have to say, if you don't stop now, we wont be going out anywhere." I gasp as his kisses trail down my chest and he slides a hand over my sensitive centre, cupping and rubbing my heat over my clothing.

"Let's leave then." He says as he looses contact with me and a small whimper leaves me.

We arrive at the restaurant and we are taken to the roof top terrace which overlooks Central Park. The views are incredible as the contrast between light and dark outlines the vast emptiness of central park. The lush green a deep grey black colour in the night.

We order our meals which arrive pretty quickly and we make light work of them, devouring the incredible tastes pretty hastily. The night is incredible, every detail is tailored to me and him. He couldn't have done it better if he tried.

"I'm having an incredible time, Mr Broderick. You've really outdone yourself tonight." My smile is wide, I don't think I could love one person more in all my life.

So I've got a surprise up my sleeve for you," he says, his smile menacing but cheeky.

"Oh really, and what's that then?" I ask, as I take a sip of my pink gin and lemonade.

"I've booked us a penthouse stay in the city." He says and when I didn't think life could get any better he out shines it all. I don't think you could wipe the smile off my face.

A small band starts playing in the corner of the roof terrace and suddenly I notice that we are all alone up here. I turn around glancing behind us to see if I've missed anything.

As I turn back around, I gasp, the wind knocked straight out of my lungs as I stare at Max, down on one knee staring straight up at me.

"Mollie Rutter," he begins and my eyes fill instantly, "You are the light to my dark, you are the sun that brightens my gloom. You have picked me, when I didn't always pick you. You are the most perfect human, that could ever have walked this earth." He says and my hand slowly rises as I place this over my lips. I'm trembling, but for once it's not in panic.

"Mollie, I want to spend the rest of eternity with you." And he pulls out a little mint blue box from his pocket and opens it, "Mollie, will you make me the happiest man alive and marry me?" He asks and tears spill over my cheeks as I nod, words failing me for a moment.

"Yes. Yes! A million percent yes!" I say as he pulls out the enormous diamond Tiffany ring and places it on my left ring finger. The fit is perfect.

He stands and takes me into his arms, cupping my cheeks and taking my lips in his. His tongue runs across my lips and I devour his taste as I deepen into it. He hoists me up, into his arms as I wrap my legs around him.

Our kiss continues to deepen and I start to rub myself along his body, trying to ease the tension building in my core.

"Fuck Mollie, I need you," he says.

"Take me back to where we're staying. Now!" I demand as he drops me to my feet and leaves $350 in cash on the table. Far too much for what we've had but we have zero interest in waiting for change.

The tension in his SUV is incredible as he brushes his hand along my thigh. We head to a building with underground parking and as Max enters, the barriers automatically lift, recognising his registration. He parks in the space named 'Penthouse' and jumps out of the car, rounding to my side in a jog.

He opens my door, and lifts me back into his arms as my legs wrap around him. Carrying me over to the lift he runs his thumb across the sensor. The lift door springs open and he steps us both in. Pressing my back against the wall, he plants kisses along the crook of my neck, his hands gripping my ass tight. The lift is quick as we arrive at the top of he building and step out into pure luxury.

He places me on the floor, spinning me to unzip my suit. Sliding this off my shoulders, it drops to the floor.

I'm wearing a one piece lace wine red lingerie outfit. I spin around to face him, the lace covering but not blocking my skin as he drinks me in.

"Fucking hell, I am the luckiest fucking man on this planet." He says as he rips open his shirt, buttons ping everywhere.

I glance around looking for the bedroom as I walk backwards enticing him to follow me.

He unbuckles his pants, dropping them to the floor, his eyes following me, I see a set of stairs which leads to a balcony bedroom with floor length windows. Swaying my ass as I walk, I reach the stairs. He begins stalking towards me slowly, his cock in hand as he pumps himself slowly, stroking his length and caressing his pre-come around the tip. I take a few steps up before I stop and glance back towards him.

"Oops, did I drop something? I say, before spreading my legs slightly, locking them straight and bending over, my full swollen heat on display for him as my crotchless outfit reveals all for him. I see his eye blaze with fire as I catch a glimpse through my legs. I reach my hand through my legs, and start to circle my clit, before dipping my fingers deep into my sex, a breathy moan escapes me, as Max lets out a feral grunt. I think I've just unleashed the animal inside.

He strides towards me, purpose in his every step as he slaps my hand, pushing me in deeper before dipping his own fingers in along side me. He pumps me deep as I remove my own hand and use this to balance myself as my legs begin to tremble. He continues to pump me as my ass is bent over. He dips his head down, removing his fingers he sucks my clit in between his lips, before running his tongue up my slit, drinking in my arousal as he reaches my ass with his tongue, he plants a playful slap.

"Get up the fucking stairs before I pull my cock out and impale you right here, right now, you naughty, naughty girl." He says as he holds out his hand for me to take. I grab this and he swirls me to face him, picking me back up in his arms, and carrying me the rest of the way, my bare pussy sliding up and down his engorged cock. It feels incredible. I plant a kiss on his lips, slipping my tongue in between his and tasting him completely.

He lays me down on the bed, our kiss never parting as he continues to mouth fuck me. I thrust again trying to get traction between us, needing the relief as my centre pulses between my legs, my wetness dripping down my legs. I need him deep inside me.

"I'm going to fuck your first orgasm out of you Mollie, hard just like your pussy is begging me to." He says, his voice husky and deep and his hands circling my nipples, "But then I'm going show you exactly what you mean to me, because tonight is about love Mollie, and you need to see how much I fucking love you baby."

Oh fuck.

Fuck.

I nod incoherently, taking in the words but needing to relieve the ache. Lifting my arms above my head he ties them together with his belt.

Unhooking the clasp between my breasts he unleashes them, cupping them in his hands he massages each one before taking my nipple into his mouth. He continues to work down my body, reaching my clit and sucking down hard as he works me with his mouth, my legs clamp shut as my orgasm builds, my walls throbbing with the sensation.

"Ahh, I just needed another taste of you," he says before standing and pulling on my legs, tugging me to the edge of the bed, the belt tightening at my wrists as the restraints keep me in place. He lines his cock up at my entrance, rubbing his head through my folds as I wait for the intrusion to satisfy me, the anticipation is almost enough to make me come right now.

"Fuck Max, please," I beg him.

He flips me over, tucking my knees under and positioning my ass up high as he brushes his cock along my slit, up to my ass, he presses in my ass slightly and a moan bursts from me, my sex tensing with jealousy. He slides back out lining up at my sex as his fingers continue to swirl at back entrance, his other thumb circles my clit deeply.

And then he slides his cock in to my pussy slowly, but deep. A moan fills the room as I can't hold myself together riding the edge of orgasm, he starts to pump me faster, his finger pushing into my ass as he fucks me deep and hard. My sex throbs as my walls take in his length and my legs tremble.

"Oh fuck, I'm going to come Max," I say as he continues fucking me hard. My walls clamp down and my release floods out from inside me.

He slows his pace, his rock hard cock still evident inside me as he slows, my pussy continuing to clamp down on his cock deep inside me. His hips continue to pulse slowly, telling that he has yet to release his seed.

He pulls out of me, spinning me back over and unbuckling the belt from my wrists, he tosses this aside. I feel drunk in an orgasm high as he trails his hands across my skin, touching, circling, caressing my nipples, before taking these in his mouth again. His hands trail down my stomach as he circles his hands around my sex, fuck I didn't think I could orgasm twice in a row but my body is telling me otherwise as my sex starts to tingle again. He runs his hand down, circling my vulva and caressing my folds, building that sensation up inside me. I reach over and take his cock in my hand, slowly beginning to pump him. I turn and look into his eyes.

"I love you Max."

## Max

She stares at me, those blue eyes a fucking desire in themselves as I run my fingers up and around her slick folds. Her body on full display in front of me, fuck I don't know how I've not come already.

She pumps my cock and I know I'm close, but needing to work her back in slowly I continue to circle her most sensitive spots.

"I love you too, future Mrs Broderick." I say, a smile covering my face. She's fucking perfect, so much more than I ever deserve. She smiles at me, before our lips lock together again.

"I'm going to make love to you, so you can remember just how fucking much I love you, Mollie." I declare, my tone sensual and gravelly.

I plant kisses along her jawline, taking in her lobe between my teeth, as my hands continue to circle her sex. I move back over the clit, she flinches as the sensitivity is still high from her last orgasm. I feel her tightness uncoiling as she starts to loosen her walls again, the strokes ensuring she can take my cock again. I need to be inside her, fuck I need to spill everything I have inside of her.

"Are you ready baby?" I ask, as I position myself on top of her, my cock edging her sex, as her arousal coats her entrance. She's so fucking wet, as I slide my head along her slit.

She nods, giving me the okay to slide home.

I press into her folds, her sex enveloping my cock in a vice so fucking tight that it's almost impossible to hold my own orgasm in, I take it slow as I enter her, getting three quarters deep before pulling back and sliding back in deeper. Her whimpers fill the room and my restraint is second to none. I keep a rhythmic pace as we lock together, our kiss deepening, the passion unmatched. My pace quickens as I near the end, I can feel her body twitching around my length and I know she's just as close as me.

"Come with me babe," I say between kisses as I thrust in and out of her folds, my pace continuing to deepen, I rub my fingers along her clit, circling and squeezing as we share the moment together. She bites down on my lip as her release overcomes her and her walls clamp down, milking me of my own release deep inside her.

"Fuck!" I grunt, before returning back to our kiss. I hold myself deep inside her still, unable to pull myself away from the kiss.

"You're so fucking perfect."

"And so are you Mr Broderick."

****

The next morning we get up early, and made our way back to our house, as I have to leave for my flight by 10:00am.

Mollie seems a little lost this morning, although her smile is still right there on her face for me. If I could stay here forever and never go back I would.

I head to the door, my army backpack full, my combats in position. She looks me over head to toe, like she's taking a mental photo of me.

"It's time." I say, I feel my heart breaking. I don't know how well this next few weeks is going to go or if I'll even be able to resign like I want to.

The situation is complicated.

I open my arms wide to ask her to come over to me and she stalks closer to me before settling in my arms. I smell her hair, embedding the scent to my memory to drive me through.

"I'll be back before you know it." I say, trying my hardest to put conviction behind my voice so she believes in me. If anything I need her to believe in me.

I pull back and tilt her head up to look at me. Her eyes beading with tears and I'd be fucked if I didn't admit it killed me off a little. I kiss her deeply. Remembering the taste of her lips.

"I love you baby," I whisper to her.

"I love you too." She says. And I take a step back, knowing I have to put distance between us before I decide to fuck it and whisk her away into hiding so they can't find me. I take a step back out of the front door as she stands looking at me.

"I'll call you when I can."

"Have you got your letter?" She asks, and her eyes are glistening with hope.

"Yeah, it's in my pack." I say. I look her up and down before planting a kiss on two of my fingers and waving at her. I turn and make my way to the car.

I hope this fucking works out. Because I need to come home to her.

Fuck.

How did I get in this fucking position?

Bile rises in my throat as I speed off away from her home. She can never know the lie I live. Because I don't think she'll ever forgive me.

# Chapter 27

## Present Day

### Mollie

I head to Maureen's having asked Sally and Gina to meet me there for coffee. I had a couple of errands to run this morning in the city but I'm so excited to tell them that Max finally asked me to marry him. I didn't feel like it warranted a text message to them. I wanted to really share the experience. I pull open the door and walk into the cafe, locating Sally and Gina in the cozy corner, our usual spot. Sally picks up and waves a cup at me, so I assume they've already picked me up a drink and head straight over to the table.

It's a cold day meaning my hands are covered with gloves which adds to the surprise for them.

"Morning girl, how are you feeling?" Sally asks, while pulling a slightly sad face towards me. I take it she's referencing Max's departure this morning.

"I'm okay, he's taken his letter of resignation and…." I whip my glove off my hand and tilt my fingers to flash the huge diamond that sits on my ring finger. "He asked me to marry him last night!" I blurt out, the smile spread from cheek to cheek. Their faces immediately become elated with shock, joy, happiness.

"Oh my fucking word!" Gina blurts out.

"When? What? Oh fuck. I need to know it all!" Sally says as she takes my hand and ogles the ring "Why did we not know instantly?" She says her tone a little firmer now, but I laugh as she continues to inspect my hand.

"I just wanted to see your faces properly when I told you." I say back, my smile still beaming.

"What is it?" Gina asks as she inspects it.

"Massive, that's what it is, what does it matter about anything else?" Sally quips, shoving Gina in her shoulder and knocking her away from my finger.

"It's Tiffany's!" I squeal, a blush creeping up my face.

"Fucking hell, the guy did good!" Gina says as she sits back on the sofa.

"Well, it's about fucking time he did." Sally says, sinking back into her chair.

I pick up my coffee and I feel so happy right now. My life if finally heading in the direction it should and despite everything that's going on with the organisation, I just can't seem to find the fucks to give. For once in my life I feel positive.

"So Sal, I'm so confused over this whole marriage to my brother. You don't see each other, you don't seem to have decided to live together. I don't get it." I say, deciding to go straight in with the question that's been on my mind since Vegas.

Sally sighs and throws her head back onto the couch.

"We're all confused Mol, and I live with her." Gina interjects. While Sally remains silent in the corner avoiding the question.

"You won't get anything from her Mollie, she's radio silent, I'd try your brother instead." Gina says, shrugging her shoulders.

Graham and Joey walk into the cafe. I asked them to join us but I told them to come 30 minutes after the girls, as I just needed to share my news with them first.

"Morning girls," Joey says as he heads over to the couches and I scoot over to make room for him. Gray picks up their drinks from the counter and joins us all in the corner.

"Has Max gone back now?" Gray says as he takes a seat next to Joey and me.

"Yeah, he left this morning." I say, a smile wide on my face.

"And, your happy about this?" Gray looks at me confused.

"Oh absolutely not, but I am happy about this." I parade my hand again to Gray and Joey.

"Fuck yes. He finally did it!" Joey says at the same time that Gray says, "Fucking finally, I've been keeping that secret for fucking weeks! I thought he wasn't going to go through with it,"

"Wait, you guys knew? And you never said anything?" I say, shocked at their reactions.

"Well, yeah, he asked my permission, and then the three of us went to Tiffany's and legit must have spent five hours looking for the absolute perfect ring for you. He would not settle for just anything." My heart melts into a puddle all over again. I am infatuated with this man.

"So, it's just us guys for Christmas Dinner? And then did you say flights to London were booked for 27th Gina?" I ask, changing the subject before I get tearful at missing Max.

"Sounds like a plan to me." Joey states.

"Yeah, we have an early morning flight to London which should get us there for 9:00pm UK time." Gina says, pulling out her laptop to go through the itinerary.

"Sara's birthday is the 29th so we land late on the 27th and then we're going to the hotel for the night and some sight seeing before we surprise her at home around 5:00pm when the work day ends." I reiterate the plans to ensure I have a proper understanding.

"That's absolutely right." Gina confirms.

"Have we just got carry ons or do we have proper luggage too?" I ask, wondering how much I can pack for one week.

"We have hold luggage yeah, so pack as much as you can fit in," Gina says.

"I'm just thinking how cold it is and know we will need layers."

We all carry on the conversation and enjoy a few more coffees as the afternoon continues. We laugh and talk, it feels so good to have these guys around me.

****

It's Monday on the final week as we head to the build up for Christmas Day this Friday. The city is heaving with tourists wanting to visit the city while it's all dressed up. It makes me anxious knowing the Organisation are lurking about targeting their next victims. Work with the police has slowed down, not because they have backed off, but more because there's not much more I can offer.

I spoke to Morgan and Verity who now go by the names River and Isabella. They're happy and safe and located in Seattle. It makes me happy that they're happy.

I have a catch up booked with Dr Rene today. Not a full session, more of a casual chat to tell her about my upcoming trip. I know as always she'll crush any anxieties I have with one of her super speeches to make me feel better. I glance at the clock as my appointment is at 2:00pm and it reads 1:45pm. I throw a text to Max in the hopes he'll be able to read it soon.

**Mollie -** I hope you're having an okay time where ever you are fiancé. I love you deeply. See you soon.

I close my laptop and head to the lift to make my way to see Dr Rene. As I arrive, Florence greets me and as usual brings me a coffee while I sit in the waiting room. After ten minutes, I watch another patient of Dr Rene's leave and continue to wait silently for her to be ready to call me in.

"Mollie, come on in," she smiles at me. I walk into her therapy room and inhale the vanilla and lavender scent filling the air.

"Is that a new fragrance?" I question, noticing the difference.

"Ahh, not a permanent change, but a feature for that particular patient." She replies.

I sit myself on the sofa and to my surprise, Dr Rene comes and sits next to me instead of across from me.

I turn, looking at her and taking her in as she starts to giggle.

"Come on now Mollie, you emailed me for a catch up chit chat, not a session. If you want to just go get some coffee we can head out and catch up." She smiles at me "So, since you aren't asking me for a session, I thought I'd join you on this side of the room for our catch up," I smile a warm smile at her, she has a point I guess.

"We've booked the trip to London. We leave on the 27th for a couple of weeks over new year. It is Sara's birthday too so that should be fun." I say as we sip our coffee and look out of the windows.

"Sounds great, I wish I could join you." She says sipping her coffee too.

"Max proposed to me," I say, a smile broad across the face although the excitement a little at bay.

"That's amazing news. You seem a little defeated though, is everything okay?" She asks as she looks at me "Do I need to swap sides?" She jokes, gesturing over to her chair on the opposite side.

I sprout a laugh "No, not quite." I sigh, "I didn't tell him about the planned trip to London. He was so against me travelling that far last time I brought it up that I just didn't bring it up again." I say, spinning the cup of coffee in my hands. "I guess I just feel like I'm lying to him, and that's not a good feeling to have" I say.

"Can you not message him?" She suggests.

"I could, but it's not often he gets messages through, he tends to not have signal or they block them from main signal so they can't be tracked or whatever they do."

"Well, sometimes you need to do things for you. And he will forgive you Mollie. It's not like you've gone off and found someone else." We both laugh it off.

"Yeah, true." I say, and I had to admit, this has been really enjoyable. I feel calm and safe, but also like I'm with a friend not in therapy.

"I know you joked about going out for coffee, but I like this room Aria. I like spending time with you and sharing without the intensity of therapy, but I still think I need this room." I say as I finish my cup of coffee and set it down on the table.

"That's okay, we can still meet here. But just put coffee catch up rather than session when you drop me a message." She replies.

I stand and adjust my clothing, before picking up my cup to take out to Florence for washing. I pull Aria into a hug.

"Thank you for everything Aria, I'm so glad you turned out to be a friend." I say as I give her a squeeze before pulling back and heading out of her therapy room.

"No problem, have the best trip away with the girls. Don't stress about Max, everything will be fine." Her smile is warm and I meet her smile with mine.

"Merry Christmas Aria, Merry Christmas Florence."

"Merry Christmas Mollie," they both say in unison.

****

The day has arrived for our trip to London. My stomach a swirl of nerves and excitement. I am desperate to get out of NYC, which I never in a million years thought I'd feel, but everything is so intense here.

We had a great Christmas Day together as a group, although I didn't hear from Max which was sad, he did manage to send an email to me late into the day which said:

***Thinking of you always. Sorry I can't catch up with you today. I love you Mollie.***
***Your Fiancé xx***

It meant more to me than I even realised as I tucked myself up into bed feeling content about having all of my favourite people close by. We have all spent the last two days sleeping at my house, not because of my nightmares but just to be close to each other. It's been really nice spending the holidays with my favourite people.

The 27th rolls around faster than we realise after a mad dash to pack everything the previous day, we're all finally ready to head out to the airport. Gray has given us all the rules of travel and made Sally and Gina promise to keep him updated on me and how I am throughout the entirety of the trip. He's such an overprotective asshole. Our flight is early doors and we have to be at JFK for a 08:00am flight. Peeling my eyes open at 05:00am after a heavy couple of days was not the one but I did it nonetheless.

We're all ready and head out into the garden to jump inside Gray's SUV.

"Have you got everything? Passport, clothes, the things I gave you? Gray asks too quickly for me to answer to.

"Yes, Gray, I have it all." I reply, trying to keep my tone light despite him acting like my dad being very irritating.

We set off in the car towards JFK. The traffic is lighter with it being a little earlier than usual so it's not too long of a trip across the bridge to JFK.

"I'm going to take a trip to visit Lola this week," Joey announces during the car journey and we all squeal with excitement for him. Lola is the air hostess he met on the flight to Vegas. He seems really smitten with her so I'm really happy for him, although I feel a pang of guilt that he's only just felt like he can go meet up with her now that I'm leaving the country and he doesn't have to baby sit me.

Gray drops us at JFK and we give out hugs and kisses goodbye. We make our way through the airport rolling our carry on cases along with us.

"Maybe we should get you shit faced on margaritas before we embark today so you don't over think the situation," Sally chimes in and we all laugh along with her.

The flight was killer but we managed to have a great time in our first class seats again. As we arrive in London the time is 9:00pm in London and we quickly exit the plane and collect our items before heading to the taxi bays. We get a taxi from London Heathrow and make our way to our hotel in the city. We have a suite room located in the city of London and according to the address Sara gave us, we can see that she lives on a street in Chelsea, so we decide to go and freshen up in the hotel and have some food and drinks while we set up a plan for how were going surprise her the following day. She's going to be so, so shocked but I hope she's excited to spend her birthday and New Year with us. We are definitely better than spending it all alone, or at least I think so.

We reach the hotel, check in and head to our room. The views here are amazing as our room is a suite, high up in the hotel, and we can see quite a distance across London.

Being back on home turf brings out the British accent in all of us and we giggle at the changes in our voices as we all freshen up. Gina opens the door to room service and wheels in our freshly made cocktails, tipping the waiter and closing the door afterwards.

"Yes, the goods have arrived," she announces, shimmying her chest as she wheels the trolly of cocktails towards us. We all burst out laughing and I'm so glad I chose to come here with all of the girls. We need this.

I need this.

It's very late, past midnight at the moment so we decide to finish our cocktails and head to bed so we can have a fresh start tomorrow. The plan is to head around some of the highlights of London through the day before we make our way to Sara's house around 5:00pm.

The morning arrives and we wake up feeling fresher than I expected. I open the curtains as the windows are exposed and I look out at the vast London City. I spot the London Eye, not too far from us and the memories flood my mind again as I locate the bar just a few steps away.

I am flooded with emotions with being in London. This trip is hard on me emotionally, I can feel it in my soul, but I know that it is a necessary trip to try and help me to move on with my life.

I head out on a tour of London with the girls for the day, eating  and drinking in some local bougie cafe's and bars. We said we would give until after work hours are done so we can try and guarantee she's home for the surprise. I feel my trembles present at points but I manage to hold myself together well which fills me with faith that I can do this.

"Imagine if we turn up at her house and she's not there, and has in fact swanned off somewhere," Sally jokes.

"Don't. Because that is entirely fucking possible." I laugh as I take in a sip of my drink.

We continue to laugh and joke and have the best time ever. We have spent a little too long drinking and notice it's now 6:00pm. We decide it's time to make our way to Sara's house. It's pitched black now so we are relying on our phone maps to navigate us along the streets once we step off the underground station. Eventually we hail a cab once we reach a busier street and ask him to drop us at the address Sara has given us.

"I can't wait to see her face when she realises we've planned a whole surprise trip on her." I say, the excitement buzzing through the car despite my trembles.

"I know, she's going to freak out!" Sally squeals besides me, "We definitely are the best birthday gift a girl could ask for," She says playfully and we laugh in unison. The cab drops us off close by to Sara's house which is fronted by a long strip of greenery.

A park of some sorts.

As we make our way across the gated grass like area which is located outside the row of houses that leads up to Sara's house, I start to feel uneasy, and a little light headed. Stopping for a moment, and putting my fingers to my temples and taking some deep breaths.

*You're fine Mollie. Pull yourself together.*

Sally wraps her arm around my shoulders, "You okay girl?" She questions, as she smiles a warm smile at me.

"Yeah, I think I'm maybe just tired and a little tipsy. I'm feeling a little light headed." I reply, leaning my head on her shoulder.

"Let's stop for a minute, come on sit down here, there's no rush to get there, she doesn't even know we're even fucking here!" She snorts a laugh and it makes me smile. She tugs at my arm and pulls me towards a bench. "Sit. Have a minute," she says as she plonks me down, dropping to sit next to me, Gina and Sally continue a conversation but honestly I've switched off from them at this point?

My head is pounding.

I start to scan the wooded area and take in its natural beauty. It's dark, and cold, the only light illuminating the area from the lamp posts lining the road besides us, the sun has set long ago in the midst of British winter.

A noise catches my attention and my head shoots to the right. Gina and Sally are completely oblivious, still full of laughter as they sit next to me. A deep husky voice pricks my attention, my heart stutters as confusion floods my features.

I know that voice.

I stand, looking to locate the sound as I walk further across the wooded area, I am sheltered by the trees, hooded by the darkness.

As I stalk through the tree cover, I see it.

The source of the voice.

“We can’t keep doing this Sara. Going backwards and forwards. What do you want me to do?” the voice sounds and I can see the back of a male head.

He’s talking to Sara.

“You keep doing exactly what I tell you that you are fucking doing until I tell you that you can stop.” Sara bounces back at the man and I am fixed on watching them, frozen to the spot.

I watch as the man dips his head low and his hands run across his temples and through his hair, his back still positioned towards me. For a moment I see Sara’s eyes gaze over towards where I’m standing, unsure of whether she can see me but her gaze averts. I assume she was just day dreaming for a moment.

Sara picks up her hand, placing this under the man’s face, lifting his chin and tilting it upwards to look at her as she stands a step higher than him. I see him glance at the door, before his face turns back meeting Sara’s gaze again. The door besides them begins to open.

Before I know it, I see her envelope him with a kiss, their lips tangling together. His hands rise and cup the surround of her face, the kiss is deep and sensual, seeming like this isn’t the first time they’ve done this.

She never told us she was seeing anyone.

They continue to face fuck, and I can't stop myself from watching. The male lifts Sara up, wrapping his arms and cupping her ass and backs her up, placing her on the concrete hand rails that line either side of the staircase leading to the front door.

Another male steps out the house, placing a cigarette into his mouth as he lights this, completely ignoring the public display of affection happening beside him.

What the fuck is this some kind of gentleman's club?

The man tilts his head up to the sky as the light outside the door illuminates his face.

It's Felix.

And then it all fucking unfolds.

The male that has just been mouth fucking Sara turns in my direction to face Felix. A breath leaves my lips in a gasp and my heart shatters into a million piece.

Stood there at the side of Sara, with his arm slung around her back placed on her fucking ass, is Max.

My Max.

I watch them, smiling and flirting, Sara leaning back with her tits bursting out of her top, on full fucking display. Tears burst from my eyes, and stream down my cheeks. I can't fucking move from the spot I'm stood on. I can't peel my eyes off of them.

Their movements are so natural together, it's clear to me they have done this for more time than I could even imagine.

I turn to run towards Gina and Sally and I find the bench they were sat at is completely empty. I listen trying to find them but I can't hear anything. Panic rushes through my veins as I scan the wooded area for signs of them.

"Gina, Sally!" I call out, my voice frantic.

Where the fuck are they?

"Gina, Sally!" I shout again, louder this time, as I turn back around and meet the eyes of Sara and Max, looking over the road at me.

Max's face like thunder, shock in his every feature while Sara's face looks callous and calculated as they stare back at me.

"Mollie," a vile voice purrs into my ear and my breathing stops dead.

*No.*

*This is not happening.*

I freeze to the spot just as a man, wearing a pin striped suit circles around to face me.

"Melvin," I whisper.

"It's been a while Mollie darling, thank you for your friends, they're such a welcome gift for your return and one that will certainly help towards your apology to me," I shoot my eyes sideways as I see two men in hoods and snoods straddling Gina and Sally across their shoulders, their heads bagged.

No, no, no. This is not happening. Not again.

Tears line my eyes as I tremble on the spot.

"Mollie, what are you fucking doing here?" Max bellows across the road, his voice panicked and fearful, "Melvin. Stop. Leave her alone," I hear him continue to shout, his tone, a pitch of desperation clear, as I turn my head to meet his eyes, to find tears spilling over. "No, Melvin. Fucking take me, leave her!" He wails, desperation evident in his voice and I turn my head to meet his tortures expression.

A bang sounds, so loud I flinch and duck. My body trembles as I process the sound.

A gun shot.

I look back directly at Max in front of me. He clutches onto his side under his left armpit before falling to his knees, his eyes glassing over. Sara stands stoic besides him. She grabs onto him as he falls, blood covering her hands as she attempts to block his bullet wound.

"Let the fuck go, Sara! Unless you want to be fucking next. I'm not against killing my fucking daughter if she protects the traitor," Melvin shouts, his voice so full of malice, it makes bile rise up my throat. "Felix, take your sister inside and leave that fucking scumbag to bleed out," Melvin orders and I see Felix tug on Sara's shoulder to encourage her into the building.

Sara stands, her hands up in the air, blood coating them, as I hear Max spluttering and gasping for life.

Melvin grabs onto my chin and forces my face back around to look at him.

"I always knew I'd get you back, Mollie Rutter." His disgusting gold toothed smile spreads wide across his smug face. A mixture of fear and anger fill me up as the ugly bastard stares down at me, like he's won the biggest prize at the fair. That's the last thing I see as two men bag me and drag me.

I find myself taken.

Again

***To be continued….***

## *TRIGGER WARNINGS*

This story contains references to:

Trafficking
Gang Crimes
Rape (only mentioned)
Trauma
Kidnapping
Entrapment
Violence
Abuse
Mental health
Anxiety
Therapy

There are no explicit or graphic scenes which involve any of the above triggers. All references are descriptive to the story.

Printed in Dunstable, United Kingdom

65772993R00201